CAPTAIN SMITH
THE TRUTH REVEALED

M J WEBER

LifeRich Publishing is a registered trademark of The Reader's Digest Association, Inc.

LifeRich Publishing books may be ordered through booksellers or by contacting:

LifeRich Publishing
1663 Liberty Drive
Bloomington, IN 47403
www.liferichpublishing.com
844-686-9607

ISBN: 978-1-4897-3723-6 (sc)
ISBN: 978-1-4897-3724-3 (hc)
ISBN: 978-1-4897-3725-0 (e)

Library of Congress Control Number: 2021914840

Print information available on the last page.

LifeRich Publishing rev. date: 08/03/2021

It all started when I was being driven across Libya's portion of the Sahara Desert, far south the coastal town of Tobruk. The men with me were Daniel an officer and a spy of sorts for the British army, if not commander in British intelligence, I had met some time ago. An officer riding in the passenger seat, known as Perkins, with him a driver named Joseph; I recently had learnt along the drive to Tobruk. Both men accompanied by Craft, a sergeant wounded in the arm from our last in counter with the enemy. And there sat beside me was Esther, a woman of course, while I sat between Daniel and her towards the rear right side of the Morris C8 truck.

The wounded soldier's arm was pressure bandaged, after had been shot and laid barely conscious, I looked back out into the desert, as we all often did from time to time on the long drive. The small open top truck we were in being part of a minor convoy of five, with a further two trucks traveling alongside us. I looked back at the one on right, as they tried to avoid the soft sand and our dust, by staying close, shaking my head as the inexperienced driver would swerve from left to right and men sat in the back slid from their seating.

Nearing Tobruk's east entrance once again, after had set out into the desert on a mission, the very same day, as it became sunset. The lieutenant officer sat in the passenger seat, known as Perkins, stood on removing his cap before waving orders to the men driving the trucks and his second lieutenant in the jeep behind, signalling them to make way for the base. He then re-took his seat, and nodded to the driver,

"We best get him to the hospital first, then we'll go see the colonel; hold in their Craft and to think we weren't long for Jorden, with the rest of the ninth division."

We drove into Tobruk and went directly to a hospital, as the driver and officer got out. Perkins quickly ran into the large brick building, with near five-foot windows along its front face and either side of a six-foot-wide entrance doorway. With rounded decorated frames made of render, that seemed to suit the sixteen-foot-high by forty-foot square building. The officer soon returned from the building with two nurses, both men bearing a stretcher between. They ran to the back of the truck, and lined up the stretchier, as the officer came over and we help assist the wounded man, suffering from loss of blood, carefully placing him upon the stretchier, thankfully finding the wounded man still mobile.

Esther said a silent prayer, as the officer took his seat and the driver pulled forth passing few streets, till arriving near a vacant area, just off the south edge of Tobruk, entering between mid-size military tents set either side of the road, that formed rows running a hundred yard ahead, where the dirt road appeared to lead out into the desert. As they stopped the small truck outside a larger tent on the right, with a slight owning out the front, we stood and jumped from the vehicle.

"Ha," officer Perkins said, "we are here, make your way in," as he pointed toward the tents entrance. We approached the owning outside, noting an arrangement of two rounded table with chairs, either side and decretive bottles of wine sat upon each. Hearing British marching music sounding from within the tent, we stood before a beaded door of different Arabian colours.

Perkins pulled the strings aside and entered, standing to the left at attention, while I stepped forth upon a large Persian rug, ling the floor, passing a large sofa to the left, lined with soft cotton materiel, and cream, brown to black collared embroidery, to match the rug upon the floor. And to the right of the tent a queen, if not modest sized bed, lined with white cotton sheets and a heavy timber frame from England, with arched ends. I turned my attention to a large desk opposite, at the far end of the rug, and six-foot map hung upon the wall behind, as wind blew in through three-foot-wide window openings either side.

And there stood behind the desk, was a large elder man, sipping water from a tin cup, held in his hand, as he stretched his left toward us and pointed with his index finger, mimicking us to wait. He finished and lowered the cup and left hand, saying "Ha, now who have we here?"

I approached the desk, "Smith, that is Peter Smith," I answered, "I'm the one who sent the letter,"

"Are Smith," he replied, "now I do understand you promised some treasure, out of this?"

"No," I answered sternly, "I don't recall."

The colonel drew a red envelope from his top pocket, producing a letter from within, reading aloud, "Are, colonel Rossby. I have managed to find some treasure on my archeologically tour of the area far south of Tobruk this side of the boarder and unstable sand, but I am afraid that some German mercenaries working for an unknown organization are trying to kill me and take what I have found. I hope you'd receive this letter on Friday morning, or ells too late.' Now Peter Smith, where's my treasure?"

"Where was the artillery I explicably requested?" I inquired, "It is like I said, but you wouldn't know what I meant by treasure, would you? No, I found nothing to take, though the German mercenaries were convinced I had,"

"Well, I'll keep a watch on you," he huffed, "and if I find your holding out, then I'll have you arrested. Is that understood?"

I saluted, as he ordered, "Now get out of my sight."

I turned to Daniel and Esther, as he commented under breath, "A right blighter isn't he what, I didn't think we'd be fight a war on both sides of the cion...?"

As we calmly exited the tent, before walked pass the British soldiers seated outside and turned left or east along the road, I urged Daniel, "Just keep going, I don't trust the British... I mean, that colonel Rossby."

We entered the civilian streets of Tobruk, proceeding down the first street to the right, before crossing the road in hope to follow it down toward a hotel at the far end, Daniel asked, "How did that pompous colonel receive the letter he mentioned, within the last twenty-four hours?"

"Boas," I commented, "the bookkeeper we saw; when here yesterday, tipped me off in a book he had gave to look at, finding a piece of paper within a military stamped envelope. I realised his plan on how to initiate the cavalry, and knowing Boas knew what time the mail was collected; at the pacific post office and all mail, bearing the stamp and red seal, would go directly to colonel Rossby. The stamp being a forge, but he didn't ask, so I didn't tell; the reason for me doing this was because of the rush we were in and Boas hesitant to trust you."

"That's ok," he smiled, "I didn't trust Boas, his to switched on and lives in an archive that hints the fill of a morg."

Crossing the street, Esther commented, "Your incredibly rood and senseless that old man was just trying to help us and save some of the treasure belonged to his ancestors."

"Well," I sniggered, "she likes to make a point, as much as the last man."

She came close and tried to swing at me, as I dogged and she struck my arm,

"Are…," I huffed, "Are you happy now?"

"That was no good," She huffed, "but I'm surprised I could get to a man not many in the German world would be able to hit."

"Not on my own ability," I assured, "but with God's help, now let's keep walking and try for a hotel."

CONTENTS

Unexpected Welcome 1

A visit to an old friend.. 8

On the way to the airport 13

Arriving at Turkey 23

The Arminian hotel 31

Interceding the convoy.. 39

Receiving information 47

Finding the ark... 53

Escaping Turkey.. 60

Landing in Italy... 64

The library.. 71

Obtaining cargo 81

Rough waters.. 91

Bringing the ship about... 101

Rechecking in.. 111

Catching a train 120

A sandy stop 127

Fighting the current 132

Sandstorm 136

The Oasis.. 144

A ride in the desert.. 153

Ducking for cover 158

Sending Word.. 161

Sabotage.. 167

Acquainting an old friend.. 174

A change of plans 183

The catacombs 189

Catching up 195

Silver and Gold 199

Hidden Treasure 203

True treasure 211
True Hope 221
Trouble in camp 227
The Hearing 234
Esther's estate 249
Tying loose ends 258
True inheritance 267

UNEXPECTED WELCOME

As we continued up the paved road, with near two-story high buildings either side of us, as the sun had set, and light faded. We came to the end of the run and turned to the right and continued up the next street, approaching a large sixty-foot-long, two-story brick hotel. That was well maintained, with six-foot windows, along the fount face of its first and second story and set of steps before its central entrance with the glare of light shining through. We approached the steps, spotting but three vehicles in the street, Esther asked, "Are so this is it?"

"Why not this for our accommodation this evening?" I asked,

"More like a week or so," Daniel seconded, "I'm stuffed."

We quickly turned up the steps and entered the doorway, into a forty-foot lobby, dimly lit by four decorative chandelares hung from a white textured ceiling, with restraint seats to our left and right upon a white tiled floor. Seeing customers sat around small roundtables, lined with white cloths, napkins and silver wear placed among whatever the people had ordered. As I saw that each table was to suet three and well-spaced apart, with a timber bar counter along the rear wall ahead to left, steel counter to the right, before a doorway to a kitchen and large white marble topped counter to its right, before the base of a stairway and each counter manned by attendants.

Following along the centre aisles' Persian rug, to the right counter, noting patterns of palm leaves carved into its front face and decretive boarder, as appose to the left counters with fewer decretive details. I noted sighs above the counters, reading to one hung above the second, 'restraint' the next, 'bar', and the one before us 'accommodation and booking'. Finding the attendant gown from behind the counter, I rang a small brass bell beside the ledger book, noting keys hung upon the rear wall. We waited as one of the waiters ran over from the restraint, wearing a butler suit and chef's toque blanche hat. He took position behind the counter upon opening the ledger book and drew a pen from his top pocket, spotted few vacancies, he offered, "Yes, mister we have accommodation if you like?"

"Yes," I answered, "for three nights, then we'll see how we're going after that,"

"Yes, mister?" he nodded,

"Smith," I answered, "I'm on the books, and used to go to the last hotel, before you relocated and maintained a contract with Mica Ashulum the owner, your boss. To stay here and nowhere else if I am ever in Tobruk, for a discount. Some deal he thought up."

He flicked through another book, grinning, "R Smith, ok," and offered a key, before turning to leave his place at the counter.

"Wait…" Daniel called.

The waiter stopped and turnback to him with a grim face, Daniel huffed, "I know Smith must have an account with you, but the sign by the door said, 'tips if you please?"

Handing over few coins, the waiter seemed nervously to except the threepence, nodding, "Thank you, koi." Before turning and walked forth with hast.

"Funny waiter," Daniel commented, "but what can you expect when someone plays chef and bar attendant as well, ha…"

I clinched the key tightly in my right hand, sighing, "I geese, now let's go."

Another waiter appeared and led us to the base of the stairway, left of the counter, we passed and continued up the polished steps, Esther commented, "Well, I'll be glad to get a decent sleep." I thanked God and prayed for protection against evil.

Reaching the top of the stairs, with few small decretive pillars supporting the roof above and entered a ten-foot-wide hall, continuing left to right of the stairway. We turned to the left and followed it along with doors to our left and widows similar to the ones along the buildings front face, to the right. Noting numbers upon the rooms doors and read the room keys' on approaching a room, I had previously used, marked 22, the same as the key and stopped. Daniel and Esther followed, as I found the numbers upon rooms door had recently been changed to 24.

I then walk down further, still not finding the room numbered 22, as I turned and begun back toward the stairs, we came upon, noting a door to the left of the stairway was left open, not for the guest, but rather to store things. I then walked pass the stairs and distinctly remembered the room not being on the other side of the hotel, swiftly proceeding and continued down the hall. Reaching its end, I turned down another to the right, with doors on the right and left-along the roadside wall of the building. Soon turning to a door numbered 22 on the left and reaching for its handle, I hesitated to grasp the knob.

"Is everything all right?" Daniel asked,

"I'm not sure," I answered, carefully stepping to the right of the door, "stay back."

They stood to the left, as I used the key to unlock the door, hearing few footsteps emit from within the room, I took out my Wembley mark VI 455 revolver and swung the door open, keeping right of its frame. Cocking the pistols' hammer and presenting it, I calling, "Who's in there? Answered me!"

Hearing no reply, I grinned at the sound of their slight movements and breathing, and stayed ready by the door, quickly turning in and firing few shots high, before ducking behind the left of the door frame, calling, "Anyone else?"

"Are..." one of the would-be assassins moaned,

I stood from the door, called, "Anyone? I'm about to throw a grenade."

Hearing no reply, I took my boot off and threw it into the darkened room, hearing the scurrying of hands and feet, searching to secure a live grenade. One jumped out a rear window, I carefully entered the fifteen-foot square room, spotting an overturned large sofa before the rear wall and two fatally wounded men dressed in brown over coats bearing German gestapo issued Luger pistols, now laid motionless, one with a heart wound and other a hit to the head.

3

Hearing a noise, I turned toward the window within the rear wall that had been shattered, and cough sight a gloved hand of a man attempting to leaving by its sill. Then suddenly heard another take a deep breath from behind the sofa, I stepped forth and kicked it over upon whoever it was, pinning him down from standing. He panicked and fired few shots toward the ceiling, as I grasped the gun within his hand and attempted to secure it, quickly amid and firing mine, skimming his arm as he released. Collecting the Luger and throwing it out the window, before jumping of the lounge and stood to the right, training my pistol toward him. The German still wearing a uniform shirt, pushed the lounge off and stumbled to his feet, knowing him likely a Waffen SS majors, I ordered, "keep your hands up, or I'll shoot the other one."

Daniel then came over and instantly searched him, finding a dagger and small pistol, similar to a Derringer in size, nodding, "Ok."

Before pocketing the items and some ammo, I asked the officer, "What are you doing here and who sent you?"

"We were sent to capture you, or kill you," He answered, while holding his wounded right hand,

"Who sent you," I asked, "they must have a name?"

He then smiled, "You won't beat us, Smith," as he quickly ran over to the open window and jumped through, I ran over and looked down to see where he went, spotting a rope hung from the sill leading to the street below.

Spotting the officer sliding down the rope, I amid with my pistol and saw him look up, as I called, "Stop!"

He then lost his grip and fell near ten feet, collapsing upon the pavement below, before getting up to re-joining another man presumably stood from the rope, though both limping, neither appeared shaken by their fellow combatant that fell's body laid dead upon the street. The man first climbed down quickly fired a pistol toward the window, as I ducked back into the room in order to conceal myself and two black W02 Mercedes passenger vehicles come from just around the corner and pulled up outside the hotel. Cautiously I observing as five men stepped from each vehicle; noting few dressed similar to those deceased, accompanied by further men if not Wehrmacht soldiers and ran towards one of the hotels' entrances. Daniel hearing multiple footsteps echo from the hall, closed and locked the rooms door behind, I starred toward the out of range, two retreating officers and watched as both got into one of the vehicles and took off. I Knew the two retreating Waffen SS offices were likely on their way to meet those who arranged the hit, and noted there no men left attending the other Mercedes.

"Smith," Daniel inquired, "we have company, and I don't think the room will accommodate,"

"No," I commented, "we best leave; you go first."

He quickly ran over and climbed out the window and down the rope, ran down alongside a drainpipe. Reaching midway down, he felt the rope to give way, as the German to last use it had weekended its frays with a piece of glass, to hinder our escape. Daniel quickly utilised the down drain, as Esther followed and I began to climb out, hearing the sound of multiple gunfire and the door splinter to pieces. Quickly grasping the drain and climbed down to the darkened street, spotting two Germans left to guard a side entrance to the hotel and the other Mercedes. Finding the men preoccupied, we stuck to the wall of the hotel and ran down toward the vehicle, seeing the driver sat within studying a map and to hadn't spotted us stood in the dark.

I ran forth and opened the passenger door, the officer gasped as I struck his face, knocking him out cold and took his place, opening and allowing him to roll out the door to the dusty path. Daniel took the rear seat and Esther the passenger, retrieving the map and finding it to be of the area east of town with destinations added, before handing it over to Esther and started the vehicle, upon taking off. The men guarding the hotels' side exit, quickly unslung their rifles and turned to the officer laid in the street, one aimed and fired toward us in vain as we sped. I kept an eye out for a public phone, entering another street veering right and reaching its end before swerving right into another and accelerating. Spotting a phone booth ahead, on our side of the street, I hit the brakes and called to Daniel, "Give the police a ring."

Daniel quickly stepped from the car and grasped the phone, while dialling the number, he huffed, "Operator, G1-2-12 it's an emergence… Halo, constable; relay message to the twenty ninth, to a colonel Rossby there has been an enemy breach of security on Marlbrough street, specifically the hotel, tell him to send men from the battalion and don't give me any late-night excuses!"

Before hanging up and running back to the vehicle, as I took off and sped toward the end of the street, Esther pointed which side streets to take, cautiously following the marked map. Finding the headlights worked well, I prayed we would find out what the Germans officers were doing and soon caught up to the now slowed, Mercedes, as it continued out north of Tobruk and into the desert.

Turning off the headlamps and seeing the darkened vehicle come to a stop, little more than ten miles out of town and keep our distance. Watching as their headlights pulled forth over a sand dune and shun upon an airplane, that appeared to be a new type either the Focke-Wulf A 38 or rather more impressive JU 160? I quickly, while hearing the plane engines start for take-off, turned on the headlamps and sped forth, spotting two people stepped from the vehicle and ran toward the plane, I near launched over the small dune toward them. Daniel drew his pistol and opened his door, as he stood upon the running board and fired at the fuselage, while I floored it toward them.

The two officers now aboard drew and fired their pistols from the rear of the cockpit and perhaps cargo bay of the mid-size aircraft as it begun to leave, a shot hitting our left headlight and another cracking the windscreen, leaving a hole in the centre, "Duck Esther!" I called, as she kept her head down and the plane accelerated as the sand slowed the vehicle, one of the officers got on the planes rear machinegun and fired toward us. Taking out the left steer tyre as we bogged and built holes ran across from the tyre struck to the engine bay, I quickly stopped; knowing it wasn't worth it.

Daniel commented, "Well, that was successful?"

"It's just fortunate I didn't get to use my Derringer," Esther replied,

"I think we're the fortunate," Daniel huffed, "and that shiny peace wouldn't have helped much... So, what are they doing or are they just ticked off we ruined their last plans?"

"I don't know," I sighed, "But I think I may know someone how dose, we best get back to Tobruk."

Reversing back as far as I could, before becoming stuck in the sand, I stepped out and saw the flat steer tyre, followed by coolant drained upon the ground, sighing, "Are, that's whey; let's take the other Germans car."

Notting it but sixty feet away and stepped from the Mercedes, as the other suddenly exploded and we dove to the ground. I stood and begun dusted myself off, suggesting, "Right, I think it's safer not to take German vehicles after all, let's just walk. Tobruk is only eight to ten miles back, we should get there by dawn."

"Well," Daniel smiled, "I'm glad we drank up and eat something, when being driven in,"

"and none wounded," Esther smiled.

Gritting our teeth, we began to walk through the desert, following our tyre tracks back toward Tobruk. Esther still smiling, nodded, "I would have to say, I'm surprised, each hotel we visit has a surprise, as though they were waiting for our return,"

"Yes," Daniel seconded, "old Huns really has it in for you smith, mind letting us in on that?"

"Perhaps we'll find our answer in Tobruk," I nervously replied, "those jottings from their last expedition may help?"

"Of course," Esher nodded, "after all the trouble they went to retrieve it, why not wish to protect their interests?"

"She has a point," Daniel seconded, "and leaving the scene isn't going to solve anything?"

"Like a true detective," I grinned, "of course you are an inspector aren't you." Staying near silent as we proceeded along the barely visible tracks holding Esther's hand as she appeared to stumble upon lumps of sand.

A VISIT TO AN OLD FRIEND

We finally neared Tobruk, finding it farther then I had estimated, and the sun begun to rise from the east as the dim light of dawn was upon us. We soon followed a road in and entered a side street, along the eastern edge of town, leading to the north, as you face the sea beyond, Daniel questioned, "The army is the other way there; Smith?"

"Sorry," I replied, "we cannot afford to waste time, I must speak with Boas,"

"Hope he has water?" Esther sighed, before proceeding down few streets while the sun rose and we arrived, half staggering, outside the bookshop and historical archives, we had visited just yesterday morning. I lowered Esther from my back, after had piggy backed her the last half mile or so and crossed its front steps to the buildings recessed entry finding the door unlocked, before entered the old shop again. Finding Boas at the counter to the left, before a four foot stake of books and parchments toward the far end of the counter, as he appeared to be translating them while contently sat upon his small armchair, with add from a small spherical light hung from the ceiling above.

I glanced over the counter and called to him, "I don't mean to interrupt."

He closed the collection of parchments and stood from the chair, grinning, "You succeeded again?"

"Sort of," I sighed, "we stopped them from taking any treasure and kept it secret, but the Nazis are still after me, and can't be sure whether they knew it was anything to do with us,"

Boas held his chin with his right hand, pondering, "Yes, go on?"

"Well," I nodded, drawing a copy of the jottings Esther had made, and handed them over for safe keeping, as he begun to skim over them, I sighed, "Baller and a group of his investor's Gestapo officers, didn't even seem to be fazed by the treasure, as we had expected. No, they were looking over inscriptions, you talked about, of the destroyed and abandoned town-perhaps city and even sent one of their members off with their own comprised copies of it,"

"I see," Boas sighed, "and did this messenger get away?"

"Well, Daniel?" I asked.

Daniel retrieving a glass of water from a convenient jug, Boas had sat upon the counter; after Esther, and lowered the vessel huffing, "He was faster than I thought and Germans were coming down the shaft, as he was going up. I couldn't get the bounder,"

"Are, this is in code," Boas replied, "constructed from two languages, I wouldn't have understood it fully, but now that I had already begun on a few books. I can now find how it was writing, in a way as to make sense, though appears coded with mixed letters, a bit like a cross word puzzle. At the time they may have been the only place to had used such language and when they fell, it was to be lost. But it says something about the arks' where abouts; you know, the one Noah built and has some information on where it can be found. I can interpret it and get it to you through our post telegram to Igdir, by the time you arrived at eastern Turkey, that giving you the upper hand, the Germans don't have."

"Yes," I agreed, "but this language; have I ever studied or got you to interpret it before?"

"Not in its entirety," he answered,

"So," I pondered, "what would the Germans want with something they cannot interpret, unless?"

As I took out my diary and flicked through, finding pages missing and closed, "They've taken some information…"

Boas then lent forward with his right hand outstretched, as I handed him the diary, he then flicked through it, "I see, I'll start making you a copy eminently and send it by post to Igdir. I'll use my special, waterproof paper,"

"Also," I requested, "do you know of any one in Germany or Italy that could be helping them with such a task, someone who is also a person, who they can use to help interpret such things?"

"There is one man, by the name of Fredric Vincent, a distinguished gentleman and keeps secretive," he answered, "I could never get hold of him, but before leaving completely, he worked as a partner, in the booking industry. But I don't believe he is any Nazi, all though he was easily corrupted by money, that's what tor the partnership apart. He was not being carefully to whom he was selling information to and sold of some ancient text of my ancestor's history, from before Moses's time even. But if you want to find him, I can also make inquiries?"

"Ok," I replied, "please do, and we'll wait on what you find, I think there's more to this than what it seems. If Baller and the others weren't after money, and the Germans are still helping them, what are they after?"

"More money?" Boas replied,

"I see your point; they could be after bigger fish," I replied, "either way, we must go," and shook his hand, before turning to Daniel offered the vessel. I took and drunk, lowered it from my lips to the counter, "Oh, and thanks for the water,"

"Yes, thank you," Esther nodded,

"good stuff chum," Daniel smiled.

As we turned for the door, Boas called, "Are you sure I can't help you with transport?"

"Well," I commented, "what do you suggest, a ship is what it'll take correct?" And turned for the door in a hurry.

"Are ships, but you could always go by plane as fare as north Agri, east Turkey," he recommended, "and then head for Igdir, now the air strips been open this last week."

I stopped and turned back, as he handed me an envelope, "May you be successful in the way God wants you to be. I hope one day you'll realise this."

Shaking Boaz's hand again and excepted the envelope, upon nodding and turned for the door, he smiled and went to pure himself a cup of water, finding the jug empty, sighing, "Theses brits can't handle the sun a mere half hour."

We stepped out and down the few steps to the street, seeing no one around and decided to see what became of the hotel situation, saying to Daniel, "The airstrip is this why," Turning to the right and up the street.

"But Smith why go back through central areas?" he asked,

"So, we won't be picked out," I answered,

"Maybe if the army is present to?" Esther agreed.

Following the street down and through a gap to the left, leading into the next over and proceeded west, crossing to an alleyway opposite. We walked with hast toward its far end and came out into the street with the hotel opposite, and turned left, cautiously following its foot path while starred toward the hotel across the street. Spotting a British privet seated in a small Morris truck outside, suddenly pull forth and turn across to our side of the street. I stepped from the curb and flagged the officer down, as he stopped before me and demanded an explanation, "What is it?"

I walked around to the right driver side door of the truck, answering, "Are, I heard shots fired from within that hotel and saw some strange car movement when we went for a walk last night, is everything ok?"

Expecting to hear a reply along the lines of multiple arrests, he huffed, "What are you talking about old man? We got an anonymous call from some pranking, lunatic. You better not be him?"

"No, I'm not him," I replied, "I'm an officer in the British army," revealing to him my meddle,

"Look," he sighed, "we searched the place since last night, I was even told to stay in the hotel on suspicion as we had found nothing. No vehicles out the front, not even tyre marks and no German mercenaries, like previously seen, that you perhaps heard of, on the hush, hush, as rumours spread from the desert?" Whispering the last part, upon spotting Daniel and Esther stood by,

"Don't worry," I assured, "they're in the army too, one an officer and captain."

The man saluted Daniel, "Yes, hard to believe isn't it, that some bounder had the nerve to call us up over such rubbish. I think you know what I mean when I say, I wouldn't mind hunting him down for the day; that's if you sirs would permit me?"

"You wouldn't survive the day," Daniel replied,

"Ha, ha…" The man laughed, thinking it a joke concerning his place in the British army, "Capital sir, capital."

"Now get back to base," Daniel snaped, "before they really do court-martial you for not being at your post."

The officer nervously selected gear to leave, I reached for his arm, "No," I ordered, "wait privet, the window in room twenty-three… Isn't there, if I'm not mistaken, few broken pains and some disordered furniture and perhaps one or more blood stains upon the carpet?"

"No man, you are very much mistaken," he exclaimed, "I talked to a waiter who was on last night and morning cleaner, after their shift you know, and maintained the room hadn't been in use for weeks. The last people in there were a family with children and never got the full story on how that window broke. They've been waiting on new glass to come in by ship ever since. The manager insisted the new pain be tinted…" then pursed, before nodding, "Well, I'm off, cheery oh."

I realest and stood back, in the centre of the street, as he saluted before driving on down the street, shaking his head at what I had bought to attention. Daniel and Esther approached, as I turned to cross the vacant road, huffing, "Aren't we glade to have him,"

"Not a very good judge of character," Esther sighed,

"A privet or general, each still human," Daniel alluded, "even those from Briton Mis Esther as hard at times it is to admit."

ON THE WAY TO THE AIRPORT

Once across the road I knew we were still a ways from the military airport, just out of Tobruk, Daniel asked, "Do you know what this means Smith?"

"That someone wasted time and a few coins, making a phone call?" Esther sniggered,

"No," Daniel replied, "the Germans could be anywhere, for all we know."

"You've got a point," I replied, "Let's stick to the side streets."

As I turned to my left and away from the hotel, passing few parked vehicles, noting a Morris Oxford and blue van, second from the end, all parked toward the corner before us. We continued around and down a side street, we had taken last night, followed it down and turned to the right, up another narrow road and continued forth, praying for safety. Continued down and soon entering a nearby alleyway to a side street, continuing northwest toward the airport.

Entering an alleyway to the left, I glanced over my shoulder, spotting the same blue commercial van previously parked down from the hotel; now enter from the last street into the twelve-foot-wide passage. We continued a hundred feet and approached midway through the narrow alley, then heard the echo of an engine, amplify off the walls. I turned to the van behind, now accelerating toward us and quickly ran for a door to the left ahead, gasping, "Get to the door!"

They nodded upon running forth, I retrieved my pistol and turned to the approaching van and fired toward its drive, as it swerved from left to right and a man in the passenger seat, presented an MP34 machinegun gun from his window. Daniel drew his pistol and fired toward the passenger, as the man stood to hang from the window and fired the machinegun in retaliation. We ran back to the door, as Esther forced it open and entered before us. I amid up and fired once more, spotting the driver heavily wounded, and the van to violently swerve back and forth against the walls of the old buildings, knocking the machinegun from the passenger's hands, before turning hard right and crashing into the wall, coming to a spot. The passenger quickly retrieved another machinegun, finding my pistol empty, Daniel leaped into the doorway, and I dove after, as the German fired and bullets ricochet of the doorframe behind.

Realising once though the old timber doorway, we had entered an old, sixty-foot square mill and perhaps storehouse, with a ten-foot doorway opposite, that had been secured shut by a large bean across its top, middle and base. Precautioning against adverse winds no doubt, and large five foot in diameter, circular motion, stone crushing wheel that would track along a thrashing floor before us. Its wheels tall mast, fashioned from a rough-cut cylindrical beam, with a large timber cog upon its end that appeared to mesh with the cog of another shaft of similar size, mounted to the sheds roof trusses and continued to the rear wall, lit by sun shining through a large square opening. With a timber mezzanine-platform ran along the rear wall and second beneath, with a tow stairway below. Noting a lifting rope ran through poleis, dangling before the platforms, from the ceiling above and two timber grain slides leading down to the mills base and crushing wheel. Each of the slides able to be turned and centred from the ground, depending on what the mill was being used for, whenever that might had been, as bust and old chaff covered the floor.

Daniel quickly reloaded, as I closed the door and bolted its damaged lock, on placing a nearby timber board across. Reloading I turned for the mezzanines' stairway closest, leading to the first platform, "Quick, to the mezzanine!" passing a number of drums stowed beneath, and noting two further by the doorway opposite. Running up the stairway, as it turned left and stepped out upon the timber beck, before truing for the ladder to the next walkway, huffing, "Right, to the second garrets' deck!"

Turing to and climbing the ladder to a trapdoor, on through it open, hearing the sound of multiple soldiers attempting to weaken the small ally entrance door. I climbed up and stood upon the creaking boards before Esther, ahead of Daniel still climbing. As the Germans brock through and disguised SS officers entered, instantly spotting Daniel, one pointed, "*Oben dort, abfeuern auf sie!*"

Daniel quickly drew and fired his pistol toward them, while proceeded to climb, I stood toward the edge of the platform and fired my revolver, in order to cover Daniel's retreat. He and Esther then stood from the edge, one or two of my shots hitting their mark. The officers swiftly fired their multiple pistols in retaliation and few men entered armed with MP 34 machineguns. I quickly jumped back from the edge, as few of their shots struck the timber beneath my feet and I dove to the deck, turning to my legs and feet, before the deck finding their bullets unable to penetrate its thick timber boards.

Then spotting the pully for the mezzanines loading doors' rope before me and quickly reached over to it, and pulled it up from the edge, before tossing its end through the loading door behind. Daniel stayed low and fired back at the Germans reloading, before diving to the beck beside as further cluster of rounds struck the celling and stone wall behind, as Esther too stayed low, while grasping her Derringer,

"I'm out." he sighed, "But tell me Smith, what is a mill doing with leaky old steel drums?"

"What?" I gasped, closing my revolvers cylinder once reloaded and partly stood, as few soldiers below begun to reload, and swiftly fired few shots toward a drum by the door, coursing it to leak upon nearby drums and ground, as further soldiers entered. Seeing what Daniel had meant; finding the mill was not that heavily secured in the cases of adverse weather, but rather the security of fuel being stowed within. I hit the deck once more as soldiers proceeded to firring back and turned to Daniel, now kneel besides, "Daniel, pass me your lighter?"

He threw it to me, as I gathered chaff from the platforms deck, nodding, "Get going, I'll see whether those fuel drubs are easy to ignite." He and Esther turned for the loading door and begun climbed out with add of the rope, knowing I was down to but five shots, as I reloaded, hearing soldiers upon the platform below and stairways.

I closed the door to the manhole and bolted it shut, as I stood and fired my last shots toward the drums below as they leaked out upon the ground, and fumes of gasoline filled the air, but hadn't ignited. Desperately lighting the hay and throwing it down, upon the saturated ground, as it smouldered yet still hadn't lit, I quickly lit and through a further hand full over the side. The soldiers now all stood upon the platform beneath, begun firing at the small door as their shots passed through and door splintered to pieces. I dropped the empty pistol and raised my hands, as two men stood from the ladder hole, one struck my gut with the butt of his rifle whilst the other presented a luger pistol and smacked me across the face with its barrel.

Two further men stood from the ladder hole and unslung their machineguns on turned for the loading door. I quickly grasped the pistol of the officer before me and turned it toward the soldier holding a rifle to my right and fired, as he fell from the platform. One of the two soldiers by the loading door turned to fire, while the other prepared to fire out the door, I quickly pulling the pistol free from the officer's hand and firing a shot at each as they fell. Then pointed the gun toward the officer, as the next climbing the ladder raised a pistol to fire, I quickly, in a split second turned and fired, striking his head. Before raising my hand to block the officer's left fist, as he swung at my face and grasped the pistol with his right.

I turned to the officer and head butted him, as I jumped forth and releasing his arm, throwing my left fist into his face, as he released the pistol and I circled to the left, quickly pushed him back first down into the manhole, before any further soldiers could enter nor fire their weapons. I swiftly retrieved my pistol and put it away, before running to the rope dangled from the loading door and grasped it, as I slid down. Seeing once out, the rope lead down to gourd before an old donkey stables to my right that made up one side of the alleyway, before continued by few houses ahead and teeing into a further street beyond.

Jumping to the alleys compacted dirt and turned to Daniel and Esther, a hundred feet ahead toward the end of the alley and street, as they ran to the end and crossed. I quickly pursued, whilst soldiers fired their German lugers toward me, narrowly missing, as I moved from left to right, till more than a hundred yards from the building. Then heard a laughed woof and explosion, as the mills base blew out and one side collapsed due to the blast, and pieces of daubery flew passed and rubble mounded within the alley, cutting off and burying their vehicles.

I dove to ground, before standing and glanced at the desecrated mill, finding its debris had struck and damaged the empty donkey stables, before turning ahead and swiftly ran a crossed the street, catch my breath, "Ha, we beast keep moving... Are, follow me," and turned ahead to the west or left end of the street.

We cautiously continued walking with hast, down the quite street and out along the road, leading toward the outskirts. Soon spotting the airfield in the distance, equipped with two small sea gladiator military aircraft and a larger civilian Ford trey engine airplane likely kept and used for evacuating local civilians: hents Boas's resourceful qualities on supplying the tickets. Silently paying reverence to God for keeping us safe, I followed the desert road toward the airstrip, "Not far now," I encouraged, while each filling our thirst take its toll, upon reaching its gate and drive leading to a small flight station at the end of a runway and temporary awning to the left, shading few trucks parked before a sixty-foot square, temporary military hangar for servicing and housing aircraft beyond.

We proceeded toward the small brick flight station with but two small windows, noting a sign before its open door, advertising the flight time tables, for flights that would leave once a week or intermittently to collect cargo as Boas had suggested. fining today was on the listing and turned for the stations' entrance on entering, finding there was a line-up of eight people, toward a small counter in the left corner. As few people sat in rows of timber chairs to the right, facing a large six-foot window, within the rear wall of the building, overlooking the runway beside a door to the right.

Finding those present to be people of biasness with one mid-age women stood near and all holding possessions within bags and small suitcases. Then spotting the women to have a paper cup in her hand, and quickly turned left, as Esther closed the door spotting a porcelain water dispenser upon the wall, over a small sink and paper cups staked beside.

Quickly walked over and retrieved few cups, handing one to Daniel and Esther allowing her to go first, she cracked the coolers tap and filled her cup, before drinking as fast as she had filled it and quickly refilled before standing aside, Daniel stepped forth, saying, "Excuse," before filling a cup and sculling it down, followed by another three cups full. He lowered the cup and turned for a vacant row of seats against the wall by the entrance, beneath one of the buildings front windows. Taking a cup of water and scowling it down, followed by another.

Daniel and Esther stood to refill, as I too followed, realising the line-up was nearly through and the last person was due. I took one last drink, suddenly spotting two men barge through the door and turn for the counter, with small black suitcases firmly grasped in hand and presented the elder gentlemen manning the counter.

Slightly lowered the cup from my mouth, noting them to both be wearing fedora stile dress hats and grey over coats, the one on the left, revealed a belt around his waists' left side, as he pulled the coat over to conceal it once at the counter. Spotting he had a small swastika branded poach upon his belt with an eagle insignia on its opening, watching as their tickets were stamped and they walked toward a far row of seats to sit, "Smith," Daniel whispered, "did you see that?"

"Year." I nodded, tacking another sip,

"So, they must be with Abwehr?" He gasped,

"Well, seeing how they're here, we now know where on the right track," I replied with a sigh, "I suggest we stay low and continue as planned."

"But what if they're here for us?" he cautioned,

"I doubt they'll do anything aboard an aeroplane," I assured, "plus we have little choice, we need to reach east Turkey as soon as possible."

Before stepping forth to the mid-aged man, behind the counter manning the booking office, to have our tickets stamped, he smiled, "Thank you," as I handed them over and he handed them back once stamped. Cautiously turning back to the bench and glimpsing over my shoulder at the two suspicious Germans, as they looked to the runway in anticipation, I saw Esther stare toward them, while keeping her hand upon the concealed Derringer within her trouser pocket.

"Take no notice of them," I urged, "lest we draw attention," and took a seat on waited for our flight to be called.

Waiting a half hour, a women air attendant came rushing through the rooms rear door, calling in Hebrew, "Flight one is ready to go, luggage besides personal small baggage must be placed to the left side of the steps when boarding. To be put into storage, below. "

Directing those closest to follow her back out through the door and over towards the nearby try engine airplane; those present seemed to understand her and begun to leave by the door. We held back to observe the Germans, as they quickly headed out with the others whilst grasping their small black suitcases and hastily crossed the runway to the five portable steps, leading up into the mid-size aircraft, originally used for cargo, and cautiously boarded.

"Ok," Daniel encouraged, "Smith, Esther let us go."

Leading as we too stepped out by the door and proceeded to the airplane, as the last passengers boarded and we began to up the steps, carefully peer into the plane, spotting the Germans to the rear. We entered and casually turned to sit in the front row of seats, as our tickets were collected and the planes door was shut, while flight attendants secured passenger luggage, hearing the engines start, we soon took off toward Turkey.

Sitting quietly for an hour into the flight, I pulled my hand from Esther's firm grip, as she had fallen asleep after a nervous take-off, and cautiously headed for the toilet facilities to the rear of the plane and passed the two Germans, now sound asleep. Knowing where they were from, due to the typical effects of staying up most of the night, as I went and came out, finding them still asleep with their suitcases sat ungraded before them.

Noting most passengers in the next three rows also asleep and the two rows to right deducted to make space for the rest room. Silently approaching I swiftly reached down and carefully retrieved the two suitcases. The officers stayed sound asleep as I stepped back into the cubicle behind and placed the cases upon the small vanity, opposite the lavatory and picked the locks, revealing papers listing their contacts, some archaeological information, ide papers on me, ammunition and each housing a custom luger police pistol, alongside knuckle dusters that could kill and Nazi daggers. Besides that, a few more papers and about two thousand marks between either case, as I thought about it and prayed for help.

Thinking of a plan, I closed the suitcases, before walking out finding the German officers still asleep and Esther approach to use the facilities, I whispered to her, whilst pointing, "Could you get Daniel?"

She still holding on, turned back and sat, as Daniel stood as though making his way to the restroom and approached. Noting a gap behind the German's seats and all other passengers preoccupied,

"Do you have any chloroform?" I whispered,

Daniel presented a small bottle from a hidden pocket, sown into the lower right side of his trusses, "Yes of course," he grinned, drawing two clean handkerchiefs, as he measured a correct dosage, going of estimated body weight and placed few props it the centre of one, carefully handing it to me and quickly preparing another.

"You get this one," I suggested, "I'll do the one on the right."

Shuffling behind their seats, before reaching over to the officer farthest away, while Daniel gently smothered his one and I the other, as they awoke only to fall asleep. I handed Daniel the handkerchief, as he stepped into the toilet cubical and dispose of them, before thoroughly washing his hands, I stood in after to clean mine.

Closing and handing the cases to Daniel on leaving the cubical, I then covered the officer's faces with their hats and left for our seats, Esther gasped, "Finally..." As she stood and punched my shoulder, while passing to the restroom.

"What's that about?" Daniel asked,

"What, that...? Or the Germans?" I asked,

"Let's go with the less complicated... So, the Germans?"

"In those cases," I replied," are German contacts and identification papers with our photographs, as they were ordered to locate and apprehend, if not eliminate us. Money and some information on what the Germans high command are up to, two knives and some ammo with their Lugers. Don't open it though, someone might see, we'll wait until others fall asleep."

He withdrew from open a case and slid it under his set, we then waited, silently praying all would work out, suggested to Daniel, "Ok, so when we reach Turkey, I suggest we follow all the orders set for the two jerry's,"

"Good idea," he smiled, "no need to second guess their next move."

As we waited and saw those seated behind had fallen asleep, "Ok," I whispered and retrieved one of the suitcases,

Esther silently seated, awoke "A suitcases?" she asked,

"Shush..." I hushed, "Yes a suitcase and one that is caring some rather interesting intel."

Carefully opening case, Daniel presented the other and did the same, as I read through some papers and explained it to Esther, "Ok, you see this map of Turkey, we get off near the small town of Igdir. The military according to these maps of the area, show they had just set up a small airfield a distance to the north of Erzurum, on its out skirts. Now going off what word Boas sends over; he believes the ark is around this area and so do the Germans. Boas giving us specially made tickets for the airport, to go to Eastern turkey. I think if Boas is correct, we may only have to travel around Turkey's countryside, likely no more than a few hundred miles."

"Yes," she commented, "but Smith, wont we be at risk of being spotted by Germans, the closer we get to the area, and maybe even once we land at this airfield?"

"Well, that may or may not be the cases," I sighed, "for I'm not aware of the number of temporary airfields. But there, according to these men's orders states, 'The colonel wants you in Igdir immediately; once dealing with Smith, be sure not to be followed. Take flight 29, leaving in the morning from Tobruk and do not delay; there will be a car parked outside airfield ten, ready for you to take to SS headquarters. PS, don't be late."

"Are, so the SS have set up in Eastern turkey," Daniel huffed, "I think we should form a plan; I say we seek transport and leave the vicinity. With this map we may be able to find our way,"

"But Smith what about Boaz's letters?" Esther urged,

"They'll be there within two days after landing," I smiled, "he uses air freight and telegrams for just about everything. But as for what our next move is, I'd say we'll have to wait and see. Boaz's letters were to be sent to a post office in Igdir, we should wait in Igdir till it arrives then make our move, before the Abwehr or SS counterparts know we're there,"

"And if the Germans get there before us?" Daniel asked,

"No," I confirmed, "they should receive their information on the sight after, because I believe they've sent their jottings to Fredric Vincent's office for verification in Italy. Who's work, if I'm correct, even if transported by telegram, would at best take a week. Though there is a possible convoy moving in, either on its way to the north-east boarder or ready to move in once received word. Anyway, like I said, we won't know till we arrive, so let's just pray it will be all right."

ARRIVING AT TURKEY

Waiting out the flight till near fallen asleep, the plan begun to descend to a dirt landing strip in the centre of a grass airfield. The airplane thrust into position and slowed to a halt, turning to the windows, spotting palm trees either side of the runway and a large tent set for the airport to the right. Turning attention from the small windows, Daniel and I stood on retrieving the briefcases, before awaking Esther and exiting the plane, following the line of passengers across the small airfield and toward the tent.

Seeing there were two Turkish soldiers posted either side of the tents' rear entry, shaded by a short owning above, propped by support pols. Noting the men had military Mauser K98 rifles from Germany upon their backs, we passed between the men and entered a thirty-foot square, shaded, arear of grass, spotting another owning out the front, with two small counters set up either side of the main exit, with an eight-foot-wide U-sapped bench between.

A number of people turned for the rear exit, eager to board their plan flight, seeing few passengers approach the booth to the right, we turned for one of the men at the right counter and had our tickets stamped, as Daniel held the luggage. Then proceeded out via the front exit, finding there a short driveway, leading to a twelve-foot-wide dirt road continuing north, with few vehicles parked up between the nearby palm and pine trees. Noting any suspicious vehicles parked nose first, along the edge of the road, as the trees shaded us from the sun's rays, I grinned, "Are, now let's find our car."

Reaching and walking along the edge of the quite dirt road, passing five vehicles, spotting a small black Mercedes and two further secret policemen, dressed in grey suits, with American still dress hats, I stepped behind one of the large Cretan date palms for cover, "Esther you wait here," I suggested, "we'll get the motor."

As she stood between few trees to the left, finding the two Germans Gestapo officers ahead had not seen us, as we casually approached, as though heading for a vehicle and entered the car beside the Mercedes. Quickly walking around to the passenger side and waited, as Daniel took the driver's seat. I looked into the review mirror and adjusted it, seeing the Germans behind us, now turned towards the road away from us.

Nodded to Daniel, he stepped out and sneakily walked around the front of the cars, while keeping his head low, spotting him now in front of the Mercedes while the German officers stepped back, and lent upon its rear trunk, still fixated on the road and those leaving the checking station opposite. I knew they'd notice Daniel enter their unlooked vehicle, before able to reach the key, likely within its ignition, and stepped out onto the road. Slowly making my way toward the officers and continuing passed, before stopping and turning to one of the men, "Would you know which way to Igdir?"

"Whys that?" He demanded, as most Schutzstaffel do, in attempt to control people.

"Are," I replied, seeing Daniel still hid at the front of the car, "I hope you took your keys out of the automobile, you know fifths are about?"

The one on the left stayed silent, before replied, "Don't worry, if someone tried that we'll kill them, and Igdir is up the road from here to the east, now will you go away."

As he lit a cigarette and threw the match at my face, I caught it between my right fingers, nodding, "Thank you, by the way Igdir is down the road, don't you know anything?" As I turned away and blow the match out.

The one who threw the match near drew a pistol, as the other restrained his arm, gasping, "His not worth it, don't blow our cover now." Then heard Daniel start the car and quickly reverse out, the officers turned and reached for their pistols as Daniel knocked them down, both winded as they drove out of the way only to be struck by the rear parcel rack and their pistols thrown from their hands.

Daniel pull-out, quickly through it into gear, as I called to Esther, "Hurry," and waved her over, whilst ran out upon the road to take the passenger seat, she lowered her derringer and quickly followed. Just as Daniel pulled forth and spun the wheels, flicking dust in the nocked down officer's faces, as he approached and slowed for us to board.

Esther quickly jumped up onto the right running board and took the front passenger seat, I grasped the edge of the vehicles roof and stood upon the left runner, waving to the Germans that had been knocked down, as they staggered to their feet. Before opened the door and removing an MP 38 machinegun to one side, as I took the rear seat, Daniel accelerated down the road for few miles, as it begun to curve left to right and the back end of the Mercedes slid upon the loose dirt, "Do we have to continue at this pace?" Esther asked, Daniel backed off with a sigh, as she grinned, "Thank you. Now Smith, is there somewhere we could go to get food before dark?"

"Yes," I answered, "and best get off this main,"

"This is a main?" Daniel huffed,

"Take the next left," I replied, as we approached a side lane to a narrow dirt road, he turned hard in and down a straight one-way section, following it a near half mile and soon begun to enter between oaks, Canthium and cedar trees.

I looked back to the road we had turned off, seeing a black 770 Mercedes drive passed, with a Turkish police Opel Olympia car in pursuit, as they stuck to the main in a cloud of dust. We proceeded up a slight grade to a fork in the road and stopped to read the signs, finding it directed further left, as appose to right-where the road appeared to continue. Taking out one of the maps, finding the road specially marked upon it, saying, "Continue right."

Daniel pulled forth and soon out into open hill country, passing few Turkish wagons on the way, noting the surrounding terrain to sharply elevate. Then spotting a small Turkish café building around a bend three mile ahead, that appaired fifteen-foot-tall with a flat roof and bark yellow rendered walls and front parking area, with a stone fence around it, "here looks like a good place for a feed," I replied,

"Why not," Daniel nodded, as we pulled up outside the yards entrance, spotting another Opel Turkish police car parked before a stone water trough outside, by the buildings' open entrance and widows either side. Seeing there were Turkish police, or rather secret police seated at a table within, by the left window with its shutters open, counting five men.

We cautiously pulled in and parked beside their grey Morris Cowley, Daniel stared in through the window, seeing them chat away before pausing at the sound of the Mercedes, as if they were expecting someone and tried to act casual, as they stared at the vehicle.

"Well, they look pleased to see us," Daniel commented, "I suggest we get going before they actually do."

"No," I replied, "I think they may be in on the SS's activities. I wouldn't be surprised if they aren't afraid of them, we should use this to our advantage. I suggest we walk in like SS and ask them a few questions."

Stepping from the vehicle and heading to the café entrance, Daniel followed ahead of Esther, I turned whispering, "Ok, we should act like SS operatives, if they ask questions, we'll say our contact is in eastern turkeys' upper land holding of Agri."

Before entering the restraint, seeing a ten-foot-long three-sided-bar in the centre terminating at a rear wall before a kitchen. Noting sets of tables and chairs either side, lined in basic red and white patch cloth, instantly turning to those seated to the right and the Turkish police to our left, with a vacant table further toward the counter, as they drank red Kavalkidere wine and eat Turkish roles.

I stepped forth to the counter and looked over a small menu board hung from the ceiling to the right and read aloud to a man in his thirties stood behind the counter, "I would like the chesses," I pointed, "Chechil, grilled halloumi, Kashkaval and chive rolls with the roast off the day,"

"So sorry," the man sighed, "we are all out of goat, camel and lamb, we only have the beef roast today. Will that be fine?"

"We'll take it," I replied and handed him more than the listed fee upon the menu,

"I'll bring it out, soon as it's ready," he nodded.

I then turned toward the Turkish police and sat at the vacant table down from them, Daniel and Esther too took a seat, as I now facing the entrance door and window, I had peered through earlier, on spotting the Turkish police. Two of their high ranked officers seated at the end of their table, stood and turned to me, one asked, "So what's wrong this time? Or is it that you have changed your orders?"

"Nothing has changed," I answered, "except, I was simply here to find out what you've done so far?"

"I've just had a speech in the village," he replied, "that if anyone sees anyone from British or Arminian society, they must contact the station immediately. But so far, we have had no problems, perhaps this person you call smith and his small army, are no match for the third rich?"

"Yes, but we like to be certain," I sympathised, "check and checkmate, for that individual will be able to evade. Now that you and your men are informed of what to look for, I have come to eat and talk about what you may know of the dig sight."

"What dig?" he asked, "We do this for your high command, I thought?"

"Are, we'll," I commented, "keep it up,"

Seeing the food was being bought out by the bar attendant, as he sat a number of ceramic bowls upon the table with a large two kilo beef roast and selection of breads. He then retrieved a bottle from the counter and sat a cup before each of us, placing the twenty-year-old bottle, nodding, "In joy," before leaving,

"Well," Daniel committed, "you certainly get value for half a mark in these reigns."

Their leading constable and the other men stood to leave, he turned to us once more, "As usual, in one of my highly recommended restraints. For any of our German friends," and left by the entrance, as the other police followed him out to the car, before driving off.

We began to eat, now knowing some more about the police and secret police, I thanked God for the food and the day, Daniel whispered, "So, Smith I think it best we get going as soon as possible and perhaps catch some sleep."

"Yes," I nodded, lowering a cup of water from my mouth, "I agree; the Aspet hotel in Igdir is but five miles from here, according to the map,"

"Well, Turkish food isn't bad," Esther committed,

"Nar, this isn't standard Turkish food," I explained

We then finished up and stood to leave, suddenly hearing another vehicle pull up outside, I turned spotting it a blue Mercedes W 21, followed by another painted white. A Gestapo in standard under cover uniform step from the first, as five undercover officers stood from the second. Seeing the first, and possibly lead officer, turn for the restraints entrance.

"Best head for a back door," I suggested on leaving the table, noting the café continued further back and made our way passed the remaining vacant sets and counter to the right, toward a door in the rear left corner of the room.

Staying low, we near crawled to the door, while the first few German officers entered and turned to the front counter. Thankfully reaching the door unnoticed, we silently entered, as I stood realising it no more than a large cupboard, lined with shelves.

Daniel quickly closed the door behind and peered through vents within the door's upper quarter, hearing the Gestapo officer ask the bar attendant, "Have you seen this man?" Presenting a photo of me,

"Yes, his one of yours's," the barman gasped, "he just talked with the police, he was just... Oh, where's he gone...?"

"What?" The officer huffed,

"I served them not a half hour ago," the barman explained, "surly they'll be here somewhere, their car is out the front. Is something wrong?"

"Two of our men here had their car stolen; that car is outside," the officer replied, whilst further men entered, "if we cannot find this man and what you're saying is a cover for Armenian resistant's, I'll have you shot. Men search every inch of this Turkish centre and see whether Smith is here! And you bar tender, I'll be placing under observation."

The officers begun to look around the cafe with pistols drawn, and we spotted the drivers of the commandeered vehicle stood guard outside, Daniel asked, "Well, do you think they'll find us?"

"I think they just may," I sighed

"Are look," Esther pointed above, "a manhole."

Daniel and I turned to the fifteen-foot ceiling, spotting the manhole, I grasped the timber shelves at chest height, lined with paint tins, whispering, "Ok, let's use theses shelves." Finding the first sturdy enough, I placed my hands together and half knelt, "Quick," offering to give Esther a lift.

She stood upon my hands and climbed up first, before Daniel and pushing off the wall to the right of the six-foot wide shelves, avoiding the gear placed upon them. Bumping few pain tins as I pulled myself up and climbed the selves, Esther opened the manhole and proceeded out, as Daniel and I followed before recovering the hole.

Finding we were now upon the flat roof, with a four-foot rendered brick wall along the surrounding edge, "Stay low," I gasped, we all ducked down, and I carefully approached the front edge of the roof, seeing there was a near half mile wide, steep grass covered hill to our right, before the level grounds of the building. Quickly turning left and finding it slopped down to a small valley behind the café, with few trees within and upon the surrounding hills.

Then saw two of the officers walk around to the front of the building from the left, before continuing around, monitoring the building and surrounding terrain. Seeing the two officers stood out the front, guarding the cars, as one looked out at the scenery to the left and the other readied his pistol, while stood before the first vehicle.

Another car then showed up and parked to the left of the vehicles, as more under cover Gestapo officers stepped out and received orders from one passing by as they begun to walk around the restraint area, "Are," sighed Daniel, "so there are more Germans coming?"

Seeing they had left another to guard their vehicle and he stood to right with a pistol, I withdrew from the edge, "Well, once the ones on our right are gown, I suggest we find a break in their movants around the sides of the building and get going through the countryside."

Turning to the left edge, whilst staying low, and finding the area clear as the officers speared out further downhill beyond the building. Spotting a previously car parked beside the building, midway along, that appeared to be a Buick master six, no doubt belonged to the restraint informant, commenting, "Look down at that red Buick convertible, with its roof set..."

Daniel turned to edge, in question, "How did that cafe, bar attendant...?"

"The Germans do like to pay with gifts, at times," I commented, "they must have given him that shiny Buick instead of a jerry car. Anyway, it's a vehicle; let's see how well it goes."

Still finding there no other Germans, I quickly climbed over the slight wall and hung down off the edge of the building, placed my foot on its protruding main truss support, and used it to get down. Daniel followed, before Esther, as I stood and took the drivers' seat, Daniel the passenger and Esther the rear, as I hit the ignition.

"Quick man," he gasped,

Esther kept her head low, gasping, "But aren't you afraid of their guns?"

"They aren't guns," I commented, "they're pistols and so long as we stay a hundred yards off…" as I took off, along the wheel track driveway and kept our heads low, on accelerating passed the Mercedes parked out front and onto the dirt road, turning left with hast. The confused officers guarding, fired few shots at the vehicle, as we became out of range and continued to speed down the road, thanking God we are all right.

"Won't they come after us?" Esther asked,

"Defiantly, " I answered, "the road curves ahead, before Igdir, where we can take a side street to the hotel there, we won't have time to make a mistake, best I take the map and Daniel the wheel."

THE ARMINIAN HOTEL

Quickly trading placed with Daniel, while keeping the vehicle in motion, I took and further studied the map, finding as suspected many of the roads listed miss represented and likely dead ends. We swiftly speed around few bends, as I directed to a side road and begun to see the village of Igdir upon the hill to the east or left. Following the unmarked road around, soon passing small houses on our left, constructed from clay and timber.

"Enter here," I suggested, as we approached an entrance road to the left and turning up the hill, "take a right," I directed, as Daniel veering into a narrow side street, with buildings either side.

We began to see through the gaps of buildings downhill; to our right, one of the German Mercedes and Turkish police cars, speeding by along the main road below. Thankfully finding the buildings below, had impeded their view.

"I think we're clear?" Esther gasped,

"Yes, for now," I sighed, as we continued to the end of the street, and entered another running left to right, across the edge of the villages' hilly landscape. We headed up hill to the right and neared the town's northern outskirts, "Now this hotel should stand out some…" I assured, spotting a near eighty-foot square, two story high hotel, with a stables built off the left wing, constructed from brick concealed by white render and orange tiles upon the roof, before a walled in front court yard.

"There's its entrance," I pointed, as Daniel swerved in off the road and entered the near acer yard, discovering a twenty-foot shed to the right of the large building or possible stable-hay loft, with a sizable dual doorway and upright within its centre for support.

"Now what, jerry will spot a red Buick a mile off?" he huffed,

"The barn," I gasped, Spotting the large, tow part Dutch doors of the loft partly open. He quickly swerved in and across the courtyard, to the right off the hotel and ramming the barn doors open on entering the loft and soft hay within, coming to a stop before turning off ignition. I turned to the review mirror, seeing no perusing vehicles enter the yard, and caught my breath, "Ok, let's see what the hotels like,"

"Honestly this far east I would had assumed this was it," Daniel smiled,

"Ha," Esther laughed, "the straw stopped us dead, I hope we hadn't roughened it for animals?"

Daniel shook his head, as we stepped from the vehicle and turned for the door, he and I threw hay over the rear half of the vehicle, as Esther helped. "Mined the exhaust system and headers," I instructed, throw few more hand falls, before stepped back, "that should hopefully do it,"

"Now to the larger barn," Daniel suggested,

Leaving, we began to cross the sixty-yard wide by thirty deep yard, toward the central main building, lined with five foot slender windows, equipped with open shutters and locally patterned curtains, coming to few rounded marble steps, before its opened twin front doors. We continued up and entered into an eighty foot long, by twenty-foot-wide lobby like atrium, with a staircase either side the entrance, lead up to second story walkways or open corridors, with decretive timbre handrails ran outside multiple arched doors, to the hotels' second story accommodation. And below the up-stair corridors were further arched doors to rooms below, with Turkish red, green and black patterned tapestries hanging from hooks between.

Noting a red, white, black and even green coloured, eight-foot-wide Persian rug lining the centre of the atriums' floor, leading toward a six-foot-wide, closed front desk covered in papers to the right. I stepped forth toward the desk, spotting a ledger book upon it, beside an ink well.

Before hearing the sound of a vehicle pulling into the yard outside and quickly turned, only to spot a black 770 Mercedes drive on by, passed the hotel entrance, before a voice greeting in Turkish, "*Tebrik*," and quickly turned.

Seeing a mid-age man stood at the desk, "*Tebrik*," I smiled, "I would like a room for tonight, one large enough for three?"

The man, dressed in a common Turkish red tunic, answered, "Why yes, we have such a room, mister...?"

"Ballery," I replied, while approaching.

He drew a quill from the pod upon the desk and wrote down the name, retrieving a key from a draw with his free hand, offering, "here up the right stairway,"

"Thank you," I accepted, before turning from the Turk and begging to walked back toward the stairway, finding the key marked four in Roman numerals and spotted its door above, before proceeding up the stairs.

"A unique accent that man?" Daniel questioned,

"You think so?" I replied,

"They're all strange to me?" Esther whispered.

"Room four," I pointed, on approach and turned back to the man stood behind the desk blow, as a Turkish policeman entered by the front entry, brandishing a riding-crock in hand, like a jockey before a race, accompanied by two further men stood behind. The man with the crock walked up to the Turk at the desk while tapping his right hand with the cane, slapping against his black leather glove, "Are, have we seen any strangers," the officer inquired, "or a man by the name of Smith come in?"

The inn keeper at the desk, still filling in the ledger book, took little notice of the policeman, answering, "No names like that on today's page, nor in the last week. But may I remind you that information is confidential and could be just telling you what I think perlite for someone impatiently clapping his hands, contentiously awaiting my reply."

The Turkish officer smacked the edge of the desk with the cane, and innkeeper looked up scandalized, as the officer huffed, "I hope you realise what I determine perlite for that withholding information, on conspirators and Armenian rebel dogs?"

The man at the desk stood, "Sorry, but there is none by that name here," he urged, "perhaps you could describe him; you know, the other thing you'd do if you were a real policeman."

The Turkish officer withdrew his crook and smacked the man at the desk across the face, huffing, as the innkeeper felt the bleeding right side of his face, "Again with the ordering around, remember," as he held the end of the crook beneath the man's chin, "I'm the one asking the questions, don't try to make a fool of me in front of my men again, or I'll have you executed...!" suddenly drawing a small photo and presenting it with his free hand, "have you seen this man?"

The man at the desk glanced at the photo, while holding pressure upon his face in order to limit the bleeding, "No," he smiled, "I haven't seen this man. Now that your questions are over with, get out,"

"Not just yet; Vivid," the officer grinned, "show us guest some hospitality, as we we'll soon be the new owners." The two men stood behind the officer drew their pistols and aimed toward the innkeeper, Vivid, the lead officer also drew a German luger and prepared to fire.

Daniel and I held our pistols ready at the sight, "I've got the one on the right," I whispered, "you go for the left," and fired, taking out the two underlings.

The lead officer turned and fired as we ducked on him frantically discharging his Luger and run for the front door, before turning back. The innkeeper quickly ran from the desk, counting the officer had just ran out of ammo and threw his left fist across the side of perpetrators face, as he swung round, and the innkeeper placed an arm around the officer's neck upon striking his back and pulling him down. He quickly stepped to the left of the Turkish policeman, as he fell and threw his right fist into the officer's face, to knock him down, followed by another as the officer blocked with his arm and pistol whipped the face of the innkeeper, as he lent forth before kicking him in the gut. The innkeeper fell on his back as the officer stumbled to his feet and proceeded for the door.

The Vivid laid whined, though quickly grasped the officer's right foot, on tripped the policeman, before striking twice at his back with his free hand. The officer moaned and quickly turned over, throwing his left foot against the side of the innkeeper's face, as he partly ducked to the left and the officers boot struck his shoulder, coursing him to relinquish his grasp in pain.

"Well..." I sighed, quickly lowering and concealing my pistole, before slid partway down the stairways' banister and jumping the last steps to the hotel entry doorway, cutting off the officer. He shook his head with a smile and threw his left fist toward my face, I quickly grasped his left arm, finding the riding crook still hung from a wrest strap, as he withdrew from my grip and I snatched the crock on swinging it hard across the left of his face, coursing him to flinched to the right, crying, "Are...!" filling it had broken the skin, I threw my left fist against his jaw before following through with a hard right as he fell backwards, passed out.

Daniel then came down and walked pass, to aid the beat-up innkeeper, offering a hand, "Ecad man, don't you know how to pick your fights?"

"Oh, I know," he sighed in English, "I was once a senior police chief constable in Armenia, before the third rich secret service came around. They have been harassing me and fellow countrymen who fled, because as a Christian I wouldn't work for the Germans. That man a sergeant and chief inspector; ahead policeman, before making deals with the enemy,"

"Why strike back now?" I asked,

"Oh, this wasn't the first time," he answered, "I'm actually with underground intelligence, for British intelligence. I recognised your photo and knew you were in trouble; they truly desire you dead. I couldn't let those thugs take another man for the Nazi's cause."

"Well," Daniel commented, "We'll talk more later, for now you best get some rest, in case any other police come. You can't appear fatigued."

An elder man entered from a door to our right, "Vivid," he gasped and quickly approached,

"I'm fine," Vivid waved, "Joselyn these men are English; perhaps I should lay down,"

"Carful Vivid," the concerned friend, urged and begun assisting him back towards the door, closest to the desk.

Vivid turned requesting, "If you could help secure Mr Sivas and leave the two officers aside, so we may sort to their brief funerals,"

"As you were," Daniel urged, before turning to me, "I'll sort this Smith, if you and Mis Esther wish to retire, I have one or two questions for our concierge,"

"Ok," I called, turning to Vivid and Joselyn, "we'll be in our room, providing we haven't cause you any further trouble?"

"No," Vivid insisted, "but don't open your door unless you hear five knocks, as the final notes to Mer Hayrenik."

"Well, I know what five knocks sound like," I replied and turned to Esther at the base of the stairs, "come on Esther, let's go."

As we made our way back up the steps, before the second story corridor to room four and entered, finding it a fifteen-foot square room, with light green walls and a king size four post bed to the left of the door, with a gold painted arched head against the front wall and white post supporting its arched canopy. I turned right to another bed and small dressing table at its end equipped with an oval mirror, before two glass-panelled white doors to a small outer balcony surrounded by a decretive iron railing, overlooking the tilled roofed of the donkey stable below. Stepping forth, noting the floor lined with a large green, blue, black, red and white patterned rug, and crimson drapes either side of the entrance to the landing.

Esther quickly entered and jumped into the left bed, "I'm defiantly going to sleep," she smiled,

"Right," I commented, "at lest you weren't shaken by the fact we had witnessed both a corrupt or well stimulated police force and far more dangerous Schutzstaffel if not German Abwehr, likely monitoring the hole area if not hole south regent?"

"No, but it seems Kuoiti was no different to societies and peoples being oppressed in many places and regens. But I pray and trust it will not be forever and, in the meantime, stay human rather than cut off all emotion,"

"Some find that last commit difficulted," I sighed,

"Witch part?" she gasped, "Pray is what we all must do, to stay human some see as optional, though to observe what is Good certainly reflects in one's actions," she smiled and begun to sleep.

Finding Daniel had not arrived, I shut the door, before turning to the spear bed as I lay on my back and waited, taking out my pistol and laying it to the right as I prayed to God, thanking him for looking after us, before falling asleep. Awoken by the glaring morning sun shun in from the room's balcony and loud grunt, grasping my pistole upon sitting up and turning toward the end of the bed, spotting Daniel asleep on the floor with aid of the cushion I had rested my head upon.

"That's a change old boy," I smirked.

Before hearing few voices emit from downstairs as I stood from the left side of the bed and turned to un looking the door, finding doth Daniel and Esther asleep before stepping out into the corridor. Seeing two men dressed in over coats, had entered the lobby below, while accompanying Vivid to his desk. Carefully sneaking towards the stairway, holding the pistol ready and proceeding down; hearing but the muttering of few words. I concealed the revolver behind my back and approached, asking, "Any trouble?"

The two men turn as Vivid answered, "Are, this is the man that saved me from Bozorg Sivas. He seems to be British and fear fighter, but as far as I know Bozorg wanted him for reasons only the German Wehrmacht have. But like us all, I would think him wanted for showing resistance, ha...?"

"Smith is the name, remember. And no, not for the same reasons," I assured, putting the pistol away and stepping to the left, "we're wanted by the German Abwehr because we are interested in finding artefacts they too seek; before they can be recovered," holding back the full detaisle.

The elder of the two men with a moustache, stood beside, smiled, "Are, so you are a rebel, ha well. We want as many rebels as we can get,"

"What kind of finds do you hope to secure Mr Smith?" the other inquired,

"Are, that isn't certain." I sighed, "Though I believe you have a local post service, that receives mail from airplane? I would like to go there tomorrow; could you tell me where I may find it?"

"It's just out of town, to the south pretty much opposite this location, but why?"

"Oh, I just wanted to send word," I replied, "and do you do breakfast?"

"I'll get the woman chef onto it straight away," Vivid smiled,

"Thanks," I nodded, "we are quite famished," before retrieving few documents from my pocket, acquired from the German officer's briefcases, "are, and could any of you tell me where this red, highlighted area is in this photograph?"

Handed it the elder of the two men, as he laid it out upon the desk and all three gazed upon the aerial image, the younger of the two men, replied, "Yes, we know this area, it's a stretch of mountain pass between Karakoyunlu about five miles out, and Hasanhan, why is this?"

"Because a convoy of German trucks are going through there this afternoon," I replied, "and each carrying equipment and loot from what the papers describe." Before presenting further papers, as they looked upon a possible manifest.

"Are yes, equipment and artefacts," Vivid nodded, "but what's in it for you?"

"Hopefully more information from officers leading the convoy and to finalise the location of an old friend. Besides, I am too considered a rebel,"

"Hem…" he smiled, "we'll study these papers and find the best area to hit them. I'll get some scouts onto it."

"Thank you, I'll be in the room," I replied, before leaving their presence and back up the stairs to our room, thanking God for the day and that it would work out with his help.

INTERCEDING THE CONVOY

Re-entering the room, I quickly turned to Daniel sat upon the left bed, to the right of Esther, as he inquired, "So how did it go? I peered out and saw you having a conversation with the Turk's?"

"Well, you know the maps found aboard the plane describing a rendezvous point for a German convoy heading in northwest from the Armenian boarder?" I commented, "I realised that even if we knew the Arks location before them, they would not be far off, and we would need a diversion. So, I explained to Vivid's friends that a shipment of valuables would be within the trucks of the convoy, to help motivate the Arminian rebels and likely number of Turkish bandits among them,"

"Do you think they'll buy it?" Daniel questioned, "And consider that we may want something in return for this information?"

"Yes," I answered, "so I clarified, we want documents from the lead vehicle, nothing more."

Suddenly hearing an increase in the number of voices emitting from the atrium and turned to the door, Daniel followed as I partly opened to overhear, spotting the three men below still engaged in conversation and two further men now stood by. The elder stood closest to the corridor, beside Vivid, suggested, "...I say we keep your guest here,"

"I agree," the younger seconded, "it's like he said, if that's a gold run; those papers Mr Smith wants, could very well lead to more equipment and priceless *tesoro*. We could use such treasures against the Germans."

A woman stood from a door opposite with a breakfast tray and passed Vivid, he raised his hand before her as she stood aside and he addressed those present, "Ok, now it's clear we don't want these guest interfering; I'll take them their breakfast," nodding to and taking the tray from the women, as she turned back to the kitchen.

"Here, I'm done with the Aksam," the elder replied, placing a newspaper upon the try, Vivid smiled and left his guest, before turned for the stairs. I silently closed the door and Daniel quickly sat at the end of the bed with his back turned, as I passed to the room's centre and concealed my pistole behind my back, before hearing a knock at the boor,

"Oh, come in…" I granted, seeing Vivid enter with the try of food held high, before placing it down upon a small fold out table, retrieved from beside the door, smiling,

"I do hope the food will be to your liking, and I've spoken to my friends, they think it best you stay here for safety. This is our war, but reassure we'll have your papers in due-course," he imposed,

"Wise move," I nodded, "seeing as I am but a simple biasness man…?" and reaching forth to retrieve the newspaper, "If you and the others insist, we do not wish to offend your generous hospitality."

"Thank you and don't bother leaving this room," he smugly grinned, "by the time we're gone, German scouts could be anywhere. You are wanted after all and we don't wish to give our under-cover group away, but we agree, it's safer if you stay here,"

"Naturally, old chum," Daniel huffed,

"Today's news?" I smiled,

"Only the best for our guest," Vivid nodded, "though I rather better news, so vag theses Turkish papers, a sure reflection of the times?" Before turning for the door, watching it shut before the sound of few bolt locks and Vivid's footsteps leave. Trying the handle and pulling only to find it locked from the outside side.

I began flicking through the paper, finding it littered with tabloids, Daniel asked, "So, what do we do?"

"We pray they'll not get there before us," I assured, saying a silent prayer,

"What's so important about the papers Smith?" Esther whispered,

"If we disable German supplies, we can slow them for a few days," I answered, "and any additional papers if I'm not mistaking, likely belong to Kikes, as he would have one of his trusted officers lead the convoy, and German expedition. Kikes being an old archaeologist friend of mine help promote him to what the Germans now consider the best chance to locate the ark. I would say he has orders for the selected Colonel leading the convoy that may tell us just where they have selected to set up site. But more Importantly why they want to find the ark's remnants in the first place and shed light on where Kikes is at this point in time."

Before tossing the paper to one side and stepping forth to the balcony as I looked out, finding it a ten-foot drop to the tiled roof of the small barn beneath. Notting no one to be seen outside and area of clear ground, before the edge of a forest behind the building, smiling, "Now come, we haven't much time," climbed over the railing, as Esther followed and I jumped to the roof, filling its timber joists creak and crack. Esther elegantly leaped down from the rail and stood upon the roof's brown tiles, once more finding its joist to hold, I quickly turned left, to the rear side of the building and grasped the roofs' edge on climbing down and dropping to a narrow dirt path ran alongside the building below.

Seeing Daniel leap from the balcony and run to the edge of the roof, Esther quickly hung her legs over and jumped to the ground, I quickly turned right. Spotting a stone railing built around a large ovular pathed courtyard, within a surrounding garden of diverse plants, including jasmine and few varieties of rose. Positioned along the outer edge of the yards stone rail, stretching fifty yards from the rear of the hotel to a set of five-foot-wide steps crowned by a decretive entry arch, leading down a slight grade from the top courtyards' garden to a path leading out from the base of the steps to the woods, beyond the hotel.

Seeing the younger of Vivid's friends, who presented a more strategic point of view, threw aside a cigarette, before turning away after had perhaps dinned in the garden, to the glass doors of the hotel's rear entrance. I cautiously approached the rail, noting once near, the garden furnished by sets of stone tables and chairs for two, along the inner edge and a nine-foot-five, tiered fountain centrepiece. Finding the man spotted had not notice our advance, I jumped over the stone rail and stayed clear of the hotels rear twin glass pained doors, seeing the men chatting within whilst facing the front entrance.

Quickly running across the gardens' grounds, Esther and Daniel followed and jumped the railing opposite, reaching the far corner of the building before turning right and running to the rear corner of the hay loft, the Buick was hidden within, passing its rear south wall to the west edge. Hearing the sound of vehicles emit from the roadside, I carefully peering around the corner, as three different coloured Zis and two Lancia-Ro trucks appeared and pulled into the yard, before halting outside the hotel entrance, followed by a blue Austin twelve passenger vehicle.

Suddenly seeing the men with Vivid, run out and aboard the Austin, to lead the trucks after had likely planned for their attack on the German convoy. Seeing the vehicle turn to the entrance and take the lead, the truck drivers followed them out of the courtyard before turning right and speedily continuing down the unsealed road, whilst maquis shrubs and Turkish pines impeded their ability to view us. Finding it clear, as I ran out and around to the loft's entrance and hidden vehicle, as I ran through the hay and jumped in the driver's seat, Esther took the front and Daniel the rear, huffing, whilst I started the engine, "Well Smith they won't recognise this car and with how little we are armed, we wouldn't want them to,"

"Don't worry, we'll be able to overtake them in their dust, hopefully," I assured, as I reverts out like a maniac and hit the drakes, slamming it into gear before taking off after the trucks well up the road. As we caught up, about a mile or so down the narrow hill road, court in the dust now everywhere, I quickly turned out and overtook the long line of trucks, just before the road narrowed. Finding them to emit enough dust, they would never be able to identify who we were as I speed ahead of the small convoy.

We then, whiles looking at the map held by Daniel, sped along the curved roads of the pass through the mountain side with hast and veered into a sideroad to the left, around a right-hand sweeping bend and proceeded east. Traveling through the mountains, saving time as we bypassed the area of Karakoyunlu and continued till not far from the suggested rendezvous point, Daniel presented the map, "If we follow this round we'll come by a train station at the village of Hasanhan and if we go from there, along a road long side the tracks, we'll end up by my calculation, interceding the German convoy, long before their marked rondavel point just hear north of Aralik; so long as we reach them not long after this railway crossing."

Turning down a short road to our right and across a railway crossing, with a station further east or right, Daniel had mentioned, upon entering Hasanhan and exited the town, while flying though a three way inter section and continuing east, passed the railway station as a train left its platform, Esther asked, "Yes, but how are we going to stop the trucks?"

"I'm not sure yet, but I'll find it strange if the resistance had the same plans we have," I replied, "so, I'd say they'll wait around till this afternoon,"

"No, I mean the Germans...?" she asked,

"We only want to get at one vehicle," I answered, "that being the lead car; though I think we may cut them off if the roads narrow enough. Even pull up and say were broken down and request a lift, if we get as far as entering their vehicle....? Maybe first see whether we can persuade them to give us their information, though unlikely, we'll hinder their advance at the very least if we're too late."

Pulling in down a narrow dirt road through the countryside, few small timber fences either side with the occasional tree and clumps of bushes. Till we came to the railroad crossing, I knew we would be waiting but ten to fifteen minutes at the most, as I drove over the crossing and parked.

Daniel seeing the road wide enough for trucks to get around and knowing we would be dealing with a Waffen SS colonel, doubted, "Well, I don't think it'll work."

Noting well established tree spurge bushes either side of the road, I suggested, "Get out and head for those bushes. I have something in mind."

Daniel stepped out before Esther and headed for cover, I quickly pulled into gear and revers across the railroad tracks, know the train was due to come around the slight bend and likely collide. Stepping from the Buick and running forth to Daniel and Esther, carefully avoiding the Canthium shrubs and hid amongst the tree spurge bushes by a weathered stone fence to the left,

"Isn't that a bit extreme?" Daniel commented,

"Well, it should block the road up farther than one carriage," I assured, "and because you suggested it: calling the notion 'extreme'... I think it just taking the next step,"

"In that case, it'll work," he nodded,

"But surly we'll be cut off?" said Esther,

"Not so long as we remain concealed, and ready to move in," I assured, before silently pray to God, it would work out.

Hearing the steam powered, black 44001 locomotive approach and its whistle blow, as the engineers held speed around the bend. We all turned to the vehicle, hearing the load screech of the conductor locking up the engines' brakes upon speeding into the Buick. Damaging its front fender and bending the Buick, as it surprisingly seemed to hold together quit well, before rolled over on its side, as the hundred tone locomotive crushed the vehicle. The trains engine came to a holt sixty yards from the crossing, with but two carts partly off the tracks and the engine half derailed, mainly due to the carriage's momentum pushing hard against it.

"I think we just wrecked a dissent car Smith," Daniel committed,

"Yar," I sighed, "if the train weren't necessary,"

"Oh, and now we're without transport?" he sighed,

"That's what I said?" Esther huffed,

"We'll see," I assured, "here comes the convoy, right on time..."

Spotting a cloud of dust emit from the southern end of the road as the German convoy swiftly approached and the lead W18 Mercedes vehicle soon came to an abrupted stop, not far to our right. Noting its roof lowered and two SS officers seated in the rear of the vehicle, driven by a privet and long line of German trucks still catching up further back.

The two SS officers cautiously looked toward the wreck before them and to the right, as the officer on the driver's side of the vehicle stepped out and the other followed. The first stepped forth while diagonally passing us on approached the derailed engine, quickly drawing his Luger. The other one turned to the trucks and stretched his legs as he waved his right arm and called to the first drivers, "Stay put!"

The other Waffen officer met with the trains' engineers, as they appeared to assess the damage before simply turned back toward the crossing, to begin their walk back to the station at Hasanhan. The officer called both men over and proceeded to speak with them, before holstering his pistol and turning back to the other Gestapo officer, calling, "Just a derailment, someone must had got their car stuck on the crossing and headed for town to acquire help, the engineers say it happens at times. They'll be able to get a crane out in an hour or so," before reapproaching the vehicle and turning around to the driver, ordering, "Stop the motor and get out."

The other SS, turned toward the truck drivers and crossed to the left side of the road, "Stop your engines and get out for a stretch and short break!" Before continuing down the side of the trucks with the other Gestapo officer and driver of their vehicle and spotting the drivers of the trucks behind jump out on turning toward those further back.

"They must be going for their supply truck," Daniel whispered, "let's move."

We carefully stood and ran across to the lead Mercedes, taking the drivers set, Daniel the rear and Esther the front passenger, as I started the motor and Daniel discovered two briefcases, similar to those taken from the Abwehr officers aboard the plane, and sub machinegun upon the parcel tray. I quickly took off, like a maniac toward the rail crossing and veered right, down beside the rails steep ballast mound, alongside a stone fence, passing the derailed engine and speedily swerved up the track's steep ballast mound, on an angle.

Straightening up on approached the rails before the engine and launched the Mercedes up over the mound, cleared the line completely, while holding my foot flat as we landed before the recently wrecked vehicle opposite. Damaging the Mercedes front bumper and severely scraping its undercarriage and running board, before sliding down the steep mound of Ballast and neatly avoiding a timber fence at its base, as I proceeded back toward the road. Daniel sat up straight, after had ben bounced around and Esther rubbed her nose and forehead after taping the bash, finding none hurt, I swiftly speed down the unsealed road and back the way we came with God's help.

Continuing along the main road, knowing the Turks and Arminian rebels would be approaching us if we were to continue the same rout we came, "Start reading, what's in the cases," I called to Daniel.

He quickly opened a case, finding another warrant and threw it upon the floor, discovering few passports and map, as he read over it, "Ok Smith, we're on the back-road heading toward the town Karakoyunlu," he replied, "this map shows we continue straight through its centre. From there we take a left, about two miles out and would appear the Gerrie's onto something there; either setting up or previously had set up a base in the hills twenty miles southeast of Igdir though keeping within the region. It also appears they've marked areas closer to Igdir, a third of a mile to the north with a line of exes including one larger than the others, in the centre. I think they may know where the ark is, but they may have moved to another marked point by now. As they numbered which area they'll go onto first and dates beside; though perhaps they haven't, according to these dates relevant to the setting up of their camp but a week ago. I'd say, giving the brief time established, that convoy likely the first to return or set out from Germany. Given the information correct, we're well in front, but if we don't receive word from Boas, we won't know if their right or where to look; unless we too wish to search the whole region?"

"No," I answered, "all we can do is wait and see what they find, but is there any where we may recon the area if need be?"

He studied the map further, "Yes, actually there are few hills and surrounding trees; I suggest we do not hesitate to survey the locations. Though what if they get to whatever it is their looking for before us?"

"No, I'd say all the exes are evident of their uncertainty, beside they couldn't have had the information processed and sorted quicker than Boas, even with their resources," I answered, "No, I'd say they contacted if not took a plane, with the information likely to Fredrik Vincent. And if that's the case Fredric would have given them what he knew of, but only what he could interpret and forwarded by radio, but don't worry, Boas is fast and as he said, it should reach us by telegram first, before post, perhaps even by tomorrow morning. Then we can find out where the ark might be."

"I hope your right," nodded Esther, "or the Germans may be after something they hold more precious than gold; war, destruction and terror." I continued driving while Daniel directed, and prayed that we might succeed in stopping them.

RECEIVING INFORMATION

Re-entering the village of Igdir, I diverted south around the hills upon the out skirts toward the local postal service, passing few small farms and pulling up outside of a small square clay rendered building, between two small Turkish huts, Daniel smiled, "Let's hope they've received Mr Linnets telegram...?"

"If not do we assume the Nazis have the location?" Esther gasped,

I stepped from the vehicle assuring, "If they have it would be by no fault of Boas; stay here and keep watch," Before turned to the building opposite and entering its small front yard, to a small dirt covered path led to its open front doorway and entered into a small room, with a counter before me.

A short Turkish postman in uniform stood to attention behind it, gasping, "Yes sir, may I be of assistance?"

"You receive telegrams, have any come from a Mr Linnets for P.S?"

"Yes," he nodded with a smile and turned to enter a doorway behind the counter, quickly returning with a letter and address printed by worn typewriter, offering, "Here sir, can't make sense of it?"

I took the letter, smiling, "thank you." Before leaving by the door as we swiftly returned to the idling vehicle, tacking the drivers' seat, upon taking off with hast down the narrow road,

"Well?" Daniel asked,

"We have it," I nodded and continued back toward the hotel.

Reaching the Arminian Aspet hotel, finding its front yard empty I swerved in and quickly re-entered the hay loft, noting the coast clear, I shut down the motor and stood from the vehicle, Daniel retrieved the brief cases as I offered to carry one,

"That was fun…" Esther smiled, "wait I smell burning?"

Daniel and I dropped the cases and turned for the vehicles' front, quickly removing the hay from the headers and engine bay, while covering the rear boot, she smiled, "That's better,"

"Quite so," Daniel nodded, "we can't have the jerry bus dying on us now…"

"Right," I replied, "grab that briefcase, we must get back to our room."

Turing for the entrance and cautiously exiting, we ran around the stone shed and cautiously snuck back to the rear of the hotel, before passing its rear glass doors, on the way to the donkey shed beyond; the same way we sunk out. Once back at the donkey shed, I quickly helped Daniel and Esther climb up onto its roof, offering a boost, before throwing the cases to Daniel as he secured them and lent a hand as I climbed up.

Hearing multiple vehicles approach from the southwest, by the main road, we spotted few of the rebel's trucks, led by the blue Austen twelve passenger vehicle, re-enter the courtyard and pullup outside the hotel. I Quickly turned for the rooms' balcony and offered Esther a boost, before Daniel, near jumping to its rail and climbing over. I quickly passed up the cases and pursed for a moment, seeing but few men leave the vehicles, while stepping back. Running up to the rooms window and jumping up as I grasped the edge of the small balcony and climbed over its railing, Esther grasped the collar of my jacket to assist.

Finding we made it unnoticed Daniel quickly ran for the bedrooms door as he took out a small lock pick, fashioned from a type of wire, Esther lowered her hand from my collar as I stood, and looked into my eyes as the softening light of the west noonday sun partly shun into the room. In fear of her and I being spotted, I placed my hands upon her alarms and turned into the room from the balcony, as she smiled.

Daniel opened the door and carefully looked down into the hotels' atrium, I lowered my hands and nodded to Esther before turned for the door, as she followed, and both peered out over Daniel as he knelt before us. Spotting Vivid enter with his two guests from before and continued forth toward the ledger upon the booking desk, where a rebel bearing a dated rifle and smouldering cigar in his mouth was sat asleep, no doubt previously elected to guard the front entrance, though with a paint of beer sat before him and turned to the hotels' rear doors.

"Stand to attention!" Vivid shouted as he approached the desk,

The reclined Turkish rebel jumped to his feet and dropped the cigar upon few papers laid on the desk before him, fretfully saluting, "Yes, sir...!" as one of the papers ignited, Vivid snatched the small paint of beer and splashed it over the now singed document, bearing a photograph.

The younger of the two men with Vivid reached forth with his right hand and clutched the saluting Turk by the scruff of his collar, pugnaciously pulling him over the desk and drawing his left fist in anger, "Why you...!"

"Leave him...!" Vivid ordered, the man to the left, still grasping the nervously saluting young guard, released. As he stood nervously holding his salute, Vivid asked the novice guardsman, "Have you had any trouble with our gest?"

"Not a peep," he replied,

"Your excused," Vivid nodded, "go back to patrolling the grounds or gardening...?"

The young man lowered his hand and quickly turned, marching with hast toward a rear door and exited. We silently stood from the door, as Daniel closed and locked it with the picks before turning away and sitting upon the bed, as Esther sat upon hers, I turned to the rear balcony and looked to the front yard, spotting two men standing guard before the hotel entrance and two further men out back that had already begun to patrol. Steeping back into the room, I quickly noticing the untouched breakfast tray and grasped it before tossing its food out the window and placed it back down on the small table.

Daniel stood and quickly hid the brief cases beneath the bed, upon hearing foot steeps followed by an abrupt knock at the door, as it opened by Vivid followed by the younger of the rebel generals, he greeted in English, "Are, so how are we liking our stay?"

"Ok," I replied, "beside someone decided to lock us in and prevent us walking around the grounds,"

"I'm sorry," Vivid sympathised, "but we didn't want any German police to search this room if they choose to look for their missing offices. Anyhow, if you'd please honour my guest; diner will be served in the garden at six o'clock, please do attend, some of the men would like to meet you."

"Oh, so it went that well?" I asked,

the general stood beside him, stepped forth and saluted, as I saluted back, he nodded, "It was a great success captain Smith. For I am instating you as a captain in our army, how you managed to get such information from Gestapo headquarters...? I've been trying for quite some time to get the amount of information you obtained. We did destroy the trucks and found much explosives, guns, tents, shovels, fuel, a generator and food to feed an army. I congratulate you, for you had told us it was gold, their cargo. But you, being a true soldier, saw these things as gold and even used the word loot, to encourage some of our more questionable, criminally eager accomplices to fight. They not being true rebels; were angered over this, but we had them striped of their positions as captains and offices. Now you are captain, whenever you fill you can help our cause, please send telegram to this hotel."

"Will do general," I answered,

he presented an envelope and offered, "I congratulate you once again and your fellow fighters," saluting once more, I saluted back, as did Daniel. The general then turned to Vivid and left the room, as he too followed and shut the door behind.

I opened the envelope, finding three medals within; two copper, for a captain's rank and one nickel plated for an officer or likely sergeants' rank, intended for Esther.

"Ok..." Daniel dumbfoundedly replied, "So what did they just do?"

"Well, despite neglecting to salute the two Generals as they left," I commented, "we are now instated as rebel officers."

Esther now stood behind, inquired, "Oh, do I get a shiny broach?"

I offered her the sergeant's metal, answering, "You are now instated in the Arminian rebel army. When we win, you'll be paid a percentage; according to this letter."

She excepted with a grin, "Hem, I think it'll match the price of a dress...?"

Daniel took his meddle and letter, revealing a small map, huffing, "And now we have shares in a rebel army."

I pocketed the envelope and mettle, smiling, "Yere, anyway let's get going." Drawing the telegram and deciphering its basic code, as the second and third letter was switched from each word to the word prior and few first letters switched to words third prior. Describing compass points from Igdir as I sketched what I could upon the maps recovered, finding his words revealed direction to an area southeast of Igdir, toward Uzengili.

Noting few roads leading toward the semi open area of sorts, with few trees surrounding and going off Boas's descriptions, then marked but three exes upon the field to form a bearing-reference line. Then retrieved a further detailed map from my pocket, retrieved from the offices of the recently interceded convoy. Finding they were a fairway off, though had written further comments upon it, read aloud, "If not, try another mile-two north, toward Igdir."

Lowering the paper, "Well" I commented, laying the map with the others, pointing, "we have the location, but the Germans aren't far off. The rebels have taken out the first convoy, but there may be a second by the time they have things figured, in as little as a week or few days. But Either way, we may have enough time to find what their after, in the field Boas has described."

I proceeded to interpret a further telegram, discovering it a translation of descriptions Esther had copied from the lost mines, with a message to start off, as I grinned before reading, "Are here; so, what did Boas write...'Smith I tried my best to translate and have succeeded well. It is a matter of finding yet another artefactual treasure, as it is written, 'The waters have destroyed all and have covered much with earth, now the only evidence of the lands' early positioning and the way the earth was shaped; was deeply etched upon stone to the sunset side, of the arks' remains. By our great ancestors and others who wrote and carved out their ideas of the lands' layout, before believing the land had not changed overly much, and so they may not forget the lands prior form.

So, they may not get lost and know where to travel, though it useless, for the earth has now changed as though made a new, for all is covered in earth. But in this washed earth we have been given a second chance from God, we will live as commanded to Noher and his family that were told to spread from the ark and all over the earth in great numbers.' See Smith, they wrote this down as a type of reminder, before their cities or towns were built, likely near the locations given; as believed a second resting place for the ark, safe from volcanic destruction over the years? This information was what the Germans had discovered, by acquisitioning help from my old friend, Fredrik Vincent. Who has gained enough information to discover the location of treasures, the Germans had wished you to find? For you have gown as far as to correct me at times…"

"Ok," Daniel nodded, "so, jerry's after an ancient-world map of sorts? Do you think it'll be on the ark?"

"No," I replied, "I think they were alluding to large stones, if not boulders, to whichever side of the ark captures the sun as it sets. Theses rocks could have been used for quite some time, till rendered useless."

Esther studying a map, commented, "Unless you were looking for treasures to dig up that were covered by the earth of course?"

"Your point is quite clear," I agreed, "the Germans want to find treasures from a time prior the flood, or around areas the water had influenced." While packing the papers within my jacket, imploring, "There's no time to lose. Let's leave before sunset and the Abwehr's Waffen SS catch up, considering they're likely not far behind?" Turning once more to the balcony and cautiously looked for men stood guards or patrolling the grounds below; praying for safety and we might plan the next move with God's help.

FINDING THE ARK

Finding no rebels present on the ground, I swiftly climbed over the railing, discover but few men gathered toward the far-left or northern side of the hotel, passed the stables of witch roof we had used to climb upon. Leaping down upon its thick tiles again, as Esther and Daniel carefully followed and stuck to the stone wall of the main building beneath the balcony, spotting a Guard step from the far rear left corner on passing the north edge of the brick stable and deviated east toward the forest behind the hotel.

Another soon stepped from the buildings' far front corner and out into courtyard, stopping but thirty yards out, I whisper to Esther, "Step where I step; to avoided further cracking the tiles."

Then cautiously crouched down and snuck to the rear eave of the roof, carefully grasped its edge upon half swinging down and jumped to the dirt path below. Noting a waiter setting up tables, on the far side of the hotels' garden and waited for Esther, as the guard seen prior continued further out, and I caught her in my arms as she dropped, assisting her to the ground, Daniel quickly jumped down beside.

We carefully snuck north away from the main hotel building, as the man stood guard approached the forests' edge to the east, and another two waiters appeared from the hotels' rear door to set up tables. Quickly reaching the far corner of the stables and continuing around, spotting two further men stood guard fifty yards out, monitoring the northern edge of the surrounding forest.

I steeped forth to the buildings front corner and peered around, noting the number of vehicles parked within the yard, outside the hotel entrance, as a further vehicle pulled in from the roadway and park behind the line of cars. Two footmen stepped from the hotel entrance to open the door of an Arminian rebel general's white Morris twelve. As a mid-aged man stood from the vehicle and passed the footmen, as both they and the chauffeur dressed in bark olive uniform, retrieved luggage from the rear of the Morris and took it inside.

Finding it clear, I whispered, "Come, before they return," steeping out and swiftly running pass the number of vehicles toward the buildings front entrance, as the general stood within the atrium was greeted by two rebel offices, whilst the chauffeur followed the two bellhops up the right stairway.

Noting the soldier to the general's right had a monocle and moustache and other smoked a pipe, as each appeared preoccupied with their guest. We proceeded to cross the courtyard to the west side of the hotel complex, before re-entering the hay loft and snuck around the concealed Mercedes; we had borrowed. I once more took the driver's seat; Esther ran around to the passenger and Daniel the rear.

Quickly started the engine, seeing a turquoise Wolseley hornet six passenger vehicle enter the hotels yard from the road, as I casually reversed out and through it into gear to take off passed few further vehicles. Seeing the second vehicle to enter likely another stolen Mercedes, all but trading paint upon passing and quickly veered right, through a gap between a red approaching Skoda 860 passenger vehicle and proceeded down the road, as none seemed to suspect a thing.

We then continued four hundred yards, before turning right as I remember the map and speedily continued up the narrow roads, and further southeast through the steep mountainous terrain. Till eventually nearing a fifty-ace field to our left and slowly driving alongside a small, weathered fence comprised from timber and stone, off the edge of the unsealed track. Stopping short of its narrow entrance gate, seeing there was open hill county beyond the meadow with a number of stepped ledges within a valley.

Seeing the ground mostly bear, with a distinctive raised series of large mounds, formed as though contours, more than a few hundred yards in from the recently used dusty track as the stern sun shun across the field from between the surrounding hills, barring few poplar trees, and further eliminated two large boulders toward the top far west side of the undulated hill, Daniel pointed, "The sun is over the far side. Look the stones!"

I drew the modified map and found my calculations correct; Boas as usual described the location to be within a hundred acres. Noting raised sections of the field I had marked with an exe and circled, as a more likely place for the location of the ark, and the site had not been excavated. Before turning downhill to further large field opposite, with a small German camp set in its centre equipped with but few kubelwagen-jeeps parked outside the main tents, likely after calling it quits for the day, and no personal to be seen.

knowing we still had plenty of day light, I smiled, "Your right, Boas has marked this point, all we need do is get to those stones…"

Suddenly hearing two German SS officers upon motorcycles, ride passed within the left field, followed by two Wehrmacht soldiers upon BMW R12 dispatch motorcycles. The officers left the field by the partly swung open gate before us, the offices then approached and came to stop, followed by the soldiers and stood from their motorcycles.

The officers belligerently brew Luger pistols and positioned either side of the vehicle, the officer by my door, ordered, "Halt, state your orders!" I reached toward the documents upon the seat, while slowly raising the vehicles engine speed from idle and turning to offer one of the warrants with my photo upon it, as he accepted and the other lowered his pistol. I quickly released the clutch and pulling forth with my right foot planted, the two men stood before the vehicle abandoned their cycles, as I rammed into them and straight over the top, wrecking the fuel tanks and even wheels upon accelerating through the timer panelled gate to the right.

The officers franticly begun to discharge their pistols, as we kept our heads low and continued well out of range, Esther then laughed. Whilst I speedily crossed the field to a depression midway and powered through, carefully avoiding the bumps and contours as much as possible, and risk of damaging the large, square, ship like contours on continuing up hill. Running over a section and causing a four-foot piece of fossilised timber to protrude from the soil. I fought for traction and proceeded to accelerate up the hill, holding momentum as the wheels spun and launched over few small boulders on reaching the larger, I quickly pulled in behind two of the largest stones.

Finding a small mound of rock piled up around its bases of the stones, I stopped the vehicle and stepped out, as Daniel and Esther followed, seeing the one on the right was about eight foot wide, by six foot tall, and other similar, though slightly rotated, "Quickly now," I gasped and begun to remove the stones from the base of the left bolder, Daniel ran to the other and begun to clear its base, discovering part of a slightly curved line engraved above the pile of stones.

Daniel begun to crouch and clear away what he could, as Esther kept watch and begun to help pull the stones further away. She and I peered out to the left while clearing, spotted the officers and soldiers now running back toward their camp, she gasped, "Look, I found something!"

I turned, seeing we had uncovered a world view of the earth, starting from the north pole down and begun to uncover variably shaped areas, finding the bodies of land marked out distinctly different, with each boundary marked as though a country or even large states.

"I found part of the world," Daniel exclaimed, "starting from the base up."

I drew trace paper, retrieved from a large carbon book, and unfolded few pieces on running over before carefully trass what I could, whilst Daniel uncovered further representations. Hearing the sound of vehicles near, I turned attention downhill, spotting a further group of several Wehrmacht soldiers upon motorcycles, accompanied by two SS officers soon to approach. Quickly handing Daniel the papers, encouraging, "keep at it, Huns is on the prowl."

He accepted both the paper and charcoal pencil, as I quickly turned to Esther, uncovering further depictions, and approached handed her a small sketch book and silver pen, liberated from the Gestapo office's suitcase, while briefly kneeling besides, "Copy it, I'll see to this lot,"

"Carful Smith..." she sighed, upon hearing the sound of their B.M.W R12 motorcycles pinging their way up the hill as I stood from the stone and held my pistol ready, before running furth downhill, to the men attempting to ride up and took a shot at the closest, as he fell backwards, and the bike rolled toward me.

Few others near dropped their cycles upon stopping and others came to a halt further down, drew pistols to fire in retaliation, I quickly jumped on the B.M.W and road across to the left or northern side of the hill, finding a remaining three of the riders still heading toward Daniel and Esther, while spread out across the hill. I quickly fired few shots toward them, managing to strike one second from the first, while slowly tacking off across the hill, firing a further three shots toward them, hitting one's headlight, one's tire and perhaps another's fuel tank, as they all diverted and came after me.

I quickly flogged the bike hard, as I near lost balance and put the pistol away, as the field roughened along the hill and instead turned down the grade, to one of the contours. Seeing smoother ground beyond the near five-foot mound and slight hole opposite, I held it flat and pulled up, as I hit the contour and jumped over the depression hole, only to landed hard, as the bikes frame court some soft soil covering the arks remains, beneath. Riding less abrupt over the next mound, whilst turning back, spotting the two men out in front attempted only to land within the ditch and came off, as the others went over the contour either side of them, to avoid the hole, upon witnessing those who fell.

Accelerating down the hill and over multiple ruts and bumps, as the rear wheel skidded from left to right and gunshots emitted from those pursuing, one bullet struck the rear tall lamp. As I approached the base of the hill and quickly headed for the entrance gate, locking up the brakes and slowing before turning left and through the grate, taking off down the narrow road.

The men with an officer among them proceeded down the hill to the gate, before entering the narrow way in pursuit, whilst one of the soldiers broke away and entered the field opposite, toward the camp. I accelerated to increase the gap between the three men pursuing, now coping my dust and found the track to further narrow ahead, quickly hitting the brakes and sliding to a halt, before lowering its stand and leaving it parked across the road.

As I could still hear the German cycles approach through the cloud of dust and stood clear, to the right of the road, seeing the officer emerge from the dust filled air, traveling an essay fifty-sixty mile an hour and tee bond the parked B.M.W, as he flipped and fell off, before another not long behind, as he slid out and was thrown from the motorcycle. The third traveling slightly slower upon a Terrot HST motorcycle emerged and hitting the laid over bikes, bounced over. Before skidding passed the officer fallen upon his back and came to a halt alongside me and one of the damaged B.M.W.'s

Spotting the officer laid lifeless upon the ground and other struggling to stand, in pain, suddenly removing his goggles while catching his breath, before a smirk of relief he hadn't come off, and believing I too had crashed. I steeped forth, as he looked toward the cycle I had acquired, though could not see my body.

"Over here," I smiled.

He quickly turned left and reached for his pistol, as I threw my right fist into his face, knocking him off the motorcycle and out cold before he could raise the gun. Quickly rolling the cycle back, upon jumping on and spun the rear tyre whilst turning around and swiftly took off back down the road.

Approaching the gate to the field, seeing another group of ten men on motorcycles leaving the camp within the south field, I skidded to a halt at the gateway they were due to exit by and jumping from the cycle, upon noticing a thick chain and padlock hung from the end post of its detreated timber fence. I approached seeing the German riders, but two hundred yards off and quickly swung the gate shut upon fastening it with the chain and jumped back upon the Terrot and road off, while few fired shot as they neared. Quickly re-entering the north fields' gate and turned up hill toward Daniel and Esther, near launching the mounds, spotting another SS officer who had previously fallen from his cycles, now quickly pursuing.

I turned down the steep embankments, before turning up hill, as he stayed close, till coming over the top of few mounds on accelerating and turned back, unaware of one of the arks larger far contours, seeing the officer in pursuit draw a pistol, while I mine before glimpsing ahead, far too late to pull up and unintentionally powered up over the fifteen-foot steep bank narrowly clearing the slight escarpment beyond and landing rough on sliding down. The Waffen officer, attempted to pull up short, only to swerve left up and over a Sothern section of the steep remains, abandoning the BMW once in mid-air, I struggled to hold the Terrot straight, before powering on up the hill. Speeding up the undulated ground till pulling up alongside the marked boulders and dropped the cycle, on approaching to see what Daniel had uncovered.

Discovering a six-foot square, full lay out of a world map; of sorts and him still copying it down, asking, "How close are you?"

"I'll getting it all, in the next ten minutes," he answered, as I turned to Esther seeing she hadn't yet uncovered all the depictions and quickly ran over to help dig out the loos rock, as she copied the next lot of markings down.

Swiftly cleared the remaining stones, I stood back and looked down toward the fields' gate, still seeing no sign of the soldiers, Daniel called, "All done!"

"You're sure?" I asked,

"Yes," he answered,

As Esther took another minute or so to finished and stood, with a smile, "Ha... Done,"

"Ok, quick, tack Daniel's papers and put the copies in the glove compartment of the Mercedes," I called, as she ran over and retrieved Daniel's papers before quickly running back to the vehicle, while I began to fill in and cover the mysterious map, Esther had discovered with the many loos rocks again, as Daniel did the same; both thankful they were loose enough due to recent rains.

ESCAPING TURKEY

I took a step back, spotting the band of motorcyclist now exiting the south fields' gate, Daniel and Esther ran pass to the Mercedes. I quickly placed a few more stones before following, upon Daniel's command, "Hurry!"

Turning for the vehicle and driver's seat, before starting the motor and took off down the hill toward the entry gate, as the men upon B.M.W motorcycles entered and we accelerated passed, through the gate. Swerving hard right on speedily proceeded up the road, before veering left down a wider gravel lane and soon out of sight, "Well done," Esther cheered, "they are no longer following,"

"Let's hope they fail to guess just whom we are?" Daniel smiled, before grasping the map and giving me directions through the network of unsealed roads, till nearing Igdir and lowered the map asking, "So Smith where from here?"

"Given, we still don't know what they're after or what treasure they are looking for...?" I sighed, "but the representations presented on the boulders are useless, unless you can interpret them. I suggest upsetting the German's flow of information, now I believe we have proof they are indeed being shown where to go by Fredric Vincent, or whatever his name is. Due to their methods and markings upon their maps, being only slightly out and identical to Boaz's. I suggest we pay him a visit, if in Italy I know exactly where he'll be."

"So, if we stop him," Esther commented, "the Germans would be stopped?"

"Yes," Daniel assumed, "and if we can persuade him to tell us just what their after; we can get there first and have the treasure saved if not secured?"

"Ok," I nodded, "though having alerted if not every member or combatant of Germany's Abwehr within this country…? I suggest we leave and fast."

Continuing downhill and through Igdir, while speeding toward the airfield we landed at; in hope to book a flight to Italy, specifically to the southeast coast. Reaching the airport, we parked outside its front entrance, between civilian vehicles and retrieved all documents before stepped out, placing few within my jacket.

Daniel and Esther stood from the vehicle and cautiously followed as we entered the large tent, noting a board upon an easel by the entrance, reading, "flight to Eastern bull, departing at six thirty tonight," careful not to saying a word, we turning back to the vehicle, spotting two further vehicles arrive and park on the far side of the road opposite the Mercedes, realising the drivers and passengers likely Abwehr, I turned to Daniel, "How do you fill about Easternbull?"

"If we get on that plane, we'll only be picked up in Easternbull," he sighed,

"What's wrong?" Esther whispered,

"Nothing." I replied, seeing but few people stood before the counter, suggesting, "Let's go out onto the airfield," passing by and sneaking around the Turkish civilians, silently to and through the tents' rear exit, out to the airfield. Looking to its airstrip with palm trees either side, spotting civilians boarding a dark blue Fokker F.VIIb passenger plane opposite and red striped, white Bloch 120 before us, bound for Eastern Bull. Then saw down the south end of the airfield to the left, was a silver German Gotha 145 twin seat biplane parked by a Volvo LV71 series refuelling truck, likely used for reconnaissance and perhaps the transport of finds from the dig sight or Waffen officers.

Then heard an SS officer, call to people as they entered the tent from the roadside, "Have you seen this man?"

I turned back to the rear entrance, as another officer turned for those stood by the counter, whilst presenting a poster of me, I turned forth, "Quick, to the far end of the field…" And begun to run down toward the distant buy plane, coming near only to notice two German soldiers stood guard, barring pistols. I quickly took out the revolver on approach and proceeded running toward them. The one stood to the right of the aircraft drew his pistol, as I fired, sticking him in the chest, now but fifty yards off and the other turned upon drawing a pistol.

I aimed and fired striking his right arm, as he dropped the Luger and grasped his lower bicep, before retreating to the left of the airfield, as we reached the biplane plane, Daniel asked, "How are you at flying?"

I kept enigmatically withdrawn, sheepishly answering, "Well I'm a bit rusty," before climbing upon the edge of the wing, to board the cockpit.

He ran over, insisting, "Shove over then. If you like, I'll try out this German wreck; if you don't mind."

I stepped aside, as he jumped and stepped to the front spar of the wing, before tacking the cockpit, Esther nervously smiled, "Another aeroplane... where do you sit?"

"Wait for me to sit," I nodded, on Daniel handing me the crank handle and I inserted to wind over the inverted Argus Mortoren v8 engine, as Daniel primed and started. I stepped upon the wing to tack the rear seat, placing the crank handle beside and quickly tacking off and folded my jacket, like a lanolin greased cushion placed over my legs for Esther to sit, calling, "Ok!"

She climbed into the passenger navigation cockpit and sat upon my legs, "Thanks, Smith!" she called.

I turned to the runway ahead, while peering out by her right side, seeing five German officers exit the main tent with pistols drawn, calling to Daniel, "Well, if we stay here much longer... they'll question our passenger arrangements. Ok, let's go!"

"The engine is still cooled," he called,

"Take my word for it, the engine will be fine!" I assured, "Remember we're only borrowing the aeroplane...!"

Daniel trusting what was said accelerated, as we begun to head down the strip, the officers stood out upon the dirt runway, begun discharging their pistols, Daniel filling the tail lift while facing the men ahead, lined up the planes specially mounted over wing MG30 machinegun and fired a burst toward them. Taking out four of the now retreating SS officers, before passing the remaining two, as they drove to the right with their faces hid in the grass.

We suddenly gained speed before partly taking off, Daniel swiftly pulling up before leveling at a low altitude and continued flying at a reasonable speed for the bi-winged aircraft, as Daniel asking, "So they hadn't damage anything?"

"No!" I called, "I guess not, well except for paint...!"

"And the noise of those guns!" Esther shouted,

Daniel and I laughed, as we continued over the Turkish countryside and toward Italy. Daniel utilised a German map found within the cock pit and followed it by compass, Esther put the belt over her waist and released the surrounding frame. I retrieved my pistol and begun to clean it, thanking God that we were safe and, on the way, to finding out answers, and stop the Germans with his help.

As the sun set on the horizon, we continued through the fading light and night, while Daniel used a torch to study a chart. Catching some sleep, we awoke to the sun rising in the east, seeing we were now just off the cost of a countries shore, while still over sea, I called to Daniel, "Where are we?"

Esther awoke, as he called out, "We're on the south coast of Grease, now heading to Italy! We're getting closer but I'm not so sure of our whereabouts or fuel getting us any farther than Italy's coast! We are already low; someone had just arrived at turkey in this plane; we may make it to the shore of Catanzaro only to land! But I believe the Germans had implemented further security, we'll want it to look as though a typical break down if we get that far!" As we continued flying over the ocean.

LANDING IN ITALY

We finally came over a beach off the southeast coast of Italy and cautiously continued till found a smother point, still slightly southwest of Catanzaro Marina, spotting 37mm Flak antiair guns set upon cement stans to the far left us, as the coast command radioed in, "Gotha 145 *pilota*, Report operations numbers and *detaisle…*"

I called out to Daniel, "Tell them we're plane zero, two and on operation SS, they may buy it!"

"Why not," he replied, upon radioing in, "Plane zero, tow, operation Waffen SS, we are having fuel trouble, *meccanica problema* and are to land at closest airfield spotted!" "Understood, *passare concesso*," the coast commander replied.

Daniel called back to me, "How did you know about that?"

The engine suddenly gave out and stalled, before running lumpy again, as we had run out of gas. He quickly spotted a flat beach, with few rocks upon it, as a possible place land, by a steep hill like bank of the south edge of a village further west. Daniel put the biplane into a controlled dive, before levelling on what fumes were left in the tank,

"What's going on?" Esther gasped,

"Nothing much! We're about to land!" I assured,

As Daniel glided down and carefully timed our decent as the engine changed pitch and the planes wheels touched down on the, thankfully compact, sand beach and continued along, till the engine fully cut out, and came to a stop. Daniel quickly climbed out and Esther stood, I could just start to gain filling in my legs, as she stretched, before stepping from the fuselage and out upon the wing enthusiastically jumping to the beach.

I stood whilst putting my jacket on and threw myself over the side as I near collapsed upon the sand, Daniel gasped, "There will be a patrol out here within fifteen to twenty minutes. Quick, we best run…!"

Stepping forth to lead, we begun to run across the beach, staying by Esther as we followed him toward the edge of the beach and steep grass covered hill. Approaching its base, we begun to climb its grass covered surface but forty yards, to a line of olive trees before a four foot stonewall along the edge of a paved road. Leading west or left and further right, curving passed the front entrances of many small stone, tilled roofed houses on the edge of the village. Hearing a few vehicles approach from the west end of the street and appear from around its slight bend, we quickly ducked to the ground, as two kubelwagen-jeeps passed, only to stop seventy yards up the road.

Few soldiers led by a lieutenant stepped from the vehicles and proceeded toward a small gap in wall opposite and followed a path leading down to the steep hill, to the beach and Gotha biplane plane. Suddenly hearing before seeing a couple of Gilera LTE 500 motorcycles appear from a narrow street between the houses, to the far left.

Ducking low, whilst they speed by and pulled up short of the parked vehicles, spotting one had a colonel sat within a sidecar, chamfered by another soldier, and lower ranked officer upon the other motorcycle. As both parked by the wall and each man disembarked, upon stepping passed the kubelwagen-jeeps and quickly down the narrow path, I whispered to Daniel, "Once their gone, we may have a shot at their Gilera motorcycles,"

"Yes," he seconded, "they look the easiest vehicle to obtain from this angle."

Waiting till it was clear, before jumping the wall and stayed low as we crept up to the motorcycles, finding the officers had all left for the downed aeroplane, and quickly decided on which Gilera to use.

"I'll take the one without a sidecar," Daniel suggested, "I think I'll only crash with that infernal thing attached." Jumping upon the other cycle without the cart, I took the other, as Esther approached and stared toward the cart.

"Go on," I smiled, "it's supposably safer than doubling,"

"Ok," she replied, before climbing in,

"Ok, so what do you think," Daniel asked, "witch way from hear?"

"I think we should go straight ahead at first, to the north and perhaps west" I replied, "but just follow me, I'm sure we'll be able to plot a safe route to avoid all military and Carabinier, even once upon the main roads,"

"Ok," he nodded, though puzzled and started the motorcycle, I stood to start mine after few tries, smiling to Esther; nervously seated within the cart and revved the engine upon taking off as fast as I could passed the jeeps ahead and down the pathed road, the side cart felt terrible, even whilst riding straight.

The road slightly curved right, as I veered and could see the Germans leaving the beach below, in attempt to run back up the grassy hill, to their vehicles, falling over upon the slip grass. I quickly turned down a side street, as we rode and followed it for ten–fifteen minutes, Esther turned around, gasping, "The Germans are coming!"

I turned, to see Daniel accelerate around to the left of me and soldiers perusing within kubelwagen-jeeps. I increased speed, as Daniel called out whilst passing through a narrow stone archway, supporting a railway bridge above, "Well Smith, I'll go ahead and take a detour! Where do we meet?"

"If they should follow, I'll meet you outside the hotel in Sala Consilina on the northern edge of town, on the via Nazionale motorway to Rome! Follow the main, you'll see it!"

He smiled upon speeding up and turned down a small street to the left, one of the perusing jeeps followed after him and another stayed close. Hearing few gun shots, I turned spotting a soldier within the passenger seat of the jeep kubelwagen discharge a Lugar pistol and turned hard left, into a twelve-foot-wide side street, with houses either side. Quickly turning to see the German jeep slide into the street, bashing into a half-crumbled buildings' stone wall and continued toward us,

"Look out!" Esther yelled.

I turned ahead to a twenty-foot-deep stairway before us and stood on the brake lever, as we slowly went down its stone steps and slid to the base before a side street. Seeing Daniel speed passed along the narrow way from the left, and continued north, as I pulled up short of the jeep perusing him. I turned to the jeep behind and saw its' driver to start down the steps, we quickly pulling forth across the street, finding the way clear as I powered on noting the narrow street continued but eighty yards ahead then teed into another, I quickly turning hard right.

We speed down the widening road, Esther with her hearing well attuned, gasped, "Smith!" I turned spotting three German motorcycles behind, two with sidecars armed with MG 30, one equipped with detachable box magazine and the other belt fed, accompanied by a standard motorcycle road by an officer in-between. I strangled the bike on approaching a hill, as the men within the sidecars begun to fire their guns, though could not aim upon the angle, as a cluster of bullets wretched off nearby buildings.

Reaching the end of the run as it teed into another street at the top of the grade and saw Daniel ride by from right to left, with two jerry jeeps hot on his trail, I called to Esther, "lean in!" As we turned left on entering the street, whilst those perusing reload and quickly speed up toward the kubelwagen-jeep perusing Daniel ahead. Noting the road followed the edge of the coast, with a stone wall to our right, along the edge of a cliff just off the shoreline below, and cliff face to the left.

I accelerated downhill toward the kubelwagen-jeep and killed the motor whilst rolling in neutral, "What's wrong?" Esther asked,

"Oh, well I thought it was obvious. Ok, we are going downhill and hopefully the soldiers manning the jeeps won't hear our approach. Once we reach them, I want you to crawl out and jump in the rear with that 41cal Derringer; once you are safe, I will follow. Hopefully Before the jerries on the bikes catch up."

"Ok," She nodded.

Soon rolling up to the kubelwagen-jeep, with a driver and passenger stood, while firing a pistol toward Daniel, well out in front. As the driver slowed for the other to fire and the road curved from left to right, "Get ready," I called, finding the road barley wide enough to pass the jeeps, and came up alongside to the left of the first, with the front tire of the cycle beside its rear.

Esther begun crawling out upon the jeep, as it skidded around a right-hand bend and managed to stayed inches off its bumper, she grasped its rear quarter guard, as I pushed her forth with my left hand upon her backside, to help her in and backed off to avoid striking the vehicle.

Seeing the road straightened ahead, before further narrowing. The jeep pulled away from me and slowed for the next bend to the left, hearing the motorcycle riders catching up, I approached the rear of the jeep once more and steadied the Gilera LTE 500 motorcycle before reaching forth and leaping over into the rear seat of the vehicle.

One of the riders equipped with a side cart, fire few shots toward the cycle as it veered into the jeep and rolled over, just before the sidecar and rider unable to weave around in time and struck the wrecked motorcycle with the cart. As it broke free and bounced eight foot in the air and the soldier left upon the cycle diverted hard right into the stonewall, as the front tyre griped and the B.M.W flipped over, down the cliff. Then saw the passenger within the jeep, turn toward Daniel ahead, whilst charging a machinegun offered by the driver, as Daniel was about two hundred yards out and begun to zigzag from left to right.

The driver turned to the noise of the cycles' crash and number of bullets that had struck the rear of the jeep. Seeing him draw a pistol upon spotting Esther and I laying low, quickly kicked him in the face with the sole of my boot, before siting up, throwing my right fist into his face, rendering him nonconscious. Quickly leaning forth to grasp the wheel, as the soldiers foot rested upon the accelerator and attempted to pull him over with my right arm, while crawling forth and over into the seat.

The German to the right, begun fire short bursts, as he could not hear over the wind, ordering, "Get closer...!"

Before noticing me and turned the MP 36 sub machinegun upon me, I quickly grasped a spear pistol upon the dash and attempted to fire, finding it out of ammo, the officer presenting a swash sticker upon his arm, laughed, "Ha, ha..." sternly ordering, "Stop, you fool!"

I saw Esther suddenly stand with a full aluminium canteen, and swung it by its leather strap toward the officer, striking the left temple on knocking him out, he dropped the gun over the windshield and fell into his seat, she nervously asked, "Is he dead?"

"No, just fast asleep," I answered, noting the other Germans upon motorcycles had caught up and soldier within the sidecar prepared to fire the mounted MG 30 machine gun.

"Get down!" I gasped.

As Esther dived low, the rider continued to approach, till but thirty foot off and the road straitened, knowing there no quarter at such a range. I quickly hit the brakes as their cycle struck the rear of the vehicle and its rider flew clear over the seats of the jeep and through its windshield, before tumbling out upon the road in front of the stopped vehicle. Instantly followed by the screeching of brakes and sound of the single rider's B.M.W clipping the rear bumper upon attempting the avoided the jeep and struck the stone wall, upon flipping over the edge, as its rider tumbled by the passenger side of the vehicle.

I leant over and opened the door to push the nonconscious Italian SS officer out, by the stone wall and turned to the soldier landed in front. Before turning back, as the officer within the side cart come to, finding the cart and cycles' front folks had been bashed in. The officer attempted to fire the gun and begun shout, "fire, you, inferior peace of mull...!" I lowered my revolver and begun to pull forth, finding he in his concussed state had not notice the machineguns barrel to be bent and its built belt and box fallen out upon the road.

Accelerating passed the other as he begun to sit up, barely able to stumble to his feet, we turned attention ahead and begun to pursue Daniel. A wile later we neared the town of Sala Consilina, about a mile downhill ahead, spotted him enter over a narrow stone bridge, followed by the kubelwagen-jeep not long after and appeared to veer right of the main way. Speeding down the hill, we crossed the bridge over the passing river thirty feet beneath and followed the main road, passing by the town's many houses and narrow streets to our right, whilst heading to a further arched bridge less than a mile ahead.

Suddenly seeing Daniel pull out of one of the side streets before us, and speed on toward the bridge, followed by the SS officers in the kubelwagen-jeep, cutting us off as they pulled out in pursuit firing pistols toward him, before the short burst of a Beretta M38 SMG. Swiftly catching up to the jeep on approached the narrow bridge ahead, I held my foot flat and came up alongside the door of the officer's exasperated driver, hogging the narrow road.

An officer stood upon the passenger seat, waved on singling us to slow for the bridge, before noticing Esther and I at the wheel, gasping,

"Halt, stop…!" quickly turned the machinegun within his hands toward us, just as I swung our vehicle hard into theirs, coursing them to veer further over, missing and clipping mouth of the bridges'. As we entered by its pillars and the enemy launched out over the steep riverbank upon falling thirty odd feet to the rushing water below.

Crossing the bridge and continued left up a milled grad ahead, Esther turned back laughing, "Ha, they are having a swim,"

"Or fighting the current," I smiled, before dropping a gear as it leaved and soon proceeded east, toward Sala Consilina in hope to gain on Daniel in the far distance, only to lose him through the winding bends.

THE LIBRARY

Heading further inland from the coast, coming down few country roads, with fences either side the narrow way and growths of olive trees, planted upon the gentle hills. Esther enjoying the passenger seat, smiled, despite the lake of windshield, as I glanced toward her, and wind blew through her silk like hear. She simply turned to me, anticipating a remark.

"Why the canteen?" I asked,

"I couldn't bring myself to shoot, it was the better decision, was it not, or was it wrong?"

"I leave that between you and God," I grinned, "but I'm glade," before turning to the road, spotting a large restraint and inn, about half a mile ahead to the right and saw Daniel pull into its frond park, with a surrounding hedge. We too approached and entered the gravel park, seeing Daniel's acquired B.M.W to our right, before few vehicles parked in closer to the front of the hotel or inn, and turned off the jeep once pulled up beside the cycle.

I looked toward the large wooden, sixty-foot-wide building ahead of us, with fifteen-foot-tall stone steps, leading up to an eight-foot deed porch, before a restraint built into its front, right of a large central entrance door. Noting five six-foot-tall windows along the first and second floors' front face, before the number of German vehicles to the left and a jeep, truck and two motorcycles, parked by a likely German officer's small blue Audi UW 225 and grey Alfa Romeo 6C 2500 parked beside a fiat 521c passenger vehicle.

We then saw Daniel appear from one of the six-foot bushes to the right, presenting his pistol, before putting it away, smiling, "Well, this is a surprise. You know Smith the idea to use German Wehrmacht marked motorcycles was bad enough, but the jeep?"

I stepped from the vehicle, nodding, "I agree, we mustn't continue drawing attention to ourselves." Noting the restraints' curtains drawn whilst retrieving a spare Beretta M38 and turning to the unmarked vehicles, as Esther followed anticipation.

"So, which one?" I asked, "we have a Mercedes, Alfa Romeo or whatever it's called, and Fiat?"

"We had a Mercedes already," She commented, "and I think it's time to try something else..."

Daniel huffed, "That should be an advert for their buckets."

I then, while considering something the Germans might not suspect, commented, "Alfa it is," and turned to the vehicle upon running around to the driver's side door and got in. Finding it set to go and concluding it an unmarked Abwehr vehicle, typically due to how carelessly it was parked and secured, such as anything given. Starting the motor, Esther took the passenger seat and Daniel the rear, as I put it into gear and reversed out upon the road, before throwing it into first and speedily taking off, quite well.

Swiftly drive the next two hundred miles, cautiously avoiding Naples and proceeding further west, we came to the VIII Municipio, east of Rome not far from castle Di Lunghezza. Knowing we were in the neighbourhood, upon entering the town of civilian houses and most other building constructed from stone and spotting but few other vehicles along the pathed roads and the occasional German soldier stood on a street corner.

Avoiding the traffic, I took the side streets in order to deviant toward the southern end of town, before taking a left into another with further earlier built houses and number of closed down stores either side, till Terminating before a large two-hundred-foot square, by sixty-foot-tall building ahead. That used to be an account's estate, surrounded by a fifteen-foot, bark roared iron fence consisting of inch thick vertical bars, crowned by sharp iron points, firmly held within a stone base and brick pillars between, decorated by small gargoyles. I slowed and pulled up ninety yards short of its closed arched gaits, hung from pillars stood either side, seeing two soldiers stood guard before the eighteenth-century masonry supporting the tall fence right way around the two-acer property.

"Witch building is that?" Esther asked,

"Is this not the library you spoke off?" Daniel inquired,

"Indeed," I answered, "and not a moment to spear," preparing my revolver, "are you ready?"

He left the cumbersome SMG aside and brew his newfound Walther P38, nodding, "Ok."

I gently pulled forth the last two hundred or so yards and approached the men stood guard outside the gates and aimed my pistol upon the left, noticed they; once spotted the Alfa, attempted to unsling their Beretta M38 machineguns. I quickly shot the one on the left in the shoulder, as he discharged a couple of rounds toward the vehicle, before firing my revolver again and struck his chest. Daniel fired at the other, too striking his chest, as I accelerated and rammed the vehicle through the front gates, to a half acer coble stoned courtyard, before the buildings central arched entrance door and passed by a large dead apple tree to our right.

Parking beneath another dead apple tree to out left, as the days' light dwindled and looked toward the buildings' front entrance, covered by a six-foot square flat brick canopy awning beneath a large twelve foot wide by fifteen-foot-tall centre window. Noting the awnings' roof firmly supported by foot square, brick pillars etherised. As light appeared from the buildings five-foot-wide, by eight-foot-tall, smaller arch windows, near twenty feet above ground level with deep sills and crimson curtains drawn. Counting fifteen windows up high along the front face of the large building, with small stone landings outside but few, complemented by marble railing.

Daniel looking to the right and left of the moss-covered garden, with over grown bushes and trees either side the large mansion, though mostly dead, he asking, "So Smith, this is where Fredric Vincent lives?"

"Well, I'm not sure," I sighed, "but I'd find it strange if he weren't here," while stepping from the vehicle,

"What's so ruddy, strange about that?" he enquired, stepping from the vehicle,

"Yes," Esther seconded, "I wouldn't like to stay here?"

We walked to the front door, noting it was becoming overcast and likely to storm, as the light begun to fade. Approaching I attempted the doors, only to find them locked and released the round iron handles, upon taking a step back, noting the glare of light within a high up window, to the left of the larger in the centre. Quickly turning to the doorways' canopy, spotting few of its pillars' bricks had large gaps between, suggesting, "I have an idea." Before walking over and testing my fingers in the gaps and grasped the edge of the bricks, upon climbing up till reaching and pulled myself up on top of the small stone owning, turning to Esther and Daniel, "Won't be long!"

"I'll move this car out," He suggested, "in case of Germany's finniest turn up!"

"Don't take long," Esther nodded.

As I turned toward the small decretive landing to the left and they to the Alfa. I quickly jumped across to its rail and climbing over, before looking up to the one above and carefully stepped up onto the railing and grasped the buildings bricks before reaching and grasping a decretive cornices, along the wall, and jumped, while pulling myself up close to the left edge of the landing above. Grasping the masonry and what I could of the buildings textured bricks while climbing up to its surrounding railing, just as I lost grip of the bricks.

I attempted to keep a level head and quickly pulled myself up and over the rail, ignoring the gap between me and the ground twenty-five feet blow as I stood to investigate the glare off light admitting from within. Hearing Daniel start the alfa on revers out of sight and found the light within the window to dim and attempted to open its arched glass frame. Discovering it locked, before kicking in a panel at the base and knelt to reach through to unlock its drop bolt and entered, moved the dark red curtains aside.

Steeping forth but a foot, finding I was upon a second story walkway, circle around the large two-hundred-and-fifty-foot square library, overlooking aisle of twenty-foot high, large timber bookshelves. Each housing books, parchments and artifacts, amongst many filing cabinets and further units lining the walls beneath the platform. As the walkway had slender shelving units positioned between its windows and continued right round to the buildings rear wall, and red carpeted central entrance to a large curved stepped stairway leading down to the ground floor and wide centre aisle between the shelving units.

The whole pace being lit by four large brass chandlers hug from the decretive plaster ceiling and illuminated the floors jasper, onyx and darker white marble or perhaps granite-cubit square pavers below. Turning to the central aisle three rows of desks set in single file, starting twenty feet from the base of the far rear stairway and ending twenty feet before buildings entrance, with books and a number of parchments placed upon them. Spotting a white bereded man seated just below at the first of the twenty-eight desks, by the left shelving unit and courteously faced the entrance whilst working by aid of a lamps upon the desk.

Spotting the end of a ladder beyond the hand railing before me, rested against a shelf below. I carefully crept forth, suddenly hearing a vehicle enter the outside grounds and the clash of thunder, as a storm of a storm, begun. I turned back and secured the window, seeing no sight of the alfa and the lights of the vehicle below turn off, and further head lamps shun from the end of the street. I drew the certain and waited, hearing further vehicles enter the grounds accompanied by an Austro fiat truck, before a knocking at the door and a man shout out in German, "Open this door, it's colonel Hendrik Snider!"

The elderly man stood from his desk and turning for the door, unbolting it he questioned a group of Gestapo's officers, as they entered passed, "What's it this time?" As he pursued the one in front, driest in a bark over coat,

"He wants to speak to you, in person." The SS officer answered.

As further officers entered and passed by to form two parallel lines, ither side of the colonels' four SS officers, as they too stood in line, accompanied by two Wehrmacht sergeants armed with machineguns, stood either side within the centre aisle. The elder man nervously standing before them, commented, "That's all right then...? Please come in..."

As a further fifteen Waffen SS soldiers dressed in olive uniform, barring swastikas upon their arms entered. Likely from Abwehr and each armed with an MP 38 machinegun as they too passed to form a line, behind the officers. Then saw him; Kicks Ritter-Schulz, dressed in full lieutenant generals' Schutzstaffel uniform, as he approached the elder man, I whispered in anticipation, "Well, Kicks..."

As he faced the elder man, and offered a folder of documents, "Well, Fredric, how are we? I would like you to interpret this one and solve the questions, it should only take but fifteen minutes."

Fredric nervously saluted, as the rumbling thunder charmed, and he turned for a desk to his right upon opening the folder to retrieve documents and begun to read over while writing down answers or rather interpretations.

Also noting the large piles of books sat on the desks behind and Fredrik franticly turn to retrieved books from the second desk down, to his right and open few pages, of parchments to be studied. As kikes walked quietly passed the desk with his hands behind his back, whilst a Gestapo officer walking behind with a knot pad, Kikes stood aside as the officer begun to cut pages from the books upon the desk, Fredric had marked and begun to copy others down. As they continued around to most of the desks, as Fredrik visited fifteen with laid open books of interest and continued for near three hours of study.

Fredric then sat with the papers and gathered parchments at the first desk, before sections and took notes upon paper and a number of maps as he finally, after a short four hours of study, stood nervously offered Kikes a diary of answerers, "Here, it's all there, you must find the village of Veneciy-Tillcar, which is between the last area; toward eastern Syria and Israel. The others are areas of Israeli catacombs, found in ruins. You must go there and find out where they had them hid; I believe it to be in a hidden valley of sand, in the regen. But that's all I know of it and as much as I had learnt about the area."

Kikes took the diary and turned to the now four other adware officers, still marking down listed information to notepads, asking, "Are we right?"

They turned to the rear of the room and officer still writing, as he stopped and sternly answered, "Yes, hare-general we've got it all,"

"I have just one question," Fredrik boldly asked, "who found all these papers and uncovered so much information on these artefacts; to fill in the gaps, even found in the ancient books recently discovered?"

"An old acquittance of mine, which is being hunted down," Kicks assured, "now Fredric, the gates out the front have been opened and two Schutzstaffle officers stood guard are unable to be located. Now has anyone been here?" Whilst lowering the diary and staring toward Fredrik,

"None, the door was locked," he answered, "as you said, both inside and out; I haven't heard any shots fired?"

Kikes turned to the soldiers, ordered, "Ok, one of you, over here!" Pointed toward one stood to the left, "You get out there and fire a shot with your pistol at the grate, make it five rounds and the rest of you, get out there and help the others search the grounds. Whoever it was will be here somewhere; if you men *finden* nothing I will be most *verargert...*!"

As the nervous soldiers moved out, closing the door behind then, Kicks then waited for the shots to be fired, heard little over the thunder and I few light cracks, faded by the wind and rain, Kikes confirmed, "Right, you're proven not guilty Fredric."

"So, I'm permitted to leave now?" he asked, Kikes turned to the Adwa officers and nodded, as they retrieve further books and turned for the door to exit, as the fifteen soldiers that had left re-entered.

Kicks drew his pistol on Fredrick, as he sat back down at the desk, "Not quite out of the mud yet I'm afraid. You see I cannot have any witnesses; otherwise, why would I not have seen you face to face sooner? No, you are the only one that could track it and expose the advice gained from you; in order to gain control, and the only one that could foil my planes by informing others, especially the allied force..."

"They found a silver flask sat by the gate," Major coronel Snider calling from the door, "it's unlikely they would had left it?"

"No mater, whoever came left with the bodies," Kikes assured, as four officers returned with gas cans held in hand and placed them before the gathered soldiers as one approached Fredrik with a role of rope, Kikes turned to the SS officer, ordered, "Tie him up."

The officer passed Kicks and bound Fredric's to the chair, as kikes yield, "And the rest of you!" While holstering the pistol and turning to the soldiers stood by, "I want this place treated as the Furore said to. Make sure that it is well rigged, to light this bonfire before leaving; so, get to it!" The Waffen SS eagerly retrieved the Jerry cans while other left to retrieve more and begun to run around the shelving unites, whilst dosing the contains with fuel as they passed, soon making their way back toward the exit with the empty gas cans.

I then saw Kicks light a match off a chair, to his left and turned to ignite the line of fuel, I quickly prepared my pistol and aimed up, as a Waffen soldier passed Kikes, as I fired unaware, and the built struck the unsuspecting officer's head. Kikes dropped the match and drew his custom Walther 38 pistol firing few shots toward me, seeing the line of gas ignite before him and lit up a line of shelving units. I quickly ducked behind the rial, seeing him pass by Fredrik and retreat further into the building whilst franticly discharging the gun, I waited for a break in his shots, before quickly getting up and ran to the left.

Knowing I wouldn't make it around to the rear stairway before the blazing inferno, I turned to the section of railing, before the line of shelving units to the left of the centre aisle, and stepped upon the banister, on leaping across the near fifteen-foot gape, to the ignited bookshelf. Landing upon its oak timber and laid down low from its edge to fire back at kikes stood about mid-way down the aisle. Firing but two rounds as he quickly ran in close toward the base of the shelving unit, I stood and ran along the large burning shelf toward him, firing three more rounds.

He proceeded to retreat, as smoke impeded my view, forcing me kneel once midway along, regaining sight of Kikes now stood behind the end of the shelving unit opposite. He reloaded and fired around the corner toward me. I quickly lay low and reloaded my revolver, seeing flames coming up the sides of the shelf and Kikes swiftly running out into the aisle.

I felt the shelf lean to the left and hole unit starting to full toward the next in line, due to one side of its base becoming incinerated. Kikes quickly fired a full clip toward me, whilst ruining for the buildings' entrance. I promptly stood and ran down along the shelving unit as it leant further over and fell against the units beside; on swiftly firing but few shots through the smoke, as Kicks reached the door once out of ammunition. I Jumped the last several feet threw the engulfing flames at the base, to the paved floor of the large aisle as the toppling timber unit fell against the second and third to forth, and I turned to the entrance.

"Is that you Smith?" Kikes called, whilst hid behind the thick door,

I ducked behind a pile of books placed upon a desk, as he fired toward me and struck the literature, "Yar," I answered, "I'm still here and you're out of practise,"

"You know Smith," he called, "I've been getting men to look everywhere for you, but I'm afraid you have just made me mad, and seeing as I have obtained what I came for, good by Smith. I couldn't have planned this better, ha, ha...!" As he went to close the thick timber doors, I quickly stepped forth and rapidly fired toward the entrance as it was bolded shut.

I proceeded to the doors, haring Kicks call over few of his men, "You five!"

"We heard shots fired," An officer gasped, "but were not gain to enter?"

"Never mind about that," Kikes huffed, "sergeant major stand at the gate and make sure none escapes from the front of this building, set up *Maschinengewehr* 30s!"

I then turned to Fredric, seeing he was still okay and ran over to him, quickly putting my pistol away and drawing the bayonet as I cut his ropes. He stood and pulled a gage from his mouth, before franticly gathering the documents upon the desks, gasping, "We must save it all,"

"No, time for that," I sighed, "to the ladder," stepping forth as he begun to follow toward the ladder seen earlier rested up the shelfs below the upper walkway, turning back to him, "hurry up!" as I relived him of one of two folders held within his arms and begun up the ladder, "we haven't much time!"

Reaching the base of the upper walkway's railing and climbing over, before retrieving the other folder in Fredric's hands and assisting him over the rail, as smoke filled the air. I turned for the window I entered by, seeing the German trucks leave through the gates and proceed down the street. Spotting three soldiers armed with scoped Mauser K98 sniper rifles, take up position by the gateway, in crouched positions, and two further manning MG30 machineguns set upon stands, to the left. As two black Mercedes speed by, followed by two kubelwagen-jeeps and continued up the street, filling the heat and lake of oxygen getting to me, I called, "Get back down!" As he turned and climbed back down, I followed barley able to see and again reached the base, both catching our breaths.

The remaining shelves begun to topple and catch ablaze, knowing there but one entrance, I shook my head, "Sorry, but they'll kill us if we leave, and all other exits sealed, it was already fortunate they hadn't installed bars upon the front windows,"

"What are we to do?" he ponded,

"Pray," I answered, before silently praying everything would work out.

"You don't give up?" he sighed,

"No," I answered, "neither did uncle Teddy I hear?"

"So that's why... though you don't match the dossier files I read?"

"Nothing bad I hope?"

"Little defence it makes now," he sighed, while attempting to catch his breath with a cough,

"Perhaps it is a fitting fate, for a traitor," I relented,

"Please, do not treat me so..." he huffed, "even in these final moments I regret,"

"Conserve your breath then," I assured.

Soon hearing a vehicle approach and laughed crash at the entrance, seeing the front of the Alfa Romeo, brake through its doors. The vehicle reversed, Fredric and I quickly steeped through and saw Daniel at the wheel whilst catching our breaths, as he stepped from the driver's seat, armed with an MP 38 machine gun, and walked pass. Before looking into the library for the first and last time, as Esther stood from the vehicle in question, Daniel ordered Fredric, "Get in the back."

As he turned to the alfa and got in, I turned to the soldier armed with rifles at the front gate, seeing they had been gunned down, and two with arms bound to the entries iron bars, after had lost position of their rifles. I quickly took the rear seat, beside Fredric, as Daniel the driver's and Esther the passenger, before turning around to the right, and passed the dead trees, before the SS officers tied to the gates.

"A message for jerry ha?" I commented,

"After had taken out the men on the machine guns they soon gave up," Daniel grinned, "those men held by Esther's notes,"

"Yes," she replied, "with cord from Daniel and their own gun straps,"

"Slings," I smiled, "but I'll let that one slide."

Obtaining cargo

We continued up the road and turned right, down a side lain, as Daniel could just begin to see the tail lamps and lights of what appeared to be the German vehicles ahead, Daniel called, "We have the tail of their convoy in sight; detour?"

"No," I answered, "keep on them."

As he slowed to follow the line of vehicle out passed the eastern outskirts of town, I thanked God we were all safe, Fredric confirmed, "So, you are Smith? And I've read a lot of your work and may be so bold to say it seems somewhat similar to an old friend of mine's work?"

"Are...." I sighed, on attempting to play ignorant, "I mightn't had known just how you came up with that. But for now, I have a few questions?"

"Of course," he nodded, "and because you rescued me, I will answer,"

"What exactly are the Germans looking for and what was it they showed you?" I asked, "And how may it fill in the pieces?"

"Are, the papers he gave me were in fact descriptions of treasure, artefacts," he answered, "Kikes Ritter-Schulz had been doing this from the start of his search. Having me interpret your work, the best I could, taking months and years of research to answer his requests and achieve all demands. I told him what was needed to be found and though made no promises, simply said 'he would see what could be done'. But the requests got harder and that is when I discovered it was not any of his own work, to be interpreted, but yours. He showed me books that had many pages marked, my letters would link to a whole world of treasures, but he wouldn't even look. But seeks the treasure that would continue to lead him to more treasure...

I had no idea what he was up to and only believed him due to receive a small two-precent off the German's finds, and a committed to the Nazis cause, though wishing to gain from it. But I heard rumours he was in the biasness of taking up higher Gestapo positions and assure his way; Hitler it would seem wanted the money, but found he was simply promoting those who liked his ideas and intern gained funds, to locate treasures by utilising the German army. But of course, a high percentage would go back to Germany, and remaining investor's pockets.

This is as much as I could gather and would also ensure the rest of the Waffen SS to remain under him, rather than to question his orders. Now back to your question, I am now showing him a tressure and continues to go off some of your papers. I have the copies in the red folder, he believes you once uncovered a town that would had been most difficult to uncover; you wrote down a description, as recommended,"

As he located a flashlight on retrieving a folder placed upon the seat, to reveal documents within,

"Stating that you dug for the lost town, of the philistines 'only to find another unnamed city, that was destroyed by flood and all that is left are its lower catacomb, that were carved into stone and a number of sections collapsed, with many writings carved upon its walls in varying dialects that were difficult to interpret. The place also seemed to have stone articles and booby traps, through out. And without the right interpretations none would survive the expedition; we had already lost men trying to determine our path. The expedition now just one of many listed sites we have had no choice but to discontinue.' Now this made me cures, it's a description similar to another three you had described similarly, in previous papers general Ritter-Schulz obtained, and another concerning your uncle, that I had not realised till now. As it talks about finds in areas, he too backed out off, but I had no idea where the SS Abwehr agents retrieved it from...?"

"He stole it from me," I conjected, "now on with answering the questions?"

Fredric presented the folder, commenting, "Well, the writings Kicks found were on such sights. Ones that you wrote down but could not or hadn't yet interpreted, as he linked them using your work; witch I regret, he could not have done without me and importantly theses listings of translations relayed by radio, by order of Kike's partner Hinrik Baller. First receiving what could be read, before pages in full, to assist the locating of the ark and in search of a world map, believed in the area that showed what our world privacy appeared, in order to find the first settlements and their treasures.

Making it possible to find great artifacts and locate treasures to be dug; lay hid beneath the surface, now to get back to the reason, he came in wanting me to find a town east of Aleppo. Near where we believed treasures were buried by armies that had conquered the eastern regens, before being kicked out of their kingdoms and forced to move around in wonder. As they eventually settled a town in the far eastern area provenance, where you found the catacombs. You see, he believes this to be that settlement, but couldn't have known it, because it was lost among many and couldn't be interpreted; even when you found it you too didn't know. But now he has the map from the stones and believes it to be the settlement, perhaps its buildings nothing more than huts and tents, called Gazae."

He then rolled out a map, showing the location near the northwest of Israel toward the boarder, marked with two names, Gazae and Tillcar.

"So, what about Tillcar?" I asked,

"Just another name for it I gees," he answered

"Are, I suppose so. Anyway, thanks for your answers."

Daniel carefully drove on whilst keeping his distance from the rear of the convoy and soon court up, as it begun to rain heavily, I pondering on points made by Fredric, "Well, now your making sense of it, especially agreeing in part that this Kicks is a Nazi and obsessed with gaining control of others, otherwise a hard act to follow,"

"I try not to make sense of mad men who burns books," Esther huffed,

"And now their trucks have finally court up to the Nazi cars leading," Daniel agreed.

I looked ahead through the windscreen, spotting Kiks's Mercedes before the convoy, but three hundred yards ahead, saying, "Don't lose him, he'll show us to an airport or docks for sure." As I pray to God that it will work out and his will be done.

Following the trucks for what seemed hours, through the rain, we came into hill country, south of Agropoli along the west shore and saw the speeding Mercedes a near quarter mile ahead, slow before turn right into a lane off the main road. We slowed and looked down the hill ahead of the Mercedes toward the shore half a mile away, spotting a large, five hundred yards wide, concert docking station. With three large gable roofed warehouses and four docking bays beyond protruding from shore and to the water lit by flood lights. Revealing two small cargo ships in its centre bays, painted in German naval camouflage, with two U-boats within the left bay and gun boat on the far right, I gasped, "Stop, they'll see us."

Daniel pulled to the left and off the road, noting the timber fence alongside before an open field between us and the base at the shore beyond, turning off the lights, he turned to me, "So now what?"

"Well, I would think they'll be leaving within the hour, " I commented, "I suggest we sneak down to the docks, through this hay paddock. It's still raining, so none should see us in the grass; yet alone the dark," drawing few documents from the folders.

"So, where's does he go?" Esther asked,

"Ok, Fredrik," I said, "once we're down the hill, you take this vehicle and reframe turning on the lights, till way down the road,"

"Yes," he nodded, "but where do I go from here? The Germans will be looking for me?"

"In that case I'll advise you leave the country," I answered, "though the Abwehr think you and I already dead. "

Esther voluntarily opened the door, becoming the first to get soaked, smiling, "It's nice, come we best hurry."

Daniel pulled the brake and stepped from the vehicle, gritting his teeth, I opened the door to follow, as Fredric replied, "Of course they know about you, I take it? Now keep this safe." As he handed me few documents, within a wax sealed envelope.

I took and placed them within my jacket amongst others, sighing, "You know, these papers are about all I have left of a courier worth of finds?"

"Sorry," he smiled, "and take care."

"You to," I nodded, "but know it wasn't up to me whether I lived or died, but God, who holds all time. Forgives me and keeps me from falling. So, I may live by grace through his son, Jesus Christ, who dead for our transgressions so we may choose to live again through him. I hope you make the right choice, as I do all; though some choose not."

Smiling before stepping from the vehicle, into the heavy rain and ran across the road, to Daniel and Esther stood by the old timer fence opposite, before the lush grass within the muddy field, gradually sloping downhill towards the docking station.

"Let's go," Daniel urged,

"And hope we are not seen," Esther smiled.

We quickly duked through the fence panels and continued, whilst keeping an eye on the entry lain, over two hundred yards to far left. Reaching most of the way down the slippery hill, seeing there two German soldiers patrolling the perimeter with MP 38 machineguns upon their shoulders, now to the far right. They then approached the rear of the docks three, forty-foot-high by hundred and twenty wide, large brick warehouses, with few high windows along their sides.

"Get down," I gasped, as I slipped over face down in the muddy grass, seeing the soldiers proceed around and toward the far-left corner of the second building, before entering a gap between the two warehouses, Daniel commented, "I hope those papers are ok,"

"Don't worry they are in wax paper of sorts," I assured, "likely made of hemp, I think."

Esther took a breath, as I begun to crawl forth, toward the buildings ahead, as she and Daniel followed, seeing the soldier appear within the gap between the buildings. We proceeded to the right, till but twenty feet off, finding we were level with a soldier stood guard to the far left, barely visible through the rain, and came to the bas of a surrounding mound before the concert pad beyond.

Carefully sneaking over and into the near four-foot-deep-drain filled with water ran off the hill and edge of the slab, I all but swam to my right and begun around the edge of the building Esther and Daniel followed while continuing forth. Finding the drain to fall away, before us and fill as it collected further water ran off the hill, filling to eight feet in depth and carefully swam through the rushing water to a build-up of earth alongside the front half of the building.

Grasping the bank while carefully crawling up and stood upon stepping forth to the edge of building for cover, as Daniel and Esther followed. Slowly we walk down toward the buildings front right corner, as the soldiers spotted earlier at the rear of the buildings, begun to appear from behind and proceeded along the wall. We quickly reached and peered around the front corner of the building, spotting a large number of shipping crates, ranging from two-four-five and six feet in height, stacked upon the concert outside the warehouses to be loaded. Finding both the ships and crew members to be far enough away, I swiftly steeped from the building to a pile of creates ahead for cover, noting each of the buildings' twin steel entrance doors closed, before turning toward men working around further piles of crates ahead.

Then to the boats, noting vehicles loaded aboard, before two unassembled Mechosmit 109s and further reconsents planes on deck, as kikes accompanied by Abwehr and Kriegsmarine officers pass those working and proceeded across to a U-boat, moored opposite the nearest cargo vessel and carefully watched for an opportunity. But as soon as he boarded the U-boat its crew begun to take off, as so did the other, before the gunboat and nearest cargo vessel as its gain planks were removed and men aboard cast off.

Then turned to the other supply ship, with many crates loaded aboard, realising all the remaining crates before us were only of previsions. Then spotting the usual team of doodlers checking the boats manifest against their note pads, before leaving via the last gangplank to be removed, followed by near twenty soldiers that had helped load the vessel and few men that had casting off the mooring lines. Seeing none left present upon the pier, and remining soldiers turn for trucks parked outside the far buildings entrance, whilst passing the Mercedes W07 and a red pinstriped, black Isotta Fraschini 8A S.S Castagna sleek-passenger vehicle left by kikes, just as few SS officers brock away to retrieve the vehicles in the rain.

Quickly realising the boats captain to be the only one out and about upon the small cargo vessel, as he left to maned the helm with the first mate within the top cabin.

"Now's our opportunity," I gasped, "let's move." As I stood from the crats and snuck by the next few staked for collection, as Daniel and Esther followed passed the bocking bays. Coming near, I found the small ship of similar dimensions to a converted boat, with a slightly lower bridge or control room, with cargo loaded before the cabin as well as behind and around the base of its' boilers flew, and upon a raised forecastle at the front of the bow.

"Gerrie's leaving," Daniel commented, "there may be but a skeleton crew aboard?"

"Hopefully," I seconded,

"and food or water?" Esther sighed.

Suddenly seeing the small ship move, and its starboard side just off the edge of the concert pier and none of the Germans at the bridge appeared looking back, before reaching the wharf and ran for it. Daniel jumped from the edge and grasped the starboard rail of the ship, as Esther and I proceeded to run alongside. I then saw Esther near trip upon few pieces of timber left laid upon the wharf from creates loaded, quickly stopping, I turned back and grabbed hold her left hand on pulling her to her feet. Before turning ahead and swiftly court up to the ship, as Esther regained her footing and I grasped the starboard edge to help pull her forth, she reached out and grasped the edge as I lost my gripe, and Daniel helped pull her aboard.

I approached the end of the dock, hearing thunder and a flash of lightning in the background, as the vessel passed and revealed its rear stern but several feet ahead, and leaped from the end of the raised pier, as I reached out and grabbed hold the edge of its surrounding top rail. Attempting to climb up, Daniel ran over and helped pull me in, as I dangled over the props more than twenty feet below bellow.

"Ok," he huffed, "no need to show off, but some might say, 'jolly good show,' old chap and capital," as he maintained a sense of hummer, either in glee or just rubbing it in; as Esther stood near, and he shook my hand as a British officer before withdrawing.

I nodded and turned ahead to steeped forth between the near seven-foot-tall piles of crates, in the dark, as Esther walked up and gave me a firm hug, I once again held up my arms high, as she released with a smile, "Glade your aboard," I caught my breath, as she appreciatively nodded, "Thank you,"

"Well as a soldier one must do these things. Are... never mind," I sighed, upon Daniel entering the gap and cautiously continued forth, whilst silently thanking God for all he had done and I was able to make the jump, to the slippery rail with his help, and prayed for protection.

As the rain poured down, we proceeded left or to port and passing between the last two allotments of cargo, before the base of the bridges' steel stairway, terminating at the rear door of the cabin above.

Cautiously kept to the shadows, Daniel drew his pistol, "Ok Smith, you take the left." I readied my revolver and begun my way around few crates before me and looked toward the top of the stairway. Spotting two officers stood within the cabin, through the rear doors square glass window, as one of the men turned attention to a large map upon the right wall and the other dressed in a Waffen camouflage coat, manned the helm.

Daniel reached the base of the stairs and carefully begun to crawl up, I quickly followed as he reached the door and opened it while presenting his luger, in his outstretched right hand, and amid at the Kriegsmarine major turned toward the map. I quickly entered behind and aimed for the one manning helm, yelling, as I slightly lowering my pistol, "You're under arrest!"

Daniel called to the man still turned toward the map, "That go's the same for you too, now raise your hands and turn around!"

The man at the helm, turned around fast, realising the camouflage coat loosely hung over his shoulders, covering a lieutenant Gestapo uniform and not his hands but sleaves tucked into his trouser side pockets. Swiftly presenting a concealed Luger held in his left hand, court by surprise, I discharged the revolver and hitting him in the stomach, as he went to fire, and grit his teeth whilst still aimed toward me. I swiftly discharged a further round, as it struck his chest and he fell to the floor. Hearing Daniel too fire, as the other had a similar idea, though Daniel his pistol reedy in case of the soldiers attempted to retaliate.

Seeing the officer fall to the floor with a single shot to the head, as Daniel's reflexes were tested, I turned back to the one I had shot and collected the pistol from his hands, as Daniel took and handed me the other's. I stepped from the room and tossed them over the side in frustration, before re-entering, ordering, "Ok, quick, take the jacket off yours. While I collect mine."

Turing to the dead Nazis, on taking their jackets and folding them before leaving both aside, I retrieved the desisted helmsman before exiting passed Esther, and down the stairs to throw the body overboard, and help Daniel do the same. As Esther entered from the rain and Daniel followed upon the steps and quickly took the helm, while I an overcoat hung by the door and offering it to Esther, "Here."

She removed her wet over shirt, and excepted the coat, inquiring, "Was that Necessary?"

"Of course," I answered, "we don't want any Germans coming up on deck to find them," and closed the door of the slightly rounded cabin. Noting a small square table to the left and padded chairs against the wall behind, with a tin box containing a chess-set sat upon it. Seeing Daniel observing a sexton and compass on a small beech in the corner to his right and shelf to the left, bearing further compasses and navigation instruments.

I sat down upon a chair by the door, as Esther took a seat opposite, whilst retrieving the tin with a smiling, "Are, it's a chess game," before opening and setting up its pieces, soon turning to a small timber cubed below the shaves behind, asking, "what's in that cupboard?" I stood and turned to it, with a smile, she huffed, "Where are you going?"

"To see what Jerry left us," as I opened the cubed, finding three shelves, like a pantry housing coffee tins upon the first, biscuits tins on the second, cheeses and even chocolate, with jars of pickles and sauerkraut. Then looked down, seeing few bottles of wine and canned fish, of expensive taste stowed at the base, "Well, now I can almost see why they didn't want us pirates, tacking their plunder," I grinned, "they had enough chesses and wine in their privet larder, for a trip to the west shores of Syria and back."

Retrieving a biscuit tin for Daniel, before three of four wine glasses, placing one within a compasses mount upon the cupboard for him, and handing Esther the other two for the table, along with cheese upon a small board and crackers. Before presenting a bottle of Primitivo wine and popped its cork, as I half filed his glass and turned for the table. Esther begun to get into the cheese and crackers, then finding what appeared a round hole at either end of the tabletop, we placed our glasses within, prior to re-filling.

I regained my nerves and took my seat opposite, holding a cracker with a generous slice of Tilsit cheese, whilst Esther finished setting the chess pieces, "Ok, let's play," she insisted, "who goes first?"

"I'll give you a gentleman's head start," I answered, as she moved the first piece and took another cracker biscuit, liberally crowning it with cheese.

I shut my eyes and silently gave thanks, as she saw and did the same, before eating the cracker, as I too retrieved one and took a bite, asking Daniel, "So are you right to manned helm for now?"

"So long as there's something to eat, I'm fine to continue plotting course, in pursuit of theirs," he commented, "I've even have a spear chair beside," noticed the chair to his left, I turned to the board and begun to play chess with Esther, as we continued through the night.

Taking the helm about mid-point through, as Daniel sat and started his game; after I managed to lose to Esther and her malty tasking ways, only to win the last round of five, I asked, as she started to verse Daniel, "So, I take it you played cheese all the time on the island?"

"No, not all the time," she answered, "but when you teach as many people how to understand English. You also show them how to play games like chess, you'll be surprised how well I can play,"

"Year," I enthused, "surprised…"

Hearing the hash of the radio, no doubt in-tuned to the other vessels, hearing but few words, "Hold… Follow… course…"

Daniel stood to switch it off as I seconded upon flicking the switch, insisting, "I've got it,"

"What was said?" Esther gasped,

Daniel took his seat and moved a pawn, assuring, "Whatever the transmission, we're best to continue as though the radio is brock."

Holding course, I stayed by the helm till the next morning, while Esther and Daniel slept in their chairs at the table, with his head rested against the wall and Esther face down in her arms at the table, by her half empty glass.

ROUGH WATERS

Esther then awoke and stood, before approaching to my left whilst I maned the helm, noting the rain had stopped during the night, she asked, "*Gulunta*... are, what's happening?"

"Not a lot," I answered,

"Can I have a go," she grinned, "you know at steering?"

I shuffled to the right, "Of course; well, it's not my boat and easier than you think once you know how to go about keeping it straight. I very rarely in those past hours looked at the compass as I rather go off the stars; of course, it may seem difficult to line up the vessel by sexton, but once you get there and know the water, its easer."

She took the helm and begun to steer, I looked down from the horizon to the cargo aboard revelled by the dawn, noticing a number of the crates upon the deck below, appear unmarked, "Hem..." I pondered, "right, just follow where the dials are seat on that compass, I'll be back soon."

As I passed Daniel, sat still sound asleep in his chair and turned for the door, holding my pistol ready, as I exited and ran down the stairs to the crates pilled in rows below, finding many left unmarked. Discovering a crate behind the first stack on the left, to be damaged and stepped through a gap to the three by five-foot-wide crate. Reefing three of its damaged sideboards open revealing further small crates of dynamite within.

Then turned to a larger crate behind and drew my bayonet, as I levered off few boards, revealing rakes of PM 38 machine guns and Mauser 98 rifles amongst quickly packed ammunition and short bayonets. With further timber boards firmly securing the tightly packed machineguns and rifles below, as I broke away further boards to retrieve a machinegun from the top of the crate. Before putting the bayonet away and collected three MP 38 sub rifles and placed them beneath my left arm, on retrieving a Mauser 98 rifle in my right hand, and quickly turned back to bridge.

Following its steps up and entering, I placed the collection of firearms down beside the doorway, calling to Esther, as she remained focused on the horizon, with had her back to me, "Is everything ok still?" She waved, with a grin, "No, everything is fine."

I turned, noting Daniel still asleep and exited, before running back downstairs on deciding to search for more ammo, spotting a smaller four-foot-long crate, to the left of the crate I collected the rifles from and grasped its end in attempt to shift it aside, finding I could berley lift nor nudge it. I knew it be of munition, before drawing the bayonet and using it to lever the edges of its top boards.

Loosening two, before sheathing the bayonet in its scabbed and ripped the remaining boards off, discovering it full of ammo. Swiftly securing a number of magazines for the submachineguns and filling my jackets' right-side pocket with more than ten clips for the rifle, barley fitting the twelfth, before turning back to raised bridge.

Entering I closed the door behind and placed most of the gathered magazines upon the food cupboard, before arming the MP 38s and 98 rifle, carefully situating them to the left of the door, Esther turned, in question, "What are you doing?"

"Being prepared," I answered, "are you still all right?"

"Yes," she nodded, "like you say, it gets easy when you get the hang of it."

I took a machinegun and turned for the door again, racing down the stairs and around to the right or starboard side of the bridges and preceded forth toward the forecastle, finding most crates appeared similar to the last. Approaching the centre of the deck and manhole to the lower engine room, I carefully opened its hatch and looked within, finding two Waffen soldiers shovelling coal into a boiler, toward the rear of the room, accompanied by three others taking a break.

Reclosing the hatch and headed back to the bridge, I raced up its steps and entered, noting Daniel had acquired a machinegun, and laid it

with the machinegun I had offered. Before opening the door to head down the stairway, as she stood by one of the crates closest and pretending to shoot the others, I called, "Are, there you are..." reaching the base of the steps.

She suddenly stopped pretending to fire toward the crates and loosely slung the guns' strap over her should, answering, "Yes?"

I shook my head and approached, "Come with me and don't shoot unless I tell you, otherwise."

She nervously followed, as I walked around to the left of the bridge and waited, as Daniel begun to turn hard to port, I knew it would not be long and ducked behind a line of crates stacked before the manhole. Esther too hid behind the crates, just as the door in decks centre open, and the German Waffen and few Kriegsmarine soldiers, begun to emerge from below deck and turned to starboard, as I counted them, finding all men present on deck.

Then carefully circled around behind, with the machinegun held handy and stood from the behind the crates, as Esther cautiously stood to the left, whilst the soldiers crowded the starboard edge and looked to the ships in the distance. I cocked the machinegun and Esther attempted to cock hers, accidently firing eight or so rounds at the deck and gasped, as the men quickly ducked behind crates for cover, and she reaffirmed the gun.

I tried not to laugh, yelling, "Holt, or I'll shot the lot of you!" They then froze and turned from amongst the crates, with their hands in the air, filling shaken, as Esther had nearly dropped the machinegun, I ordered the men, "Ok, now over the side with you and don't worry, the Kriegsmarine are on their way."

They quickly turned to the starboard side behind and begun to jump overboard, till the last, Waffen officer, starring toward Esther, grinning, "You will pay..."

She then ran up to him, demanding, "Get over the side or I'll shoot again!" He widened his eyes in fear, as he must had thought it was I who fired at their feet, and quickly threw himself overboard.

I turned back to be sure no others had come from below beck and turned to Esther, upon decoking the MP 38, "See, the guns self-loading. So, if you want to shoot a single round, take out the magazine or slid it down from the receiver."

As I slide my magazine slightly down and fired into the water, about thirty yards out, and watched her as she prepared to fire the machinegun, commenting, "and hold it firmly in doth hands and to your shoulder, so you can use its sights." She then slid the magazine down slightly and aimed up, ready "Wait," I grinned, "it'll be better if I help, position the gun," slinging my gun over my shoulder, and turning to her as I reached forth to elevate and pulled hers further forward, saying, as she looked toward my hand upon the for-end, "Don't look at me, look through the sights and get ready for the kick."

As I quickly used my left hand to push the magazine propyl up into the receiver, nodding, "Fire," she fired a round, as I watched and she asked, "So, am I doing it right?"

"Ok, it's all done?" I commented, "but you must check there isn't another built in the chamber and if you have slid the magazine down enough?"

As I released and she instantly aimed up again, believing the chamber empty and fired two rounds in shock, before lowered the gun to catch her breath and put on a brave face, nervously turned to me, "Is it ok now?"

"Not quite," I answered, "you see, the gun fired because the magazine wasn't free, you have another two rounds,"

She then pulled the magazine, saying, "I'll make sure this time." As she fired the last round into the water, then went to fire again whilst lent forth only to hear the click of the firing pin, she smiled, "You see, safe," before putting the magazine in and slinging the gun over her shoulder.

"Yep," I grinned, "real safe now,"

Seeing the gunboat in the distance alter course from escorting the cargo ship, as it proceeded our way, till about a mile and half out and appeared to be diverting in order to pick up the men overboard and turned for the manhole in the decks' centre, to check the boiler. Reaching and looking down into the manhole, with a seat of steel steps, upon a ladder lead down to the boiler rooms' floor and quickly proceeded down. Noting the coal aboard allocated in bins, either side of the ships fifteen-foot-wide, by six feet tall, boiler's chamber. Approaching the fire door, while retrieving a prodding iron hung to its right and used its hook to open the door, finding the chamber well fuelled with coal and dropped the iron turning to a large pill of coal, to the right.

Spotting a large shovel, stood in the fuel, and knowing the design of boiler to be well efficient, due to its unusual, curved shape likened to a large cylinder and adjusted its main pressure output, to full steam. Taking off my jacket, I turned and retired the spade as I begun to stoke the chamber, noting the wall opposite had a doorway to few sleeping quarters and continued shovelling a while.

Soon seeing Esther enter the manhole and came down to watch in her usual inquisitive manner. Keeping it up another forty minutes, till stopping and tossed the shovel back into the small mound of coal, before grasping the iron and pushing the fire door shut, on calculating how much coal it would take to keep at full steam, as its chamber was already well over capacity and threw the iron a side, assuring Esther, "That should do for now,"

"If you say so," she smiled, as I turned and passed to the ladder to climb up, she followed me out on deck and I drew the small map from Daniel to study, whilst turning for the bridge.

Entering the helms room again, Daniel turned from the wheel and glanced out a small window to his right, before the maps upon the pine board, "They had of course changed course for the survivors otherwise they would had caught us by now."

I stepped forth and retrieved the telescope, seeing the gunboat had continued its cruse, "Are, but the gunboat is still on its way," I sighed, "any message or they dear not break radio silence in these waters, it would seem?"

"Only threats and the order to cease," he replied, "though this jerry barge seems to be pulling along. I do not know why, but could it be much slower than that small cruiser pursuing?"

"No," I answered, "not at all, well so long as the boiler stays steady. I checked it just then; but must set a faster course, I don't want any German Luftwaffe planes to show," presenting the small map from Vivid and pointing to few locations, "According to the map we may find allied help, within the coastal town of Guzelyurt, Fevziye or perhaps Zeytinler...?"

Turned to the maps upon the wall, I begun to plot out a course, before resetting the dial on the compass, for the shore of southwest Turkey, close to the town of Zeytinler. I took the helm as we proceeded to divert northeast and away from the gunboat at the same time, while Daniel calculated distances and Esther asked, "So, what's wrong?"

"Oh, nothing much," I commented, "just that we're in an old boiler job, crossing a great distance in the shortest amount of time, at full steam, while transporting dynamite and other explosives, amongst munitions, I imagine. With intent to arm Armenian rebels, all while being chased by a heavily armed Kriegsmarine gunboat- if not light cruiser, no doubt equipped with eighty-eight milometer guns, able to destroy a light tank out to a mile and many MG 30 machineguns, despite also being faster, and intent to pay us a visit,"

"What if they catch us?" She gasped,

"Well, theirs's being a large vessel and likely full Nazi crew," I sighed, "just pray they won't."

"I'm afraid I would have to agree," Daniel seconded, "death or death, depending on their questions Mis Esther."

Proceeded to follow the course, Daniel had set, for nearly two hours while keeping watch of the German ship, as Daniel left to restock the boiler, I said to Esther, now sat at the table, "Well, they haven't caught up and we're coming in close to our destination,"

Daniel then returned, with my jacket, huffing, "Ok, she's stoked," and through me the coat.

"Right, I have also been keeping track of their movements," I assured, "now heading in a straight line, possibly hoping to fire upon us, as soon as we're within range, but I have a plan to slow them down. We can start leaving sticks of dynamite in the water, it may stop them, even as a scar tactic. have your Evens lighter?"

"I suppose; here you go, I'll take the helm..." As he approached offering his lighter, I put on my jacket and excepted, as he took the wheel. I nodded and ran forth out the door to the create at the base of the steps; where I had seen the gelignite, quickly opening the crate and pulled few sticks, finding some primed with four-foot fuses to detonators, that appeared slow burning and water resistant.

Drawing my bayonet, I carefully cut the fuses off several sticks and joined them together, to create a lengthened fuse and fastened the gelignite together, before prepping further bundles: all with different length fuses. Making the last distinctively longer and turned for the rear of the ship collecting and tying off the explosives to boards and pieces of wood from the crates, lighting the waterproof fuses before carefully lowering the sticks into the water, hoping the wake would not move them to far about, despite the reasonably calm sea.

Then turned and ran back up into the bridge as I waited to see how close the timbers would get, before exploding, tacking the telescope and watching on, as their ship neared the first sticks, before actually passing by unnoticed but feet from their starboard bow. Then saw the dynamite come in toward the rear of the ship, due to the wave of its wake and sighed, before lowered the telescope, suddenly hearing a faint explosion. I held the scope to my eye, seeing the heavily armed gunboat slow, as the first set of dynamite sticks had gone off, to the rear of the vessel and second set detonate to port, likely coursing damage. The ship then all but ceased not far from the second set that had detonated, as I pray that one might damage their tub.

Then saw the last sticks, now floating up before the ship, till but feet off their hull, as it exploded, producing a loud bang and far dent, likely followed by a rip in the forward compartment of the naval craft. As the near four feet of damage, rapidly filled with water and it bow appeared to sink, till barfly float. Knowing they could no longer purse without submersing the ships forecastles' heavy gundeck, I grinned, "That should do it,"

"Their boat has sunk," Esther gasped, while turned to the wreck,

Daniel too turned and secured the telescope from my hands, inquiring, "What? How did you manage that?"

"I didn't," I answered, "I just threw few sticks over the side."

"What?" he questioned in disbelief, but then realised it a miracle, the sticks had come so close to the ship even to travel in our wake with such timing.

I turned to the wind shield, "Are, the coast is dead ahead. I think we should find a quit area to dock this thing."

He then put the telescope away and turned to the helm, before manning it once more, replying, "I know just the place."

I stood back, leaving it to Daniel's discretion and walked over to the chair opposite Esther by the door, as she looked out toward the patrol boat, "That's a relief."

I then heard the sound of an aircraft emit from the air to port and seemed to become increasingly louder and louder, before a burst of machinegun firing to port, as I leaped for Esther and pulled her to the floor, gasping, "Get down!"

Lying beside the three machineguns, Daniel quickly duked, as the cabins' top was shot multiple times and the aeroplane swooped down, riveting the cabin with further bullet holes. I quickly grasped the rifle to my left and ran out the cabins' rear door, down the steps, and hid behind few crates for cover. Daniel quickly followed, before Esther, avoiding all jalopies containing munitions, I passed Esther and manoeuvred around to starboard.

Daniel and I stood before the crates, seeing it a Fait CR32 biplane diverting further out to starboard and coming in for another manoeuvre, we quickly ducked behind the small piles of crates not far from the bridge. Hoping the Italian Regia-Aeronautica pilot would not target equipment aboard, waiting but seconds as the Fait CR32 biplane came in, letting off another burst from its twin 7.7m Breba-SAFAT machine guns. Daniel stood to the left and I to the right, resting the rifles upon the edge of the crates, whilst the plane's shots passed overhead.

We quickly aiming up and fired toward the planes' fuselage and engine bay, as it passed the desecrated bridge and banked hard right on spiralling out of control, toward the ships starboard side. Daniel and I quickly ran forth and dived towards Esther still hid behind the crates further to port, just as the airplane's left wing collided into the right side of the bridge, before passing over the deck and struck the port side rail.

Esther quickly approached to see we were safe, "Smith, Mr Daniels?"

"Not Daniel's; madam," he snuffed,

"Though any closer and we'd cease to care what you'd call him?" I sighed, and thanked God we were all safe, as I stood noting the devastation imposed on the ship.

She just smiled in relief, "I'm glad to see you're all right,"

"Likewise," Daniel agreed, before stepping forth,

"I hope you are fine too," I sympathised, "sorry I had to push you so,"

"If not, it would had been both our heads," she smiled.

Bringing the ship about

Daniel, now at the front starboard side of the ship, called, "Smith, over here!" We quickly ran over finding him stood to the right of a large, six-foot square crate; reading its' contains description marked by an eagle insignia, he commented, "This crate has aircraft munition and bombes, bound for Grease. That's where this blighter came from, I'm not so sure as to what ells is here, but this monsteras crate behind, described a large M1931 76mm anti-air gun. That's capable of taking out small ships, you realize, though it'll take a day to assemble, and no doubt lacing ammunition."

"So, we're giving the rebels a fine deal" I grinned, as he stepped between the crates and stopped before opening a six-foot wide, by two-foot crate, drawing an MG 34 machinegun and handed it to me, whilst grasping another and small, yet heavy box of ammo belts. Handing me the tin box as he retrieved one for himself, placing the large machinegun upon his right shoulder, I placed the other on mine.

"Ok," he nodded, "let's take these to the cabin. Boy, don't these things weigh more than expected...?"

"Well, it is your idea," I replied,

"Yes," he huffed and steeped forth.

Esther turned to the crate to help retrieve something of use and attempted to lift the last of the guns, finding it harder than anticipated, before retrieving Daniel's MP 38 he had left and a tine of munition. Daniel and I quickly went about setting the machineguns up on crates to either side of the ship. I took the starboard edge and Daniel the port, while Esther offered munition belts from the crate, and I accompanied her back to retrieve the last of the large machineguns, and further tin of ammunition, before setting it up on a central stack of crates before the manhole to the boiler room.

As we left for the bridge, Daniel quickly took the helm and steered us back on course for the southwest coast of Turkey, finding even the wheel badly chipped from shrapnel, with windows shattered and cracked. I turned to the table, choking up a damaged leg with the wounded biscuit tin and begun resetting the chess pieces, Esther entered, huffing, "Those built boxes, are hard carrying; don't expect me to do that again..."

Daniel begun to study a coastal map, looking for a suitable area to beach the ship, and Esther near threw the sub machinegun from her shoulder, placing it upon the pantry cupboard, as I asked, "Are all women the same?"

"What?" She quizzed,

"Never mind," I grinned, "let's play chess, I'm already five games to one, your way."

She then sat back down and begun to play chess again, shakily asking, "You act pretty casual after what just accord Smith?"

"You don't do so bad yourself... Are, check," I brashly replied,

"Hem, but not mate," she replied, countering my bishop with her queen,

"Well, basically when a soldier or man achieves something," I committed, "he may loss interest in it after achieving it, likely due to sacrifices made," moving forward with my bishop coming across from the left, as my knight covered the square before the king and took out her queen,

"Well what kind of a man is that?" she replied, "But one doing things from a worldly perspective, where there is no accomplishment, not even a cause, and possibly no better than the ones their fighting, or no better than when they started. Whether building wealth or fighting a war against good and evil." Taking my bishop with her king, commenting, "But a man that has a cause, that's for a greater being and fights the good fight with his hart given to God, will not regret the sacrifice he has made along the way or if he had to de for justice."

"I suppose that makes sense and the pressing question is which am I, now?" I pondered, "the latter, I'd hope...?"

"I wanted to ask you this question; since I met you," she admitted, "and few of the tribe's men on Kuoiti island, felt the same for Daniel?"

Daniel overhearing, answered, "Why, I'm with Smith on that one, but surly you'd say that...?"

"Just thinking aloud, I guess," she sighed.

As it became evident, she was yet to trust me, after just asked such a question concerning my heart, and if I felt at all for those I killed, which was as I hoped, a yes, and quickly added to my last comment, "But I would only kill for justice, even in war, I hope and pray..."

Daniel then pointed toward a small inlet ahead, he had first discovered upon a chart, barely wide enough for the vessel, "Here we go...!" he cautioned, and made his way for the mouth of the creeks' inlet, a near two miles ahead. I cut off her king with my queen, suddenly hearing the raw of another aircraft, this time a far more distinctive, inverted Daimler-Benz V12 engine of a Stuka JU-87.

Daniel quickly lined the ship up, best he could, gasping, "Make your way for the deck chaps...!" As I stood and lead Esther out, he quickly followed and leaped from the stairway, as the bridge was hit with a devastating run of machine gun fire, from the aircrafts twin MG 17 machine guns. Spotting the typically grey panted, dive-bomber coming in a quarter mile out to starboard, we all hit the deck as it passed over, "How many of these iron birds?" Esther gasped,

"An eagle stalking a duck," I sighed, noting the passing plane equipped with two torpedoes, and if not multiple one hundred- and ten-pound bombs, "Stay low and prepare to abandon ship, once he sees us armed, he will likely torpedo."

Quickly running forth passed the bridge to starboard, and turned for one of the set machineguns, hearing and seeing the plane now sharply gaining altitude before banking around, to observe the wreck, and reapproached from over the shore. knowing his next move was to radio in and finding the gun set in the centre conveniently aliened, quickly reaching and charging its bolt, upon letting of a short burst towards the plane, as its pilot instantly dived.

I fired a stream of further shots, following but few tracer-rounds as it pulled from the dive on approach, I near emptied the belt, as the Stuka, court on fire and exploded on passing but a hundred feet above the surf as a shower of derbies fell from air.

Smiling, I took a breath and called to Daniel and Esther in relief, "Perfectly safe now...!" hearing the rumble of a further airplane, as they stepped from the ships rear edge and turned to port, barley spotting an approaching Messerschmitt 109 fighter firing a long range bust toward the bridge and even deck, before me.

Ducking down as the shotes reluctantly ceased and re-stood, seeing we were due to enter the inlet ahead, and quickly turned the gun towards the Forcer Wolf passing over as its pilot bucked back toward shore, whilst gaining altitude. I quickly fired upon it, each shot barley scraping its camoflarsh paint work, and swastika defaced tail. Firing till out of rounds, I quick threw the feed cover open and franticly fed a further belt into the gun, as the roaring, out of range airplane contrived its manoeuvre similar to the last, only this time readily prepared to fire upon the deck, with a likely equip 20mm canon.

I carefully aim high and fired a burst, discovering the belt without tracer rounds, and held the trigger down, as I oscillated the barrel. The pilot of the 109 came in fast, firing a burst in retaliation, striking the water before the bow of the ship, then forecastle. I dove to the deck, just as the crate was struck and the thundering shots ceased, only to hear the comforting sounds of planes' engine cough and splatter. Daniel nearing the gun set to starboard, quickly turned fired a full clip from the MP 38 he had, as the fighter barley passing over the bridge and dove to the sea, dissipating on impact.

I stood while taking a breath, only to fall forth, as Daniela called, "Brace yourself!" just as the boat entering the shallow inlet, but few hundred feet and came to an abrupt stop on beaching its hull. Noting we had begun to enter a narrow valley with steep ledges either side, Esther ran forth to assist me to my feet, believing I wounded. Finding me unscathed, she simply hugged me before releasing, as Daniel handing me a spear MP 38, "Come now, we aren't in the business of admiring our work, but good show all the same,"

"It's a miracle," I smiled, excepting the machinegun, before retrieving the nearby rifle, nodding, "let's get going,"

"Right behind you," he agreed, before too retrieving a Mauser 98 rifle and slung it over his shoulder with his MP 38,

"And I'm glad you're alright," Esther smiled, in relief,

"So long as you are Mis Esther," I assured, noting the near vertical ridges either side the inlet, before gathering rope and hanging it over the port side, quickly climbed over the rail and jumping to the shallow, sandy water and assisted as she and Daniel followed.

We turned northwest and begun to hick across the undulating terrain as the grad dipped down to the base of a lesser grad covered by native shrubs and tree spurge bushes, a near four miles in, with still a band of steep ridges to our right, Daniel pointed, "Ok, I think we should continue, before attempting to head up along this ridge, for the town of Zeytinler if I'm not mistaken?"

"Yes," I seconded, checking the small map, "not far off now,"

"Are, and appears a leaser grade ahead," he smiled, "well at least the wrecks well hid,"

"I only hope they do not find us," Esther replied,

I turned to the steep hill, "Ok, let's go; we haven't much time. The Germans will still be heading for Syria and we must prevent them looting the catacombs."

Proceeding along the sandy shore of the stream, I prayed it would work out with God's help. Daniel and I still barring a rifle and machinegun, were sinking in the sand, while Esther walked with ease, encouraging, "Come, *ecla* that means to hurry,"

"Save it for the hill," I huffed, continuing for what seemed like few miles, along the chasm and found the stream begun to thin. Noting the grade to the left lessen, upon spotting few huts and buildings, a mile up, before the town of Zeytinler, nearer to the summit and stopped.

Daniel stood behind, asked, "What, why have you stopped?"

"Look, it's Zeytinler," I pointed, "and by the looks of it, well secluded. I'll say Turkish police won't be present."

"That assumption is but a hopeful estimate," he huffed, "but we shall see?"

Esther stood before me, cautioning, "Is it safe?"

"We'd best stealth it up there through the tree spurge," I replied, "be sure to stay low."

As I turned to the hill and begun to sneak up the steep grade, between its shrubs and stones soon approaching the huts, before the town and found there to be local women, hanging out their red, blue, yellow and other die-coloured materials. We cautiously kept two hundred yards from them and stuck to a line of shrubs on passing the spaced-out row of houses, ran along the grade and proceeded a hundred yards to the next line of buildings.

Finding there a further two rows beyond, with many of the huts staggered among trees, before a weathered section of a ten-foot-tall stone, mortar surrounding wall at the cresset of the hill as it planned off. Realising the town itself to be small, with few overgrown pine trees, we cautiously passed between the remaining well-spread houses, and reached the towns' wall. Spotting a large seder tree midway along the wall to our right, we stayed low and crawled through bushes toward it.

Hearing the voices of people emit from the towns' premises, I stood to peer through an opening in the wall, seeing no one stood before a line of larger square buildings and rear of the houses, fifteen feet within, positioned either side a narrow dirt lane. I turned to the wild conifer tree and reached for a branch, upon climbing up and onto the wall, as Daniel and Esther followed. Halting, I stood still spotting two women and a man, dressed with a fez hat pass by on entered between two of the houses to the left, tacking no notice.

I quickly jumped down from the wall and continued across the road, to rear of a mud houses beside the first of the larger square buildings to my left, Esther and Daniel followed, suggesting, "Now would be a good time to seek transportation,"

"Well, let's see what we can find," I replied, then turned from him and looked up, finding the ends of the square buildings' roof rafters protruding two feet out of its rear wall, above few shuttered windows. Passing and quickly jumped up to grasp the end of a five-inch beam, fourteen feet up and took hold, pulling myself up to stand upon it and swiftly climbed over the roofs four-foot surrounding wall, finding its surface tiled, to walk upon and verity of desert cacti, within large pots, towards centre.

Turning to Daniel climbing up, and assisting him over the side, before Esther, as he steeped forth to the front edge of the building. Staying low, we cautiously followed, finding the roof belonging to a fruit and cloths store with stands seat up beneath. Noting few local civilians passing by, before turning toward the tone of incensed voices, spotting a Fiat 521c Turkish police vehicle across the street, parked opposite the store and possible hostel, with a red and black Maybach SW35 SS vehicle pulled in behind the fiat, facing toward the right end of the town's main street, Daniel huffed, "So much for unoccupied, what are the blighters after now?"

"Whatever their target, they'll find them soon in a town this size," I sighed,

"Are there men in the motors?" Esther gasped.

I turned to the vehicles, suddenly hearing the voices below and two Turkish police officers detaining a man dressed in a brown suit on our side of the street, likely the owner of the building we were hid upon. As they dragged him across the street and hand cuffed him, before directing him into the rear of the fiat and made their way to the front of the vehicle. I then noted two policemen sat in the front of the Mercedes, as its rear driver's door open and a German SS officer stood from the vehicle and raised a hand to salute the two Turkish policemen that had made the arrest, ordering, "Halt!"

The two Turkish police officers turned from the fiat passenger vehicle and stood to attention on saluting back, as the one before the passenger door ran around to face the saluting SS major, asking, "What is it head major Gestapo?"

The SS officer approached, drawing a small photograph from his top pocket and opened the rear door of fiat, to verify the man arrested; reconcealing the phot upon closing the door, "Well done," he congratulated, "now we have him, being one of the head rebels. We'll be able to secure the rest, soon as we search his restraint for information and of course question Mr Bardiose, my way. We'll soon have the whole lot of them arrested and shot."

I quickly unslung the rifle from my shoulder and Daniel his machinegun, as I ordered, "Take out the drivers."

He quickly aimed up and opened fired, each shot striking the front windscreen of the Maybach, I too aimed the rifle upon firing at the Gestapo Major, hitting his chest and turned to the Turkish police, shotting the passenger, attempting to draw a pistol. Then ducked, as the driver drew his and fired toward me, whilst retreating for the driver's door of the fiat and those present in the street ran by for cover. I fired on remerging, only to strike the door of the vehicle, while avoiding the last of those running by and ducked as the officer franticly fired toward us.

Daniel quickly reloaded the MP 36, hearing the shots ceases and vehicles start, I quickly stood and shot the front tyre. The Turkish officer now armed with an MP 38 machinegun, begun fire at the building in retaliation, as I ducked and he took off, about two hundred yards down the street, toward the edge of town. I carefully aimed up with the Mauser 98 rifle, whilst the officer slightly veered left to right and slowed once three hundred yards out, believing he was out of range. I fired the rifle, seeing the car violently swerve into the edge of the surrounding stone walls' entrance, coming to an abrupt stop, Daniel congratulated, "Jolly, well shot, old boy."

I reloaded and re-slung the rifle, commenting, "Yes, I think I finally blew the grease out of its barley," seeing Esther unscathed and turned to the front edge of building, "Let's hope the passenger of that one-way taxi is breathing," and handed Esther the MP 36, from my shoulder, "glad your safe, mind handing this down,"

"Of course," She smiled,

Daniel offered her the rifle, "If you may."

Carefully climbing over the front edge of the buildings' roof to the ends of two trusses and lowered myself down to the street, as Daniel followed, and Esther prepared to lower the MP 38 in her hands, calling, "Were there any wounded?"

"None, apart from civilian ears," Daniel smiled, and jumped to the pathed road, just as an SS officer stood from the far rear door of the Maybach and approached, on presented a machinegun. Daniel and I quickly split upon drawing our pistols, suddenly hearing and seeing a burst of bullets near struck his feet, fired from the MP 36 Esther had in her hands. The murderous officer turned to shoot her, I quickly raised my pistol and fired, hitting him in the chest, as he leaned to his right and fired few shots, before falling to the ground dead.

I quickly turned to Esther, in shock, seeing she had ducked for cover, "Esther, are you there?"

"Yes," She called, "is he dead?"

"Yes, thanks and no thanks to you?" I sighed in relief, knowing Esther had hesitated and thought he may have stopped; not realizing the man a crazy Nazi, "hurry now," She then lowered the rifle and slung the machinegun, before climbing over and down.

"Thanks for the decoy, Mis Esther," Daniel congratulated "he just kept coming?"

"Crazed Nazi," I assured, "well, we might as well take the Maybach,"

"Right, you are Smith," Daniel nodded, as he walked up and used the butt the mouser rifle, to cave in what was left of the windshield,

I turned to Esther, "So you de cocked it without firing?" Putting my pistol away,

"No," she replied, "but it stopped,"

"Here," I insisted, offering a hand, she gave me the gun to check its chamber, finding it had mis fired with five rounds remaining and replaced the magazine, smiling, "Keep it safe," offering it back, as Daniel threw the body of the deceased driver from the vehicle, and quickly wiped down the seat, I turned to the passenger side and remover the other, upon wiping the seat with the lieutenant's cap and through it aside, taking a seat.

Daniel started the vehicle and hearing Esther close the rear door, quickly pulled out and speed down the street toward the crashed Fait, instantly spotting the driver's side rear door had been opened and the man arrested, now running down the dirt road, more than a hundred yards ahead. I stepped from the Maybach and approached the Fiat, as I opened the driver's door, finding the Turkish officer dead, fatally wounded by a shot to the chest, and built hole through the centre of the door.

Then searched the officer's pockets, finding keys to the man's hand cuffs, Daniel commented, "Well, I though you got him twice?"

"Yes," I replied, "it would seem, anyway; let's get that prisoner," retaking the passenger seat, as he turned up the road and floored it up to the man fleeing for his life, I quickly wound down the window, and instructed Daniel to come alongside, calling to the man as he huffed and puffed, "You speak English?"

He stopped, as Daniel pulled up, "Are you fighting Germans?" the man huffed,

"That's a bit of an understatement chap," Daniel called,

I stepped out and use the keys to free his cuffed hands, assuring, "We're in with the rebels. I am, and Daniel in the driver's seat, are captains. The woman: Esther, is an officer."

"Ok," he smiled, "I'll go with you then."

I turned to the rear, offering him the passenger seat, as Daniel pulled forth and the man pointed ahead, gasping, "We must get to Igdir, there I'll be out of reach and those searching will not find us. There we must go to headquarters, at the Arminian Aspet hotel."

"Step on it Daniel," I commented, "and you Mr, what is your name?"

"My name is... Well, what is yours?" he demanded,

"Peter Smith," I answered,

"And mine's Joseph Bardiose," he nodded, "as you can guess I'm not a full blood local, I'm actually one of the few that are still in contact with ally forces."

"You mean Briton, America, New Zealand and Australia?" I inquired.

"Why yes," he answered, "they are the countries we stayed in contact with, since the world wars' end. I was their eyes and ears, and you may say; Armenia and Turkeys' future swaying. And in return others working with Briton, would assist to keep our country safe. This came about when Hitler started a ruthless and violent campaign. Now the allies have been sending, few weapons for us, mainly ex-war guns and munition, nothing of great number or use. Though the fight hasn't started for them, so in a way Briton has forgotten us for now. But still relays snippets of updated information."

"Well don't worry," I commented, "I'm fairly sure things are about to change." Saying a silent prayer

RECHECKING IN

We continued driving for the remainder of the day and took turns at the wheel, pushing on through the night and following morn till near evening, with the aid of Josephs directions. Till finally re-entering the hills, before the town of Igdir, as we came in from its southern outskirts then through the town itself, whilst the setting suns' light dulled to our back's.

Reach the southern outskirts I quickly diverted to the post office again entering the small clay rendered building by its front door to a foyer and short Turkish man stood at the counter, prepared to retire for the day, I asked, "Any, packages for Smith?" The man at the counter, answered, "Are Smith, this came in today." As he placed a mid-size parcel upon bench and presented a clipboard with a quill, "Thank you." He smiled, as I signed before collecting the parcel and walked back out to Daniel, Joe and Esther in the car before swiftly proceeding.

Soon reaching the Arminian hotel Aspet, relieved to find nothing had changed, with few vehicles parked within its front yard. Daniel cautiously, pulled in and parked before the buildings front entrance, noting men dressed in Arminian uniform stood guard at attention either side, "Guest again, do they ever leave?"

"Paying customers perhaps?" Esther suggested,

"No, I doubt that" Joseph commented.

As we stood from the vehicle and turned for the door, I seconded, "I agree with Joe, and am relived."

The men bearing old Turkish Mauser 88 rifles from prior world war, instantly aimed upon us, as I raised my hands and Joseph walked on by, calling to the men, "Lower your weapons, his with me," before turning in to seeing Vivid sat at his desk tending the roll of an inn keeper. The men lowered their rifles and I my hands, whilst Daniel presented the medal given by their superiors and Esther hers, as I entered, and Joseph called, "Vivid!" with open arms, "how are you?"

"Joe," Vivid greeted, and stood from the desk to approach, with a slight hug.

I turned to see the guards quickly stood to attention, whilst Esther and Daniel enter the lobby Vivid lowering his arms and turned to us, "Are, so I see you have met the new captains that were here as guest, but mysteriously vanished in the night? As they would not have any part in our cause and dishonoured us greatly."

"My dear generally, do you not know they left on urgent business?" Joe objected, "Why, when the Germans found me; due to that meddling traitor Dontiro, who has run to Italy, just to return with further weapons and Nazi sympathisers, to kill us all. Theses captains ambushed the secret police vehicles and killed a Schutzstaffel major and the other murders at the same time. Foiling a key part of Dontiro's planes to have us hunted and executed,"

"That's a relief," Vivid replied and stood before us, saluting, "I may have mistaken you, captain Smith and your friends in arms." Lowering his arm.

"Though Joseph's theory should not be taken lightly." I assured, "Since the first men signalling you out, and now this attack at Zeytinler and perhaps disrupting all surveillance operations along the west coast; likely due to men on the inside that will stop at nothing,"

"Dontro," he sighed, "I never thought a man would be so blind as to turn traitor, even a lieutenant and aid-de-camp as he, we are gathering tonight to discuss the dire situation,"

"We best discuss matters outside in secret," Joseph urged, "these few can come. Now about our ammunition statues and gathered troops?" turning for the rear doorway to the hotels' gardens, lit by a number of lanterns upon polls, as a number of waiters entered and few left to set the tables within the ovular gardens centre.

112

Exiting, Vivid answered, "Well, our ammunition has been toped up. But after our raid on the railroad yesterday, to uncover a Nazi general traveling by an armoured train, had failed due to hitting a second locomotive, after the general's had first passed by over-night. Not so much as scratching the front carriage, filled with Wehrmacht soldiers lead by officers. That put up a huge fight and we were forced to retreat into the hills, losing both men and ammunition, prior a third train, with more Boch aboard.

While Azad with our larger patrol managed to close the track down further, but by that time even the civile-police arrived, once fast out of ammunition. It was bad enough to had lost the first train, but the second, to an overwhelming force. Kisha, Roume, Ebim, Husham and few others bravely stayed, whilst we out of ammunition retreated uphill for the trees; leaving them completely out gunned."

"Yes, I see," Joe shook his head in frustration, "and the German's gun shipment could arrive any moment, with more men. It might be best, we discuss a retreat and way out of the area, till the police die down."

"You, being a minister, how can we do nothing?" Vivid replied, "You know they will not stop and keep imposing their ideas on us, with their filthy Nazi religion. Yes, we'll be oppressed, but we must try to stop them, as I am a policeman and now general, it's my duty to stop them; at least till the war starts. We may seek help from the ally forces again; either way our goal is still the same. How many men, women and children have been murder since their transition and airfields. There must be something we can do to stop them now?"

"Of course, as a minister, I must fight the fight with weapons not of this world, we can see the evil behind the sense; many are drawn in because they can't. We must never give up on pray and as for you and your men, I'll be careful how you choose."

"You speck truth," Vivid replied, "but I'll also pray, I might save lives, by stopping them as a general."

"I'm also for that," Joe agreed, "but, we must be careful how we go about it, to keep the fight for justice and you're prays may be answered...."

"Beg your pardon," I butted in, "but my colleagues and I have, with God's help, not only foiled the capture of Joe here, but also managed as it would seem. To capture a German freighter, loaded with weapons bound for Greece,"

"What are you talking about?" Vivid asked, "Are you saying you've stopped the shipment of weapons, that had been mandated to destroy us?"

"Yes," Daniel answered, "we beached it down within an inlet to the river south of Guzelyurt, prior rescuing Joseph."

"What a coincidence," Vivid gasped, "I'll instruct men to loot and gather what they can straight away," and quickly passed Daniel, Esther and I, before the waiters and re-entered the building, calling two the men in uniform, stood guard, "Nathalie, Hezik follow," The two men instantly accompanied Vivid to a Mercedes, as he took the driver's seat and switched on its headlamps, before taking off across the yard and south out the front entrance.

Seeing more guest arrived and entered the rear gardens' ovula pathed seating area Joe assured, "There's no accident about it, you people saved us all from death. You see; if the Germans got their hands on such weapons, we would be done for. So how much was aboard the vessel?"

"As an estimate, few hundred machineguns, a large amount of dynamite, Mauser 98s, aircraft bombs, and oh yes, an M1931 76mm anti-aircraft gun, likely to increases Greece's defence; but it's to safely aboard."

"Praise God," Joseph said, "is there anything we can do for you, young men in return?"

"Well, this has somewhat held us up," I sighed, "you see, we've actually; on last leaving this hotel, took a German plane to Italy, to safeguard information and files within a library. As I am an archaeologist or treasure hunter of sorts and to my surprise, I could only save but few documents, it was not till attempting to leave, that we were able to board the Kriegsmarine vessel moored at one of many secure Nazi military docking station. Appropriating the last of a number of vessels, and attempted to pursue the others, though it the only freighter bound for Greece. Then once sighting, a gunboat thought it best to divert course and immediately pursuit our alternat heading, in hop to liberate the shipment from enemy hands, and so we diverted again, this time for southwest Tricky,"

"That's incredible," Joe commented, "what do the British call you, or whoever's army you are in listed to?"

"The last army, Smith, Captain Smith."

"Well Smith," he smiled, "where were you heading, before being diverted off course?"

I tried to withhold information, suggesting, "Perhaps a military dock, ran by allied forces near Assyria, in hope to slow the enemy's advance, if found."

"Then, you may get there by train into Sierra or should I say the morning express train that heads through Kurtalan." He commented, "I'll be delighted if you stay and perhaps tell me more of your adventures."

Esther near opened her mouth, as I cut her and Daniel off, insisting, "There isn't much to tell."

He stepped between Daniel and I, placing his arms upon our shoulders, as we turned towards a far vacant table, to the rear of the gardens surrounding stone rail, insisting, "I'm sure there will be something, please join me in the garden for diner,"

"If you insist sir," Daniel excepted, Esther followed with a smile, as I prayed that all would work out, with God's help, noting more than eight of the fifteen officers present, were dressed in uniform for the occasion.

Taking a seat at the vacant table with a wine cooler and bottle in its centre, Joe retrieved the bottle of red and called over a wondering waiter, who had just attended the other nearby tables, "Waiter!"

The well-dressed man approached with a notebook and pen, "Yes, Joe sir?" Whilst stood to attention,

"Are yes," Joe answered, "we would like to have the kinsmen's dish, dolma, basturma and mante for me and my friends, and if you could open this..." presenting the dottle, I suddenly heard a suppressed gunshot, emit from the far right, within the tree line of the woods beyond the yards' rear stone rail. As the top of the unopened bottle was shattered and the waiter's notepad thrown from his hand,

"Everyone down!" I gasped, as all jumped from their chairs to the pathed ground and manicured turf, thankfully reacting to the call. Taking out my pistole, I turned to Daniel now drawn his, "Stay down and keep me covered, aim high; I'll see to it." As I stayed low and quickly snuck left, over to and along the gardens' stone railing, as

Daniel turned and fired few shots out into the forest. I once out of the light of the lanterns, climbed over the stone rail and stayed low to the ground as I snuck down a grass sloop, towards the rear of the ovular yard, and entered the jasmine bushes at the base of the woods tree line, before standing in the dark.

Hearing few supressed shots fired in retaliation, I carefully snuck further to my right and determined where the noise had emitted, hearing few supressed shots fired in retaliation, between Daniel's unsuppressed shots, emit from a large alder tree ahead. I carefully took note of where Daniel was firing and stopped, before running across and behind its large trunk, quickly looking up to spot a person's boot, stood upon a branch twenty feet above.

I put my pistol away and jumped up, grasping one of the over hung branches and pulled myself up and carefully climbing higher towards the dole thuds of the assassin's weapon, seeing it was a man in Turkish uniform, holding a silenced German P-38 Walther pistol, equipped with a short stock. I knew it would be better to take him alive and proceeded to climb out from him, keeping the rear half of the tree and cautiously back in toward the assassin. Staying in the shadows till level with him, though barely able to make out branches before me.

As he attempted to shoot an impatiently stood general, lapsing his concern, peering through the leaves, concealing the short-range sniper. He then noticed deflection in the branches and turn, as I struck him with my right fist, near losing balance, he quickly kicked me in the stomach. I fell back and grasped a branch, pulling myself up, as he begun to climb down.

I stayed hid behind the trunk of the tree, as he thought I had fell and quickly drew a further unsuppressed luger pistol, looking to the ground and surrounding underbrush. I climbed around to the right and stump of a broken branch to swing off, as I swung down and kicked the would-be assassin in the chest. He fell back through the branches upon discharging the pistol and landed upon the ground over fourteen feet below. Noting him winded and likely nonconscious, I calling to Daniel, "I got him, quick his at the base of the Alder tree, you shot last!"

Quickly climbing down, Daniel, Joe and a few others jumped the gardens stone railing, whilst others ran down the garden's rear steps, on retrieving lanterns and swiftly approached to apprehend the assassin. I leaped to the ground from the tree and ran around to the assailant, as Daniel collected the fallen Walther 38 pistol and held a bead on the apprehended man, with his own. Swiftly concealing the other, whilst joe collected the standard luger fallen from the man's hand, finding him concussed, as the further men showed, I huffed, "Year, he was defiantly well devoted,"

"I'll say," Daniel snuffed, "he near went for the gun, as I came over, but lacked the capability,"

"Finders, Gorge, Mara lets tack him in," Joe called, as two of the men present picked the assassin up and the man's face was revealed to joe by a lanterns light, "You!" he gasped, "Take him away. We'll see what he knows, but don't allow him to drink, while concussed."

"Yes sir," "head generally," the men replied, before tacking the assassin back toward the gardens steps and continued up, before passing by the shaken crowd of further generals, lieutenant officers, accountants and waiters within the garden, to the rear doors of the hotel.

Daniel then asked Joe, as he stayed by the base of the tree, "Friend of your?"

"Yes," he answered, "actually an old friend, bought out by the SS; due to him being someone I had trusted for a long time."

I rubbed my stomach, commented, "Yare, well he had fight in him and kick,"

"Yes, he was one of the men we trained, after had joined both the Turkish and Arminian army," Joe sighed, "he knows everything you might expect an officer to know or secret police. He was like most of our men, an assassin, but now just a paid one without cause. I really did see more in him, though he was always suspicious?"

"What's going to happen to him now?" Daniel asked,

"Seeing he likes the Germans so much, we'll banish him the rebel way…",

Esther than stood from a nearby bush,

"Where have you came from?" I asked,

"Hush," she gasped, "there's someone ells out there, in the trees,"

"Hardly mam, we saw no one," Joseph doubted,

"No," Daniel intervened, "she may be right,"

"His moving," Esther gasped, and quickly turned for the trees to the right and begun to run in pursuit.

"Keep watch," I huffed, and followed after her entering the tree line and proceeding further into the woods, barely keeping up,

"Smith!" she called, followed by the distinct echoes of two shots, first from a 41 calibre Derringer and second a German 9mile Walther, fifty yards ahead.

Quickly navigating through the trees and light underbrush, aided by the glare of the dual moon light, hearing three further shots emit from between one of the pine-trees and an oak, not forty foot ahead to the left. I carefully circled around, in fear that Esther may had been hit, and hearing light footsteps, saw a man dressed in Turkish uniform, near limping forth whilst presenting a pistol. I moved in between the trees, as he turned to his right, I aimed upon him; but twenty feet before me, calling, "Halt!" As the man fired, followed by a shot emitting from Esther's Derringers, as I too fired, striking his chest, coursing the man to fall dead.

Quickly running passed the deceased, "Esther!" I gasped,

She stepped from behind a Cedar tree not more than fifteen feet from the body, "Smith..." she gasped, stepping into the moon light, revealing she was unscathed,

I near reached forth to embrace her in relief, but remained composed, "You are all right...?"

"Yes," she smiled.

Suddenly hearing the trudging of Daniels boots, "Get the blighter," he called, "it sounded as though there were more?"

"On the ground," I answered, he quickly turned to the body,

"Did I kill him?" she sighed,

"Wounded," Daniel assured, "though it's any man's guess as to which shot was definitive."

Joseph then approached with few men, "There's your phantom Joe," I huffed,

Approaching, he apologised, "Mam, I truly am sorry; you most certainly have that sixth sense,"

"The common one," Daniel replied, "this fellow was your assassin's spotter, he most certainly would had told the Germans of his partners shortcoming, in taking yours' or the lives of the decided target's."

Joseph waved the men forth, "Gammon, Hovnatanian, Simonian have the body bought back to the gardens for a burial, thank you again, especially mam Esther," As he saluted,

"Yes, thank you Sir Joe," she saluted back, as he turned with a smile and followed the men back, once retrieved the body.

Daniel came over nodding, "Good show, but I must emit, for a gutless wander he sure sounded to of had put up a fight,"

"Yes, gutless wonder," I remarket, "the makings of a Nazi assassin," grinning at the sarcasm before offering a hand to confit Esther's, "well, how's this diner coming on?" In order to change the subject, as she smiled, and we turned back for the gardens of the hotel,

"Quiet, so Smith," Daniel seconded.

Catching a Train

Reaching the hotel grounds, we proceeded up the rear steps of the garden, Esther smiled, "At lest you court the other traitor, in uniform?"

"Yes," I grinned, "it would seem we did. But what we haven't court is dinner," on spotting the waiter from early, in search of his notepad, calling, "waiter, another bottle of wine with our meals please!"

He then stood, whilst writing it down, nodding, "It'll be here soon Sir Joseph Bardiose, now the other guest will not be dining, this evening." And turned for the building's crowded rear doors,

"Let us take our seats," Daniel suggested, sitting down at the table, finding Esther appeared nervous,

"Don't be frighten," I assured, "I'm sure they are all just a bit tired,"

"Oh, no," she replied, "I know there is no men in the woods,"

"After that ruckus," Daniel nodded,

"They do not understand…" I replied.

On the waiter returned, with a bottle of fine wine and glasses, filling one for me first, she asked, "What is it they do not understand?"

"My trust in your judgement," I answered.

Joe then approached from the hotel, "Pure me one, Petters," he called to our waiter, and retrieved a chair, noting a hole where a built had passed through its back, and sat, "It's settled then, you are defiantly to be trusted and may leave in the morning. I'll get you on the rotating shift, when the locomotives come into the station, at Van, last stop before the boarder of Syria." Raising his glass to toast, as Esther's was half filled, and diner was being bought out.

Leaving the gardens after had eaten and re-entering the lobby Joe offered, "Please, any room you like, providing unoccupied,"

"I think we have an idea," I replied, passing to the stairway ahead and continuing up and reached the door of our last room, finding it locked. I turned back to the one beside and entered, discovering it much the same as the other,

"Want the bed Smith?" Daniel shook his head,

"I could take the floor," Esther insisted, "it's similar to what I'm used to, on Kuoiti island,"

I wearingly lay down upon the carpet, grinning, "Discus it amongst yourselves..." saying a silent pray as I fell asleep.

Awaking early the next morning, before rising to awake Daniel and Esther, "Time to get up!"

They doth awoke and stood from the beds, as I retrieved my revolver and turned for the door, spotting Joe on his way up the stairs, as I greeted, "Morning Joe, we're right to go,"

"Please, no hurry, the train will be departing in three hours," he assured,

"Are, so we have but an hour before we leave?" I affirmed,

"Yes," he concurred, "given twenty minutes. I just sent a telegram to one of our men; he's a second foreman for the local civilian rail depo, he said the engine is scheduled to stop and gain a load of timber. You should use the opportunity to climb aboard the guard car, for it is an Austrian SB 109 locomotive and may be watched by the SS of the railway roads. But there is a nearby accessway, leading through the forest, south of the tracks. I'm just waiting to see if he confirms."

The waiter from last night entered the down stair lobby from a door by the service desks opposite, calling to Joe, "He says yes, but you must leave Igdir now, or you'll not make it!"

"Right," Joe called and offered me a map, "follow this and take my car, it's the silver jaguar, mark four; I had bought in better times. If you could conceal it by the tracks, he believed there a service shed. My men will pick it up," offering the keys,

"Your too kind," I replied,

"You must leave," he smiled.

Daniel stood from the room and Esther followed, as he asked, "When do we leave?"

"Now would be the time!" I answered, while nodding to Joseph and passing to the stairs, before running down to and through the buildings front entrance, between two men stood guard, seeing Joe's vehicle parked by a grey Lancia-Ro truck and Austin six out the front. I drew the papers Joe had gave and glanced over, while Daniel and Esther caught up. I then observed the map and commented, "Ok, this isn't the only region we're leaving, now the train will stop before the Astrain east boarder, according to these papers," offering them to Daniel, on approaching the jaguar.

He excepted and took the passenger seat, whilst I the driver's and Esther the rear, he asked, "Are, but how does he know where it isn't stopping?"

"We have an insider on it," I replied, before starting the vehicle and taking off out the drive to the west or right, somewhat recklessly, eager to make the rendezvous and of course test the vehicle. Speeding ahead while Daniel directed and continued out of Idgir, toward the town of Van along a number of winding unsealed roads, for a fear while. Till entering a corridor of trees with the entry road to a station in the far distance and neared a faint side-track, concealed by ferns though marked upon the map, as the one said to have led to the railroad tracks, along the edge of a forest.

"Are," Daniel pointed, "here we are Smith,"

"Right," I nodded, hitting the brakes and sharply turning in, between the pine trees and cautiously followed it a near mile, spotting a small open front brick shed amongst the tress and evergreen bushes ahead, as I entered and parked the Jag within.

Daniel stepped from the vehicle, as I followed, before Esther and left the silver, chrome out lined mark four on exiting the small shed, increasing its value a some of four thousand pounds. Daniel passed to the right of the old shed and turned to his left to pear through the surrounding bushes, I and Esther followed, spotting a two lain railroad, with a long line of logs piled up before a tree line beyond. Daniel pointed towards a locomotive stopped two hundred yards ahead, having logs loaded upon its two rear carriages before a further four carts bearing timber slates, two with lengths of steel and three in closed carriages, before the coal cart and engine, "We almost missed it, quick, while she's still being loaded," he gasped, and ran forth, through the shrubs toward the train.

"Do you suspect it under guarded?" Esther asked, as we followed through the underbrush,

"If not by soldiers, the engineers themselves." I affirmed, coming to the edge of the trees and thirty-foot-wide clearing, alongside the tracks, looking to our right and left, discovering it clear. As those rigging to load had left, and we ran down a slight slope, before crossing to the trains' preloaded lumber carts and quickly climbed aboard the last.

I then turned and carefully crawled up the pine logs, to view those on the far side, seeing there were five Mercedes trucks lined up toward the front of the train, as men present unloaded cargo from the vehicles to load the train. Five Gestapo officers stood among them, suddenly turning after had inspected the crates and proceeded down passed the open top cars, as I ducted low and they walked by; to two black KDF Volkswagens,

"What's over there?" Daniel whispered,

"Five trucks," I answered, "accompanied by a small group of police that appeared to have escorted the convoy within two vehicles, far less exiting than the ones we drove,"

he climbed up and peered over the logs, commenting, "Quite so, ha…ha…."

The carriages shunted as the train begun to move, Esther crawled up beside and peered over, on hearing one of the Gestapo vehicles' backfire and turned to the trucks as men present prepared to leave. But when she turned, to see the police in the Volkswagens take-off with a further backfire, she near laughed, uncontrollably, "Ha…Ha… Ha… Hem…" Covering her mouth, while Daniel and I kept composure, knowing the seriousness of the situation, as the engine built up to speed, I silent prayed, thanking God, we made it on time and for protection.

Crawling down from the logs, "carful now," I cautioned, "to the caboose and guard cart" and turned to the rear of the open cart, before the caboose, jumping to its forward landings' railing and climbing over, as Daniel and Esther followed.

Offering a hand as she stood and turned to the entrance door behind, Daniel quickly drew his pistol on entering, and called, "Hands up!" finding a Turkish officer sat upon a chair to the right, before a series of levers within; dropping a tin cup of tea upon the floor in shock. We entered noting a tin kettle upon a burner, seton a small bench in the rear left corner.

The man raised his hands and stood from his seat, "Wait," I called, before turned to the officer, Daniel maintained aim, as I asked, "You understood us?"

"Yes," he replied, "I suppose I do?"

"Of course," Daniel huffed, on lowering his pistol, "you must be one of the rebels?"

"Yes," he nodded, "the foreman told me to wait for you, but didn't say where or when. You are friends off the resistance?"

"Are yes," Danial answered, "what was his name now...?"

"Oh, you know?" the officer replied,

I then noting the man to have a Walther P38 pistol carefully concealed beneath his opened work shirt, swiftly raised my revolver toward him, "Yes," I affirmed, "he knows, but you don't. Tack that gun out and drop it on the floor, now!" Coking my pistol, as I watched him carefully retrieve the counselled pistol from his belt and partly lowered, before dropping it at my feet, as it fired and nicked the tip of my right boot, as I jumped back. The Turk quickly turned for the carriages unlocked rear door and out upon its landing, near head butting its rail as he dove to the deck.

I quickly stepped forth in pursuit and aimed toward him, before grasping the coward by the scruff of his shirt and pulling him up, holding the pistol to his left temple, "Ok, at least tell us how you came to be here, before you get off?"

"We just arrested the foreman," he gasped, "no doubt, you saw the cars parked beside the train, in case. To prevent saboteurs, but I thought you weren't going to show."

"So, what happened to the man who was to meat us?" I demanded,

"The foreman?" he nervously answered, "his going to Igdir to be questioned, is that what you wanted to know?"

"Not yet," I commented, "you stood guard if we were to board; but how were you to contacted others down the line, if the railroad between Van and- Assyria was sabotaged?" Pulling him to his feet, with the pistol on him.

"Through Morse code," he gasped, "a wireless transmitter behind you, to the right of the levers, in that steel box."

I decocted the pistol and put it away, he at once swung his right fist toward my face, I quickly blocked with my left arm, as he swung with the other and I quickly belted it down with my right, throwing my fist up hard against the side of his face. As he fell back off the edge of the platform and into the bird of paradise bushes and shrubs, along the right side of the line.

Seeing the sun rising behind us, revealing a range of small hills either side of the track, covered in hardy grass and pine shrubs, before re-entering the carriage,

"Nasty blighter," Daniel sighed, "wounding a leg would had been too good."

I turned to the Morse code transmitter hid by a blue steel cover, as he asked, "So, what did he have to share?" Tacking a sip of tea from the officer's cup.

Finding the cover locked I drew my bayonet and levered it open, discovering few pages listing a number of seatings, for secure lines and small book, by an envelope of two hundred marks, "Are yes," I answered, "he said they captured the foreman, we were to meet and had took him to Igdir for further questioning. But with this we may send Morse code to the hotel, given there are papers here the Germans must not had realised, on how to tune into a number of local frequencies, including Igdir,"

"What are they going to do to him?" Esther asked,

"The usual questioning and ways of inventive torcher," I answered, "followed by the usual death as a result of their methods," finding there two listed under Igdir and it pre-set to one, "but don't fear, Lord willing I'll get through."

Turning on the transmitter and placing the headphones on to send message; nearly four minutes later, Daniel asked, "What did you send?"

"Basically 'German convoy of Volkswagens caring rail foreman for questioning to Igdir, from the last point of stopping, I think they'll get that; I even sent it in Turkish," I answered,

"How would you know that?" Esther asked,

"Well, these papers helped," I commented, placing the transmission key and the deutschmarks within my jacket pocket, "I think I'll hold onto them."

Retrieving a chair for Esther, from five stacked in the corner beside the forward entrance and one for myself, smiling, "Here we are," offering it to her, "let us go out the back."

She then walked toward the rear door and put her chair on the left side of the rear platform, before a safety chain, I followed and took the right, Daniel accompanied while offering cups of tea, "Tea...?"

"Thank you," Esther smiled,

"You can fill the dryness in the air already," I nodded, "we should be right till the next station, south of Mosul a hundred miles on,"

"It's been a while since I had tea," Esther smiled,

"So, you didn't have tea on that island you came off?" Daniel inquired,

"Yes," she answered, "we grew it wild in some areas. My father started a small crop, before it seemed to go wild."

Daniel took a sip, snuffing, "Willed tea, barbaric." I smirked to myself as he handed around a biscuit tin, no doubt belonging to the foreman we were to meat.

A SANDY STOP

We patently waited for the train to reach its destination, observing the varying scenery behind for few hours as the landscape had changed to desert with but few shrubs growing around the base of the distant hills and the plants themselves appeared to differentiate. Heading the charm of a bell, I stood and re-entered the carriage followed by Denial, spotting there a small bell hung from the white ceiling above the levers. Knowing we were due to stop and finding the brake lever labelled in German, I gently pulled it to my right and felt the train decelerate, before pulling it on hard, coursing a loud screeching of metal as we came to a near holt. Daniel stepped through the forward entrance to see ahead and re-entered, calling, "We're stopping at some kind of Arab town, with a river to its back!"

I stood from the lever and peered out the door, spotting the locomotive had enter the town of Sultan Abd, on passing by a number of hundred-year-old Ottoman buildings. Noting the sand piled up around a recently erected station platform to the right ahead, and a further build-up shingle either side of the track, along the walls off the square buildings and narrow alley gapes in-between, beneath joining arched walkways above. Spotting a fertile green area beyond the right line of staggered, ode-size buildings, before a large body of water a quarter mile out.

Then turned ahead spotting a platoon of soldiers on the plat form, accompanied by a Wehrmacht officer, whilst further men begun down alongside the carriages, led by three SS officers with pistols drawn.

Realising them in search of us, as the screeching stopped and suddenly heard the crunch of sand under boots, as two officers leading a party of five Waffen soldiers bearing rifles, stepped from a narrow alleyway between the left buildings, not more than eighty feet ahead. I quickly re-entered the carriage, as one or more caught glimpse of me and turned to investigate. I quickly released the brake lever, and the train proceeded to move, "Quickly, out the back," I gasped, on retrieving my pistol, "move now, it's a trap!"

Passing Esther, as she and Daniel followed out upon the rear landing, I observed the line of houses before the fertile land beyond and grasped her left arm on removing the safety chain, encouraging, "Quickly, jump; and head for the gap between the buildings to the river," coming up level with the next gap between the buildings, we jumped from the platform to the soft sand and proceeded into the narrow alley, beneath an arched walkway, as Daniel drew his pistol and followed.

I turned back and peered around the edge of the building to see those left from the platform a near two hundred feet down, spotting their officers turned toward the passing timber cars, still oblivious among those turned to the caboose and guard cart. Quickly turning around, "we're clear," and begun running down the gaps' sand covered walkway, passing under a further arch at its end, before a moderately crowded street and halted to peer in.

Spotting there three German Wehrmacht soldiers to the far left and five Turkish soldiers to the right, among the passing civilians, not more than forty feet down the way. Knowing there but one line of buildings with similar gaps between, before the river Tigir beyond. I observed those monitoring the street, finding their view impaired and backs slightly turned, Esther asked, "Now what...?" Suddenly seeing the five Turkish officers pass to the soldier on the left.

"Ok, now," I signalled, on entering through a break in the crowd and quickly cross the street to a gape in the buildings opposite for cover. Cautiously running through, we came out into a large open floodplain, where civilian locals farm their produce and ran their livestock, with but few assorted houses eighty feet from the town's busy street.

Notting each dwelling to have its own vegetable patch, before meadow grass populated by goats and series of dirt tracks, leading to the shore of the river. Continuing with hast along the nearest dirt track, I soon saw there an old fishing dock on the bank of the river, to our far left ahead, mooring a number of small boats, upon the water and two larger bearing freight, pointing, "To the dock, down there!"

"Seeing you there," Daniel huffed, as we ran forth, passed the last of the houses and through the cheyenni grass toward the timber docks,

"Transport, and way across…" Esther nodded, noting the few small fishing boats tied off to the piers, amongst surrounding reeds.

Turning back, seeing there a party of Arab and German Wehrmacht running out from the town's buildings, in search of us. We kept to a narrow dirt path and approached the sixty-foot-long narrow pier, discovering four men repairing nets laid upon its deck, and further six unloading the freight carried by the two thirty-five-foot slender boats.

I quickly turned to a fifteen-foot, unattended sailboat, sixty feet to the left of the dock, wedged between the reeds, realising the Arabs and Egyptians on the dock preoccupied, unloading their supplies. I ran to the small boat, finding a rope tied off to a peg from the boats bow, just off the sandy shore and oars readily laid over the side, "Climb aboard,"

"Jerry's hot on our tail," Daniel called, "hopefully the water will cool them off," as he and Esther entered the water, to board the boat,

"They mightn't pick us out," she gasped.

Quickly I drew my bayonet to cut the rope, while Daniel and Esther climbed aboard and I turned on throw both my jacket and pistol to them, before entering the water. Unaware, I placed the bayonet over the side and attempting to push off, only to find the boat wedged in the reeds. Daniel quickly retrieved an Arab scimitar sword; found aboard, before jumping over the side, into to the water, and swiftly begun to hack through the reads.

Esther climbed over the far side to help push, soon turning from the boat, gasping, "Look out Smith!" I turned to shore, seeing an Arab driest in black with yellow silk out lines upon his kurta, and braid upon his head, approach presenting a raised sword, clasped in both hands and swung down at me.

Quickly stumbled to the left, as he struck the water with the razor-sharp blade and I jumped up to reach for my revolver, only to grasp the bayonet. He quickly stumbled forth in the water and swung at my legs.

I Jumped up once more, whilst still gasping the side of the boat and kicked him in the face with my right foot, coursing him to stumbled back, I quickly realised the side of the boat and retreated to shore. He followed and thrust the sword from the right, I narrowly avoided and blocked the blade with my bayonet, near dropping it from my hands, as I leaped back and allowed his sword to pass overhead, before throwing my left fist into his face.

He stepped back, only to swing back at me from the left, as I jumped back further from the water and the blade skimmed passed. He again swung across, while I proceeded to withdraw onto land, frustrated he quickly raised the sword and ran at me, swinging down and to the right. I blocked and diverted his blade, as it touched the edge of my shirt and instantly cut through, barley scraping my arm, as he laughed, "Ha... Ha...!" and continued to push.

I stepped forth and elbowed him in the stomach, throwing his pressing blade off, as he stepped back and begun to swing across from the left. I jumped back, as he continued to swing back and forth, shoulder to shoulder, narrowly missing as I stepped back; timing each stroke till the third downward thrust and quickly swung in from the left, instantly using the force of his sword as an advantage to divert its blade hard down.

Seeing he had a Nazi badge or likely cufflink pined to his arm, knowing him an Assyrian allied with German intelligence, then holding his sward down, spotted an Arab from the dock dressed in white, aim a breech-loader musket toward me, whilst the man before me stood with his back to the water. I quickly, on just caught glimpse of the knelt gunman, stepped to the left of the swordsman, as he followed my steps and quickly thrust at my neck.

The far Arab fired, unintentionally striking the aggressors chest, as he near turned around while falling and I to the boat, seeing Daniel and Esther had begun to move, now already climbed aboard. I quickly grasped the port side and climbed up into the boat, as the current begun to tack us out, Daniel grabbed an oar and I lowered the bayonet to take mine and passed other boats moored at the dock, but several feet off and around to the front of the pier as I looked up. Seeing the Arab marksman, run along the dock presenting a sword raised above his head and forwarded to jump.

I rose the six-foot oar, just as he leapt for our vessel and shoved it forth, on him headbutting its paddle and falling upon a boat before the dock; breaking a number of crates and cages housing birds such as parakeets of many colours, as they flew out. While an Arab man owned the boat, being to shout at him, as he lay barely conscious, Daniel asked, "Wasn't that the crazy blither I saw fire a flint lock just now, when boarding; only to wound his fellow Arab?"

"Yar," I answered, "you may say, he was quite accident-prone."

"Ha, ha, hem…" Esther laughed, "I mean; yes, accident-prone. But if you ask me, they were both crazy, especially the tough one with the sword"

"Oh, not to tough," I commented, as I sheathed the bayonet and massaged my wrist.

"So, how far down this river do we go?" Daniel asked,

I looked at the river and where it continued ahead, answering, "We follow it for as long as we can, till the town of Ash Sharqat along the right bank. Away from any German activity and where we can get supplies, before journeying southwest,"

"Well, at least we are far away from the Jerry's for now," he smiled, "and can make use of the current." I thanked God we were ok and that we might catch up to the German Nazis and stop them from prevailing.

FIGHTING THE CURRENT

After three hours, following the current of the Tigris River we begun to note four or five sail boats catching up, from a third of a mile off and closing fast, Esther pointed, "Is that…?"

"Yes," Daniel nodded, "Trust them to have faster vessels,"

"Keep rowing," I huffed, spotting a twenty-five-foot fishing boat ahead,

"Good idea," he commented, "but how are we to outrun them?"

"Perhaps not," I commented, "steer her alongside that fishing boat and prepare to jump ship. No one will know where we're going and the current will keep the boat straight, long enough to swim for shore."

Seeing there a small village just off the right bank in the distance, with a slight wall, in case of a flooding and swiftly steered the boat toward and passed the larger fishing boat, then pulled in front on lowering the oars, "Ok, now!" I called and stood to put my jacket on, before diving overboard as it created a restrictive drag, Esther gracefully dove after, Daniel quickly set his oar as a ruder, before jumping over the side.

Staying under till clear of the larger fishing boats' unsuspecting crew, we quickly begun the quarter mile swim to shore. Reaching the sand bank, we kept to the water and turned to see the pursuing sail boats proceed on by, maintaining course for the adrift vessel. Stayed hid in the water, before cautiously stepping out upon land, noting a small dock a mile downstream, with many local men attending fishing boats.

We turned for the small mud wall before us and groups of houses, with shading date palms grown between and a road leading passed. Spotting there a small market set up between an open row of mud clad buildings, to the far right.

"We are here," I announced, "Ash Sharqat or it's eastern out skirts at least,"

"But now what?" Esther sighed,

"Ha, that's the way no need to catch a breath," Daniel encouraged,

I turned to those gathered within and leaving the marketplace, commented, "Ok, lets gathered up some supplies and source a map of some kind."

Jumping the wall, we begun down the dusty road to the marketplace, noting a fish market to the right of a central unsealed thoroughfare, and stores of all sorts of fruits and vegetables on the left. Passing the fish markets, whilst caught sight of a canteen store ahead, I quickly approached and picked out six, "Here we are," I exclaimed in German, handing two to Daniel and Esther on paying the bearded Arab stood by a neighbouring hat and cloth stand,

"The pound is always welcome," he nodded,

I presented a further Deutschemark, "And a detailed map of the south lands?"

He turned to retrieve rolled parchment and offered, "Yes, sir," I took with no further word spoken, and turned ahead, as Daniel purchased a bag of dates and apples, before passing through the crowding locals.

"Why did you speak in German at the store?" Esther Asked,

"They may be paid off by the enemy, to report any suspicious tourist," I answered,

"But they sold us food and were so perlite?" she asked,

"Oh, don't worry about that," I commented, "they still do business, that is until they stop taking your money and call authorities."

"Right, you are Smith," Daniel agreed, "now what have we for transport?"

Then spotted a camel merchant, down the far end of the street, with trained camels tied and sat by the right side of the way, I opened the map, "Well, we have only a bit over a hundred miles south to go. I suggest seeing no sight off the twentieth century, we go by camel,"

"How do you ride a camel?" Esther nervously asked,

I concealed the map and drew my compass to hone our bearings, assuring, "It's different to a horse and you're up higher, but they're fairly well behaved when trained. And don't worry, you'll only fall upon the sand."

Lowering the compass and proceeding to the camels, noting five; I quickly concluded the best three, and a bearded Arab with a red vest and fez hat, tending the animals approached, greeting in matted German, "Guten nachmittag, you will buy?"

"Ja," I answered, pointing to the furthest camel and one second from the end, before stepping forth to retrieve the best saddle off the MewarI camel closest and swapping it with the other Dromedary camel.

"You are no fool mistier," the Arab replied, "but I'll charge extra for the saddle."

I handed him a hundred Deutschemarks from the wax envelope, as he excepted and ran back into the building behind whilst counting the damp bills, seeing him gone, I turned to Daniel and Esther, "Come on, take a camel; Esther you best take the one resaddled."

Daniel ran to the one at the end and I the fourth, freeing the ropes from the stakes and Esther hers, before getting on as the well-trained camels stood for us. I tapped mine on the hind leg with a switch, found upon the saddle and he walk forward. Esther nervously copied and we began to move, slowly take off out of town.

Esther loving every moment, secured the canteens to her saddle and Daniel his, as we road on and the sun begun to set in the west, she commented, "I like camels,"

"Well, yours being a female would help," I commented, "Daniel's and mine can be a bit nasty, though gelded."

As the sun finally set and its rays reflected upon the sand as though glass, till inevitably growing dark, I followed the compass, Daniel replied, "I hope these vagabonds had enough to drink, before left?"

"There's a well not long ahead, according to the map," I replied.

We continued to ride on for over three hours, till spotting what looked to be a stone well in the moon light, with a trough beside. We approached and dismounted, as the camels knelt down, before running to the well, I followed and lowered its wooden bucket to draw water for the stone trough and the camels franticly begun to drink, Esther patting hers, asking, "But how did you know it still flowed?"

"It was marked on the map, as working," I answered,

"So, where are we heading from here?" Daniel asked,

"We'll travel through the night, westward," I commented, "and by day we'll be within seventy miles of the lost city of Tillcar."

Esther whilst patting her camel, pleaded, "Oh but she doesn't want to walk much more?"

"Trust me," I assured, "her design is that she can walk a lot more, especially in the dark."

Finding the camels had drank the water up, I waited before retrieving further loads of water with the bucket, till they were calmly satisfied and begun on the grass grown by the well, while I replenished our now empty canteen. We thoroughly checked our saddles, as I took of my jacket and used it as extra padding, before mounting up and continued around the four-foot wells' ancient trough, and continued through the desert terrain, going off Polaris and compass, as moonlight illuminated. I prayed we might stop the Germans and not fall to sleep, and of course the health of our camels.

SANDSTORM

We road till dawn, as Esther asked, "Can you here that?"
"No," I answered,
"Ha, I can," Daniel nodded.

I then heard the faint rumble of multiple engines, through the approaching winds from the north, beyond one of many large dunes, gasping, "Yes, I hear it now. It's on the far side of the dune."

We carefully road to the large dune before us and proceeded to its crest, noting the distinct sound to increase and the clunking of metal, followed by few squeaks.

Coming to a halt at the top, "Dismount," I called and jumped from my camel, Esther and Daniel instantly followed, and looked downhill ahead, through the dust forming in the air, finding it an open area before a large string of dunes about half a mile out.

Instantly turning to the sounds emitting from the foreground, faintly spotting a squadron of German tanks; the same if not similar to ones seen in Eastern Lidya prior. Counting but the faint out lines of five units equipped with large 75mm KWK 40 guns, no doubt panzers' mark IV, roaming through the large area.

We dropped to the ground, as Daniel huffed, "Tanks, we won't get passed them, not to mention there's always a patrol beyond them. But I do fall to see why they are here; the last lot we saw were out on patrol, in case of resistance or perhaps to prepare for an assault. These may be the latest variants?"

"Hem, yes," I commented, "likely part of anything up to a small division."

The sound of the panzers' V12 Maybach engines and squeaks were then silenced by the ever-increasing winds, as a sand storm was due to approach from beyond the far dunes, called, "I can see an incoming sandstorm on the horizon, when it comes over we may sneak passed. It'll be here in under tween minutes, I suggest we get prepared, and cover up."

Seeing the increasing sand propelled by the winds and quickly crawled back down to the camels knelt upon the stand, I retrieve my jacket and material hung from my camels' saddle to cover my face, Arabian style. Daniel did likewise, as I turned to offer Esther material and back to the crest ahead, "Ok, just follow me, we'll be able to sneak right by once their commanders shut down, to limit sand blocking up their air filters," and quickly mounted up, awaiting the sandstorms' coming, "Quick!" I called, before ridding up over the crest of the dun and down toward the tanks, as the storm begun cover each unite, turned westward, spaced near sixty feet apart maintaining formation.

Nearing the tank third inline, we begun to ride passed only to have its gunner turn its' turret, firing the 75mm gun toward us, narrowly missing due to lack of vision and perhaps our being to close. I quickly road to the right, as another still pulling forth, turned our way and prepared to fire their MG 34 machinegun, on the sand in the air thickening as they could no longer see, and fired a short burst in frustration, few shots struck the ground before my camel's hooves and passed overhead.

"Quickly! Dismount, they may not see a smaller target!" I called to Esther and Daniel,

Each quickly jumping from our camels, "turn them loose!" I called, as we each turned to loosen their saddles and I mine and Esther's bridle, allowing them to run out of the storm and gunfire, as we could hear the tanks.

"Stick together!" I gasped, carefully walking forward through the thick sandstorm, as a tank passed to our right, I pushed Daniel and Esther out of the way, just as it drove by and begun to turn.

"They are too close," Esther gasped,

"stick with it!" Daniel called and turned toward the tanks' rear.

I stepped forth as another panzer approached from the left and quickly dived out of the way, just as another came in from the right and straight towards us. I stood from the sand upon grasping Esther's right hand and pulling her to her feet, before Daniel, as we leaped forth and the tanks' tracks narrowly missed my left heal.

I quickly turned and ran up to its rear, offering Esther a boost, "Get on!" Knowing it the only way to get up off the soft sand, as I helped push her up, she quickly made it upon the engine compartment and Daniel begun to climb, as she assisted. I quickly jumping up and grabbed hold of its edge, to pull myself up as Daniel and Esther offered a hand, before sitting whilst attempting to catch our breaths.

Then saw another panzer come in from the left, as it accidently rammed into the side of tank we were upon, as both drivers stopped, doubtfully able to see more than ten feet before them. Counting to twenty, I drew my pistol, as both tanks stayed stationary, and reached forth to bang on its turret hatch, waiting as an officer opened and stood. I quickly pistol wiping him with the revolver, to knocking him out, as he gasped.

Seeing him collapse, before quickly peering into the open hatch as he struck the floor and half dove in with my upper body, seeing another turn from re-loading and swiftly present a pistol. Quickly I struck him over the head with butt of mine, rendering him nonconscious, just as the driver stepped from behind, waving a pistol toward me and I quickly backed out as he fired only to strike the turrets' inner wall. Before climbing up, as I ducked behind the hatch and put the pistol away, the officer instantly spotted Daniel and Esther, just as I slammed the hatch hard upon him, coursing him to drop the logger and fall nonconscious.

Then signalled to Daniel and Esther, "Get in!" and quickly re-entered the tank.

Hearing the voice of their lead officer, "Weygner, Schreider, Hinn's…" Finding the operator gone from his seat and turned as he struck my left shoulder with a large wrench from behind, and allowed myself to fall out of the way beside a rack of 75mm Panzergranate shells. He assisted the officer to his feet as he stood, aiming his luger toward the open hatch.

Hearing further transmission from the tank that had crashed, "Officer Hunsen, commander Benzer, we accidently rammed commander Schneider. His bravely volunteered to check the damage, outside,"

"keep a look out for civilians spotted," the head commander ordered, "none must know we are here."

The operator then quickly reached for the hand peace, before spotting Esther at the hatch, I presented my revolver, as the operator turned to fire and shot, striking his chest, suddenly the operator knocked the gun from my hand and swung the two-foot wretch toward me. I shifted right as it struck the edge of the munitions rack, and stood throwing my fist to his jaw, knocking him out cold, as he fell upon the fatally wounded officer, who had released the Luger. Seeing both laid motionless, as I retrieved the revolver and Esther reached the floor, followed by Daniel closing the hatch.

The dust and sand cleared, "Esther," I asked, "would you be so kind as to take any firearms off these Nazis," and begun to bind their hands behind their backs, with use of their uniforms and belts, on retrieving their earmuffs.

Daniel pulled the sand covered material from his face, "Well, that was an experience, how did you find the crew,"

"Yes," I commented, "I didn't relies them invulnerable to the conditions? And It's crew alike,"

"Are," he nodded, spotting the deceased Waffen officer, "I see what you mean,"

"Take the turret," I ordered, "we have some work to do," and turned to the driver's seat,

Esther approached and took the forward machine gunner position, asking, "So, you need someone on that gun to drive?"

"Not to drive," I answered, finding I could barely see out the glass viewing slots, as she looked through hers. I pulled forth from the tank that had struck the side, and turned to face another, ninety feet ahead, calling to Daniel, "Keep elevation standard!" and turned to Esther on covering my ears, "And it's going to get loud," offering the spare earmuffs.

Daniel then fired, hitting the right side of the tank in front, as I turned left and rotated back around behind us, seeing the tank that had crashed, now pulling away through the storm with its back to us. I proceeded to follow in order to stay near, calling to Daniel whilst he reloaded, "Ok, amid up and come to your right, few clicks and fire!"

Daniel finished reloading, fired striking the rear engine bay of the panzer ahead, I turned hard left, spotting a fourth tank sixty yards out and its gunner now turning its' turret toward us. Prudently I reversed, calling, "Quick! Reload and turn to target on the left, keep a medium standard no more than six digress off horizon!"

Seeing the tanks' turret keeping up with us, more sand suddenly filled the air and rose from the ground between, as its gunner fired and struck the ground in front, before losing visibility. Pulling forward, I called to Daniel, "keep ready!" As we emerged from the impeding sand, to see the offending tanks' turret still aimed near thirty yards back, in anticipation to our past movements. As we aliened and they attempted to turn their gun upon us, Daniel fired striking the left side and seemed evident the shot reached the engine bay,

"Ok, where's the last one?" Daniel asked, on preparing to reload, I turned back into the storm and proceeded south west toward the far side of the near thirty acer area.

Approaching the line of dunes seen earlier, not sixty feet ahead, hearing a loud bang to our right and turned slightly around, discovering no sign of enemy units among the large range of dunes and called to Daniel, "See anything?"

"No," Esther sighed,

"All clear on the horizon!" Daniel seconded.

I turned ahead and raised idle, on continuing to and up the steep dune before us as fast as I could, suddenly hearing another loud bang emit from the far right, seeing the large body of sand level with tall dunes either side and gap between. Quickly turned into the narrow pass, we begun to follow it for two hundred yards. Till approaching another large dune ahead as the gape continued either side and heard another loud bang echo from the right and shot wiz passe striking the edge of the left dune, I halted, "Can you ascertain from where it originated, before it hit?"

"No, wait; actually yes," Daniel replied, "it would seem to have come from the left, before turning,"

"With the echo it could be anywhere?" Esther gasped,

I then knew now, the enemy tank was within the gap behind and our turret still forward facing, "No, behind," I gasped.

Daniel quickly turned the turret and I pulled forth, hearing a further echoing bang as a shot struck the sand behind, just off the rear of our tank, "He was up on the dunes the hole time," Daniel huffed, "using an elevated position to fire down on us, as we were coming up the gap!"

"Ok, well let's copy them," I replied and turned hard left into the gap between the dunes ahead for cover, before diverting up the one to our left and neared the top, as the storm begun to pass and the air cleared of sand.

"No sign of him yet!" Daniel called.

I began to turn around, spotting the front of a tank driving up a large dune five hundred yards to the far right ahead, noting the enemy tank still had but thirty feet to go before the large body of sand would be level enough to fire. As its gunners focused down on the gap between the dunes and raised elevation toward us, I ducked and pulled Esther from her seat, as its crew fired; hitting the sand before our tank and shrapnel cracked the observation glass.

I quickly reversed till level and called to Daniel, "Increase elevation by three digress, at least middle range, for four-thirty-meters." As he aimed up, just as the enemy panzer reached the top of the dune and stopped to aim upon us, Daniel fired the 75mm gun, and the shot struck the rear of the tank on the far dune, igniting its engine bay if not reserve fuel supply.

Seeing two Gestapo offices jump out of its turret hatch and retreat into the deserts' miner dunes beyond, Daniel smiled, "Well, that got them, no wonder we had trouble seeing them." I turned and proceeded down the step side of the dune and through the gap below, before tracking up the larger dune ahead, as we reached the top and found it to level, with narrow gapes between the lesser dunes ahead, that we could follow.

I took out the map and compass, as the whole landscape seemed to elevate slightly, announcing, "We'll continue to an oasis north of the location," thanking God we were safe, and we would be able to reach the catacombs in time.

Driving on through the dunes for nearly two hours, "She's a might bit faster than a Matilda," Daniel commented, "but still a tank; how much further?"

"About another hour I hope," I retorted, then begun to hear a loud clunking of metal and pulled up, on stepping from the driver's seat, "I'll check it out."

Opening the hatch and exiting the turret, spotting scorch marks up the side of the tank, where the other tank's shots had near struck the hull. I stepped down from the spare track links mounted upon the front of the tank and circled to the left, finding the track partly damaged, with the outer edge of few plates bent, a cracked locator and loos joining pines. Then walked around to the right, viewing blast marks and severely dented rear guard, before finding one of the tracks' roller locator wheels' axel bent and track plates missing.

Coming near, I gave the wheel a kick, discovering the locator to move about loosely and tested the next wheel beside, finding it firm, before proceeding around to the rear, finding it to scorched by one of the blast marks and slight amount of oil leaked upon the sand beneath. I knelt and looked under, seeing it a slow leak that would likely not hold out and quickly stood, to climb upon the tank, pulling myself up. I turned for the hatch and climbed in, Daniel asked, as I passed to the driver's seat and sat, "What's wrong Smith?"

I raised the idle speed and grasped the levers, replying, "We have an oil leak and not much time till it'll need its engine replenished, as well as that the right track is badly damaged and might begin to stretch. Could you fill the motor with what oil we have...?" And turned from the chare to open the small floor hatch to ditch the spent shells,

Daniel begun to climb out the main hatch, assuring, "I'll see to it,"

"Not that I should ask...?" Esther sighed,

"Go ahead," I insisted,

"We don't have wheels," she pondered, "so are these machines hard to maintain?"

"Only after what we've been through, but I fear we haven't seen the last, if the journey doesn't kill it first!"

"I hope not," she gasped,

The Waffen lieutenant officer of the German crew, mocked, "Ha, you're bound to fail," "Makes little difference to you..." I huffed, disposing of further shells, discovering an extra casing and depletion of ammunition from the storage rack, "and why all the shortage of panzerganate 39 rounds?"

"Practise," he huffed,

"All good for now," Daniel called, "I hope jerry bosch here wasn't making trouble?" "No," I replied, and turned to the driver's seat to presume driving, through the deserts sand with God's help.

THE OASIS

After an hour odd of driving, we could see the oasis in the far distance and slowed, retrieving a pair of binoculars from the commander's neck, as he grumbled, "Stupid Englander, how dare you!" I ignored and opened the side hatch to view the waterhole, whilst Daniel observed from the top, finding it surrounded by palm trees and shrubs, with a convoy consisting of five German Kublewagon jeeps and two trucks forming a convoy to the west, beyond. Before noting two Hanomag halftracks, one armed for an anti-air and the other a 75 mm gun. With a fair number of Arabs gathered, and horses tied off by the date palms to the right, starring toward the pool, longing to drink of its untainted water. Then noted a faint cloud of smoke in the distance beyond, likely the fate of an up raw.

Refocusing upon German Wehrmacht soldier occupied the far side of the oasis with Waffen officers among them and few portable beck chairs set, similar to that found upon a cruise ships, and few men swimming in the water in shorts, after leaving their uniforms and guns a shore. Whilst the Arabs sat by the water and sharpened their swords with stones, as others lined up at a truck, to be issued Mauser 98 rifles from few soldiers, as those receiving looked over the fine rifles and turned for the next truck. Receiving ammunition belts and clips from two further Wehrmacht soldiers, as few were instructed to form a line before an unarmed men dressed in Arabian cloth and presented arms on firing to execute.

"What's wrong Daniel, Smith?" Esther anxiously asked,

Daniel climbing down, answering, "I'll tell you what's wrong. Those filthy Huns have populated the oasis and its water."

"What did they do?" She gasped, "Poison the water or something?"

"No," I replied, "but they're swimming in it and have an overflow of munitions."

"Exactly," Daniel seconded, "I say we go in there and give them jolly what for,"

"The oasis," the captured gunner gasped,

"Best you stop now Englanders," his commander grinned, "you are well out numbered,"

"What of the smoke beyond?" Daniel huffed, "Your, doing?"

"A combined effort," he answered, I re-entered and nodded to Daniel, before turning to the driver's seat.

"You haven't even a vorwarts maschine gunner," the commander huffed.

I turned to Easter, seated beside, "See this gun," as I reached over and charged the bolt of the MG 34, "fire at any who retaliate,"

"Yes," she nodded, as the commander stayed quiet.

I took the controls, smiling, "Things made easier with a tank." And begun to drive forth toward the oasis.

"How much ammo do we have?" I asked,

"Well, three shots on the main gun and about two hundred rounds on the machinegun," Daniel answered, "but we best not get too hasty,"

"They may think we're with them," Esther called,

"I hear you perfectly," I seconded, driving on towards the oasis, as we approached its eastern edge and entered between the trees, seeing the trucks and VW jeeps unattended and halftracks, with men nearby, over a hundred and fifty yard out opposite our position, decorated with swastikas and flags. Pushing over few small date palms, as they fell nearby Arabs and Germans sat by the water's edge, as they turned to the sound of the tanks' damaged tracks. I diverted from crushing any with the tank, seeing the other soldiers within the water, before driving forth into its shallow shore to gain a better view of the vehicles, through the row of trees adjacent.

The men ran from the water, as I stepped from the seat and took the turret MG 34 machinegun and fired few rounds towards the unattended kubelwagen-jeeps as a warning. Men by the bank then instantly retaliate and the halftrack armed with a 20mm KWK 38 ant air gun, begun to fire upon us, striking few men. Daniel aimed up and fired the 75 mm gun, striking the halftrack's front, as those manning its gun were blown from their seats.

Soldiers forwarded from the trucks and shore, throwing grenades in retaliation, with few killing one or two men in the water, whilst others fired, and a mist of water sprayed over the tanks sight glasses. As I fired toward those approaching and Esther followed, firing her gun, Daniel proceeded to reload the main, then spotted the second halftrack through the trees, had repositioned to fire its deadly 75mm gun.

I took out few more men armed with grenades and turned to check on Esther, while holding back their advance. Seeing the captured Waffen commander had made his way to her and kicked her from her seat, with the sol of his boot whist laid on his back. She quickly turned from the gun and grasped his other boot, before falling forth throwing her fist against his jaw, rendering him noncaseous as his head struck the floor.

I quickly turned back to the 75mm equipped halftrack, as it fired and struck our front left guard and its projectile continued through the hull, passing through the other captured officer as he stood to retaliate, before exiting the panzers rear flank. Daniel now reloaded, quickly turned the gun on the halftrack, as its crew franticly prepared to fire a further round. Aiming up, I fired a burst toward it, taking out its forward machine gunner and driver as Daniel fired, and struck the vehicles engine bay detonating few shells aboard as the guns' turret head blew off, on firing, and the shot struck trees to the left before us.

Daniel proceeded to reload the final round, as we were suddenly engulfed by men with grenades and Esther fired toward those remaining, whilst others begun to retreat. Though still found the tank heavily under attack, as water splashed up either side and our engine bay was struck. I turned to the trucks, seeing the officers had formed a line of five mortars with men stood by open crates of shells taken from the rear of the truck behind the first and retrieved further launch tubes.

Swiftly firing a burst toward them, managing to take out and defer further men from the trucks, as the gun jammed and found it out of ammunition, calling to Daniel, "Take it out!" As he had finished reloading and quickly aimed on firing, blowing the truck to bits and nocking the Germans to the ground. Then saw few Arabs to the left of us, to still throw grenades, as they ran across from behind; retreating toward the horses, I shouted to Daniel, "Behind you!"

He quickly turned the turret whilst I fed another belt and fired toward few as the others dropped their rifles and retreated from the area to the north, with hands raised high. As further soldiers appeared from the trees either side and threw grenades, on retreating to the remaining jeeps left in tack, believing they were super soldiers, as the grenades on detonation further damaged the tank.

I fired a short bust toward those on the left and right, as few reached the VW jeeps and fired upon us with their large MG 36 mounted machineguns. I quickly turned and shot up two of the vehicles, as their reserve gas cans exploded or munition supply, and a third pulled forth, as I fired, causing the vehicle to swerve and crashed hard into the rear of the first halftrack upon rolling. Just as few Waffen officers took off in the munitions truck passed the rolled jeep, as I fired only to strike the halftrack in the open and few surrounding trees. Seeing it proceed in a straight line to the south and recaught sight of it once three hundred yards out and aimed up firing what I could toward the speeding vehicle as it ignited and blow up.

"Their getting away," Esther gasped, as Daniel turned around spotting two Arabs ride off on horses to the far right; knowing they would send dispatch. I amide up between the palms, as they neared the two-hundred-yard mark and fired a shot burst, as they fell, and the horses turned back for the water they were deprived off.

Daniel then opened the hatch and got out as he stood upon the tank, noting, "Well the water is clear at least."

I climbed out and stood besides, seeing there no bodies in the water, before oil streaks leaching from the Panzers' rear engine bay, replying, "Yes, I best move," quickly re-entering to the drivers' seat, seeing Esther release the smoking emptied machineguns' handle in relief, "Are you all right?"

"Yes," she nodded, grasping her right hand,

"You get used to that," I smiled, "and rest assure most of your shot performed as a deterrent,"

"I only fired in retaliation," she assured, "as you said."

I attempted to drive the tank forth from the water, finding its tracks to slip on the way to the sandy shore as its right track snapped and we turned to the right, before coming to a halt. I turned the V12 engine off, sighing, "Right, let's get the prisoners out,"

"Of course," Daniel nodded, helping the dazed commander to his feet, "Up jerry, on your feet."

The commander barley stood, whilst I secured the engineer, before turning to the side hatch and climbing through, to assist the first soldier out with help from Daniel. Lowering the engineer, I followed upon an out brake of multiple gunfire and pushed the soldier to the ground for cover, at the chime of few shots striking the tanks' hull, as I pulled my pistol. Seeing the shots of MP 38s emitted from a line of soldiers concealed behind a contour of sand, before the desecrated vehicles and the men laid before me had been struck.

Daniel quickly ducked back into the turret and manually rotated on firing a burst along the line with its machinegun, fatally wounding as many as fifteen–sixteen soldiers, before ceasing due to lack of ammunition. A soldier stood from the contour firing an MP 38 as most shots struck the tank behind, I quickly aimed and fired, striking his chest. Another armed with a Mauser 98 rifle fled from the line to the vehicles, before turning back and knelt down to retaliate, firing a shot at the sand before me, and another toward the wounded man. I held the revolver firm in booth hands and fired four shots toward the soldier knelt over a hundred yards out, the first went high, the second low and third struck his left shoulder, before the fatal fourth hitting his chest as he fell to the ground.

Daniel fired a further few shots over head, from the turret hatch and finding the area clear, jumped to the ground, gasping, "Smith, are you right?"

"No," I sighed, as he pulled me to my feet and I turned to the tragically shot gunner, "unarmed and now dead."

The wounded man mound, "Please," reaching for his right pocked,

I searched inside, retrieving a small gold cross upon a chain, commenting, "It's against the Third Reich to have religion,"

"I'm a soldier, not all are Nazi and have been discharged from their position..." he huffed,

"Very well," I nodded, "pray to Christ for forgiveness, and to be part of his kingdom now,"

"Amen," he agreed, breathing his last breath,

"Stern fellow," Daniel commented,

I shook my head and stood, "And saved my life without knowing it,"

"Is it safe," Esther called,

"Yes, for now?" Daniel nodded,

"What happened out here," She gasped, seeing the engineer laid dead,

"Nothing," I assured, "Just a result of the few men we had missed forming a line,"

"Their officer has passed out," she replied,

"Leave him and pull the radios' wires, then grab a shovel," I sighed, as we retrieved shovels from the rear of the tank, dragged the body before others nearby, including Arabs, back to the trees to be buried once search for intel.

Leaving the shovels at the sight and turning for the water, Esther beside me asked, "What are we going to do now?"

"We're only a bit over fourteen miles east of Tillcar or rather Veneciy," I commented, "but who knows what's in-between. I suggest walking or each take a horse before letting the rest go?"

"To the horses," Daniel encouraged, as we followed him over and turned loos the animals dying of thirst, finding fire of their Arab owners' bodies laid among the bushes beside, with throats cut. Daniel approached to inspect the deceased before me, consisting of likely murdered civilian farmers or perhaps traders of sorts,

"We may had done without bearing the enemy," I sighed,

"Filthy bandits," he sighed,

I turned to one closest, seeing the head was all but decapitated and Daniel turned to another, as I noticed the saddle of a horse beside to have the edge of few concealed papers pocking out between the blanket and pulled them on unfolding one to read aloud, "This message must go to none, but colonel Stirling-fourth regiment. Dear colonel I may remind you that remaining in the area after a direct order from your superiors, is a blatant offence. Leave the western region immediately, we have spotted tanks northeast of the base, your assistants may be required in time."

Daniel turned to another of the horses and drew further documents from beneath its saddle, gasping, "It is the same message. But what's the idea, weren't these orders supposed to be brought to this colonel? I suppose few didn't make it...?"

I passed the chestnut thoroughbred gelding, seconding, "Yes, I would think it sent from Percorsion outfit; caution an officer who hadn't obeyed a superior's orders. Unless they of course believed the messengers unreliable or interceded by the enemy? Though they were sent in a group of five, in case of local bandits or rather a hopefully deterrent."

"But usually, they would send out military rather than civilians in such cases?" Daniel commented,

I turned to the body and pulled the flax material from the head, discovering an officer's cap, "Right again," I assured, "they were soldiers sent by allied forces. The thieves may not have known, though obviously had not searched the saddles. Rather their killers were in co-hoots with the Germans, employed to tack out any allied dispatch, but I am still not sure why? If it's clear on these messages there's no apparent allied enemy activity in the area; why risk making it seem there are enemy forces at large, by taking out these messengers?"

"Well," he huffed, "that's why they had theses Arabs tend to it, so there's no ties if they were caught in the dirty process."

I stepped to the front of the horse and untied the rope from his bridle, so it could reach the water's edge, before another, "Anyway," I replied, "I'm sure the horses are thirsty,"

"I'd say, left to die more like it," he sighed, as we untied the remaining and Esther approached to settle them from running off. I then passed Daniel to the last, being a silver Arab mare and freed its bridle, giving a pat on allowing her to turn for the water.

Before too approaching the edge and removing my jacket, placing it upon the first horse's saddled, and patting his side, smiling, "Who was thirsty…?" As he ducked his head and continued to drink, seeing a further five horses, two grey, one bay and two black or perhaps bark bay, stood to the left, by the two trees I had rammed down earlier. Silently walking up to them, I begun to remove their saddles and bridles, as they grazed the grass growing amongst the many palm trees, surrounding the ovular waterhole.

I rubbed each one's bridle marks upon their faces and left them be, on retrieving few spare canteens from the saddles and turning back to Daniel and Esther. As she was now patting the grey mare and Daniel a black gelding, asking, "So, you explained the Island of Kuoiti, you came from, to have a diversity of tribes. And few of which with cannibals among them?"

"Yes, with different islands," She replied, "the Elpharit people, the tribe that took me in, being the larger with none practising the evil practise of sacrifices, though not all the miner tribes are cannibal but those that fear the Elpharit." she explained and turned to me, "So when are we going?"

"After we have a wash and something to eat," I answered, removing my Thomas cook boots and socks, before running into the water and dove in to swim around, Daniel then followed as Esther jumped in and cooled off a while. We then got out to pick dates from the downed palms and climbing others, soon regrouping at the waters' edge, to eat further provision found. I relived the chestnut of his saddle, as Daniel did the same for his gelding, while I assisted Esther with hers, noting the dust upon each horse. I turned to mine and unfastened his bridle, before jumping on and running him through the five-six feet deep water, as Daniel followed.

Esther attempted to jump upon hers, making use of a nearby stone and the mare ran in as she fell off into the water and stood to regrasp the bridle, before splashing the horse down and releasing the rains. Before turning back to our horses, as I raced Daniel out and along the waters' edge, quickly turned back as we passed and road out to dismounted and tie them off to graze in the shade of the trees. Gathering more fruit, I offered it to Esther and watched as few of the horses released, rolled in the water and ran wildly around the oasis,

"Quite refreshing," Daniel commented, "though I believe my steed has more speed about him then yours,"

"I doubt it, but Esther's certainly cleaned up well," I replied, "and now we must get going, it's been near two hours,"

"I think it's always fun," Esther smiled, I then resaddled the horse and loaded up few canteens, as Daniel did the same, I approached to help Esther with hers and she watched, remarking, "Are, so that's how you do it, well at least I had practise on those camels,"

"Yes, I suppose you have," I commented, "but to get on a horse, face opposed to the way the horses is and only from the left. Oh, and hold the rains firm, I'll hold them for you as you get on, and don't be nervous."

Esther put her left foot in the strip and swung up, before correcting herself in the flat saddled, I proceeded to explain, "Now if it gets bumpy, don't hesitate to stand on the stirps, but remember to look ahead in order to maintain your balance and hold on with your legs, but not too tight. Because as you do, you are telling her to go faster and always keep slight pull on the rains and lean out slightly when turning, and apply pressure to the side of the horse you want it to walk toward, maintaining slight pressure with the other, and don't worry, they seem well trained,"

"Ok" She replied, as I ran back and jumped upon mine, as Daniel approached once mounted and we rode out of the oasis, proceeding south-southwest. I then drew the map, of the land before the flood and compass from my jacket, to carefully keep to a direct route. While Daniel and Esther followed, I prayed for safety and the horse's strength, that we might stop the murderous Nazis and others from succeeding in time.

A RIDE IN THE DESERT

Taking a swig from the canteens and Esther found to stay firmly upon the mare, before slowing to a walk, I lowered the canteen from my mouth, "Well, it's a good thing we're not in a hurry,"

"Whys that?" Esther asked, "I thought we were...?"

Daniel lowering a canteen, huffing, "What he means is; we can go faster,"

"Yes," I commented, "but I now realise, we have little point in getting there sooner, as the absence of the supply convoy would surely slowing them to a halt. It's never so easy when you have to dig; as appose to blasting sand and earth,"

"What an earth do you mean?" Daniel questioned, "I thought you said you've been through the catacombs?"

Once more lowering my canteen, I answered, "Yes, but I have a rule, to cover everything so it may be blasted open, in case of anyone locating the entry spot, and I tell you now, there was little more than that of intrinsic valley discovered,"

"Intrinsic?" Esther sighed,

"Architecture and inscriptions of value only to the few concerned with its unique historical origins," I replied, "and now the revelation of the sights true significance, deduced no less from the map we had discovered concerning the worlds previous form and potential landmarks."

We began to ride at pass towards the destination, soon finding the ground to level before the slight grade of a large dune, more than half a mile ahead and continued on. Suddenly hearing the shouts of men's voices, and recognising once neared the dune, a large four-hundred-foot sand covered mountain top, supporting ancient brick buildings and ruins upon its summit, I pointed, "See, the ruins built by a much later civilization, that weren't so civil, on that lager mountain top. You may not think it, but it's essentially over half a mile square.

The ones that built the former ruins were all killed by the next foreign army of the same Persian genealogy. But at the time, after the last of the sixteenth century Arabian civilizations before Ottoman rule; some may had been spared, or if not wiped out completely, 'The Arab's plunder remained within its bores and water catchments; so, they say,"

"So, Huns seeks the treasures inside," Daniel affirmed, "being of larger quantity to the last treasure uncovered?"

"No one knows," I replied, "I'd say we only saw a very minute amount of Solomon's wealth. So, I would say; even everything these people had, still would not be of even similar size...? But it's always confused me this place; you see, if there were treasure hid why hadn't remnant of its people's descendants return to loot. That's why I think it likely a tribe of Assyrian people who build the later city upon the rock, for protection against other small Kurd settlements and Baz tribes, among few later forming parts of the Ottoman empire. They may of had no idea of what they were sitting on, perhaps utilised the vast found wealth, or it could just be the family line of initial accumulators died out before able to return. But now I have the translations and we may be able to read what was scribed upon the walls of the catacombs; in the more ancient parts of the city's ruins."

Pulling up short of the dune, finding there another beyond, Daniel drew Carl Zeiss binoculars from a pouch, while I too utilised a pair hung from my saddle and examined the mountain ahead. Spotting a large number of Waffen and Wehrmacht soldiers utilising narrow walkways carved into the side of the cliff to reach the top, and a series of ropes dangled down from the cliffs' edge to hoist equipment. Turning to those of the Wehrmacht soldiers that had reached the top, finding a number had gathered to search what they could of the ground's larger area covered by sand, no doubt in search of that sealed off.

"Well, they have been buzzy," I sighed, lowering the binoculars on hearing an airplane approach to the far left or south of us, spotting it a biplane descending to land, putting on my jacket, I shouted, "Yar... Yar...!" to the horse, as he pulled forth, Esther and Daniel followed, "Yar... giddy get...!"

"*Qwa...Qwa...Adler!*" Esther called,

As we road forth and up over the dune, pulling up at the base of the next, I called, "Quick, take the spare flax tunics from your saddles and conceal yourself, in case they're watching."

Gathering the material hung over our saddles, in case of a sandstorms, and wrapped our faces, Arabian style. I turned to the far left, spotting there a desert-coloured Bucker Jungmann bi-wing aircraft, coming into land, before turning up the dune. See just over, were numerous crates scatted among trucks, halftracks and kubelwagen-jeeps parked before the base of the cliff and oasis like spring with palm trees either side, but three hundred yards ahead.

"Dismount," I called, spotting a number of Arabs and officers inspecting the crates caried before the ropes used the hoist equipment and jumped from the saddle as Esther and Daniel did likewise. Our horses stood still before wandering toward the water, while we noted the eleven soldiers stood guard, instructed the Arabs in moving the crates sat in the sand, by the Hanomag SD.KFZ 251 halftracks,

"Waffen officers," Daniel cautioned, "have your face's well hid,"

"Better wrap up," I assured, "ok, there aren't many Germans left at the base, I think we may sneak passed and head for the ropes."

Observing the small group of Arabs preparing the ends of the ropes, lowered down from an over hung lattice frame above, before pooling upon a line to signalling men upon the cliff to hoist up their load. While others appeared busy setting up a further winch system at the top, to assist in take up further soldiers, if not equipment and supplies.

"They appear quite prepared?" Daniel commented, as we carefully approached and stayed clear of those stood by. Passing few piles of cates, I turned to the east; where the first biplane had landed, spotting a larger JU 52 tri engine passenger plane smoothly touchdown before coming to a halt. Few officers than passed, as we turned as though to collect few of the crates, seeing them reach a 770 Mercedes passenger vehicle, modified for desert terrain, and swiftly set out for the aircraft, as few men followed in five VW kubelwagen-jeeps, to receive the awaited passengers.

Knowing it an opportunity, I turn for the remaining four Wehrmacht soldiers, seeing their major had left to give orders to the Arabs gathering crates, to continue strategically loading a spear winch platform with equipment from the rear of a nearby Mercedes truck, nodding, "We may be clear,"

"But how long till their officers return?" Esther questioned.

spotting our horses had reached the waterhole undetected, the officer stood by the truck to the right, yelled, "Here... you!" I turned and quickly walked up to him, as he turned to retrieve a four foot by one-foot-deep crate and handed me an end, whilst struggling to lift. I knelt, placing the load upon my left shoulder and turned ahead, as the officer did the same for Daniel. Esther approached to thankfully retrieve a smaller box, as we turned for the winches' timber platform, seeing it hoisted with few Arabian diggers aboard and lowered the crates on waiting for its return to ground.

Seeing few of the nearby soldiers looking away, while preoccupied, I noted some crates with loosened tops behind and carefully turned to hinge one opened, discovering it full of German Wherein and French wines, before closing and noting the platform lowered. Quickly loading up ours and few crates nearby, as the other men passed to load the platform with theirs and turn for the well occupied Wehrmacht officer. We stood upon the platform and pulled its ropes, singling those above to hoist the load and were lifted.

"So, Smith," Daniel asked, "what will we be doing up there, I'm afraid we've arrived late to this picnic?"

"Well, I'm still not sure," I commented, "but if we can defer them from discovering the entry points, they will slow down long enough for us to borrow a plan and get some help. Though the only problem being to locate divisions to the south, and they are sure to want a cut. So long as it is kept a secret, we won't have any more problems with people tacking treasure, to be used for immoral objectives."

Esther looking out, seeing the vehicles had reached the landed JU 52 airplane to the east and its passengers disembark for the VW kubelwagens, "Who are they Smith?" She pointed,

I retrieved the binoculars, seeing a number of Waffen officers, Abwehr, accompanied by men and women from Balers party hosted in Germany, we had imposed on, answering, "The people from hotel Begin Berg Germany, near every last one from officials, generals, colonels, officers of high rank and even Gestapo; members of Abwehr. Most bearing swastikas upon their arms and others perhaps insignias, making their way to the vehicles," before handing her the binoculars to silently view,

"But what are they doing here?" Daniel huffed,

"They're obesely involved," Esther affirmed,

"Right," I answered, "I'd say the shareholders have come to collect or inspect their gold."

Staying silent on passing few men within the clefts walkways and approaching its top and overhung A-frame gantry, with men gathering to collect and quickly picking up our crates, before stepping of onto a suspended platform and carefully passing the crowd of Arabian works. finding we were now in a gap between the large ruins of two three story tall, stone forts either side and rows of two- and single-story civilian buildings ahead, noting a fair number of Arabs and German soldiers pass by completely unaware, we proceeded along the open if not main road.

Passing the many Wehrmacht accompanied by Abwehr officers guarding the larger of the buildings, with varies flags upon short polls they had already set, and systematically flagged down Arabs to inspect their crates. As some crates were decorated the only way, the NAZIS believed all should be and then spotted a larger four-story building to the right ahead, decorated by swastika flags positioned either side of the main doorway and a soldier stood guards either side.

Noting the larger buildings beyond, I slowed, "hold up," I whispered,

"Yes, but not for long," Daniel urged,

"They'll see us," Esther gasped, whilst further Arabs and Germans passed through the street and officers continued to inspect what was being carried, I patiently waited and carefully observed their movements.

DUCKING FOR COVER

Staying low as the bustling foot traffic continued by, quickly placed the crates down upon the sand covered paving stones, while looking toward a four-story building sixty yards ahead to the left, that appeared a likely radio building, with twelve foot tall, aerials set upon its roof. Seeing there a large break in the wall of the buildings third story and German operators sat at desk, whilst others walked to and from radio panels, hardly taking note the large number of soldiers and Arabs baring crates, like clockwork below. Each forming a line, passed the many SS officers and soldiers ahead, including men stood guard upon roofs tops to the right and left, suddenly suspiciously hearing the faint sound of music emitting from one of the far buildings.

Then seeing an officer approach from the right, I quickly turned, "This way," finding there an unoccupied side street, and walking to and around the corner of a building to our left, into an open walkway, thankfully none were observing. As Daniel and Esther followed, ignoring the officer as he appeared to peruse, "Keep following this street down and get into a building," I gasped,

"Right," Daniel seconded as they proceeded passed, I waited for the officer to appear from the corner, noting the line of men carting goods ended but fifty yards on, once passed the narrow aisles. The officer came around the corner, ordering, "Halt!"

I quickly struck his jaw with my fist, followed by a hard left and he fell, knocking out cold, before dragging him back and pulling him to his feet on throwing him through an open window of an abandoned building to the left. Just as a further line of people passed along the main road and the Wehrmacht officers detaining those opposite, had not seen nor suspected a thing.

I quickly turned and ran down the street, a further fourth yards, hearing Daniel call, "Quick, in here,"

"This way," Esther gasped,

I turned left and into a doorway of a large, thirty-five-foot two story high building, mostly filled with debris from its collapsed and weathered, limestone ceiling and second story floor, as light shun in through two four-foot windows in the buildings front face above and either side of the entrance. We turned to a large rear doorway opposite, passing the remains of stone staircase and exited into an isolated courtyard, and crossed to a rear doorway of a building to the left. Finding it too open though with a roof, stairway set along the wall opposite, doorway to the left and its brick right side wall mostly collapsed, revealing a narrow upstairs walkway between the houses ahead.

I stepped forth, finding the doorway sealed by rubble and turned for the base of the stairway to the right on following its weathered steps up. Quickly entering an open room above with ancient stone shelves and large table in the centre, filled with light shun in from windows before us, "Well, at least we know the floors secure," I smiled,

"Furnishings of stone," Esther commented, "how they ever managed to move such things?"

I turned for the windows, similar to the last buildings' and looked out, finding I could hardly spot a passageway below, that would lead still between the ruins. Before turning left, noting there a further stairway and stepped forth, as my right foot fell through the floor and quickly pulled myself up to continue, as Daniel and Esther carefully followed me to and up the crumbling steps. Exited the likely rear of the building as the un-railed stairway continued up to the doorway of a moderately taller building crowned by a slightly peaked stone roof.

We quickly and carefully continued up and entered through the doorway, finding it an open room, with windows all around, an ancient bench to the left and early Arabic patterned muzak decorating the floor. As I turned back and looked out the doorway, with the joining stairway below we had just came up and out further, to the Wehrmacht soldiers and Arabs in the main street, still well busy, and rubble filled areas around the building, whilst staying in from the doorway, as Daniel and Esther stood by.

Sending Word

Once caught our breaths, I turned to the surrounding windows behind and gassed out, observing the line of buildings and ruins beyond the side street we had entered, seeing there a number of small communications towers, if not also used to relaying messages received, set upon the taler of the buildings, with multiple windows and deteriorated walls.

"What now?" Esther asked,

"We wait," I answered, "but no doubt they'll send a patrol to locate the convoy and a dynamite shipment; limits our time."

"I say we take out their communication," Daniel suggested, "it disables two armies in a desert,"

"I think your right," I agreed, "we don't know their strengths or number of back up units. But from here we may just time their men's movements in order to take them out,"

"Or distract," He smiled,

Esther noted the number of men below, on shaking her head, "But how?"

"I'd say we wait for the right moment," I replied, "and perhaps rig a number of explosives derived from gun powder. Then once taken the radio out, we'll be in the clear to find and take-out Kikes,"

Suddenly noting the number of passing Arabs in the street to slow, "Right, let's go." Before turning to the stairway to follow its steps down to the last room and carefully across the unstable floor, to the next stairway, reaching the bottom floor and continuing back the way we came.

"Faces covered," I called,

Soon coming to the doorway and back to the narrow way, turned left fining it ended a hundred yards out, before a cliff and right, finding none caught sight of us. Quickly spotting the entry to a walkway ran between the building's opposite, on the other side of the narrow way, "The gap," I gasped, quickly running across and into the walkway, Daniel and Esther followed, noting the ruins of buildings either side would prevent us from being seen and saw the taller of the buildings, with the relay towers but sixty yards ahead. As we came to a forty-foot line of collapsed buildings to the right, long since fallen and quickly ducked low, whispering, "One at a time," and ran for the cover of the buildings ahead, as the sand covered path continued between further buildings and terminated at a street forty yards on, one at a time, Daniel and Esther followed.

Then heard the voice of soldiers as two passed by the walkways exit before us, taking no notice. I held my breath, before proceeded to the street and looked left, to see the two Wehrmacht soldiers, now near the corner of the thirty-yard squire building beside, with their backs turned to us. Then entered and turn right, following the passage down a slight grade between the rear of the detreated buildings ether side, and slowed before the main road, noting the number of Arabs bearing crates. I quickly reached the corner of the left building and continued around, keeping alongside the buildings, knowing the one equipped with short wave towers ahead.

Approaching the rear corner of the large four-story building, we quickly turned left and entered a six-foot gap between it and a smaller beside, and proceeded down to the rear corner of the buildings. Finding it teed into a wider lane ran between the rear of the buildings, hearing voices and spotting the backs of two soldiers to the right, silencing on passing two Abwehr officers stood by the rear entrance of the large building, to guard communications headquarters and generator with in.

The men once passed the officers continued their patrol further down the lane, before turning right to circle the buildings' far side along the street. Turing to Daniel, as he retreated from the corner, "You go first." He took out the suppressed Walther P38 pistol he had retrieved from the assassin at the Arminian Aspet hotel and reloaded few magazines. Tacking a breath as he nodding to Esther and I, before passing around the corner and carefully aimed up, firing at the Gestapo officers three times, striking the farthest before the nearest, and farthest again in the chest, as he drew a luger.

Daniel quickly recharged the magazine, as I entered the lane and we forwarded up to him and the unguarded well weathered door. I kicked the door open for him and he found it clear on entering, Esther approached and assisted with the deceased, as we entered and closed the door behind. Discovering it a large room, or rather walkthrough atrium before a doorway leading into the front half of the building, and a recently set up Generator, with a flight of stairs to the right, leading to the floor above. Suddenly hearing the steps of an officer come down the stairs, as he spotted us and turned to run back, Daniel quickly ran forth and belted him on the back of the head with the butt of his pistol, rendering the man nonconscious, as he fell-down five of the steps.

Daniel carefully continued up, while Esther and I dragged the Waffen SS soldiers' bodies inside, before quickly bounding and gagging the unconscious man with aid of his hat and belt, on hearing the suppressed thuds of the Walther 38 pistol once more. Before too running and up the steps, as Daniel peered out the floors' entry hole and fired few more shots on entering. Esther and I followed, entering the second story, with few surrounding widows and cement like walls of clays. Instantly turning to Daniel stood before a large desk and Gestapo lieutenant officer seated behind, with both hands raised, cowering at the prospects of the last two shots fired overhead and a perhaps fellow officer laid fatally wounded, to his left.

Daniel turned right and procced up the next stairway, while I trained my revolver on the lieutenant and noted a small roll of electrical wire on the floor behind, quickly pointing as Esther entered, "Esther if you'd be so kind, as to detain him with that wire,"

"Yes," she nodded and ran forth, before wrapping and tying the shocked officer tight like a transformer,

"*Schweine!*" he huffed.

I placed the pistol upon the desk and searched him for useful ammunition, picking up his 9mm defaced cap from the floor to gag him with, and swiftly retrieving the revolver on seeing Daniel enter the floor above,

"He won't move," Esther nodded,

"Though mad enough to conduct, good job," I grinned, knowing she would not have got the joke, and turned for the stairs to the floor above, quickly followed its steps up. We cautiously entering another large room, lit by few surrounding windows and left side furnished by a number of eight foot, fold out benches, to cater for a seating area with a line of crates beside. As food appeared to be prepared at the far end, with burners set upon three of the bench tops beside a desk and base of the next stairway.

We quickly followed Daniel, as he continued up the stairs before further supressed thuds emitting from the pistol. Reaching the top of the stairs and entered the next floor, seeing it a smaller room sectioned of from the rear half of the building. Spotting two deceased SS officers, with pistols in hand, laid either side a portable strategic battle table to the left of the entrance, with a large map of the aera upon it and additional tables set along the walls either side with different folders laid upon them and crates beside.

Lit by a light shining down through a hole in the ceiling and doorway to the right leading into the next room and front half of the building, just caching glimpse of Daniel as he entered. I quickly ran forward and entered, seeing there five technicians seated at separate compact radio units upon tables set along the far wall opposite, beyond two central rows either side. All powered by a series of wires ran through one of many windows and down to the generator.

Noting the three men and two women operators, preoccupied with sending message, I presented my pistol, as a man and the two women raised hands on seeing us and stood from the desk. One of the other two turned to Daniel and I, before quickly turning back to the unit in attempt to change frequency. I leapt forth and struck him over the head with the butt of my gun, as he fell nonconscious upon the officer sat to his right, he gasped and went for his pistol. I quickly managed to whip him across the face with the side of the revolver before he could draw and knocking him from his seat.

I aimed my pistol toward him, he through the luger pistol aside and stumbled to his feet, placing both hands upon his head, as Esther presented her 41-calibre Derringer and stood to the left of Daniel. I lowered my pistol and turned to retrieve some wire from leftover roles placed in the corner, whilst Esther trained her pistol on the officer and Daniel kicked over another quarter role, "Here, you best do it." maintaining his aim and drawing his SA dagger, ordering, "Turn, *Drehen!*" in German.

Each tuned as he approached and cut their belts on ripping them free, as their guns fell upon the floor. I cut lengths of the thin wire and tied the first, Daniel had disarmed, with hands behind his back and legs together, as Daniel and I worked our way along. Till securing the stood officer and nonconscious sergeant in the chair, as Daniel turned for the end radio unit, nodding, "Keep an eye on them, if anyone so much as whispers...."

Esther kept her aim steady; I directed the officer who had caused trouble, "You, stand with the others." He shuffled across, as I asked Daniel, "Mined if I borrow that gun?"

Daniel handed me the long barrelled, Walther 38 silenced pistol, as I turned and handed it to Esther, observing the German operators failed to take the threat of her unsuppressed silver derringer seriously, "Use this, it won't make noise,"

"Thank you," She nodded and sternly turned to the captives.

I turned to Daniel as he sat before a unit, "Don't worry," he assured, "he hadn't stop during conversation, it would seem." Then stood and passed by Esther and me to the central operators' panel, double checking their frequencies, before retrieving a short leftover roll of wire from the floor and reapproached on directing the officer into his seat and tying him in, before directing the other.

Spotting few spare cables, I took and handed them to Esther in exchange of the pistols, "If you could secure the women, you tie better then I anyway."

Taking hold, the Walther and shiny derringer, the officer shook his head again, as I lowered the decretive piece, as Esther finished and reclaimed hers and I handed Daniel the other. Quickly I drew my bayonet and stepped forth, the officer cringed, as I cut the sleeves of a spar Wehrmacht over coat and utilising the marital to gag the captives.

Daniel looking over the cables then toward the ones delivering power and carefully turning to the right window, and looked out beyond its broken away weathered sill, to the people traffic in the main street below, smiling, "So much for the need to dismantle telecommunications…"

"Wait," I replied, "although there more than enough Germans present to start a fight. I suggest you use the radio to call for help, if not a distraction. If those messengers came on horses as far as the oasis; their origin battalion couldn't be far."

"Your right," Daniel agreed, whilst stepping from the window, "best see if there are any allied forces nearby before I cut, Huns off."

I drew the Arminian rebel code book, from the train, and offering, "See if you can tune to a secure frequency?" before quickly passing toward the operators and retrieving each one's surrendered pistol, on throwing them aside and turning for the radio unit Daniel had first examined, discovering a short list of frequencies they may had been monitoring, and attempted to adjust its dials' settings, in hope to pick up any further incoming wavelengths. Persisting near fifteen minutes till picking up one they and the Arminian rebels had marked upon their long list of frequencies, hearing the voices of ally forces, "Eagle to falcon, over," "Falcon here; how is the hunt?" "Cold, over…"

I quickly butted in, "Alert, allied forces, to eagle."

"Eagles hearing loud and clear, over," A soldier replied,

"Group of supposed mercenaries, at…" I pondered and turning for a small map laid upon the table beside: to gain reference, "German grid two, nine, four, five over."

"What's the situation, over?"

"Hostel and jerry is looking for something, over," I answered,

"Eagle will be thinking of you, over and out," the soldier replied.

I switched it off and stood, turning to Daniel, "Do it now!"

He cut through the wires with his knife, as I approached the window and looked out toward the south side winch, saying, "Ok, time to be Arabs again." Reconciling my face and turning back to the door and ran through, Daniel and Esther swiftly following me down the steps and re-entering the lunchroom, before turning for the next flight of stone steps, on carefully continuing to ground level.

SABOTAGE

Once back at ground floor, I turned toward the Nazi flag hung within the entrance to the front half of the building, to signify an importance; or rather prevent dust. I approached and pulled the rag aside, finding it a semi open room, the generator to the left and no wall opposite, but few supporting pillars, and thankfully a leaser crowd passing along the main thoroughfare by preoccupied soldiers.

Realising the main body of workers to had turned back for the winch, I said, "Ok, they are returning for the winch." And concealed my pistol before face, whilst stepping forth, as Daniel and Esther followed close behind and exited to walk along behind the large group, toward the end of the busy street steered by the continual volume of foot traffic. I prayed to God they would be stopped, as we came to the lift of the hoists frame, seeing the Arabs continued to pick up boxes and crates, staked before the lift.

I quickly walked through the crowd and toward the boxes that were being over ran, noting the large crank wheel for the rope of the try pully steel A-frames' windlass, firmly mounted within a pegged down timber frame. Quickly evading the crowd of men collecting the equipment and supplies, I ever so slightly drew my bayonet from its sheath, while feigning to trip upon boxes and purposely leant over the rope, to cutting through the underside of its heavy braids. Before reaching down to pick up a crate, whilst the platform was being relowered and sneakily passed to the right of the crowd along the overhung stone edge of the cliff.

Looking down, to see the men below prepare a number of crates and Jerry cans of fuel, presumably for the generator, all though there appeared a fear collection of cans and the crates to be hoisted, retrieved from a tarp concealing a stash of explosives; they must had caried in their first convoy. I quickly turned toward Daniel and Esther now stood beside with crates from the nearby pile and nodded as they followed me away from the edge. Suddenly hearing the distinct rumble of a Daimler Benz 602 v16 engine emit from the far right, or east face.

We re-approached the entrance to the main thoroughfare, as Daniel gasped, "Well, that sounds like...?"

"What?" Esther asked,

"Like my Rolls Royce straight eight," I confirmed,

"What...?" Daniel asked,

"Never mind..." I replied, "Just wait," I then saw the large beast again, rising from the far edge of the cliff beyond the buildings ahead, seeing it the same air ship that had boomed my house in England, and manoeuvring over toward the Nazi flagged, main build on the right, toward the end of the street; seen earlier. Passing low over the remains of an ancient city detreated by millennia to millennia, before lowering the anchor lines and accurately descending behind the main building.

"Good grief," Daniel huffed,

"What is that?" Esther asked,

"Trouble," I affirmed, noticing the street to the north appeared to continue around the outer perimeter of the ancient buildings and cliffs eastern edge. Whilst preoccupied men passed to enter the main, "Quick," I gasped, "while no one's looking," and dropped the crate upon the sand and turned down the street to the right, Daniel and Esther followed as we ran the first eight yards and turned for an open entrance door of a building to the left. Entering to see an Arab busy setting up an old stone bar top along the right rear wall of the sixty-foot square building, with five other men and five Wehrmacht soldiers setting up tables and shelves along the walls, under the watchful command of three Waffen officers.

Realising each far too busy to take note of us enter and open rear doorway opposite. I quickly ducked to the left and passed behind few crates and set tables, staying together and proceeding to the rear door.

I quickly peered out, finding it led into a narrow rear walkway ran between the rubble and decayed buildings to the left. Swiftly exiting the building, as we ran down along the narrow passages' sand covered pavers. Then spotting the rear doorway to a building along the main street at the end of the narrow way, where it turned and continued right or west, and heard the laughter of men in high cheer emit from within, as we carefully approached to pass the doorway.

A drunk Wehrmacht officer stumbled from the door, as I accidently barged into him, and the intoxicated man fell into Daniel's arms, he caught the major and held him by the scruff of the uniform, "Are..." the man uttered, as Daniel struck his jaw and knocking him out cold. I looked through the doorway, seeing there a number of likely Abwehr operatives accompanied by Gestapo officers and Wehrmacht attending games of poker and Schafkopf with their backs turned. I quickly passed, as Daniel and Esther followed and continued running cautiously along the dished sand covered path, spotting a stone staircase to the right, fifty yards ahead, leading upon the roofs of surrounding single story buildings.

I quickly reached the steps and carefully proceeded up onto the roof of a thirty-foot square building, finding there further roof tops we could follow, and those caring goods in the street to lefts' view impeded by a series of buildings. "Come on, we best see who's arrived with them," I urged, seeing the airship only a further two hundred yards, nestled amongst the ruins and ran forth upon the next roof top, before confronted by a ten-foot gap, where a fragile section had collapsed between the next. I quickly ran and jumped the gap, noting there a narrow stone elevated walkway leading across the roof tops of a number of two-story buildings ahead.

Daniel and Esther, seeing the roof had not collapsed, quickly followed across, hearing a loud explosion echo from the winch at the cliffs south edge. Carefully I continued up the thin elevated bridge, before Daniel and Esther, "Follow my foot marks," I called, and reached the top before running across the forty-foot building onto another of similar size, before jumping a gape to the next and proceeding across a further three. Seeing the large three story, flag marked building and now branded, improved designed Zebulun, but fifty yards out.

We stayed low and continued across the crumbly clay roofs, toward the large buildings third story outer left wall with an arch window eight feet above and stopped to catch our breaths once stood upon the roof of the joined neighbouring building, seeing the airship to far right, landed upon a mound of sand concealed rubble.

Noticed all of its passengers had disembarked and must had entered the building, leave but few officers and aviation mechanics stood by. Quickly I turned for the large window within the wall of the building, on being sure no one in the main street to the far left, appeared to had notice us, but rather made hast for the thoroughfares west end and winch. I carefully stood and jumped to grasp the three-foot thick windowsill and pulled myself up to investigate, seeing within two Abwehr officers leaving an upper terrace along the front wall of the building and down a stairwell opposite. The steps leading down to a second story, large operations room below, with large middle eastern maps upon the rear wall and operations table in the centre, with few surrounding desks.

The officers reaching the second floor, continued straight down the stairway to the ground floor, finding the room left unoccupied, I carefully entered the window, as Daniel followed and turned to Esther as she suddenly entered and stood upon the sill. "To the gallery," he huffed, seeing its but eight feet to the left of the sill and jumped to its rail, as I and Esther followed, clinging to its edge before climbed over, approaching and continuing down the stairs to the second story operations room below.

Daniel franticly turned for a desk, with few maps and documents laid upon it, soon discovering flight plans. Whilst I peered further down the stairwell into the first floor, seeing a large hole in the rear wall of a large hall below, where a doorway may had collapsed and its rubble cleared out, with Persian rugs lining a stone floor. Hearing the muter of voices, I turned to the right side of the room, spotting a crowd of German officers in including Wehrmacht, Luftwaffe generals among Waffen, members of office and Abwehr operatives.

Each from the party Baler had hosted in Germany and no doubt disembarked from the airplanes seen earlier, toasting champing glasses, while standing around two parallel rows of banquet set tables, with a ten-foot gap between, likely arranged by Kikes, now stood among his guest with a raised glass. Noting there also few individual round tables bearing foods and bottles of wine for those present to be served. I carefully lay low upon my stomach to farther increase my view of the front half of the room, spotting a fourteen-foot arched entrance, as three Abwehr officers entered by a large Nazi swastika flag or brutally defaced silk. A first lieutenant saluting the crowd, "Here general, there's been an accident. The explosion you may have heard, was that of an explosives pallet being hosted up before the winch lines tragically gave way."

Kikes stood forth, addressing the officers and members of the present crowd, "See, I told you nothing's wrong and travel by both airship and aircraft are safer than most conventional means, wouldn't you say major Zishberg?"

"Oh... Yes," The officer who presented the news, agreed, "no, there's nothing to worry about."

Kicks then turned to the guest, assuring, "You see, there wasn't even a welcome from allied patrols; now a toast to our find." As he raised his grass and drank, all guest in the room followed before lowering their glass's, as Kikes noted five more officers approach the entrance, inviting the guest, "Now I'll show you where I've been digging, majors Donaldson, Snider, Rich, Benz and Fischer will escort you, while I consult my lieutenants, here." The excited crowd eating but few handfuls, stopped what they were consuming and headed for the men stood at the doorway, before followed them out, leaving Kikes with the three lieutenant officers that had come to inform him of the explosion.

They nervously stepped forth, whilst keeping their distance form him, as Kikes tor a leg from a baked chicken to his left and bit into its flesh, on purposely dropped his Champagne grass to the floor, before lowered the fibula from his mouth. Turning to a couple of chefs from the airship, stood opposite the stairway, dressed simply as waiters, "You two, go back to the ship." They quickly saluted and ran back toward the airship, as he took a further bite, sighing, "You know...?" Before hurling the bone out the rear exit, narrowly missing one of the retreating chiefs and snatched a silk napkin from the table to wipe his mouth, before tossing it toward the base of the stairs, continuing, "When I was on site for, I don't know? Maybe the last hundred times, at least... I never had a rope from the Gleistein company fail, despite hoisting *schwere* quantities of weighty equipment, vehicles, treasures. Now tell me major, how many explosive crates are left?"

"Well, there were three pallets worth," The officer called major Zishberg, answered, "and now we're down to one,"

"And who was supposed to be guarding the lift?" Kikes asked,

"Well, you said it yourself," pleaded the unnerved officer, "we're away from any allied forces. Even if you hide the fact, we took out the British patrols in the area. The Arabs have hindered any messenger returning with information and the ones returned simply say Jerry will take a while, as the British colonel had already sent word and protested the idea of falling back. So how were we to believe we were to place guards around the area? It's not like there's an army out there waiting to come in...?"

Another officer entered the building unannounced and stood before the major, on saluted kikes, "Sir, the supplies and Flake ant air guns have arrived and will be up top as soon as we lower new rope..."

"Yes," Kikes butted in, "get on with the report?"

The major now caught his breath, continued, "We drove along the eastern road, you instructed us, and coming to the last oasis before here, located a Panzer and Minenwerfer platoon wiped out and an irreparably damaged Panzer from the eighth platoon, with all other vehicles destroyed along with our dynamite shipment. We were not sure what had happened, but it would seem as though the enemy had left few alive, we found a tank commander inside. A major Hinrich from the eighth was spared, the man simply asked to speak to you about what he had witnessed?"

"Well, where is he?" Kicks demanded,

"Coming," the officer answered,

Kikes then saw the tank commander enter through the doorway, gulping water from a canteen while passing the officers and lowered jug to salute Kicks, on taking a breath, "Sir, I had to tell you in private. We had set out for Jorden and were caught up in a sandstorm after had sighted three camel riders; must had been part of an army. Colonel Ivens ordered to pursue, I remember Arden's tank bashing into us, as the sand was thick, then heard a knock on the hatch before opening. An awaiting adversary knocked me out, I awoke at an oasis and managed to stand within the tank, before hearing vehicles outside and was picked up. Witnessing the devastation done by the meddling allies and our illustrious tank."

Kicks grown short of patience, snapped, "Get out of my sight and don't mention a word to anyone!" before relenting, "Of course you've done well to bring this to me in secret." As the two officers walked out and the remaining three of higher rank, nerveless trembled, as Zishberg replied, "So the allies are upon us. We must leave,"

"Go ahead…" Kikes answered, drawing his pistol and shooting him in the chest, the two men remaining nervously stood aside, as he lowered the custom engraved Walther model 38 pistol, "No one is leaving, it will take more than that to frighten us. We have more weapons to set up, I have arranged in case of such matters, like armour units being spread and monitoring of income transmissions. Get everything brought up, but more importantly have your men on patrol!" The SS lieutenants saluted "*Hagel* the *fura*," and left by the entrance, as more men stood guard outside followed.

ACQUAINTING AN OLD FRIEND

"Stay up here for now and ignore the sound of gun fire," I whispered to Daniel, still gathering documents and Esther studying the large maps, and drew my pistol ready on carefully sneaking down the stairs. Kikes poured himself a glass of red wine and lowered the bottle as I reached the base of the steps and I slowly approached, noting his back to me whilst stood between the two rows of tables. I cocked the hammer, as he turned around and dropped the glass, gasping "Are... Well, well; you escaped the flames,"

"Not the way you're going," I huffed,

"Well, it gets the job done; unlike you," he boasted on stepping to the right,

"Enough about me, what about you?" I huffed, "Before I shoot, I might as well say you're a manipulative, murderer, clamming the lives of all in the industry, who knew of your selected treasure interests."

"It comes with the job, not that it would surprise you, how many Germans have you killed for the treasures?"

"Wrong," I answered, "I wasn't after it."

"That's one thing about you Smith, you were just to dam expensive..."

Quickly he ducked, as I fired, and instantly redrew his Walther 38, I dove to the left just as he fired over the table, shattering bottles of schnaps and Champaign. I aimed through the white table clothes and fired at him, as he ran for the door, each shot thrice narrowly missing. I stood and fired, striking the right edge of the doorframe beside his head. He stepped to the left and turned firing twice in retaliation, striking the table as I dove for cover and quickly fired my last shot, as he stood from the line of fire, and discharging a further two rounds in retaliation, on forwarding to the exit.

I reloaded one last round and inaccurately fired, he quickly turned firing his last shot, as I leapt upon a table and accurately aimed upon him, calling, "Halt!" He stopped and dropped the empty pistol, "This way," I ordered, directing him back into the hall, before approaching and stepping from the end of the table, "I have a confession to make Kikes,"

"What's that?" he asked,

"I hadn't yet figure out how to go about your demise." I smiled, "Well now I know, as I'm too out of ammo…" He quickly drew a spare luger from his belt, I swiftly threw my revolver at his face, and stepped forth, grasping the pistol and flicking it free of his left hand, as he struck my back with his right fist.

I turned back around, throwing my left fist into his face, as he stepped back on threw a hard right to my jaw and both took a further step back. He huffed in frustration and quickly attempted to kick below the belt as I blocked with my hands and grabbed hold of his foot. He jumped forth to elbow my forehead, as I blocked with my left arm to lessen the blow and he fell upon his back, drawing a double-edged custom dress dagger, likened to a small sword.

Swiftly thrusting its deadly blade toward me, I jumped back, as he stood to advance and I quickly drew my bayonet to block his blows, thrust from left to right, carefully angling the bayonets' blade down hard upon his, nicking a button from my shirt. Drastically, I belted and flicked his sword up, as he withdrew and swung in from the left, swiftly lowered the bayonet to block the following thrust, whilst he proceeded to swing from right to left, before plunging toward me, as I blocked and he withdrew.

Swiftly I thrust the bayonet toward his neck and advanced to plunge, as he belted my blade up and pushed me back against the row of tables, whilst applying further force to my blade. I held firm, as he laughed "Ha, ha, do you really think you're a match for a real *schwertkämpfer*," "However said I was a swordsmen," I replied, grasping a large silver platter of or-dervs with my spear hand and swung it into his face, as he stumbled to the left and I thrust toward him as he withdrew, before angerly swing down hard toward my face, as I blocked and stepped to the right.

He ruthlessly pushed against my blade, as I through my left fist toward his jaw and he stood aside to avoid, on pushing me off. Quickly I swung in from the right with the bayonet as he bogged, swiftly thrusting down and across, narrowly missing as I withdrew. Quickly blocking his blade once more as he plunged for my chest, and struck my face with his fist, on attempting a second plunge whilst I remained firm and blocked. He flicked the bayonets' blade aside on steeped up onto the solid table beside. As I swung at him and he withdrew, before thrusting down with full force against the bayonet and knocked it from my hand, coursing it to fall beneath the tables, before thrusting the custom weapon at my face, as I ducked and grasped the edge of the tablecloth, as he went to swing down at my face and ripped the material out from under him.

He fell back upon some food, and I tipped the rows' middle table he was stood upon and reached for the bayonet fallen to the right. As he pushed the table back over and caught my hand between the next, half crushing, as he stood in the gap at the far end of the table and went to pass between to the next, in order to run me through. I quickly pushed hard against the dens timber table and caught his legs within the gap before he could step through and freed my arm. Retrieving the bayonet, as he attempted to pry the tables apart and quickly approached, he stopped and thrust the dress sword toward me, as I blocked and thrust it down hard upon the table, he angrily released and surrender.

I held the bayonets' blade to his throat and secured the small sword like dagger, and threw it aside, he huffed, "Well what's the matter? Remember your training…" I suddenly pursed as though for some kind of reason, noting Daniel and Easter had reached the base of the stairs.

I lowered my bayonet, shaking my head, "Not an unarmed man, why I had failed to kill you when engaged, the same as any other opponent, is beyond me…?" Hearing the distinct sound of multiple boots trudging upon the sand and number of German soldiers enter by the front doorway and rear opening led by Abwehr officers with their pistols drawn and each man's rifles trained upon me, as I dropped the bayonet and Daniel and Esther their pistols.

One of the officers came near, Kicks ordered, "I want him alive for now, and will somebody get theses bloody tables off me!" As kikes pushed his way out and two soldiers came to assist,

"What should we do with them?" an officer stood behind me asked Kikes, once he was free and sheathe his dagger before stepping forth to retrieve the bayonet,

"Put them with the those aboard," he ordered, as I was struck on the head from behind and fell nonconscious.

Awaking to the sensation of being brutally nudging in the ribs by Esther's elbow, while sat to the right of me and Daniel to the left, as Kikes was stood behind a fifteen-foot countertop bench before us, equipped with a small wine rake to his left. He then truing from a collection of papers to gaze out one of the airships twenty-five, four-foot windows along the wall opposite, with MG 34 machineguns set upon removable stands within every second. Before realising we were sat upon a well woven mediaeval rug covering but a minute part of the forty-foot wide, by sixty-foot ovular rooms' floor and aluminium benches along the walls opposite, few filled bookshelves, and collection of inverted munition crats to the left of us. Kikes proceeded to utilise the central bench, as I lent further forward and spotting a large number of suitcases and cargo, beyond the munition crates and two officers stood by the ships entre door ten feet away. Then turned right, noting a central ladder stairway to upper deck, with pinboards displaying maps either side an entrance in the rear wall, to a forty-foot large bomb bay.

Before noticed a table housing a control panel, few maps and well-crafted timber desk with a red armchair to the left of the centrale bench top, before the ladder stairway. Leaning further forth to gain a better view, Esther assisted with her shoulder against my back, allowing me to spot two Allie soldiers tied and seated beside the boom bay entrance. Nodding to Esther, as I silently sat back against one of many tin ammo boxes, stowed beneath the bench and prayed that we would be able to stop them and all wound work out,

"So, you're awake?" Esther smiled,

"We're alive," I smiled, "I suggest we wait for an opportunity when Kikes is gone, and don't worry, they're not going anywhere without their German head archaeologist, or rather treasure hunter. Even though he stole from the archives, like Baller."

Sitting quietly, as kikes soon turned from the counter and approached, "Are you well wake?" he asked.

"Hardly," I answered, whilst attempting to appear dazed,

"And these new friends of yours?" he continued, "I like that one, what is her name?"

"Esther," I sighed, as though had given up all hope, "and the other is Daniel."

"So, Daniel," he questioned, "an officer I take it...?"

"And so is Esther," I answered, "in the Arminian resistance."

"Yes, perhaps," he grinned, "all though I found theses papers on his person, they seem to be written in code, condemning him a spy for British intelligence. So where did you meet him?"

"Aboard a Kriegsmarine gunboat, I had captured. Anything else...?" I asked,

"No Smith," he huffed, "but I'll tell a story of my own; and would you believe, it's all about you. You and I though arachnologist, were by force or choice, in listed as Abwehr operatives of sorts; you of course trained and exceled more than others. I underwent such training ahead of Baller, after a year or so, you however believed it possible to make more money as a privateer and turned down the high commands offer and admiral Schizthme. As you ran away and where reinstated in the British infantry but remember; before leaving you had orders from headquarters to find the translate. Orders which you so well covered up, before defecting and making plans to visit island XV in the Indian ocean, despite what you yourself suggested them.

As though to discover it in a typical solo attempt, we would have never guess your reckless unwillingness to show at pear 143, that night you cut all ties and the crew of kanonenboot 1248 cast off, unaware once loaded and none the wiser to the floor in their highly secret mission. Just as the well-funded previous expedition of theses catacombs, they believed not even you would have fathomed the significance, however, knew the Kriegsmarine were too not yet given their full orders. But your plans failed, for you had no idea the high command were looking to replace you for some time, due to you're holding back of finds, because you knew they wouldn't pay as well as others within the circle of potential buyers.

Likewise, proven when the boot 1248 left pear 143 without its second captain aboard, it was I who radioed to confirm my own suspicions, as you thought me but one in the group of privateers and treasure hunters. But what's this; Smith isn't aboard or at the hotel, that is when I had become first in command and as planned, promoted by order of the high command as the new head of operations, in the securing of archaeological treasures, and thanks to you, they didn't want the same thing to befall.

So, they offered five times your cut, though it was not all easy; you see, I like you had to go through offices that are now firmly under me, as appose to once over me, in cases I should fail buying each off overnight, with aid of our library. I knew the first thing was to find all your work, where it was hidden. I knowing you had presumed the library a safe place, as all partners appeared non-German privateers,"

"There were experiments being performed by a major Mullar of the SS, who himself had gown utterly insane," I snapped, "and I guess by some chance; you had something to do with destroying my houses?"

"Actually, yes and no." he grimed, "You see, Baller and I joining Abwehr remained a secret to the other privateers, while working for the Germans; because they themselves had not become Nazis nor joined the third rich in their stubbornness.

Baller was simply tolled to destroy the house to send a message, and if you were sighted, to leave you alive for capture. But Baller, he truly wanted you dead, becoming a bookie of sorts as well as a full Nazi or loyal investor, and wished I would simply run out of information, only to turn to him for more. Now you were presumed dead, and he insisted on being promoted to my leave, as apos to beneath. But I knew of his intentions once received a full report, detailing the killing of anyone sighted around the house and him instigating the destruction of a building next door, to insure your death.

We although it was done and bribed to have Baller quickly promoted and sent on expedition to locate treasures, while I attempted to secure rear finds. As soon as word got back to me by telegram and the testimony of two Gestapo officers that had survived an encounter with allied forces, at the sight further south than-east of Tobruk, Baller had uncovered. My doubts were confirmed, as I predicted my one liability, was you.

For none known where we were and even if they had, we would have been long gone before they arrived. But one of the two survivors from site claimed last he saw Baller, he was having a fight of some kind with you in the dark, to prevent him from leaving. Those two gentlemen quickly raced back by biplane to Tobruk, landing their airplane and stayed hid in the desert, before getting a lift into town and organising a way of killing you.

But they, not knowing what they were up against; even though made up most of the people within the Marlbrough street hotel and claimed to have sent you to a room of gunmen. Still made it possible for you to escape, and not only this, but also peruse them even to the point of tack off in the airplane. Would Daniel have anything to add to this by any chance?"

"You only get name rank and a single serial number from me," Daniel huffed, "but due to the fact you're humbugging anyway. Before meeting Smith aboard, the gunboat, you yourself spoke of, I found out all about you Germans and your secret band of treasure takers. Well at that point I had orders to intercede but one highly ranked Abwehr officer, before any others marked by intelligence.

According to information obtained in Czechia and Poland, he was supposed to board a patrol boat marked 1248 to be taken to a highly secret destination and soon to become our next point of interest. I was ordered simply to board the boat and observe before reporting, as such vessels had been implemented in concerns arising the disappearance of civilian ships.

I was also to determine the right time, either not long disembarked or docked at the location, to kill this treasure hunter and prevent further backing for the Nazi war effort, and I recall you that man not Smith. Your very Walther pistol chambered in 45 Cal. Given majority of the information mentioned, obtained firsthand. An improved silver 45 cartridge was found at a radio desk in Czalvarkia, the mark of the man I was hunting. And let me tell you something, you murderous wretch, if you had stayed for the voyage, you would had been but a poor breakfast for sharks!"

Kicks then drew his pistol, exclaiming, "*Ich siehe, ja...* Once thought a gift from an old friend. *Aber nur...* To Incriminate me to the allies..." As he pointed toward me, just as another officer entered, asking, "Have you found where to dig, *herr*-general?"

"Oh yes..." Kikes answered, leaning forth before taping me twice upon the head with the Walthers' barrel and rising on putting it away, commenting, "Smith here has given us some great information, I just had to take it from him." Then turned to retrieve the papers from the counter, carelessly dropping my jacket upon the floor, nodding to the Gestapo officer at the door, "I will be out soon, have them ready. I trust they returned to scoff their faces?"

"No," the officer replied, "they were all done ten minutes ago,"

"Oh, well time dos get away; now get going!" Kicks ordered, as the Gestapo major left and Kikes reached for the jacket, briefly observing it before turned to me, "Smith," as he held it to the right and compered it against his full Waffen generals' uniform, complete with a dark leather over coat he had for show. I carefully thought of what to say, in order that he might drop it before me, as he shook his head in question, "Really, Smith?" While show off his clean clothes, worn for his guests,

"Yar," I grinned, "it's amazing what those Nazis make you give up, all that self-respect and dignity."

Kikes threw the jack upon the floor, with the bible and original translate Diary and bent down towards me face, huffing, "I will teach you to have respect," on throwing his right fist against my face and stood to put on his gloves, relenting, "Are, I should have been more careful,"

"Ha, ha..." Daniel laughed, whilst shaking his head, Kikes now infuriated ran over and struck him twice in the face, before standing as Daniel spat blood and I rubbed my face upon my left shoder, as my nose slightly bleed.

Kicks took a breath before commenting, in a disturbed yet calmed voice, "You know, I'm going to enjoy talking to you all in Berlin, especially her. But now I see why you teamed up with this man Smith; he, certainty has a lot to talk about."

He then smiled and turned to those stood by the exit and stepped upon the jacket on passing with the papers firmly grasped and reached for the handpiece of a radio intercommunications box by the door, calling, "This is general Schulz speaking,"

"Hearing, *herr*-general," A voice replied,

"Transport the prisoners to the cars on this next pickup," he ordered, "and don't worry, there are two officers stood guard to watching them, Stuba and Hinnsworth that had returned from Turkey." Before hanging the handpiece and turning to us, "You will be watched by the vary man who gave us a copy of the ancient writings, revealing the arks where abouts and the other, SS lieutenant Hinnsworth, an assassin from the hotel of Tobruk."

As the men announced stood from the entrance door and proceeded before the central bar-top, whilst keeping their eyes trained on us and saluted Kikes as he exited the airship, just as its large OF-2 V12 diesel engine begun to roar. One of the men slightly limped toward me and throwing his right boot into my side as I leant forward winded by the hard blow, he spat at me as the other officer too approached and struck me across the face with the back of his hand noting his left fist bandaged, he too spat, "*Schweine* and *ratten* have more honour than you,"

The man who struck my side laughed, "You threw a shoe into a room to fool us, SS lieutenant Buerkle was stupid enough to jump from a two story building in fear of a *granate*, but you are the *narr* that returned to us now under *herr* general Kicks," "This time there is no *hoffe*, you will pay by *blut*, *hagel* our *fura*...!" he brashly called, raising his nonwounded hand and too belting me with his boot, before turned away. I caught my breath and waited quietly for the right opportunity to do something, seeing one of the officers leave to properly close the door, and returned to step behind the bar and retrieved glasses, as the other took a bottle of white wine from the rack, on pouring and both begun to drink generous portions from their crystal trophies.

A CHANGE OF PLANS

I felt my wrists handcuffed behind and the airship had begun to rise, followed by the beating of a strong eastern wind, as the large craft moved from side to side. The officers heled their wine glasses firm, to prevent a spill, only to splashed it upon themselves and turned to search beneath the bench for napkins, I rolled forth upon my right shoulder and grasped my jacket, as I hid before the bar.

Filing through each of the jacket pockets, then heard one of the officers ask the other, "Where did he go?" and foot steeps approach, I carefully rolled further to my right and partly around the far end of the bench, on releasing my jacket, so as to allow it to partly lay around the corner and turned back firmly grasp one of its sleaves in my hands.

The footsteps once left by the gape in the opposite end of the countertop, come near, before halting. I instantly felt the weight of a man upon the jacket and sound of a pistol drawn, quickly pushing my feet against the end of counter and while partly rolling over, on pulling hard, as the airship tousled about, and officer Stuba fell to the floor.

Quickly I stood and ran passed the desk to ladder stairway and quickly up its steep steps, as officer Hinnsworth discharged his drawn pistol, with each of the three shots narrowly missing, perhaps due to his wounded hand, before turning to assist Stuba. I reached the top of the steps and second level, finding it a large sixty foot wide, by ninety long living quarters, with a dining galley for the first forty feet ahead, consisting of light weight side beaches and serving counters along the walls either side.

Noting there a number of chairs before a door in the centre of the frontal wall beyond the galley, quickly stepping from the cylindrical shaped structural stairwell and continuing around from the cylindrical covers ovular opening. Spotting a series of bunk beds, set within rows, to the rear of the room, parallel to the walls either side and sturdily built to hold three men each.

Then heard the officers climbing the stairs and turned back, to stand to the left of the stairwells entrance, just as officer Hinnsworth approached the second story entrance, while presenting his pistol. Carefully timing it, as I kicked the gun from his hand and kneed him hard in the jaw, rendering him nonconscious as he fell down the steps and hit the floor, before Stuba. As he recklessly fired his pistol in retaliation and I dove from the doorway, as few rounds pierced the aluminium flooring and again narrowly missed.

Finding my knee to bleed after had struck Hinnsworth's partly open mouth and stood, hearing Stuba begin up the stairs, and quickly stepped to the right of the stairwell entrance, on Stuba reaching the top of the steps. Carefully peering from the entrance as he stuck his head and pistol out, before turned to the left, I quickly booted him in the face, as he grasped my foot in reaction and I fell forward down the tubed stairwell. Unintentionally landed upon the officer fell before me, as he had dropped the gun and my knees struck his chest with the assist of my body weight, before falling forth hard against the deck.

I then stood, discovering him dead and Hinnsworth laying beneath nonconscious, quickly I turned for the deceased officer, as Daniel approached before Esther, she gasped, "It's horrible, and they may had killed you?"

"Well Smith...?" Daniel smiled,

"We haven't much time," I huffed, "we must stop them from getting to the treasure," whilst kneling down to search for keys within their uniforms, Daniel turned to the kitchen like bench and retrieved a set, on un-cuffed himself and retrieving our pistoles, before reliving Esther and I from the cuffs.

Retrieving the Bible and incomplete copy of the diary, I had kept from the floor hearing an officer call from among the other men held captive, in a Scottish ascent, demanding, "Why are you un cuffing the enemy? He should be shot, you've gown soft! His's a trotter, the Jerry said so...?"

"Yes," Daniel answered, "but not all Jerry says is true,"

"I'll stop you traitor," the officer replied, "I'll make sure your hung!"

"Well, well, I'll get to you gentleman lather," Daniel assured, before pocketing the keys and a set of cuffs, while following me, as I turned and ran back up the stairs, and Esther following close behind,

"Come back!" the officer cried.

Once back upon the second floor, I quickly ran toward the door seen earlier opposite, on presenting my pistol before entering a narrow hall, ran left and right leading to steep stairwell at either end, to the upper deck. Also noting the closed doors to toilet cubicles and individual quarters along the wall opposite likely unoccupied. Cautiously I turned left, and back to Daniel as he entered, "You take the right," then proceeding to the steep steps ahead and climbed till neared the top, before peering out a side entrance to a curved outer port walkway, leading left to right, with few windows similar to the last along the sidewall of the customised fuselage.

Spotting an Adware officer approach from the left, I pulled back from the entrance to the steps and waited as he passed on by. Quickly I swung my pistol and struck the officer over the head, knocking him out cooled before cuffing him. Then entered the walkway and turned to a window, finding we were high in the sky and heading southeast from the site, toward a temporary air strip in the desert to land, noting there few Germans on the ground waiting by vehicles, Kikes had provided for guests.

I turned right and ran along the walkway, toward the ships' frontal control room, reaching the last door on my right and silently entering, seeing the back of a Luftwaffe oberst-colonel stood before me, another officer beside the piolet at the helm ahead and forth sat before an instrument panel opposite. Quickly passing few desks and instrument panels, while keeping to the rear of the cabin, none had yet noticed me sneak forth passed the row of desks to my right and few of the radio's panels. I carefully aiming the pistol toward the piolet and ordered the officer stood beside, "Hands up!"

Watching his hands rise on spotting me and the other sat at the desk followed, just as Daniel entered the room by its starboard doorway, seeing the fourth officer reach for his holstered pistol, he presented his luger, "Don't be so hasty, remember we were brutally treated by your kraut friends."

The major released his engraved Walther pistol, as the pilot remained with his back to us, then half turned, demanding, "Surrender or we crash to the ground!"

"*Einverstanden!*" the man stood from the desk encouraged, as the Nazi pilot manoeuvred the ship downward. I stepped forth and hit the soldier at the desk over the head with the butt of the revolver, to knocked him out, as he fell into his chair. Then quickly turned to the pilot and too rendering him nonconscious with the butt of the pistol, the man stood beside with his hands raised leapt at me as I threw him off on taking control and quickly steered out of the crosswinds and back around toward the cliff.

"I didn't know you could fly this thing...?" Daniel gasped, aiming his pistol toward the man who attacked, as the other stood surrendered swiftly went for a knife. Daniel quickly stepped forth and pistol whipped him up the side of the head, as he fell to the floor and released the dagger, before cuffing him and securing the other.

"Neither did I," I answered, before turning back to the large, curved glass window panels, to observe our approach of the cliff, nodding to Daniel and Esther as she entered and cuffed the officer at the desk, "This air ship is far too dangerous. If the ninth regiment come, they'll be killed, I think I have an idea."

"Oh?" Daniel asked,

"We'll fly back over the roof tops, while keeping low," I suggested, "I'll hold it steady, as you and Esther get off... Quick the man by the desk," I gasped, spotting the officer sat in the chair came to and Esther quickly turned her pistol on him, "Got him," she smiled,

"Right," I called, "if you could secure him and the other, before escort theses four below, ready to be lowered, there's also another Waffen officer through that portside door, down by the stairwell. When below if you could source some extra rope, there should be plenty around, perhaps within the boom bay itself, and bring it up to me?"

"I'll check the boom bay for rope, though why the need for it up here?" Daniel inquired,

"So, I may exit over the side once you're off," I answered.

Daniel then secured the knocked-out pilot and Esther the other, "Right oh then," he nodded, "but I hope you know what you just suggested. You better pray that by the time you leave the controls a sudden draft doesn't take this glorified weather balloon away, Esther would you direct jerry from the chair."

Esther then directed the man from his seat, and Daniel the other three toward the port side exit and left to secure the officer mentioned. I continued to manoeuvre the ship around and into position, as Esther returned from the starboard door with a role of rope, "Here's some rope, Daniels coming up with more," and placed it to the right of me, before gazing out the glass, commenting, "This is amazing, to think I hadn't flown before, but now have twice in less than two weeks,"

"Well, it's not every day for some people to be fighting off a lunatic and his companions," I replied,

"It was for me and came without warning," she reminisced, "Smith, was what that mad man said true? Were you really...?"

Daniel entered through the doorway he had previous with a roll of rope hung over his shoulder, "Here Smith, all the rigging we could spear," and approached to retrieve the role from Esther, "the colonels been instructed to tie off the remaining below. Where would you like it secured?"

I turned to Esther, answered, "Tie it off to the hose real, by the doorway you just came from, before the window and get ready."

Daniel then left to tie the rope, before hanging its end out the window, opposite the riel mentioned, spotting its end dangled over the ancient buildings more than a hundred feet below. Esther stood lost for words, he re-entered, assuring, "Ok Smith, I believe its long enough. I'll tell you when you're flying low enough for us to climb down, by the radio system below, then wait up to five minutes for us to getting down, unless I tell you otherwise,"

"Go now Esther," I nodded,

"I will see you on the ground," she sighed and reluctantly turned to follow Daniel as they left.

I focused ahead, seeing the soldiers among the Arabs in the main street and powered on toward the digging sit, they had begun at the northern end of the street, before steering right and over the tops of later constructed buildings. Then begun to descend, while holding the ship steady in position, Daniel called through the intercommunication system, to the right of the starboard door, "That's about right Smith, see you on the ground…!"

I adjusted engine speed and carefully held against a north wind, praying it wouldn't go adrift, as I took a chair from my right and used it to jam the wheel and picked up two of the officers' caps left upon the floor. Before leaving to the starboard door and seeing the rope, fastened to the red hose real, left of the entrance and a crossed the starboard walkway to a square window opposite, Daniel had dangling it from. Finding its end laid upon the roof top of a two-story building the ship had come over, with sixty feet of slake.

I knew the chair only jamming the controls one way, as I grabbed and held the two officers' caps as rages for my hands, and jumped through the window, on rapidly slide down the rope. Seeing the air ship slightly alter position, before gaining altitude, as I neared the end of the pore, now about eight feet above the roof of another building. I slowed and pass over a gap to another on releasing and landing upon and through the clay roof to a second floor of the building, as I lay and looked up to see its ceiling mostly collapse and the airship rapidly gaining altitude and drifted further south.

I stood and dusted myself off, finding the room to have few windows and small hole in the right corner for a stairway, quickly approached a window before me, as I stood upon its cell and grasped the edge of the newly made hole above. Pulling myself up onto the remains of the crumbling roof top and stepped forth, as it further collapsed. Hearing a voice call, as I turned to the right and spotted Daniel, Esther and the three men held captive from the aircraft; stood upon the roof of a three-story building, east of the one I was upon. Then jumped the eight feet gap to the next and raced across the buildings toward them, soon approaching as I caught my breath, "Right, follow me," I huffed, before leaving the officers captured and carefully continuing northwest along few roof tops, toward another larger building two hundred yards to our right, with its far side partly collapsed.

THE CATACOMBS

We quickly reached the sixty feet wide, rear wall of the building ahead of us, with three seven-foot square, large windows cut into it and observed the wide street to our right, surrounded by stood ruins and the remains of buildings opposite. I approached the central windows' chest height sill, Daniel and Esther caught up, though the three men we had liberated halted, and their colonel huffed, "If you're thinking about entering, we'll keep you posted out here," and saluted Daniel,

"What are you playing at?" he questioned,

I stayed turned ahead, the officer pointed to me, answering, "It's that two-timer, his mad; you can't stop them…!"

"Man up and follow me," Daniel snaped, "I out rank each one of you!"

"No," the officer shook his head, "we'll met you off this mountain and arrange transport."

I turned to Daniel, as they retreated across few of the roof tops, before entering a further one by a stairwell, "Let's hope they don't get court,"

"I hope they get court marshalled," he huffed, as I turned back to the central window before me and carefully peered through, finding it open with a series of narrow stairs leading down anticlockwise around its inner walls, and two Wehrmacht officers at ground leave, stood by a left entrance door and hole within the building stone floor.

The two soldiers stepped toward the doorway whilst lighting cigarettes, Daniel noting the buildings peaked roof and a hole in the wall opposite, where an east wing had long broken away, on collapse, "What's this place Smith?"

"Yes?" Esther asked, "It's a tower isn't it...?"

"When I came to this place on expedition, we dug our way through; only to have it blasted," I replied. Turning from the window and spotted an eight-foot square clearing amongst further buildings to the far left, the Nazis' dig crew had begun to excavate. As soldiers keeping watch stood and sat drinking from left over wine bottles, I pointed, "See over there, where that line of Arabs had stopped?"

"Yes," Esther nodded,

"That's the area we unearthed and marked upon a map; I had kept records of in the archives of the library in Italy." I nodded, "Now whenever I excavated anything, I would rebury. But little anyone knew, I had other ways of going underground, as those who helped excavate the area would rebury. I would find and generally dig in through vents or another form of entry point, such as this tawer like building revealed upon one of the maps, given by Fredric; now in Kicks' possession."

"Are, blast..." Daniel concluded, "So when he took your jacket, he found all Fredric had hid from them?"

"Yes, it would seem," I assured, "of which I wasn't counting on."

"Well how do we get down there," Esther commented, "they are guarding the only entrance into the building, and there may be more present?"

"Not the only entrance," I commented, "follow me, I think the walkway still be strong enough," then turned to the window, seeing the guards below otherwise occupied and entered upon a stone stairway, as Daniel and Esther followed me down. I drew my revolver and prayed the ancient steps would hold, before reaching the base and centre of the wall we enter by. Seeing the soldiers stood through the entrance, not yet finished their cigarettes and backs turned, we quickly snuck over to the hole revealed by the removal of a large paving stone and kept an eye on the two lieutenant officers.

Nodding to Daniel, I carefully walked up behind the soldier on the left and he the right, hearing the light crunch of sand under foot. The men turned as we struck them in sequence, rendering both noncaseous, on catching and dragged them in, seat them beside one another to the right of the entrance. I quickly turned toward the hole and steps leading down within, from our side with the present glare of lanterns hung from the walls and touches within stone holders, lit by Germans entered.

I quickly passed Esther and begun down the steps, as she and Daniel followed to the base and entered a ten-foot wide walkway that continued ahead of me, with further lit touches and lanterns hung every twelve feet along the walls. Before cautiously proceeding, as it widened and led to two doorways, with small inscriptions upon the wall between, with an arrow point left and right beneath each article, to either doorway. Unable to decipher, I drew the translation book and flicked through, till finding a match for the langwidge, "Are, it's a basic code, 'River' and the other, 'upper hall.' I would say Kicks has gone through the one marked 'upper hill' that I had previously marked, on attempt to figure out the way to enter the catacombs. Follow me."

I took a torch from the wall before Daniel and proceeded through the right doorway to another hall, finding it slightly declined thirty feet in, Esther and Daniel stayed close, as he asked, "So what's the plan this time?"

"They've gone the way I had already come once from their very dig sight," I assured, "but leads only to a large room, with few narrow passages to follow. One leading to a catacomb that had been booby trapped by a confusing collapse-away floor. Though beyond the short section it was deemed safe, till a trio of doorways; one leading to death and the other two quite safe, despite designs of passed booby-traps.

But this particular way appears to go down and thought it led to a hidden underground stream, they called a *nihr/rudkhaneh-zer* that translates as river, once unjumbled. But this translate isn't always correct, with missing pages and all. Either way we may beat them, before they even figure out the first booby-trap; though each quite straight forward."

We then approached and entered a doorway into a forty-foot square dug out, with two further entrances to the catacomb and small four-foot tall square pillar before us. Blowing the dust from the stone misandry, stood between the two entries and reading aloud with aid of the torches flame and translate diary, "Follow the wind and you will die,"

"What is it saying?" Daniel asked and begun to look for an arrow or further marker.

Esther noted the touch I had raised, pointing, "The flame," I turned to the torch, seeing its flame alter left before right, as she smiled, "That's what it's saying, the winds coming from theses catacombs."

I turned to the entrance right of the pillar and observed the torch, whilst holding it out before me, finding a gently breeze to blow on it slightly. Then turned to the left catacombs entrance, as the torch's flame stayed still, Daniel commented, "Are, so that must be the way?" pointing toward the catacomb,

"Unless there was a cave in up further," I replied, "though the right would seem to have the greater volume of air coming through."

As I cautiously entered the left catacomb, discovering it like a large tunnel, varying in width from fifteen-twenty feet, soon approaching an entrance to a narrower catacomb to our left, and the larger continued on. I stopped and carefully entered the narrower tunnel, as it widened before an eight-foot pile of golden objectless and large portion of diamonds to our right. Once concealed within detreated ancient chests, opposite a seven-foot arched doorway, cut into the catacombs' left wall. Daniel quickly passed to the collection of amalgamated metals, spotted the handle of a sword stuck out of the mounds' centre, that appeared to have fussed together over time, as he attempted to collect a golden wristlet, finding it stuck fast before grasping the ivory handle of the sword. I turned to the arched entrance and interpreted few inscriptions above, "To upper and lower level,' and 'The well of armour.' I wonder what that means…?"

"Are you sure?" Esther doubted and studied the inscriptions.

Quickly I spotted and blew dust from a plaque to the right, "To the river and lowered level.' I still don't know what river is being avowed?"

"Perhaps we should look," Esther suggested.

I turned from the entrance and prudently followed the catacomb down further, Daniel released the handle of the wedged sword and followed Esther. Discovering after but eighty feet, the tunnel further declined down a steep grade and narrowed with a row of broad footed, four-foot-wide pillars, along the walls either side, comprised of square chiselled stones, erected with no mortar.

Catching the glamps of daylight ahead, I continued down and between the pillars, toward the light, finding it but a dead end and the glare emitted from between two large stones. Approaching to look out through the gape, only to seeing the tops of few date palms below, I quickly turning back to Daniel and Esther stood by the pillars, "Dead end. I suggest we continue through to the upper and lowered level,"

"Right oh," he seconded, before turned back the way we came, ahead of Esther, as I followed back to the arch entrance opposite the mound of treasures as he and Esther entered through. I turned to the ancient gold articles and noted a glimmer as though a sudden presence of moisture on that beneath the sword handle Daniel had touched.

I quickly entered the opening and proceeded along a narrow catacomb within, till caught up to Daniel and Esther, on nearing a set of stairs and followed them up to another doorway, "Wait," I called, spotted an inscription above, as I jumped to wipe away the dust, before drawing the diary, reading, "The well of Csbare." Before entering and spotting a fifty-foot diameter, large circular hole in the centre of the room, for a deep well and raised the torches on approach to see water a foot off its stone brim.

Esther pointed to rooms' curved wall, "look at all these weapons." we turned to spot a number of ancient swords and armour hung from the walls, deuterated bows and further weapons within well fashioned stone holders below. Covering up all, apart from a small doorway to our right, left and other ahead, marked by inscriptions above.

Noting a shimmer emit from the water, I turned with the torch, discovering a large number of bronze and copper pieces of armour with decretive gold plating, laid in a large pill about twenty-thirty feet beneath the surface, "The best of armies would have come here," I commented, "only to ditch their armour and all they had, before continuing. From this point, it will defiantly be booby trapped, as it was on the way to 'the lower levels."

Then turned to the doorway on the right and read its inscription, "To treasury's', I don't think it'll be that easy...?" Then turned to the one ahead, opposite the way we entered, nodding, "Are, this one says, 'To exit' and..." as I pursed and proceeded around to the next, "to lower entrance."

"I would wonder as to why they might label an exit, but nothing on the way in?" Daniel questioned, "unless there is no exit nor lower entry, for that matter"

"I scouted this whole area," I assured, "there is no entry point from below, so there must be an exit. I would say those who once entered, weren't seeking an exit and likely took another way. So, I suggest we try this exit for ourselves?"

Esther then approached and undusted finely etched inscriptions below that I had ready, above the supposed exit doorway, calling, "Over here, there's more."

I quickly came over and gazed upon the heavily inscribed stone, unable to interpreter, nor decipher its code. I flicked through the diary, sighing in frustration, "The pages Baler had torn, and to think Kikes has the copy from Boas,"

"No, that's not it," Esther assured, "This is like the ancient people of Kuoiti and another tribble language,"

"Are yes," I recalled, on handing her my torch, "now I remember, there were many inscriptions similar to dialects used by natives to the island. So, what does it read?"

"This is a confusing language, only the first tribes used, as it is pre-Dutch-low Franconian," She elucidated, "Enter through and deposit wealth…" She then turned and ran back to the first, I had interpreted, uncovering few markings upon the stones right of the doorway, "If you enter, you will meet the ground and your maker," then ran passed to the way last interpreted, uncovering further inscription to the left, "Beware of cave in." Before turning to me, "What do these last two mean?"

"The prior explaining, I'd assume a booby trap where the floor may give out beneath the victims, at a certain point," I answered, "and I think the last, warned the walls may cave in around the victim. They really weren't taking any chances, well beyond anxiety. But your first interpreted, still spells exit and would seem my guess was right; it will take us to the treasure,"

"Right," Daniel nodded, "I think you have something there,"

Esther conceded and handed me the torch, I took and turned on entering through the central doorway, praying to God we would be safe.

CATCHING UP

Once twenty feet in, I noted ancient torches within holders every fifteen feet along the right wall and begun to light them as we passed and saw the stone floor partly raised ahead, as each paver sat four inches proud. My smouldering torch revealing an array of inscriptions etched into the stones, of Egyptian origin, lighting a torch on the wall beside as mine burnt out and opened the diary to affirm the significance of the basic depictions, reading, "Are you on our side?" I took out my compass, to check where it pointed east, as I knew the ancient occupancies were indeed Persians from south-eastern Assyria.

"What are you doing?" Daniel asked,

"The past civilisation's army were originally from the east and north is straight ahead," I answered, as I walked along the foot square pavers to the right and cautiously avoid the central inlays till a cross the thirty-five-foot stretch of elevated pavers, as few of the floors' central stones gave way disclosing a number of sword blade with bases firmly mounted to a much lower floor.

Daniel and Esther ran across the way I came and turned on spotting the broken away section, as he huffed, "Theses mongrels really didn't want there to be any remains of trespassers,"

"Yes," Esther agreed,

"Yar," I nodded, "and it usually gets worse the further you go; in these types of places."

Then walked ahead and looked up, noticing large stone blocks textured with iron spicks, hung from the ceilings by chains, and carefully walked forth. Till seeing few pressure plates within the floor before me and smalling set of blocks suspended from the ceiling, held firm alongside the walls by lugs. Though half the size of the last blocks, this time their spicks resembling that of double-edged swords, "Ok stop!" I called, before pointing with the torch, "There are pressure plates ahead; we can run and stop when the first of these large stones swing down over head, as the second set relies on the first to brake links of a copper chain; in order to realises the stones at pinnacle swing. We must stop only for a second as it does, before running forth between each swung, as the next swings down before us."

"Great idea Smith," Daniel replied, "but I think there is no need for us all to go at once; besides, we'll only miss time, I suggest one goes first."

"Ok, you two stay back," I agreed, then waited till they were safely stood between the second and first set of stones, before taking a breath and leaping forth, to engaging the plate and ran to maximizes my time to get out of the way.

The first set fell and the blades of the second swung down, narrowly missing and as assumed, engaged a further set ahead. I quickly turned and leaped back out of the way of the second set of blades, toward Daniel and Esther,

"Dive for it!" she called.

I dove, landing but three foot short and two of the stones blades scarcely cleared my feet, before crawling forth, on being assisted to my feet, Esther near hugged in relief before standing aside, I turned ahead, as the blades swing back and forth, till eventually slowing and coming to a rest, Daniel commented, "Well, I think that's as closes as I wished to engage that."

"Yes, not a bad thing you and Esther stay, instead of trying at once... In case you did notice, it wasn't to be beat."

"Of course," Esther replied, "what would have I done if you had... I mean, what would have we done...?"

"Well, you'd have to guess the way," I answered, then turned and walked towards the stationary blades, as I checked my front pocket finding its cover near completely cut off and prudently continued, sighing, "Be careful."

Passing the sharp blades, as Esther and Daniel followed me between the next set, as I held few blades aside and Esther turned ahead, gasping, "What is this?" As she saw the floor ahead had begun to fall away and continue toward us.

I released the blades, calling, "Stick to the walls!"

Noticed there a deep groove along the base of the left wall and anther nine feet above, I quickly turning left and Esther right just as the floor gave way between, I reached out to her, "Run to me!" As she jumped across the void and grasped my hand and large volume of rock and debris fell from the ceiling, while nearly throwing her forth to the wall. She grasped the groves and pulled in, as I covered her and held firm while Daniel clung to another set of grooves, fourteen feet back, and following debris struck and broke through the remaining floor and revealing a deep caesium, before ceasing,

"Are you right smith?" he called,

"Yes," I replied, as I stopped covering Esther and took the torch she had, finding the grooves continued ahead, nodding, "Right, this way now." and continued to shuffle forward to my right,

"Another close call," Esther sighed, "and miracle we're alive," as she and Daniel followed, with aid of the torch in my had to see.

We then continued as pieces brock free and fell more than a hundred feet down, I reaffirmed grip and following the wall ten or so feet, before seeing a complete stone floor ahead, on coughing due to dust and called to Esther and Daniel, "Cover your faces, the dust off the stones may cause dizziness, before fainting."

Reaching the floor ahead and carefully stepping out upon its pavers and quickly continued toward a doorway ahead, residing the torch to view inscription above as its flame grew faint. I swiftly stepped through, knowing oxygen was to run out, and turned back to Daniel as he caught up and entered the doorway, then saw Esther not long behind collapse to the floor, ten feet from the edge.

Filling faint, I quickly re-entered and helped her to her feet on throwing her over my shoulder, then quickly turned and ran back through the doorway, as Daniel half turned back and waited. I ran on by and saw the tunnel partly widened to three doorways ahead, with inscriptions to the right of each, drawing the diary on attempt to interpret, finding each in Esther's language, I quickly asked Esther, as she came to, "What do they say?"

She struggling to look up, though begun to decipher, as Daniel wiped dusted from the stones, "It's a way to an atrium, and the other two are doom…"

Not sure of which one was the way to an atrium, I quickly flicked through the diary as we both begun to heavily cough, then pointed, "Quick, this way!" And ran through the centre doorway, as Daniel followed into a hallway and the torches' flames dwindled to a smoulder. Spotting the floor ahead narrowed to a foot wide bridge, over a deep drop and noted an inscription upon the left wall. Knowing we were too far in to turn back, reading, "One will entre' This stone bridge is only strong enough for one," I gasped,

"I'll go first then…" Daniel commented,

"I'll follow," I nodded, "be sure to run."

Praying the bridge would hold out long enough, whilst Daniel started across its narrow pavers, determining it firm, and reached the far side, "Come on smith!" he called, I quickly begun across and found the bridge to not falter, till mid-way as a six-foot section crumbled and swiftly leapt forth to solid stone, as sections cleared gave way and what remained shook. I continued to make hast for the other side and floor ahead, as Daniel near collapsed and stumbled down the last fifteen feet of hall, before entering a doorway, with water flowing over its entrance within.

I stumbled on through and stood upon the top step of a stone stairway, within a sixty-feet wide, by forty deep room and turned to the thin blanket of water gushing from a fountain hole in the wall above the doorway entered, that had no doubt widened over the years. As water gently flowed over a vacant section of the step and down into a shallow pool also feed by collected water running down the wall, above a large pile of stones to the right and diverted from the pool to a semicircular drain hole in the rooms rear right corner. Suddenly catching our breaths, I thanked God we were alive, and the air was now clean.

SILVER AND GOLD

I gently lowered Esther to the wide step, entered upon, and turned to Daniel stood at the far side of the pool ahead, by a pre-lit torch upon the wall and nine-foot doorway. With the sudden glare of multiple torches emitting from within and noting another doorway in the rooms' front left corner. He stood from the door, as I carefully help Esther to sit up and she caught her breath, "Har... Well, I don't think I'll trey that again,"

"Ha, ha…" I laughed in solace,

"Wait I hear voices…" Daniel hushed us, while I helped Easter to her feet on too hearing the German voices and raced down the steps, on leaping across the ten foot wide poll to Daniel and doorway ahead, "Overhear Smith," he whispered and quickly turned to the left of the stairs, concealed by the darkness for cover, discovering an array of assorted diamonds within a large silver cistern, he dosed his torch with a grin, "If this is the entrance, I would like to see what's inside?"

"Yes," I replied, whilst concealing my torch, "but don't touch anything, there are booby traps everywhere."

Hearing the voices fad, I turned to the doorway within the left corner ahead, spotting inscriptions above that had recently been dusted off and read aloud, "Welcome, rightful owners,"

"I don't understand?" Esther asked, "wouldn't have it been just as hard for them; especially if they had to know the native languages, I know?"

"Yes," I answered, "unless Kikes found a way to have it translated by Fredric."

"Or their way was just easer to enter," She huffed, "I doubt they couldn't had come through such traps?"

"Possibly," I nodded, "otherwise they may not had made it this far?"

Daniel drew his pistol and huffed, "Well I'm sure we can ask the scoundrel, when we find him." I then entered the darkened doorway, noting the mutter of German voices had grown all but silent, finding it a near ninety-foot square room, with a tall arch ceiling and large pills of treasures to the left and right off us, before further mounds consisting of silver and gold articles along the far wall.

Then quickly spotted a gathering of officers among soldiers at the far-right end of the room and watched them pass through a large open doorway. As two Waffen SS officers entered and stood by a doorway in the rooms rear left corner. Quickly we ducked behind the piles for cover, on seeing more men enter by the far-left doorway, thankfully not spotting us, I whispered to Daniel and Esther, "Ok, I was hoping to catch them nosing through the loot and hold them till the cavalry arrived. But it seems they're not after the common treasures, either that or Kikes is that much of a devoted Nazi, that he wouldn't allow them to delve in such articles?"

"Well," Daniel commented, "do you think any Wehrmacht will be on their way down to help gather this loot?"

"Unless Kikes tries to keep it a secret," I confirmed, "just be cautious, there's something different about this treasure hunt and it's not just the Krauts."

Then snuck forth, as the soldiers to the left proceeded to decrease, and turned right in hope to closer observe the first group of officers and strike once found what they're looking for, as I prayed to God, we might stop them and for safety. Carefully running across toward the doorway, the officers had entered, hearing the sounds of multiple foot steeps echoing from the room we had entered by and halted on turning back to Daniel and Esther, "Quick, in amongst the treasure."

They ducked between a large pile to their right and kept to the dark, spotting the glaring number of flashlights entering the refuge, the way we came. I threw the smouldering touch upon the stone floor and stomping it out, before kicking it aside and retreated into a narrow gap between the two large piles of ancient articles, to my right. Then carefully peered out to observe the incoming Wehrmacht soldiers, bearing stretches to transport whatever deemed most valuable, as two once loaded instantly turned for the doorway entered by.

I waited about ten-to fifteen minutes for them to load portions and make way for the surface, as few Arabian diggers entered. Cautiously peered out further, to spot a band of Waffen officers tacking notes and cataloguing each peace collected upon clip boards. The Arabs entered begun to assist the soldiers re-entering and relieved them of stretches, Daniel whispered, "Are they gone yet?"

"Shoos…" I hushed, "Not yet and I don't think they will, until taken every last piece."

Seeing an officers stood before the line-up of Arab stretcher bearers, call, "Hurry up!" as the Wehrmacht soldiers stood aside to catch their breaths, the Arabs suddenly tumble over there loaded stretches, drawing scimitar and shamshir swords in rebellion on viciously cutting down the officer and nearby soldiers. More Germans ran into the room, just as the group had killed off close to thirty men, before forced to surrender at gun point, one of the surviving Waffen officers stood whilst clasping his right arm, and shouted to the Arabs, "On your knees!"

The men dropped their swords, and each faced the soldiers entering to form a line, with their backs to a mound of treasure. Twenty-five of the Wehrmacht soldiers lined up, with their MP 38 machineguns trained upon the twenty-four Arabs. The partly wounded SS colonel then drew his pistol and stepping forth, demanding, "Now, who is your leader here?" before instantly pointing and shot a man stood in the centre, whist further Arabs entered the room to loaded stretches.

A bearded man dressed in blue silk at the end of the line nearest to us, bravely stood, answering, "I'm Casper Anzor-Bahadur their leader, leave them…"

The officer approached and violently struck him across the face with his pistol, as the man stumbled back and the SS colonel huffed, "How dear you, after all we promised you and your survival, why?"

The Arid kept his hands upon his head, answering, "Because this bounty belongs to us. We are but few survivors of the clans and you offered us half a percent. We could have been living like kings, but we couldn't find nor safely return, due to the foreign invaders that thieve this land."

"Yes, you mean the allies and remnants of communities once loyal to the Ottomans," the colonel replied, "and just what was your plans?"

"To sabotche and have the place collapse," the man answered, "if we can't have the treasure, none can, despite all securities, we've placed many explosives within the catacombs entered."

The officer turned to the Arabs loading stretches, as they nervously went to leave the way they came, the Arab with his hands upon his head, went for his sword upon the floor, and others knelt within a line scrounged for theirs. The head Arab swung at the distracted officer and knocking the pistol from his hand, as the soldiers open fired upon the others.

I quickly fired few shots toward the soldiers, muffled by the defining echo of gunfire and Saudi Arabian battle cries, Daniel and Esther turned to me as I lowered the pistol, gasping, "Ok, let's go," finding I had managed to wound few soldiers and ran through the large doorway, the group of officers had entered and came through to a sixty foot wide, by thirty deep room, with a similar arch ceiling and fifteen foot doorway to the rear left. As the large room was housing more treasures and a number of artefacts. Suddenly noting writings inscribed upon its walls and steeped forth, discovering the doorway led to a darkened hall, and quickly entered before waving Daniel and Esther to follow.

HIDDEN TREASURE

I once near two hundred feet down the hall, could see the glare of light emit from a doorway at its end and quickly reloaded my revolver on entering through, finding the hallway continued before turning left, Daniel whispered, "They fought with vigour, but their attempts futile,"

"And all for gold?" Esther sighed,

"No, not gold," I whispered, "for men who had lost identity; the treasure itself becomes a symbol to remind them how great they once were, now be quite..."

Approaching and carefully peered around the corner, where light had shone from, spotting the Germans party from the airship, gathering before a fifteen-foot tall, large ceiled arched doorway at the end of the short run. Noting Kikes stood before the group with the translate diary, attempting to figure out the doors lock, swearing under breath in German and tossing the translate upon the floor. I turn back to Daniel and Esther, whispering, "Well, that's sorted," and begun back down the hall, before seeing a large group of soldiers entre ahead and proceed towards us.

We quickly looking around, finding there no vantage point for cover, Daniel sighed, "So, we're going to be captured again?"

"Not if I can help it," I assured, "maybe we can talk to them."

Quickly turned back and following the hall around the corner on put the pistol away as we approached the preoccupied crowd, quietly I whisper to Daniel and Esther, "Just act as though you're in agreement with me, you too Esther."

Then walked in close, while keeping to the back of the officers, officials and otherwise investors, as a brigadier second class general stood near Kicks grumbled, "But you promised us? When we return to Berlin, we will expose you to the general *feldmascholls* and high command. How dare you mislead us, I will tell the *fura* himself,"

"I'll have the next man who speaks of exposure; shot and his body left in the desert!" Kikes snaped,

"Having trouble with my translator, are you...?" I inquired.

He quickly drew his pistol and turned, every person in the crowd stood aside and followed once caught sight of Daniel, Esther and I stood in the shadows, Kikes shook his head, "It was you, wasn't it? You left out the one language needed to open this door!"

"Yes, that maybe," I commented, "but curiosity has bought us together. I know you're looking for a different, far more valuable treasure then the enormity of priceless artefacts, in the previous rooms,"

"Yes, go on...?" he cautiously replied,

"Well, that's just it, isn't it; how can I if there's nothing in it for me?" I huffed, "I may want a cut, before a deal."

Kikes stepped forth, as the soldiers seen earlier caught up with no Arab prisoner present, the Waffen major with them, gasped, "Sir, should we have theses spies, or however they are shot?" while directing his pistols,

"Putt that away..." Kikes ordered, and passed those stood aside as each obeyed, "No, he is working for us."

The Waffen major stood before the soldiers, informed, "I Also beg to report *herr*-general; the Arabs are traitors. They have placed explosives upon the exits. Their leader believed the treasures to belong to his family tribes, however they've been silenced, and the booms are being taken care of."

"Keep up the good work, major," Kicks saluted, as the men turned and promptly left the way they came. Kicks once again pointed his distinct Walther toward me, ordering, "Ok, drop your weapons."

We drew and dropped our pistols upon the floor, as I unsheathed my bayonet and released so its blade stuck between a gap in the pavers,

"Now you will interpret," Kikes ordered,

"Not without striking a deal," I bargained,

"I know you Smith," he replied, "you could not care less about yourself, many soldiers looked up to you. So now…" as he aimed the pistol toward Esther's head, and observed as I sneer at his gesture in utter contempt for his injustice, he boastfully continued, "I see you have recently found an appeal for justice and undeniable soft spot. Now then, wouldn't it be better if you survived, rather than die and leave her to us as a farewell gift?"

"Don't make things any harder," I replied, "If you kill her, you won't get through this door; you will be wanting all three of us to translate. Now about my cut, I'll open the doorway for you so long as you hear what I have to say in full, once you find the treasure you set out for, whatever it is…?"

"Don't play stupid with me Smith!" he huffed.

"Wouldn't dream of it," I replied, stepping forth as he escorted us and others in the crowd redrew pistols,

"Don't worry," he assured, "he is all part of the plan. Usually, things run smother without any further delays, in order."

Finding the door secured by runs of thick alabaster stone as part of an intricate locking mechanism and number of inscriptions midway up and further upon the walls either side, with cubit square; perforated stone covers of possible vents beneath. I quickly turned left and drew a pencil with the incomplete diary, instantly handing both to Esther and whispering as I slowly passed, "Interpret the writing on the wall and if you can't, write as though to solve a puzzle or something."

She turned to the inscriptions etched into the right wall, whilst Daniel stood to left of me and I attempted to figure out how the door worked, as Kikes and the group stood back to watched. I prayed all would work out, and picked up the diary Kikes had thrown aside, to begin reading through. Kikes smirked to those stood in the crowd, "This should be interesting?"

Swiftly looking over few languages, as I had before, Esther soon approached once written down what was upon the right and left wall and handed the diary opened to its' rear page, I excepted and announced, "Ok, here's the answer, on the wall to the right, 'Walk back, turn back and you will be free at thirty on the wall.' And upon the left, 'You may only run half the right side.' And that inscribed upon the door, 'Look at this height, the height the writing stops."

Kikes raised his pistol again, huffing, "You know Smith, I am patient, but you're teasing me. What type of peoples write like this?"

"Give me a moment to think," I replied,

"You have but fifteen minutes, no more." he snuffed.

Quickly resuming up what was presented, in attempt to figure out each inscription and turned to the wall, only to see each of the other cubit square bricks bare and the perforates indeed covering shallow vents. Still trying to re-puzzle, the wording, Daniel asked, "What if it's for two people to find and presented in such a way to find it?"

"Well, let's see," I commented, then figured it out, as I turned to the inscriptions upon the right wall, before that on the large door and begun to step back whilst keeping to the right walked. Counting out thirty cubits to the last brick, within the corner; where the hall turned and continued right, spotting further inscriptions upon a paver, in yet another native dialect.

Turning back to the anxious crowd and Daniel as he approached, "Go about midway down, you'll find some faint etching upon a brick."

Daniel turned to head right and continued back down the long hall, Kikes and officers, amongst investors intently followed behind, with weapons ready. Esther came near to interpret the newfound inscription, as I used the diary and read under my voice, "Go back, look down in shame, for forty years we could not retrieve our wealth."

I turned to proceed down the hall and court up to Daniel, as he called to me, "Yes, there's more written in a different tong."

I approached, to see him studying yet another of the floor pavers by the left wall, in the hallways corner, as I knelt and interpreted the inscription, aloud, "There being enough to sustain and build a city, whether it takes fifty years, just to build the many roofs." Then turned and continued down the hall, as Daniel followed ahead of Kikes and the Nazi crowd, while Esther stayed behind.

I cautiously studied the floor and walked forty cubits, spotting there text etched upon a paver, again by the wall. So, faint it would had been all but invisibly, I carefully blew the fine dust off and read, as it was once again of a different language, "Take a lamp stand for your trouble."

Daniel proceeded out of the hall, on re-entering the room second to the treasure we had come through earlier. I followed, immediately spotting a large brass lamp stand in the shape of a bare tree; of all things, positioned against the rear walls' centre. Daniel looked up and stepped forth, noting a large chandelier hung from the ceiling, bearing the likeness of an inverted tree, before proceeding to the unique lamp stand, as he asked, "I don't understand Smith?"

"That would make two off us," I replied,

"What is going on with the chitter, chatter?" Kikes shouted on approach, "Get on with it, you two!"

"Stand back," I replied, before grasping the lamp stand and pushing back hard against it, whilst placing my feet against the wall. The chandeliers' chain then dropped down, till stopped a foot off the floor, as I could fill the lampstand push against me, Kikes ordered two men forth to assist, one took a position between the stand and wall, too pushing off with his feet.

Daniel turned to the chandler and saw a plate in its centre, where it was attached to a chain and called out, "Over here Smith!"

I stopped pushing, as the two Waffen officers took my place, and ran over to inspect the two-foot square gold plaque upon the chandler and drew the diary to interpret, "You must take this lamp holder with you, as well." Then noted a thick copper pin going through the thick supporting chain and pointed top of the oil lamp chandelier.

Kicks came near and presented his dagger to lever the pin free, I held up my hand, "Wait," before turning to the Germans at the lampstand, "Get out from in-between the wall."

Kikes quickly levered the pin free, as the men got out of the way and the gold coated chandelier struck the floor, coursing the candlesticks' pressure too great to hold as it threw back, and hit the wall hard, knocking out a layer of bricks, revelling a large opening within the wall as the remaining sections fell. Seeing a slight amount of water gush out and waited for the fine dust to settle, as it filled the area.

I knew it was our opportunity and ran through the dust to Daniel, then quickly back around the dusted-out crowd, toward Esther, "Follow me" I whispered, as we retreated back out into the treasure hold, before the final section of the main hall and swiftly entering a gap between two large piles of treasures, on knowing we were liable to be seen and silently hid in the darkness. As the thick dust settled and revealing the crowd of both worried and confused, coughing krauts.

"Smith!" Kikes yelled, presenting his pistol and turned to few Wehrmacht no doubt and agents of Abwehr stood within the crowd, "Snider, Roped, head up that hall, they may have run to a dead end. Torrance, go back and take Goring with you, I want the others alerted and Vergers men to search for them. But do not engage alone, weapon or no weapon; they even though securely hand cuffed, were able to elude men with strict orders aboard the *luftschiff*; where I had personally left them. Now go, we' le proceed ahead and check the way is secure!"

We then waited, before hearing Kikes address the crowd, "Do not be alarmed, the way is now open, Follow me!"

Once those given orders left, and heard two sets of footsteps approach, spotting the two officers, Torrance and Goring about to pass. I quickly grasped a silver vessel and whispered to Daniel, "Take the one on the right." I quickly ran out and belted the man on the left as he passed and Daniel knocked over the other, before simultaneously grasping our enemies by their colours, as they reached for their pistols and through a fist to their jaws in order to render them unconscious.

Esther released a gold tray before assisting to drag the two men into the gap and bound their hands and stayed low as we waited, hearing no sound of German boots. I held one of the pistols secured and peered out of the gap to find that Kikes and the group had begun to enter the unsealed wall, as he shun a flashlight to examine the structural integrity of the opening. Before proceeded forth ahead of the intently following group of investors.

"Now what?" Daniel asked,

"I doubt there's a second way out," I assured, "we have them, so long as we can keep them from coming back out,"

"So long as we can...?" Esther sighed, "But more soldiers are sure to come for this treasure,"

"Have you found out exactly what they're trying to find?" Daniel inquired, "I mean, with Noshes ark and all that?"

"Yes," I seconded, "you have a point, whatever it is, it must be from before the flood and likely further lost riches, they had urged me to find. Something I refused them that was to do with Nosh's ark, and a number of other discoveries, including the location of the lost mines. But I didn't understand, what else could they have wanted besides wealth?"

"To buy weapons?" Esther suggested, "But I was thinking; what if they are clamming these treasures for that and attempting to keep other treasures a secret. Like what we saw earlier at the mines?"

"Of course; why would Kikes settle on a small percentage...?" I pondered, "No, I think your right and that's exactly how he can afford to keep a reputation, as fare as investor's go. Though we already knew this, but now what is it their looking for, is there not enough to melt down here...? Unless Kikes is interested in ceiling the rest off, so he and only few under-ranks could return to have it dug up. Of which your presumptions would explain as to why his kept this much a secret, as appose to the rest,"

"Well, let's follow them in, to be sure they don't have an exit," Daniel nodded, "I hope to get them all that is coming to them."

"That's not a bad idea," I seconded, "let us go, but when I say to leave, we leave. I'm sick of being caught by the same Germans and knocks out; I'm thankful to be able to walk a straight line, yet alone remember details of this place, or places alike..."

We then saw the two Germans, Snider and Roped; Kikes had sent up the hallway, return and run to the openings' entrance and climbed over the rubble before following down a previous hidden hall, taking no notice of us, re-entered the room. Stepping forth, I quickly turned to retrieve a lit torch from the right of the doorway, as Daniel commented, "We best let them run and get our weapons,"

"Right," I nodded and turned back up the hallway they had searched, till following it back around the corner to its end, discovering our pistols and blades still upon the ground and quickly retrieved them, offered Esther the luger, "Here, you may need this,"

"If you say so," she nodded, on taking it, "but only as a deterrent."

Before running back to the corner, were the hall turned right, spotting a light shying from the now opened hall and quickly ducked back behind the corners' edge, just as Snider and Roped exited the opening and begin across to the rooms' entrance and out into the treasury. Seeing it clear, we held our pistols ready and begun to sneak down to the room and opening Kikes had entered.

Soon approaching and peered into the once hid narrow catacomb, with stalactites covering its ceiling, though sections of wall and floor manmade. Then saw a light shining in from an opening within the left wall ahead and dropped the torch, before running the next hundred and fifty feet to the opening, and finding the hall terminated ahead. I carefully peered in, whiles staying hid in the dark, seeing the hall continued a further sixty feet to a large arched doorway and cautiously walked up toward it, as Daniel and Esther stayed nearby.

True Treasure

We carefully snuck to the corner of the doorway, before peering in to find it a ninety-foot square room, with a thirty-foot tall, curved ceiling, decorated by biblical depictions and a four-foot hole to an indirect shaft to the surface of the mountain top. Then looked down from the patterned ceiling to a large pile of treasures, copper armour, swords, diamonds and jewels, sat upon a mound of soil and stones surrounded by water. Supporting a small clump of trees that appeared to bear a kind of red fig, or possible pomegranate, judging from its spread limbs.

Noting most of the trees sprouted from the stumps of fallen vegetation, that had lay in the moat and quickly turned to the voices of Kikes astonished investors. Noting there an ancient three-foot-wide bridge before us, leading on from the doorway to the sun lit mound of treasures with a further bridge leading on toward two doorways within the far-right wall. Suddenly spotting a light, at far side of the plants, seeing kikes and the group of officers accompanied by officials step from among the trees, as Kikes stood before the larger of the exotic plants, toward the islands centre.

Boastfully presenting one of its fruits, within his right hand while joyfully shouting, "I've done it! I've delivered as I promised; a fruit that generations had passed down. Gentle-*herren* and dame-frau, long ago, as the oldest dated record shown, the tree of knowledge was written to have given worldly enlightenment. Now if we found the source of that knowledge...? Of course, inherited from the time the first of mankind had gown against their apparent creator, but I say the first time we had become our own and to us, our own gods."

As he held the fruit high, before lowering it to his lips and took a large bight of its red peel and inner pulp on swallowing, with a grin, "Now with that, we may know all and be our own gods among men." Quickly picking more fruit and throwing it to the crowd, as they near fought over it, like ragged dogs and eat of the fruit, in a misconception alluded toward the garden of Eden. Though evident each had read or heard of the biblical account, at some point, only to believe a lie, nevertheless.

Esther turned to the floor behind, gasping, "Are Smith..." I turned, spotting a series of sunken pavers,

"That can't be good?" Daniel huffed,

"No," I replied, once again noting the two ten-foot-tall mysteries arched doorways within the darkened far right wall. Then heard a cracking of masonry and the first stretch of the catacomb we entered by, begun to cave in and stalactites fell to the floor, as the whole section of ceiling caved and we were blocked,

"I knew those stalactites manmade," I sighed, "like its wall and floor."

We covered our faces as the dust emitted from the collapse and turned to hear Kikes further address the anxious group, "Are, the way we came is shut, but the way to go is now open to our minds. I can now tell you exactly witch doorway to take, but there's no rush."

"I can no longer run from my past," I nodded to Daniel, "indeed it has overtaken me. Now I must confront that I have been freed from, with one perfect plea. You must stay hid till I am finished speaking, and under no circumstance may you approach. Few officials and perhaps account Vincent Luxe among Kike's guest may be the next men to lead once Kikes has been taken out and I with him..."

"But why," Esther sighed, "there must be another way?" shedding a tear,

I turned to her and near reaching toward her face to comfort her, only to withdraw, sighing, "It isn't over and all though it is difficulted, emotions will not win a war. Nor can I bear to burden you with what might had been..."

Before quickly turning ahead and running forth through the dust spread from the doorway and across the bridge, Daniel and Esther voluntarily followed. As those in the crowd drew pistols and Wehrmacht if not Abwehr officers trained their MP 38s, Kikes assuredly called, "People, we are now above them and they are still unarmed!"

Each then put their pistols away, neglecting to note our concealed weapons, as we reached the far end of the bridge, while Daniel and Esther stood to the left of me. I ran up the eight-foot-high mound of treasures with trees upon it and silently prayed before turning to Kikes, as he looked down to my approach, "What is it, that you persist?" he called,

"I almost forgot myside of the bargain, made earlier," I huffed,

"Go on then Smith?" Kikes smiled,

"Well, hear what I have to say." I replied, "You and your party have only showed a repeat of the mistake Adam and Eve made in the beginning, when God made the heavens and the earth. God tolled the first humans not to eat of the tree, of the knowledge of good and evil. This begging a test to them, as they fell for the lie from satin, the very lie that stays between humans and getting to God, till this day for some, but not for all.

God has made the sacrifice, he sent his son begotten of the father not made, to live among us, and take the punishment for our sins, as he was nailed to the cross over two thousand years ago, as glory died for us all and perfection, that we may be forgiven for our sins. Every bad deed we have done, whether murder, adultery, stilling, lying, malice and cheating or breaking any further of God's commandments. As he took the punishment for us, that we may not perish but have eternal life with him."

"And what are you saying Smith?" he smirked, and the crowd chuckled amongst themselves,

"Only this, anyone can be forgiven!" I exclaimed, "All God asks is that we accepted this free-gift, so we may be right with him and live the way he commands us to live. Praying for Christ to come in and be Lord of our lives, helping us to see evil for what it is and to stay on the right track with his help. Please change your ways Kicks, is what I'm saying. I beg you and this party to stop this evil; for all without Christ and those who turn away from him, will perish in hell. Now I've done things as a soldier, but I'm now asking you, as I had tried to for Baller, please stop this and change your ways; give yourselves up, so we may help you get out alive. Soon the ally forces will be here and as of this very moment, the dust from the entrance collapsing is taking away our oxygen."

Kikes then heard the crowd starting to murmur, before yelling, "Ha, you Smith think you could outwit me, I...? After eating of this fruit, the fruit that no doubt you noticed and believed originally grown by an ancient Midian society, to ancient Syrian and perhaps Persian to Arabian, such as what was built up top. Taken by the Arabs only for other tribes, joined with the Otomman empire to take over, and rebuilding but half of its edifice. The trees being grown and regrown, as the flood hadn't destroyed all trace!"

"Kicks I'm warning you," I replied, "don't go down this road any longer."

He drew his custom Walther 38 pistol, huffing, "I'm still in charge here Smith and I alone give the orders...!" As he turned to observe each doorway and heard a load blast from the above surface, commenting, "Since that blast proves you partly correct, I say we go through the doorway centre left." And turned to the onlooking crowd, "You, my fellow treasure hunters and investors, leave now, I'll catch up as soon as I have dealt with Smith, *dauerhaft!*"

Spotting them turn for the doorway left of the other, with what appeared further inscriptions of a basic language etched into the wall above, reading aloud, under voice, "Choose wrong and you will find death." then turned to Kikes, "Stop, you'll kill them!"

But only few took note and slowed, Kikes suddenly turned, as one questioned, "But sir...?"

"Go now and live," he huffed, "or I'll have you shot!"

The concerned group continued to the doorway, as I quickly pick up a square four-foot copper shield and utilised it as cover on running up to Kikes. He quickly fired at me, only to strike the shelled. Before coming near as he went to reload another magazine and belted him in the face with the decretive metal, as I half leapt toward him and knocked him nonconscious.

I searched him for his rank identification papers, quickly taking and holding them high, calling to the crowd, "Stop, what are you doing! It states above the door if you chose wrong you will die! Now drop your weapons and follow us. I am now ranked as your superior officer, again in the German army. Please stop, and if any fear a court-martial, you may declare to be under orders, none in Germany will deny it. And if the allies are here, you will not be killed for miss cooperation, now please consider and think on what I said, I beg you!"

"How dear you, swine," a Waffen SS officer with a machinegun called and turned to fire, as I presented my pistol and another officer drew his, upon both being shot from behind and fell to the water.

As a man stood by account Vincent Lux, with a smoking Mauser 32 pistol drawn and distinctive scare down one side of his face, and stepped forth while cautiously looking around the room, calling, "I feared him, but as a member of the Nazi part myself I now only fill ashamed, because I fear more what you had just said. Once men of honour, I had worked in the cervices of Kaiser Wilhelm, but now I as others live with regret. Please do not judge us so..." before throwing his pistol into the water by the bridge, as the others followed and the lieutenant general, saluted, "Yes, *herr*-general, we'll do as you say."

I saluted the surrendered Wehrmacht officers and quickly picked up Kikes to cared him upon my back, as if a wounded soldier and walking along the bridge, as I lay him down on the four-foot walkway before the doorway and large step the crowd were stood upon. I then passed through the unnerved crowd to view an inscription left of the doorway, stepping by the crowd as I interpreted the first, "To the life 'After life' or 'death after death."

The offices and officials stood shocked at the clarification made concerning the doorway kikes had chosen, with few nervously whispering whilst taking a steep back, as I turned to the door on the right, reading, "To far exit and life," Daniel and Esther approached as a sergeant handing me his flashlight, I took and carefully entered to a hall within and continuing eighty feet whilst praying for safety. Daniel instructed two men to carry Kikes and ran forth to me, then heard a sharp crack and felt the floor drop a foot, as I leapt ahead to the stable floor.

Quickly turning back to the crowd, seeing the ceiling behind had begun to crack, as large pieces fell, "Run!" I yelled, *"Ausfuhren!"* And swiftly proceeded to a doorway at the end of the hall and entered, finding it a seventy-foot diameter, round room, with three doorways leading into the wall opposite. Sprinting forth to the doorways as Daniel followed by the crowd, men caring Kikes and Esther entered. I began to interpret inscriptions beside the entries, from left to right, "Go this way and die rich…' 'Go and die poor…" And the third, "Live for but a moment and bye rich."

Those over hearing of the approaching crowd begun to speak their thoughts on the interpretations amongst themselves. I seeing the fine dust enter the room, from the doorway entered, yelled, "This way!" Before stepping through the central doorway, with the inscription, 'Live, but die poor'. Entering a further hall that appeared to continue sixty feet ahead to yet another entry and swiftly approached on entering a forty-five-foot room, though finding no further exits, as the crowd caught up.

"Look," Esther pointed, "in the floor."

I turned, spotting a narrow opening within the centre of the paved floor and approached with the flashlight, revealing it a steep walkway leading down to a lower level. I quickly begun to follow it, finding it continued as a narrow hall ahead, cautiously following the passage down, as the others promptly followed. Descending further and coming out at a lower level, finding we had re-entered the very hall, Esther Daniel and I had first entered from the building above ground.

I turned right and looking up the sloped halls' grade, determining we were midway down, calling, "Follow me!" as I felt the whole catacomb shake and thunderous explosions erupt above. Quickly running up the grade in attempt to reach the exit at the far end of the hall, before hearing a loud explosion on passing the doorway to the treasury, entered earlier.

The way ahead suddenly collapsed, and the crowd begun to panic, and gasp, "We're trapped…" "What's up this way…?" "We're *zum scheitern verurteilt…!*"

I turned around to addressed those in despair, as they looked to the doorway on the right, "No, that way leads back to the treasure hold, and you do not want to attempt it."

Daniel approaching the treasure in the corner he had tried to remove earlier, noted water seeping from it, "Smith," he asked, "what are your thoughts on this?"

I quickly approached, answering, "I'm not sure...?"

Esther then interpreting faint inscriptions upon the wall above the fused treasure and blew away the dust, before wiped it clear, announcing, "You may leave, but take a portion of wealth with you, before you die..."

I then knew the section of hall ahead collapsing; wasn't simply due to an explosion, but more than likely constructed with the intent to do so, commenting, "So they made it that all exits were to be blocked in this way. But only the first people, involved with the tunnelling, would had known about such a trap, and must had left in the confidence that only members of their own clan could possibly still or recover such amounts. I'd say that's why the way we had entered was so well booby trapped, but even if entered the other way, you couldn't follow it back either, as it too has collapsed. But for now, it is a miracle this has worked out so far."

Then dropped the light and grasped the handle of the sword, protruding from the pile of precious metals and attempted to leaving it free, as Daniel helped, and brock the seal as highly pressurised water shot out, "Hold you're breathes!" I yelled, as we gave it one last pull and the fused articles cracked in half as more water flowed, and we were swept back. While the crowd stood against the walls and Esther to the right, Daniel and I re-stood, as the water surged passed our feet.

I looked to the ceiling, finding it had begun to crack and water spayed in from between its fractures, and the hole sealed off by the remover metal, had further opened to rapidly fill the area, "Quick!" I yelled, "Follow the current down!" Then ran down to follow the water, as Daniel and Esther kept close behind, and the fear struck crowd stepped from the wall, I knew the pillars down farther would not hold for long.

As a whole section of the wall broke out and the raging water pulled us down, barely able to keep my head up on passing between the pillars ahead as those behind collapsed, and quickly lay on my back. Seeing the halls dead end, discovered earlier, had broken apart and we were washed out the side of the hill, and followed the torrent, forming that of a waterfall to the small oasis and landed between the palm trees of its overflowed spring fed water hole, I saw earlier below.

Finding the frothed water brock our fall, before the those of Kike's party and the stream of water continued to pour out upon them, like a large fountain, as the officers caring Kikes had dropped him. I quickly swam over and pulled him free to the edge if the sand, then heard Esther cry "Smith…" as the overwhelming forty-foot stream covered her, I quickly swam around the falling water and retrieved her from the coarse sandy water, and pulled her to my right, as she swimming to the shallow shore.

I turn back and retrieving few trapped by the water, as Daniel followed and proceeded back and forth, then heard an airplane approached from the east and looked up from the rocky cliff face, we had exited from. Spotting a British hawker hurricane, as its pilot swooped down and flew back around the corner of the cliff, to the far right. We then continued to rescue servicers from the fast-flowing waterfall, till exhaustedly crawling from the sloshy sand and back onto the dry, as Daniel and I caching our breaths, and turned to Esther sat by a date palm thirty feet from the water's edge. As each, including the officers, laid collapsed upon the sand, utterly weary though unwounded.

I prayed to God, thanking him we were alive, as I laid upon my back and assured Kicks's investors who had stayed to attend those half-drowned, as appose to few men futilely limping west, "Don't worry, help will be here shortly and perhaps refuge, unless you rather face the desert."

The man with the distinct Liechtenauer influenced scare, sat up saluting, "Thank you general Smith,"

"As I said before, a miracle by God," I replied,

He took a breath and looked to the survivors either side of him, nodding, "Yes, well then thank God for you have shown us a different path, as you went from a higher rank position than many present here, or so Kikes said, and a bank shattering wage. Seeing the truth of it all and now opening our eyes, I don't know when the Nazi regime nor Hitler will be held to account, for the disruption in Europe, the genocide of many innocence. But I refuse to be a part of it, and it's corruption any longer." Before saluting again, I sat up and saluted back, as he lay, and I reclined to the sand to rest.

About five minutes past then heard the crunching of sand beneath German Marschstiefel boots and looked up, seeing Kikes stood to my left, presenting a Luger pistol he had ferreted away, blustering, "You… You *einmischung unterer* wolf *hund Australisch schwein*, have ruined everything *Ich gehalten gesehnt Ich glauben*… All I had wanted!"

"So, you no longer…?" I asked.

He brought the pistol close, exasperated by my remark, as I noted those of the party lay asleep and Esther asleep by the tree to the far right, "Don't temped me Smith, I'm not finished…"

"You were wrong about the way out and the fruit of the tree; if anything, you have become more argent," I provoked, "the fruit had no power, just as you are powerless. No matter how much you call yourself God."

"Your wrong Smith," he arrogantly replied,

"If I were wrong, I would be already dead. For how can a mere man stand up to a god, who wants him dead? No, there's only one God, everything else comes from the devil and evilly delusions is what they are."

"So, what now Smith," he asked, "you're about to be killed…"

"No, I shall never die, but live for ever in heaven and will not perish. But those without Christ will be in hell, in eternal fire, as I too deserve apart from accepting Jesuses as Lord and shall now go from this earth if you pull that trigger. Because I love God and Christ is in my heart, unlike those living in darkness who hate any who tell or practice His truths and gospel.

But if you are going to shoot, pleases, I beg and implore you, turn to the one who saved me, or hell certainly awaits. No one knows when their life's up or how it will come but come it will. Why not take the free-gift, so that death will not sting… I'm just sorry I made a stench of myself that you may follow it and pursue my past reputation, only to fall to greed as I once did and conform to evil."

Kikes then begun to shake, I closed my eyes as I suddenly heard a Morris C8 GS utility vehicle arrive and the crunching of many boots running through the sand and voices shout, "Stop, halt, *aufgeben!*"

I opened my eyes, as a man stood to the right of my face concealed by the brightly beaming sun, then turned to soldiers in British uniforms approach from the left, with pistols drawn. I sat up as they passed to apprehend and captured Kikes, ahead of further allied forces inclosing armed with Lee Enfield mark III rifles trained upon us. One of the British offices apprehended Kicks, ordered, "Everyone up slowly...! Hands above your heads...!"

A further three recently arrived Morris jeeps appeared from behind a nearby by dune, downhill to the east of us, that a portion of the party had just come from, and small band of soldiers stood from the vehicles once near and begun to search us for weapons. I waited patiently with Daniel now stood to the right of Esther as she approached. I prayed to God, thanking him we were still safe, and the group would accept the truths said earlier.

TRUE HOPE

A British brigadier if not major general stepped forth from the first jeep and passed the men who had searched us, taking both weapons and documents, he ordered their lead officer, "Gibs take this lot to the trucks, and we'll return to headquarters!"

The moustached captain saluted, before proceeding to escorted Daniel, Esther and I to the first vehicle, likewise to the enemy under guard, due to our lake of ununiform and general appearance. While the remaining vehicles begun to be loaded, the head officer soon finished giving orders and got up in the back with us. Under the watch full eye of an officer brandishing a Tomson sub machinegun sat in the passenger seat, as Gibs started the vehicles' three-point five letter engine and drove fourth and soon around the left or eastern side of the cliff, like mountain.

The officer offered me a canteen, as I took and gave it to Esther; the brigadier smiled, "Well, if this isn't another interesting surprise. You are the ones the lieutenant picked up at Tobruks' outskirts. What are you doing here or are you hunting down more mercenaries?"

Daniel drew a document hid in the fabric of his uniform and presented it to the officer, as he took and begun to study, "You remember Smith here," Daniel commented, "but you don't seem to recall my position?"

The officer handed the document back, "Yes," he commented, "but you'll need more than your rank to push me around. Your friend here on searching his coat; was found possessing two German Gestapo papers,"

"They are mel-inviod," Daniel replied, "he retrieved them from an officer in order to keep the other Nazis under control."

The officer turned to Esther, "And is this true?"

"Every word," she answered.

He then proceeded to look me in the eye, commenting, "Well, I guess your allies are off the hook, but I'll file you under suspicion, till known otherwise."

Our convoy came around to the Sothern front or of the cliff, spotting British Morris trucks on the ground, two hawker fury biplanes and hurricane fighters interceding the adrift airship and fired upon it. As the trucks formed a line and soldiers from each begun to escort the prisoners, as men approached to hand cuff those bound and ran a length of 3/8 chain to each stood in single file rows, before being led to the rear of vacant trucks ahead. "Aims you and Melvin give Phil a hand,"

"Eye, sir," Melvin nodded, and both left,

"Now this way," the major called, as we stepped from the vehicle and followed him passed captured men stood in line, toward a lieutenant colonel head office, seated at a small portable desk, thirty yards from the rear of the trucks and end of the line. As he marked off each prisoned on receiving their name and rank, on demand.

Then spotted Kikes at the end of the well-guarded line, as allied soldiers begun running around like crazy, picking up M1 Bren machineguns they had set up along the dunes, beyond the line. We were then escorted passed a line of serjeants and privets stood guard on approaching the lieutenant colonel's desk. The major who picked us up, stood to the left and informed the colonel, "Sir, I found theses three at the north side of the mountain, lying in the sun..." pointing toward me, "a German officer was threating this one, we know as Smith sir."

Recognized the colonel, as the same who had escorted us when picked up south of Tobruk, the colonel asked, "Are, do you not remember me?"

"James Perkins," I smiled, "and glad it's not Nathan Rossby that costly underestimating officer over you."

"You get use to my superior, when you're the one mostly living outside camp."

The major handed Perkins the documents found upon me, informing, "He was caring theses, but inspector, commander Daniel here and the women say he used these papers to keep the Jerry officers at bay."

Perkins took and skimmed over the papers, "Which officer did you get theses off?"

I turned back to Kikes, as those in the line proceeded towards the Morris trucks, answering, "One I fill was dismissed,"

"Dismissed?" Perkins asked,

the sergeant impermanently answered, "An aussi or yank term used in place of dead sir. The papers found in Smith's possession I of course believe not his own,"

"May I be excused now sir?" I pleaded,

"Yes," Perkins nodded, "you are clear."

I saw Kikes pass and head towards the rear of a truck ahead and pursued him, calling, "Stop, wait!" Kikes then turn to me with both an angered and broken manifestation, I called aloud, "I'm sorry," Knowing this all a result of my past, and offered my bible, "I might see you some time," he then took hold with his right hand.

"Hurry up!" one of the two British soldiers; stood either escort German prisoners aboard, yelled,

"Please read it," I urged,

Kikes then looked toward me in anger and turned to walk but three steps, before throwing the bible upon the sandy ground to his right and spat at it. Before turning ahead to the soldiers loading prisoners aboard the canopied truck, as one to his left said, to another stood to the right, "...I wouldn't say the futures to promising for theses, jerry's,"

"Year," the other seconded, "prison for some, but all tractors will finally get what's coming to them, at end of a four-in-hand leash."

Kikes then stopped after two further steps, noting the truck at the end of the line's engine start, in preparation to leave. He amazingly turned to his right and pull upon the chain with all his might, causing the line of eight officers to shuffle back, as they were influenced, and he dove to retrieve the bible from the sand with an out-stretched hand.

Then stood, ripping the swastika from his Waffen uniform to wipe the cover and threw the peace torn from his arm aside. He looked toward me, on recollecting my presence, nodding, "Well, I'm going to want all the help I can get, thankyou Smith."

"No," I replied, "thank God. For I would to be lost without him." He smiled and with a relinquished face, turned to follow the line of prisoners to the truck. I stood watch till they departed, silently thanking God for all he had done and for what was yet to be done.

"I can only hope he may survive the adjudicators and courts," Daniel replied,

"All can change for the better," Esther reminded.

Perkins approached from the left, asking, "What are you staring at? Or is it that you cannot figure out why you didn't just shoot the ones that are to be hung; one is a nobleman no less and traitor to the crown?"

I after witnessing Kikes leave more alive than ever, turned to Perkins, "Listen colonel, you are not to tell of the evidence concerning those identification papers. So, the courts may rule them as rebel civilians or mercenaries, arrested in the area and not to be sentenced to death."

"What?" Perkins asked, as Daniel and I stared at him, he nervously saluted, "I'll send word straight away," on leaving for the desk.

We turned ahead as Daniel commented, "Be glade Smith, I think all has worked out rather well, in the end for us,"

"Yes, it's a marcel we're alive," Esther replied, as I turned to observe Perkins reaching the line of trucks and boarding one with his second in command at the wheel. Whilst further vehicles were being heavily loaded with gear and as many soldiers as they could seat.

"Well, let's find our rides," Daniel suggested.

I turned to the north, seeing the silhouette of the horses we road in on, by a small water hole. As the crimson sun had begun to set in the west, Perkins reapproached in the truck and pulled up alongside us, smiling, "Oh by the way, we set up camp at quarter point south-west of here, sit on the bonnet; it'll be fine,"

"No thanks," Esther objected, "we rode in, we'll ride out,"

"Well, you heard her," I replied, as Perkins nodded and the driver pulled forth, with a smirk. Esther then ran across before the second line of vehicles and continued toward the horses, as we followed and quickly remounted up to peruse the convoy.

"Better than being a hood ornament," Daniel laughed.

Keeping with the convoy, the sun soon all but set as the party stopped upon a slight rise ahead and we slowly approached to see a camp formed of circular rows of tents set around a small oasis point. Flying a British, Scottish and Irish flags upon poles and may tents yet to be assembled on the outskirts of those set and the base of the slight hill.

We rode on up the grade to the camp, seeing the first jeep of the long line, pullup by a series of unset grey tent at the eastern edge of the sight and road on passed the stationary vehicles to approach, finding it Perkins's Morris C8. He stood and pointed toward a tent to the left off the jeep, calling out to us, "We've only just set up, so I'm afraid one of these will have to do, of course we're only here a short time. I'll have water and food sent form the supply trucks for both you and your horse!"

"Typical," Daniel huffed,

"That well be fine," I nodded.

Perkins then gave the driver the signal, "Onward," and proceeded forth towards the oasis. We dismounted and begun to assemble the ten, as it neared completion and soldiers drove a truck down to drop of supplies and large piles of hay with a wash tub and filled it with water from a drum.

Esther and I help reposition the tub aside, as she turned to me, "Smith," I silently turned to her as she starred toward my eyes in wonder, "can a man truly change...?" My horse stood between to drink of the water, cutting her off mid conversation.

Daniel taking a crate from the truck, called, "Could you help collect some supplied of these chaps?"

I stood up as Esther pattered the horse, not game to comment, I nodded to Daniel, "Right," and approached the vehicle, to receive a small crate of supplies,

"The cans are pubbing for the lady," one of the men smiled, "and there should be a couple with milk in there too sir,"

"Be sure to tell him she gives her thanks," I grinned, "though simply despises English weather."

"Will do sir," he laughed, before waving and tacking a seat as they turned and left the way they came and I to the tent and sat the supplies down within.

We then continued to set the tent, before tying off the horses, as the sun was now set and entered to roll matting out over the sand and begun to sort through the supplies, soon eat was palatable. Before playing cards with a deck Daniel had conveniently acquired and took places upon the large mat, as the horses half entered the opening. I lay there and looked out a slight opening toward the stars in the bark blue sky, with Esther and Daniel asleep to the left and right of the front entrance. While one or two of the horses lay upon the matt before me, weary from running the long distances. I thanked God for the day and that everything would be ok and how I might possibly answer Esther's questions, as I slept.

TROUBLE IN CAMP

Then awoke to foot steeped outside of the tent, as the horse whose back I had adopted as a pillow, stood and I rose to hear the steppes followed by the voices of men gather outside, "Shal we kill them?"

"Of course, should they resist,"

"Why wouldn't he... Wait isn't this their tent...?" Another replied.

I shook my head and cried, "Yar!" spooking the horses, as they ran out and knocking the men over in the dark.

I turned to Daniel and pulled him to his feet before Esther, as he stood once again with pistol drawn, demanding, "What's wrong?"

"Quick, someone's after us," I answered, and drew my bayonet on cutting through the tens rear side, as Esther and Daniel followed, before turning and running up a slight grade, toward the further set tents and turned back. Discovering the intruders of our tent to be a number of British soldiers, as they discovered our way of retreat and quickly pursued, I suggested, "We best find Perkins."

As we ran ahead of the soldiers and between the camps four rows of tens, in a zigzagging formation toward the central water hole, as their leading officers quickly lost track. I then noted a British flag outside a tent in the centre of the camp, beyond the reeded oasis and stopped at the edge of its open ground lit by lanterns upon poles, spotting a further party of soldiers leave by narrow rows between the tents to the right. Whilst few others from the former group passed, unaware of our presence in the dark and turned toward a nearby captain, stood by the edge of the oasis.

A second lieutenant leading the men, huffed, "We stopped them from leaving on horse, but their now in the camp..."

The captain raised his pistol and turned in the direction of the men who had just left the lit area and entered the dark, ordering, "Hurry, we must find them and keep the noise down." Watching the men bearing Linfield rifles, re-group and enter the slightly moon lit rows.

"We best find Perkins," Daniel whispered, "he's their acting commander and lieutenant colonel of the battalion,"

"Do you think he'll be around, looking for us," Esther gasped, "might it be for a harmless reason?"

"No," I affirmed, "they left with pistols in hand. Quick, we best see whether his in, before they return." Then stood and quickly ran across to the head tent, marked by flags and toward the centre of the open assembly ground. Cautiously entering its open entry discovering it dark, before the lighting of a match and kerosene lantern upon a desk in the centre, followed by the striking of two further matches and lighting of lanterns held by officers either side of the first. Illuminating the room and a table before us, on revealing an officer previously rescued from the air ship, who accused me a tarter seating behind the desk. Instantly noting the well-dressed officer's, recently half shaven face in the light to indisputably matched his photo, realized he was none other than Jason Tallery, whom I had previously worked on digs with at times, as I remembered back to the pages of warrants, I secured from men searching through my portion of rubble.

The well-dressed officers stood either side, revealing themselves from the air ship and sternly presented pistols. Tallery snuffed out his lamp under moustache and attempted to disguise his voice, once again to a fake east-Scottish accent, precariously greeting, "Are, gentlemen, traitor and accomplices. There's now just a little mater of your death by firing squared to be carried out, that is when the men get back to have a quick court, where I'll do all the speaking."

"Where's officer Perkins?" Esther demanded,

"No need to worry about him love," the man agitated, "his out, I presume on a brief patrol, after had taken us back to camp..." As he pursed, to drink from a large glass of water held in his right hand, before huffing, "That is after walking a considerable part of the journey. But with him gone, I am superior acting officer,"

"Well," I urged, "I think you'll find we're ranked high enough, to not face trial till court in England."

Jason using the system, asked, "But have you any proof of such rank?" Knowing Daniel and I out of papers, Esther then presented her Arminian meddle from Turkey and stepped forth placing it upon the desk, Daniel placed his badge and I mine with a folded blank sheet of paper on tacking a step back.

Jason gazed over the brass and tin medals, "What's this?" he asked,

"We are enrolled in the Arminian underground resistance," I answered, "of which should come under the British law, as one with Briton,"

"I'm sure if you look into it, you'll find we're neither traitors nor spies." Daniel insisted, "But assisting the fight against Nazi Germany."

"There's no time," Jason snuffed, releasing his glass and reaching forth to gather the metals and untouched paper, swiping them toward a small material sack within his arm.

As a staff sergeant entered, after had given up the search, calling, "We lost them... Oh, you have got them sir,"

"Yes, you incompetent soldier!" Jason huffed, "Now go and rouse the men, we've finished the prisoner's trial and are convinced by their pleads. We'll now forward to a hanging, now hurry ha, ha..." he laughed, as the officer left, Jason then turned to Esther, "Such a shame, but I may be persuaded to show you fair lady mercy."

Infuriated, I quickly drew my bayonet and pined his left hand to the desk, before he could conceal the medals and presented my pistol on cocking its hammer and held the barrel to the left of his head, Daniel drew both Walther 38 and Luger pistol. The officers either side, not having time to cock theirs, released and rose hands to surrender, as Daniel aimed toward both and Esther drew the derringer, Jason gasped, "Are...! Don't shoot, don't shoot! I will do any think; you can go free, yes... I'll let you go."

I looked him in the face, huffing, "You know who's a real traitor? One who diverts justice and is thought to be just,"

"Yes," He nervously replied, "whatever you say. Men throw down your arms now; right now. I mean it... His dangerous and will kill you too. I didn't know he was armed, honestly or that he was going to react so."

Hearing the crunching of sand under foot approach, I assured him, "You're going to regret this!"

Filling the urge to pull the trigger, as Perkins's voice demanded, "What's going on here Smith?"

I lowered the revolver and uncocked it's hammer, putting it away, Jason exhaled in relief and was freed, I sternly retracted the bayonet from his closed fist, as he stood grasping it in pain, yelling, "Are! Err...!"

I turned to Perkins, finding him stood in the doorway and Esther aside, as Daniel lowering his pistols, answering, "This bonder was about to hold a kangaroo court with Esther, Smith and I the victims. I suggest you have him shot immediately,"

"Smith, is this true?" Perkins asked in disbelief,

"With such events," I huffed, "you shouldn't be questioning a superior officer, who had just told you the truth,"

"Of course," Esther seconded, "and he tried to take our metals."

Jason cunningly stepped around the desk and stood to the left in prideful protested, "Theses men attacked me; a superior officer, in hope I would alter the course of justice of which they are all guilty. As told most emphatically by the commanding general of the German battalion and eighth crop; that took over our camp and held us his captives. He informed us that Smith here is an operative for German intelligence of sorts and was helping the Germans locate lost treasures, to fund the war and kill innocent civilians,"

"I wouldn't take his word for it," Daniel huffed, "nor what came from a lying German, quite obsessed on killing Smith,"

"Well, what rank do you hold inspector?" Perkins asked,

"At this moment, a highly ranked captain, as is Smith," He replied.

"It doesn't count," Jason huffed, "for the accused, I'm also a high-ranking captain and I say they're both just as guilty as each other."

"Really," I replied, "I thought you were attempting to accuse Esther earlier?"

"Yes, her too," he nervously gasped.

"I'm afraid there is some incriminating evidence on you Smith already," Perkins sighed, "with the papers found on you earlier and all." Esther near burst into tires, covering her face with her left hand, whilst supporting her elbow.

"But we must go to court," I insisted,

Jason then stood between Perkins and I, smiling, "And that's just what I was doing in your absence. Seeing I was the highest ranked officer in camp, and might I continue to deliver justice as you say?"

"Don't temped me to finish what I started," I huffed, Jason nervously stepped to the right and more toward Esther, as she stepped further away from him,

"If this is as sires as you say, captain Tallery." Perkins emphasised, "We must settle this as a further investigation and hold court in England. Till then you will all be held as prosecuted, or suspect." He then turned and calling out few soldiers, "Crafted, Tints clean up this mess and tell the men to go back to their tents, we leave in the morning. Also send for Gibs and Mc Philips, we have four more prisoners to be put under guard!" Then turned to us, nodding, "Ok, surrender your weapons," and approached Daniel first.

Daniel declined the request, "I'm a spy and can't be accused of being among German forces and am sure to be of higher ranked then this bounder."

Perkins passed Jason and proceeded to Esther, as she surrendered her pistol and flint dagger from the island, he then turned to Jason, who protested, "Are you kidding, not while his got a weapon!" He then passed to secure weapons from the two supposed officers and small sake, Jason had carelessly dropped upon the desk with our meddles.

Perkins then dropped the dagger and pistols into the sake once unloaded, and turned to me, as I too freely surrendered my weapons, nodding, whilst placing both the pistol and thirteen rounds of ammunition with in, "I don't need any weapons." And stared toward Jason, as he nervously relinquished a 32cal smith and western.

The other officers Perkins had previously called for, arrived and entered the tent, "Sir," one saluted,

"Search and secure these five suspects, lieutenant colonel" Perkins nodded, to be thorough the men briefly searched Esther and I before the officers, finding nothing; Perkins pointed to Jason, "Captain Tallery too." watching on as they retrieved a further silver plated Bulldog pistol and small knife within Jason's uniform pockets, "Here," Perkins snapped, "place them into the bag," shaking his head at Jason, as one of the officers placed the two weapons and box of cartridges into the sake, Perkins closed it off, "Take the two parties to separate tents and guard them overnight."

The major general and captain begun to escort us from the tent, Daniel accompanied Esther and I, as we begun to cross the open area and pass the glistering oasis, with its read surrounded water reflecting the moon light and exposed lilies in bloom. Perkins and officers Gibs and Mc Phillips split to direct us back to our tents, turning left I silently pray to God that it would be fine and all work out, with his help. Reapproaching our tent, Daniel stood by Gibs assuring the officer, "You may keep a man stationed outside, or rather allow me to guard the suspects?"

"Good idea," Gibs nodded, "I'll catch up with Mc and send for men to guard outside."

Daniel stayed outside as we entered and soon two men arrived with Thomson machineguns in hand, as Daniel left to attend the horses, and eventually said to the men, "Ok men, I'll take it from here, if you rather find a vacant tent to sleep and no fear, if they escape, I shall be held personally responsible," Offering a bill.

The soldiers excepted the generous tip and saluted, before leaving to set up a small tent within the out-circling row of tents opposite, before lighting a small fire for warmth and to further illuminate the area. Daniel cautiously entered our tent and holstered his pistol, whispering, "I don't know Smith, are you sure you want to go through with this? I mean to convict an officer you yourself must also stand trial,"

"We have nothing to hide," Esther gasped, "why should we be afraid, or don't you think we're innocent?"

"It's not that," Daniel sighed, "I just hope you know what you're getting into, but from what I have seen you are no traitor,"

"Traitor?" Esther snapped, "We stopped the Germans plans to buy more weapons, to help with their war efforts. How can anyone accuse us of such things, officer Taller said to be true?"

"I want to get this over with," I urged, "I put things off for too long. You find a few treasures; you two I had already answered and got mixed up in a country that is now going to war against your homeland. Sleepless nights just waiting for the enemy to find me, all because I was blind, blind enough to make deals and even promises to a colt like the third rich. Disregarding my inner foes, it was all as though hid from me, till my heart was changed and my life begun, starting in a small leaky boat stranded for more than two weeks at sea.

If it were not for that time, I would be dead and others would remember me as a great man, whilst may others a puppet and there would be those who would see me for what I was; blinded, naive of the origins nor what evil the third rich were up to. So, Daniel, Esther, I will stand trial though my name is cleared, and I'm no longer blind, but to help others to understand. I don't care what people think of me, but it's what they think of God and the ones who follow him; therefor I must clear my name no matter what the courts rule."

Esther then began to cry, and Daniel hid away his emotion, simply assuring, "Well, in that case Smith, it will be all right, whether firing squared or hangman's noose. You show what you said, even for just turning up to trial, when you could have gone free. But pray it will be ok Smith, I don't want to lose the one soldier I could stand having around, even though you seem a bit mad, such as I, but only to this world,"

"I don't want you dead, either Smith," Esther sighed, "and I'm sorry for calling you mad, when first met you. For it's a miracle we survived, but you trusted we would be safe in God's hands, it's a hope I almost forgot, back on Kuoiti island; till you arrived and helped believe me answers to pray,"

"Well," Daniel suggested, "Let's get some sleep then, this camp moves out to morrow," as we went to sleep again, I prayed everything would work out for the better and as was planned.

Awaking the following morning, soldiers entered and escorted Esther and I to a vehicle within a small convoy of trucks, led by Perkins and Jason with the two lieutenant officers in one of three Morris C8 utility trucks further back, before swiftly seating out from camp as two companies, whilst the majority of the battalions' soldiers remained, with many of the camps' tents still being packed.

THE HEARING

We then after a few hours, crossed the board into Jorden and soon arrived before an airfield west of the town Ruwaished, where Perkins had radioed ahead to arrange an airplane. Leaving the vehicles and we were escorted over to a small Electra 10E aircraft and boarded, taking our place on separate seats, while under guard. As it was equipped with fold away benches along its walls, accompanying soldiers offered Jason water and Daniel canteens for us, as we were not permitted to move, and hand cuffed once seated. By mid-flight the officers sat opposite relinquished their tendency to stair, drifting in and out of consciousness due to lake of sleep, Esther and I though dare not underestimate the severity of charges made against us, by the inferences of a silky end.

Remaining relatively calm, barley saying a word to one another, she grasped my right hand, whispering, "Whatever happens Smith…"

"Do not say such things," I sighed, "I cannot promise happens; even to remark on things I dear not, for the sake that neither's hart would forever be wounded by scares that may not heal. I dye silent, I live silent in hope these days will pass, and peace will come to be. But please, for you and I; you are better not to love me…"

She realest my hand with a tear in her eye she could not seem to wipe clear, nodding, "You are right, another time and wars will not last; you'll see…"

A man then entered the cargo/passenger bay from the cock pit, greeting Daniel as he awoke, "Sir is it really you? I should have known…?"

Instantly recognising the co-pilot to be sergeant James of the USAAC Daniel near jumped to attention, James simply waved, "Don't let me stop you enjoying the long ride, we're barley passed, Molta,"

"James," he smiled, "last I; we saw you was off at the dock, in Djibouti what the blast are you doing here?"

"Blast, is about right," he sighed, "I've just come in from Djibouti; it's shore and Malta's have been pressured by that Mussolini kraut's man; the limey's say... Sorry, British manning Hargeisa; non were to return bar fighter escort. I sooner assumed the lousy airstrip to be cleared all the same, but on return, the best I could manage was a fly-over through the thickest cloud of smoke you'd ever seen, planes mangled, and gasoline pumps ignited.

To make all matters worse the plane was struck, flying through the shot filled air; it was mine and Richey, my co-pilot's, only hope despite the very heat of the flames literally reached our tail, by the time we managed to bail out our load of supplies for men on the ground and limp her to that Jorden air base for some light repairs."

"And Gideon, lieutenant Morgan... John?" I asked, he shook his head.

"That's horribly," Esther gasped, "even in a plain coming to aid civilians?"

"Hardly a likely event," Daniel doubted.

James smiled, as an officer beside Perkins seated opposite, asked, "You know that man?"

"Yar," James answered, "and what kind of con is this, to handcuff these two?"

"He was arrested under charges of being a no-good traitor..." the officer snapped,

"You sure got your wires tangled; next thing they'll be boing Hitters work for him."

A second officer stood to reframe the other from approaching James, as Jason smirked, "Of course a man such as yourself wouldn't understand, but what to expect from men who lack the level of education, such as a man who dear counter accuses an officer of treason. You had to make up even your own emphatic exaggerations, of oh so brave events. But in court, we will see,"

"Besides, all that," Perkins inquired, "you'll testify what you know of this man in court?"

"Maybe then you'll see…" James replied, suddenly hearing the gush of air and slight loss of cabin pressure, James retrieved a roll of Scotch tape and turned to Daniel, "Sear."

He moved aside from the noise emitting from behind, and James quickly tor stripes to reseal off few holes formed due to extensive machinegun fire on the fuselage' main body, before nodding to the officer and saluting Daniel and I, "Ma'am, captain," and returned to the cockpit.

Eventually we come over Britain's eastern shoreline and landed in Heathrow airfield London, where we were escorted from the Electra 10E plane and to a line of C8 jeeps and military adapted passenger vehicles. Perkins had requested no doubt on Tillery's behalf, the officer at the wheel nodded, "Are theses the prisoners reported,"

"No," huffed Daniel, "but rather unlikely suspects," and took a seat in the rear opposite us as we were driven off the runway and down along the Bath Road, before continuing on toward London and deviated down few streets. Eventually stopped out the front of the old baily, London courthouse and main hall of justice, our side west of London wall. With the iconic lady justice with here sword and even-scales raised in the left hand, the engraved coat of arms presented upon the front facade of the buildings large gable roof, supported by two large sandstone pillars positioned either side the buildings large, curved entrance door. Leading out to the streets' foot pathed path, as we stepped from the vehicle and crossed the path, ahead of those escorting Jason and his two loyal officers.

Few people stood within the streets, dressed as in common everyday clothes, stared as Jason once left the vehicle, he yelled, "All you good people! I have uncovered one of the worst cads! One who helped fund the German war machine, to kill us all. But was he German? No, he was from ailed ground; even now he has a plot of land, a piece of English soil. I give you a traitor, one accusing me now as his last hope to gain mercy. Don't list to a word this fool has to say, he is deserving of his folly, help bring him down; don't let him live…!"

Seeing a number of men and women approach in anger, whilst others continued to walk away, but soon others joined the mob and the soldiers ran us inside. Fearing the growing crowed of down cast people, in search of someone to blame, an officer escorting Jason, ordered, "Will you be quite!"

I knew it was Jason's plan to kill me, once entering the courthouse atrium, two of the soldiers outside ordered, "Stay back!" To concerned members of the public, as they begun up the stairs to the front door. The officers drew pistols and fired in the air, scaring the peoples back, and closed the large timber door.

Earther and I stood before a seven-foot-wide oak counter not far in from the entrance, with a coat of arms carved into its front panel, maned by a British MP lieutenant. Perkins with us, handed the officer behind the counter the keys to our cuffs and identification papers. The officer quickly read through and examined the metals, Perkins called to those stood guard, "Take them to the lock up, their trial starts tomorrow." The lieutenant behind the counter, pursed from reading and looked up in concern, Perkins assured, "Yes, we came as soon as we could. A durry is being called, but the final vote goes to the military courts' judges, being Stefan Anderson, Phillips Mores and Davis Loans."

"Philip and Davis Loans, the field marshal?" the man gasped, "I wouldn't had thought you'd had the time to organise the big wigs?"

"We did," Perkins nodded, "and the small wigs."

"If what you say is true, we're dealing with a very sires mater indeed...?"

"This way," an officer stood guard ordered, and lead us passed the counter to a door in the left side of the rooms rear wall. I prayed to God that everything was going to be fine, and the truth would be revealed. We then walked through and followed a corridor of vertically bared boors to cells either side, as the soldiers opened two of the doors and directed us into separate cells midway down. Esther entering a cell opposite and Jason to a cell right of me, one of the men who escorted him locked the cell doors, before leaving us to sit upon hard timber benches mounted alongside the cells' stone wall, in the dark and laid down to sleep.

I awoke early in the morning to Jason pacing back and forth within his cell and rose from the bench to find Esther still sound asleep opposite and asked Jason-captain Tallery, "So, why are you trying to accuse me?"

"I'm a soldier and you're a cad," Jason huffed, still attempting to mask his identity, "figure it out for yourself,"

"I understand now," I smirked, "you are a soldier and I a traitor."

He stopped pacing and went back to sleep, as I after few push ups did the same, we were then woken by the sound of two MP soldiers bought in food; basically, consisting of bully beef and biscuits offered upon tin plates and large tin cup of water. Before slamming the doors and locking up, as one was a brigadier superior officer, and announced, "Your trial has moved forward."

Daniel then entered from the far end of the corridor, reminding them, "His trial, sir do not forget about officer Taller, his too on trial," as the officers left, Daniel approached mine and Esther's cell door opposite, "His right, your trial starts at eleven. I called in a favour, and you will have a hearing for as long as necessary, to find out the truth. I give that about an hour or so,"

"Good," Jason huffed, "a short hearing is a death hearing,"

"Well," I replied, "when the time comes, I'll be true,"

"I'll write down a few statements of what I've seen over the time I had met you," Daniel assured, "and I'm trying to get further references,"

"Thanks," I nodded,

"I pray they listen," Esther sighed, as Daniel smiled and turned to leave, and the same two officers re-entered to escorted us out and through a door at the end of the hallway.

I saw, on stepping first through a midway side door into the court room, while Esther grasped my hand and found it a large room with timber clad walls and many benches occupied by civilians and soldiers. Before instantly being directed to the front threshold and four-foot-tall stage, where three full-dressed military judges sat at a large desk and noted many of the people were seated along the walls on either side of the room, and each faced the judges at the front.

Leaving but a narrow aisle between before the rows of benches stopped short of the durries' stand along the right wall. Then passing the threshold noted two interrogation stands equipped with high iron rails. As the soldiers guarding, escorted us toward the question booth and short bench, to begin the hearing, Esther and I took our seat by the stand, and Jason at a desk to our left, as the officers stood either side the thresholds' entrance and the crowd of people sat.

As we faced the judges and they began to read over documents of case notes within folders, we patently waited, and pray I would know what to say. An MP officer stepped forth and stood before Jason, asking, "Do you, officer Taller swear that you will tell the whole truth and answer truthfully all questions?"

"I do." Jason raised his hand, with a smirk upon his face,

The officer turned to me, "Do you Peter Smith, swear..."

"I shall not swear by anything on heaven or on earth," I avowed, "I simply give my word."

The whole room begun to speak amongst themselves; the judge on the right grinned, as the general in the centre, yelled, "Order!" And all silenced, as he pointed toward me, "Your word Mr Smith, as a soldier?"

"As whatever I am," I answered, "which you men decide once I have my say."

Those in the room begun to mutter to one another again, the general yelled, "Order! I want this done quickly!"

Noting his facile expression was well hid by a thick moustache, though believed him to leer, and nodded to the MP brigadier officer stationed to his right, the officer turned to Jason in order to confirm, "Ok, I believe this man Peter Smith was charge first, him being the opposite character to you, officer taller. What have you found this man guilty off and explain the nature of this conclusion?"

Jason stood and pointed toward me, exclaiming, "This man is a traitor to the British empire!"

"What is he American?" The general snapped, "Explain further detail man and hurry up."

Jason, now agitated, begun to elaborate, "I have come to the conclusion that he was involved in the seeking of priceless treasures for the enemy's war efforts,"

"Treasure hunting?" The MPC officer asked, "You mean like palm tree Islands and oil wells? Please explain further?"

Jason, knowing they were quite tuff, continued, "No, I mean artefacts and lost treasures consisting of precious commodities. Finding theses treasures and being elected a member of Germany's Abwehr SS operatives of sorts, the enemy. And in such a way has betrayed the allied forces and obtained a plot of land, here in Briton, with royalties awarded for no less being actively enrolled in the German army. Even highly promoted for assisting to fund Germany, so the enemy may develop and purchase further weapons."

"So how did you come to this conclusion?" the judge in the centre inquired,

"I was told by a Schuztzstaffle general captured," Jason answered, "and in my own time of capture, after a battalion of German soldiers overran my squad and took over our camp. The highly ranked officer, by the name of Kikes Ritter-Schulz, discussed business deals with the traitor openly. While they thought we three survivors of colonel Stirling's fourth brigade an unlucky threat, in hand cuffs. But waited till opportunity came and amazedly, overpowered the soldiers guarding and escaped, getting out prior our men hitting the Nazi dig site, the enemy had well set up. I as a civilian put this before you, only to reveal a murderous wretch."

The MPC judge on the right, turned to me, whilst a staff sergeant continued typing everything down, "So Peter Smith, or Captain Smith it would seem. Have you anything to say against this charge?"

I stayed silent, as he went on to say, "Well then, either way," before re-examining the papers, "someone, who I'm not permitted to say, has something to say about your conduct that may set you straight. But will not list dates, due to the severity of this charge and the arrest of a supposed, German military funder. Because intel from allied British intelligence, shows the Germans were indeed being funded, but weren't sure just how…"

"Why are you wasting your time on this matter?" Jason butted in,

"Quiet," the general in the centre, ordered, "the woman a Mis Esther Limos is to be held an accomplice and for a later hearing depending on the outcome. We have received word from highly ranked officers stating a series of reasons he could not be a traitor. Now due to the severity of this case, I would like the alleged offender to step forth and start explaining himself, due to numbers of certain references made by highly ranked officers of the royal navy, US counterintelligence and specialised production services. And not to include statements given by agents of British intelligence and key allied espionage groups. So, I give the offender a chance to explain himself, no matter how long, till all written down is cleared. For today, we would like him to be questioned about his whereabouts."

The MPC officer on the right, turned to me, inquiring, "To the offender Mr Peter Smith, I would like you to explain your whereabouts and actions, starting over three months prior to Date and will stop at each point you have covered. For we have quite a patch work of scenarios many informally documented, due to national security and given the severity of the cases, and as the honourable general Manfred said, we will not stop this hearing till we see fit that you are guilty or otherwise pardoned.

So, Mr Smith, may you begin to enlighten us over events concerning these past three months, explaining not only officer Talley's accusation. But the otherwise misconduct of your inept unattendance and missing for that period of time, many popping up in the most bizarre of places and your house, of which you were stationed, destroyed and five men killed. Along with that, you have quite a few deaths to answer for and if you fail to give reasonable explanation, I fear its life imprisonment or the noose for you. Please do add any reference to the woman Mis Esther Limos outlying her involvement sir?"

I stood and thought of the past months as I took the floor and faced the three judges before turning to address the crowded room, "Please, ladies and gentlemen, I hope you'll listen to what I have to say, then announce what you find me guilty off, as a soldier."

Turning to the judges, general Manfred in the centre demanded, "In detail Mr Smith, we are not going anywhere."

I prayed I might be able to explain events truthfully and well, as I began my recount, "Well, it all started, when..." As I explained to the court and the judges, all I had done over the past three months, while being careful not to give information on the treasures Boas had requested to remain secret.

The hearing lasted three days and the trial was coming to a close, I stood before the judges again, and the MPC officer on the right informed, "This hearing has lasted three days and is funnily enough, correct on points. But we still do not have any more proof about you telling the truth all the way through, apart from yours and Ms Limos's statements?"

"I must protest," Jason objected, "they are accused and are offenders."

"Now who's using big words," the field marshal on the left replied, "or are you the judge?"

Jason then sat back down, huffing, "Not sorry your honour."

"Thank you," the judge nodded, "and mister Tallery is correct, we cannot take the words of an offender or supposed offenders, at face value nor literally. But if the accused's statements for or against him are indeed correct, then and only then would his charges for a sentence be complete. Now the first part of the statement; about a Zebulon come over and leveling your property, kill off fireman. We looked into it, the Zebulon clamed was indeed sighted, but radioed in as a publicity stunt, not a weapon, all though it was believed to have guns aboard and afterwards were instructed to return the way they came, though they were not sighted again.

Other residents around the town of Falmouth and of your street, also made statements about its attack and were sent to RAF officers, reviewing the case. But as for statements made concerning captain Mandarins, we have also sourced official statements from him and have confirmed all you have referenced of him, and your participation in joining the fight and helping to overcome German forces. We also have a statement from James Right; the pilot mentioned whom is now in the operation of testing new aircraft technological advances. Officer Fibs as you called him when mentioned in your statements, clams you are a hero, as dose officer John Peterson and lieutenant Frank Morgan.

We are still waiting on officer Gibbons Mains reply, though you have been truthful about that much and we have been given statements from the military base, in Tobruk, miraculously too proven correct. As they affirm us that you gave the head officer, colonel Nathan Rossby information on supposed German mercenaries, at work in the area, and of which his second in command officer lieutenant colonel Perkins agrees, although states at the time your motives were unclear.

We not long received word from the Arminian underground based in Eastern Turkey that you received yet a second captaincy, under agreements made stipulating them an allied force. Now we come to the conclusion that there is too much missing to be sure, so this trial will be postponed till after the war, as you'll be placed under house arrest, due to lake of evidence."

"What!" Jason yelled on standing, "House arrest! I think the noose suits him well." After had grown quit on the first day, along with his two accompanying officers hardly gain to say a word.

Hearing the crowd of people present murmur to one another. General Manfred seated in the centre, slamming his hammer "Order!"

As the whole room silenced and the MPC field marshal on the left, turned to Jason, "Ok, officer Tallery, have you anything to conclude or further statement?"

"I can produce my requested witness," Jason grinned, "officer Kikes; who's now in custody,"

general Manfred turned to an MPC officer stood before the thresh hold, ordering, "Captain Mc Paterson, allow the witness to enter." Before turning to the crowd, as the officer turned and ran down the aisle to the side door. In order to organise and permit Kikes to enter under guard, after had been taken into British custody and secured as an officer, general Manfred suggested, "I believe it's now time for a recess."

I then prayed everything would work out and patently waited, as Esther nervously turned to me from the stand, and I to her with a smile of questionable a surety. Kicks soon entered the court room, while under guard and hand cuffed, dressed in the trousers and shirt of an SS Abwehr office, little would those present know. He passed the threshold, Jason nervously stood from his booth, as Kikes was directed by the MPC officers to tack the stand. An officer had the *herr*-general say a vow of truth, as I had reminded that none should swear by God.

The judge on the left asked Kikes, "Officer general Kikes Ritter-Schulz as you are known,"

"Yes?" He asked, Manfred reading over a statement Jason had written throughout the break, inquiring, "Did you or did you not speak of a business proposal with Peter Smith, while aboard a military aircraft, presumable airship 1485, and inform officer Jason Tallery here; that Peter Smith was working with you in presumable assisting the German war effort."

Kikes turned to me then clockwise to the crowd and simply stared at them all for a second, then around to Jason as he smiled, before turning to the judges, saying, "Business deals? You mean discussing business deals with Smith and officer Tallery, at the same time. Only my business with Smith was due him withholding information from us and I tell you now his no SS officer in my eyes, but an allied captain. But it is true, I was discussing business with officer Smith, I was merely telling him what he could be, but he chose to ignore it, and wouldn't agree with the third which."

"Ok," the judge said, "you are excused."

Just as Kikes was being taken away, he turned to us and half smiled, Jason then took the stand and the MPC judge on the right announced, "And now for the case, of officer Tallery."

Esther released my hand as I stood from the stand to cross examine, "Officer Tallery, as you know him; is in fact doctor Jason Tallery, an archaeologist that hired out to the Germans for some time. His two close officers Halfway and Fields; he was captured with were simply obeying orders. But I'd say one thing for Jason; he must have refused to assist the Germans any longer. No, I would think he priced himself too highly and, in his mind, why not. He is a trusted officer with family influence and has done this before."

"What did he do before?" General Manfred seated in the centre asked,

"Ignored the very enemy he was supposed to be stopping." I answered, "Allowing the enemies forces, in this case archaeologist expeditions, to enter allied held or monitored locations, and made sure to transfer once received message from his benefactors, of no less the German high command. But he had a few problems; you see he let the Germans in, as they would not pay otherwise, but the enemy overwhelmed them in number. Officer Tallery was forced to drop his price and keep silent, in fact the Germans couldn't trust him any longer, and that's why he was held captive, I presume?"

Jason nervously shuttered, as the judge asked, "And what of this statement I have against him? About diverting justice?"

"Yes," I commented, "once I was in the camp of the ninth battalion, post me and colleagues being picked up, and all the while officer Charles Perkins was out on patrol. Jason, once in the camp, announced himself as senior officer and devised to murder Esther Limo and the officer only known as Daniel, no matter how you see it. And of course, hang me as a traitor after a short debriefing, but no court. Again, once officer Perkins arrived back in camp he arrested Jason over such crimes, and believed him untrustworthy, after being informed by a superior officer of Jason's criminal act in the perverting of justice."

Then retook the stand and sat beside Esther, as the judges looked on toward the crowd, general Manfred announced, "Now, we must process the information of the two cases and will regather within the hour."

I waited, as the judges rose and all stood, while they turn to a doorway to their right; the same doorway the durry would enter, all watching whilst the durry were directed to follow the officers, before taking our seats,

"So, what will happen now?" Esther asked,

"We'll except the sentence they give," I affirmed, "going off most cases Jason will go free, and Daniel may be in some trouble."

"But I believe you," she sighed, "and I prayed the truth would be revealed; the new you."

One of the five MPC officers stood guard behind, second from the end closest, steeped forth whispering, "I believe you officer Smith, in truth if what you said really happened, you're an inspiration to us."

"No," I answered, "I'm not, it wasn't I alone but Christ in me, you wouldn't have recognised me before I came to Christianity if anything you would have shot me on sight. No, do not worship me or say I am an inspiration, for it was all through Christ and not me, that I have now been able to see. But do as I do and worship the true inspiration, the one who gives life to those who are dead. I just pray I might change for the better and live for him that I may love him more. I hope you have found him as I have, but if not, please do so and find hope and stretch in him."

"Ok," nodded the officer, as he stood back in place, "I'll trey."

We then waited till the crowd returned in greater number to tack their seats, before standing, as the jury and the judges walked out. The general acting magistrate, sat with a hand full of pages, the MPC officers to the right and left followed, as did we, general Manfred announced, "The cases and hearing of the charges made against Mr Smith, on him being found guilty of murder, treachery, fifth and abandoning his posed in time of war.

Have been concluded as suspicion and now, as we have found from reliable accounts numbering no less than fifty from different sources, to confirm his own statements made, conclude officer Smith not guilty of the following. As even statements relevant to moral standards he himself had spoken on the first day of the hearing; suggest he once found out what Germany third wright stood for, indeed fled knowing the potential threat to Britain, not to mention crimes against humanity and freedom."

The MPC judge to the right concealed a grin, as he knew what I actually had meant and it was by a change of faith and hart, I was definitely shown the right way to live. As I had already explained to Daniel and Esther why I wanted and was compelled to go to court, the general continued, "You may now keep your rank, as a captain of the allied forces, if you are not put up for promoted of course."

"But what about his past!" Jason protested, "You diverters of justice! How dear you show mercy to him. That filth isn't worthy to be a number among mongrels!"

The judge slammed his hammer to maintain order and turned to Jason, "And the charges against officer Tallery here. Being accused of treachery and assisting enemy funding, has been seen only as suspicion and without evidence to back up the accusation. But the cases of officer Tallery perverting justice and his attempts to commit murder, and usury of those threatened to an unjust trial. We have found Mr Json Tallery, guilty in all accounts. As was pointed out by four statements, two of which from officers under Mr Tallery and two from higher ranked officers, also confirmed by evidence found in the camp he was detained. Officer Tallery would you have any other weapons, you would like to hand over before you are taken away into custody?"

Jason looked as though he had just awoken from a nightmare and quickly turned to run toward the crowd, the soldiers stood guard restrained him and brought him down to hand cuff. Two of the MPC officers begun to lead him away toward the courthouse holding cells, he yelled to the judges at the top of his voice, "I know now! I can prove what I said to be true, I think! The car he mentioned, the Rolls Royce; the papers he gathered are prof he is a living traitor; they will tell you whether he was ordered as a soldier for the Germans, or not! There is my prof that he is a traitor and working with the enemy, as a Gestapo conspirator...!"

General Manfred turning to me, demanding "Is this car in Briton? If so where, it must be checked as evidence?"

"No," I answered, "the automobile, passenger vehicle is not in England. I myself am not initially sure of its whereabouts."

Daniel emerged from the confused crowd and crossed the floor, Esher and I shocked to see him unannounced, suddenly stated a plea to the judges, "I can assure he is right. We do not know the whereabouts of the car."

Manfred questioned, "Can you second what officer Tallery is pleading to be true?"

"No," Daniel answered "I cannot, and to base it on evidence outside off English occupancy, concludes the evidence here say. As officer Tallery had once more forwarded just now, in attempt to form conclusions on top of his own assumptions."

The judges then spoke amongst themselves, and Manfred announced, "You are excused, court adjourned." And slammed his hammer, on turning to an MPC officers stood guard be side, "Have officer Tallery taken to his new quarters." The judges then upped and left, as we all stood and the crowd begun to vacate, quite pleased to see Jason taken into custody.

Esther and I silently waited, as Daniel stood to the left in approbation,

"It's a miracle," I nodded, "and thankyou both for not giving up on me,"

"Don't thank me yet," he replied, "I am yet to talk with the judges."

"You are going to convicted Smith?" Esther asked,

"More like reposition Smith," he assured, the MPC judge with a slight beard, who sat to the right of Manfred, re-entered by the doorway beside the stage and approached with a pen and legal documents, before presenting to me, "Please sing these to be re-instated," I read through and signed each of the five documents.

The officer expounded, "As Daniel has explained to me, you are found trustworthy to work alongside him, as part of the ally's eyes and ears on intelligence, linked with Germany. You will be tested in this position and by the truth in what you said here, as you both work to end the Nazi German campaign. Daniel here will contact you when you are needed to intercept enemy treasure hunting, for the allied forces as information comes in. But for now, you are given three months leave and I now promote you as a lieutenant colonel and second to officer Daniel, by order of field marshal Worth's recommendation to Field marshal Fletchings,"

"Thanks," I answered, "I'll try to be of help, but for sure, it was a miracle we had survived."

The lieutenant general retrieved the papers and left, I smiled, "An interesting man, and no doubt a key officer for the SOE. Praise the Lord, for all things are possible through him."

"Amen," Daniel agreed,

"Amen…" Esther seconded,

"Now what do we want for lunch?" I asked,

"I don't mind, so long as we get to lunch fast," commented Esther,

"I know a restraint that gives a good feed," Daniel commented, "and isn't far,"

"Well, let's go," I smiled, and stood as we left the plat form and down the centre aisle, towards the main entrance, by the atrium like hall. We all smiled with grins of joy, assurance and relief, now forever in God's hands.

Esther's estate

Once out we saw a crowd of gathering people talking among themselves, while stood upon the steps and front foot path. Passing the building outer pillars, we quickly avoided the crowd, knotting a Morris eight military vehicle parked alongside the sidewalk thirty yards to the right. Daniel led the way to the vehicle and opened a side door for Esther, she entered to take the small rear bench and I the passenger. Daniel swiftly jumped in, handing Esther a sealed envelope and drove us down the cobble stones road, with weathered buildings made of sandstone either side and tiled roof tops.

"Is this the documents?" Esther inquired,

"From your father's trust, as per instructed by his will," he nodded, "you don't have to open it now, the responsibility remains with you solely to collect."

We soon arrived out the front of a brick building, stretching near ninety feet in length and fifteen in height, lined with square reassessed windows either side a glass panelled double doorway, with few concert steps. Pulling in left of the entrance doors, we stood from the vehicle and followed Daniel up the steps and entered, finding it a med-size restraint, with few cafe stile furnishings, he insisted, "Take a seat, I'll order," pointing us to a spear square table for four, pre-set with cutlery and gold collared condiments, beneath a window by the entrance.

Esther and I took our seats, opposite the busy entryway, Esther sat to the right pointed out Daniel before a small six-foot counter, to place an order, "To order your food, rather than to hunt nor gather. The fish we caught on the Kuoiti where the sun is always shining, except in the case of a monsoon, as my father would call the seasons,"

"I take little notice since my first impressions," I sighed, "but I can understand the unwillingness to adapt to climate such as this?"

"I can get used to it, you'll see, now it's more than just abnormal weather," She replied.

Daniel returned to take a seat opposite, noting the restraint near packed and waiters running to and from large doors to the left and right, and collecting dishes from a leeway counter along the rear wall. Esther nervously noted the snobby people within the restraint, Daniel smiled, "Well I hope they won't take too long, quit the turn out today. So, what's on your mind Smith...? If not the next mission?"

"I can't say," I answered, "but I gees we should help Esther locate the family astute, left to her,"

"Yes, I would like that," Esther smiled,

"Well, after lunch, let's get to it." Daniel encouraged, "After all I thought we were going to help with that before we had left and I apologise, it wasn't gentlemanly to leave so suddenly,"

"No, it was ok," she commented, "even so, beside the threat and dangers, to view the change in scenery; it's actually a pity we were in such a hurry."

"Yes," I replied, "but at least we are on leave for three months, perhaps I'll figure out what to do in that time."

"Yes; but do keep in touch," Daniel commented, "I know wars split up friends and acquaintances, but I hope we can continue to do our duty,"

"Yes... And thank you," Esther agreed.

A waiter then came around and placed a bottle of wine in the centre of the table and slender glasses before us, on filling each with a surpluses bottle, Daniel asking the waiter, "Much longer now?"

"It's coming sir," the waiter assured, before walking away toward a kitchen entrance.

Daniel raised a glass, "He may return by next year. But now a toast to the one who made this possible, to God." And sipped, as we retrieved a glass to follow, while waited for the food to come. The food was then brought out to us, as a smorgasbord of sea foods and roasts, we dished up generous portions to eat. A waiter then bought a black forest cake for dessert, coming in a near foot tall and well flavoured by brandy, we shortly finished up and the dishes consisting of leftovers were taken away.

"Well, despite haven't eaten a decent meal in days," I sighed, "this was rather filling, the cake alone could kill,"

"Ha..." Daniel laughed, "and if it didn't, the price might, at least that's what the MPC secretary by the counter told me."

Esther tacking a sip of wine and lowering the glass from her lips, smiled, "that was wonderful, all though you two eat like the workers in the village, maybe even more. I can barely finish half a slice of that dutiful cake; I hope it won't go to waste?"

"Don't worry," Daniel commented, "it's been well paid for, as the war yet to mature; may cause it to become harder and harder to indulge such treats, so enjoy while you can."

"The culture of wealthy England," she replied, "so different to the lives you live, while on a mission. Unlike Kuoiti island, where we eat to survive. But I suppose it's a space between occasion. But Smith, was there any truth in it, the trial I mean...?"

"Yes," I answered, "all I said was true, but near all Jason said was false."

"Oh, on what points was he correct?" She inquired,

Daniel then seeing three more people enter the restraint, to join the world of fine dyed woollen and mink stows, commented, "No use tying up the table, I think we should be going."

We then stood and left by the entrance to the Morris, as I curiosity replied to Esther's, inquisition, "I can't trust anyone with too much information, but I'm as I said, no longer in with the crowd."

We then drove off, as Daniel asked Esther, "So how about we find the estate you inherited, Mis Esther or would you rather Lady Limos?"

She grimly opened the envelope and drew few papers, answering, "It's down walker street in Chelmsford, on the out skirts according to your map."

"Walker Street, hem..." Daniel commented, "Wait, I know the area. Do you realize you inherited a house in one of the most upper-class streets in England?"

"Walker Street?"

"Yes," Daniel answered, "a funny name for a street where it's residents haven't walked anywhere in the last hundred years,"

"It sounds like a place for snobs?" I commented,

"No," Daniel commented, "only the poshest of people,"

"Anything else?" I asked Esther,

"No," she nodded, "but there is a caretaker at the moment, who is to run my great aunt Lucie's house until I or my father would ever return."

We headed down country lanes and roads for hours, till we entered the east end of Chelmsford village of larger size and diverted up a side street from the main throughfare, passing areas of poorer people, with few desperately door knocking for food and children running around in the street. Some likely parentless and suffering from the first impacts of the awaking war. We turned up hill, to our left, avoiding the people and proceeded two miles farther from the village centre, on entering well-built semi open streets, with mansions upon larger blocks either side, ranging from two-three stories.

"What are these houses?" Esther asked,

"Other than compensation," I huffed, "they do bare social statues,"

"Rather the humble home of an account," Daniel replied, "but with that a status passed down by generations. They are not all namedroppers, though many indeed the social elite; that I doubt you'll have the displeasure of dealing with Mis Esther."

Then spotted a larger, possibly four-story mansion to the left ahead, with a large, rounded east and west wing either side an eighty-foot sandstone front face, equipped with sharply arched, tall, recessed stain glass windows and a distinct central bule main entry door. Noting few white marble steps before the entrance and all three stories of windows with dark green curtains drawn, included the few upon the lesser forth story. Before a dark grey tiled roof complementing the building constructed from large bricks once rendered white, halting outside the properties stone mounted iron bared fence panels and decretive arched twin gateway to a drive of white granite. Discovering its property numbers in order and further confirmed by numbers 64 stamped into a copper plat, mounted to the right of the gaits.

"Are, here we are, my lady...?" Daniel gasped.

"Are you certain?" She smiled,

"Right, you couldn't have expected more." I congratulated, "Though don't forget looks can be deceiving?"

I stepped from the vehicle to find the part way opened gaits unlocked and swung them clear, before walking alongside the jeep, as Daniel drove towered the front door along the entrance drive and passed the properties two acer front rose garden. Pulling up outside the mansions' front door, with a second driveway veering further right, toward a small shed and condemned stables, about a hundred feet from the house. Daniel and Esther steeped from the vehicle, as we observed the gardens' white roses, with a small surrounding hedge, and diversity of geranium flowers aligned in two ten-foot square fertilised beds, nine feet in from the well-manicured meadow grass either side the driveway, spaced six feet apart.

Turning from the vehicle, we approached the front door as Daniel knocked and an elder woman opened, snuffing at the sight of the jeep, "I already told you people, his over the age of sixty,"

"Who?" Daniel asked.

She then noticed Esther, gasping, "You're not from the government, to take Aldrich?"

"Aldrich, no... no," Daniel assured, "my dear lady we have come to assist Mis Esther Limos; the rightful heir to take possession of the estate,"

"Esther, who's she?" the women asked,

Esther stepped forth, answering, "I'm Esther Limos, my father Jonah Limos gave me the entitlement papers before he was murdered by German hands." And offered the documents to the women, "Here are my father's last wishes."

The women raising a pair of glasses, read over the will and testament, gasping in shock, "Jonah's daughter... We thought you were killed by Irish rebels, how are you still alive? I mean... This is such good news that you're alive,"

"It's a long story," Esther answered,

"Please come in, come in," the women insisted, "we will discuss it over tea. I don't want the neighbours to see you like this."

We entered into a thirty-foot square atrium, before two curved staircases running up along the left and right wall, with well carved banisters, leading to a second story walkway, with a decretive ceiling forty-feet above and doors to the left and right. Knotting few portraits of the women, tacking pride of place upon the walls, she proceeded to a double doorway between staircases and showed us through. Esther led while Daniel and I followed across the orange tiled floor, partly concealed by a tightly woven rug laid in the centre. Before entering a thirty-five-foot square living room, with large lounge chairs to the left and right, with flower like patterns embroidered on white back grounds.

Then saw an older man, start to play a grand piano, in passed the furnishings, while busy formulating scales and making up a song of sorts, as light shun through a large window opposite, similar to those out the front of the mansion. The man stopped playing, as a mid-aged butler entered through a door to the left and the women sternly ordered, "Jeffry, please fetch us some tea, we have gests. And Aldry stop what you are doing and get over here. Esther, the daughter of Jonah Goldberg Limos, is here to see us about the inheritance."

The elder man stood from the piano and dumbfoundedly approached Esther, "Esther? Is it really you? I thought you lost alongside your parents, so long ago. I still remember you when you visited the mansion, when Uncle Samson; your father's brother was alive. Ha, I must sit down."

Taking a seat on the sofas to his left, we took a seat upon the sweet opposite and the elder women commented, "We have been the caretakers for over fifteen years. We looked after this house as if it were our own. So please forgive Aldry when he has to take a breath..."

"No," Aldrich clarified, "it's not like that, Vera and I are overjoyed to see you're alive and that you, one of the last known relatives can finally do something with this place, beyond the upkeep only to be an empty home..."

"That is if you don't like the atmosphere of a manor house," Vera butted in, "with a rich history, known to entertain guests?"

"Rich history?" Esther asked, "Just how much did I inherit?"

The butler returned with the tea and the women took a small cup and soccer as she offered each a cup, answering, "It would seem as though you have inherited a large fortune, one many would love to have, up to twenty thousand pounds, in one of four accounts invested over time, as well as the house and furniture, if you wish to inherit. After all its such the effort to have these things finalised?"

We silently drank tea, as the women stared toward Esther in malice and Aldrich with love, like that of a loyal servant to a master who treats him right, and the butler staying present in the background, awaiting further request from the women, Esther smiled, "Thank you all for having such high hopes for me and it's a miracle I'm alive, so much to ask, so much to tell. But now I must talk with my friends in privet." Then stood and turned for the door to the foyer we entered by, Daniel and I stood to follow her out into the atrium.

"Pleas, what are your thoughts?" she asked,

"Well, I believe it's between you and God, what you choose to do." Daniel encouraged, "As Smith I tack it would agree?"

"Yes," I nodded, "find out what He wants you to do."

"Could you two sort the paperwork?" She asked, "I don't want them to know how behind I am in the culture times."

"I'll be right onto it," Daniel answered, then re-entered the room to retrieve the Certificates and her documentation.

"What would you do Smith?" she inquired,

"I would hope to use the wealth wisely and invest in God's kingdom," I answered, "seeing the face of that greedy woman in there and portraits upon walls. The way she must fill, as a candidate to hoard materiel wealth. I can only suggest this; if you ask me, I would fill compelled, after seeing those made poor down the street, to make the place a refuge and donate to charity, before God and in front of that snob. I'd say the money was likely il-gain anyway, only saved up by those like Miss Vera, hesitant to give away to charity, but rather hoard everything.

No, I'll rid myself of it and the environment of which it was consumed, by cold heated snobs. Well, there's enough of them about; I would ride myself of it due to the nature it came, so I would not be accused of hording, in such an il-manner and I myself would not fall into their traps of greed and darkness. That's why her husband Albury was near in tires, he wanted to be ride of his wife's obsession with the place, the money and even though the caretakers live like those who build up wealth and loosed trust in God. He is relieved, just because you are here to take what is; if misused a fool's earn without spirituel blessing and love for God. Pleas be on your guard of such things, I know these times are troubling, but please I implore you, for I love you..."

Gasping at the last words, uncontrollably said, she leapt forth to embrace me, I kept my hands from her, as she smiled, "Oh Smith, I've been the whole time looking into your heart, to see where it lies. Now hug me and I will know."

Daniel then entered through the doorway, as she quickly released and stood up straight, as though in a military fashion. Daniel continued to look over the documents in his hands, whilst we stayed quiet and he asked, "What's wrong...?"

"Nothing, are they the papers?" I inquired,

"Yes," he commented, "and lists the family's solicitor in Witham too,"

"Well," I commented, "let us be off,"

"Right oh," he agreed, before walked pass to the front entrance.

I turned to Esther, sighing, "I don't believe I deserve you, but through faith we are made spiritually rich, time will tell God's answer. Please don't worry, it will come to you in faith, and I'll see you soon."

"Have I miss judged you?" she asked, ever nearly in tires,

"I hope not," I answered, then left.

Daniel already outside, started the jeep, as I ran out the front and jumped in, he shook his head, "Women ha," then turned around, before taking off, "well did she say anything to you?"

"I don't know," I pondered, "the elder lady, Vera only said what you heard,"

"Not her; Lady Esther when she embraced you?"

"Only that she frivolously believes me worthy of her." I responded, "But I still do not believe I am and uncertain I would ever be, only time will tell."

"Was that before or after you appeared to have refused her?" He huffed,

"I'm not sure," I sighed, "but enough about me, how about yourself?"

"Well, I'm already engaged as such. She waits for me though I have not yet come, but one day; even soon, I should rather like to marry her." And reached into his top right pocket to retrieve the photo he had kept concealed and offered it, as I found it a picture of a women with fare hair, of similar age to Esther and too well proportioned, handing it back, he smiled, "It depends so much, on whether she's the right one and how strongly she believes, as life goes on and now this war. How can I or anyone know the right time for such things, or whether it should be?"

"Just as well I'm not engaged then," I answered, "but I do understand."

"Perhaps," Daniel simply grinned and continued down the streets, before the eastern outskirts and passed further victorine stile buildings of the social elite, I prayed all with Esther would work the way God planed for her life and the better.

Tying loose ends

Approaching Witham I directed as we soon arrived outside the collectors office, thankfully still in business, with a phone booth at the far end of the street. Pulling up outside, I nodded to Daniel as we stepped from the vehicle, "You go in, I'll be with you in a sec."

Daniel passed by and entered the dark tilled, sixty-foot wide, single story, brick office building. I diverted to the booth to make a phone call, feeding it coins whilst staying connected and self-funding the service, till spotting Daniel exit the building and stood from the booth, "I thought you were going in Smith?" he asked, before running around to the driver's side of the Morris and I the passenger.

"Did I miss anything exiting?" I asked,

"No more exciting than the way these things go, however Mr. Wells in there clarified the amount inherited had not matured as it should had, since October 1927. Then discovered, on bank statements entrusted to his office alone, that a sum of eight thousand had been withdrawn by Sir Samson order on March 1929," he answered and dumped the clutch to take off, at a pace he should had felt ashamed of attempting, "I think one of the reasons we might had held off with war as long as we did, was due to despatch-messages arriving by morry,"

"Ha…" I laughed, "Are well, I haven't seen to many around."

"That's because in a country of this size, why crawl when you can walk?" He answered, then passed by an eighty-foot-wide brick post office building, with a couple of arched windows either side its door and second floor, on pulling in. I voluntarily raced out to post what

I believed letters of confirmation and returned as we proceeded back toward Esther's estate.

Pulling up out the front in a similar manner, Esther ran out, as Daniel handed her the papers, "Here you are," and turned form the vehicle as I followed, she then begun to read over the deeds and amount she had inherited, he further commented, "Well it will take a few days, before the name is transferred."

"I, a half islander has inherited the estate," she gasped, "and near eighty-seven thousand pounds?" With a grin that could not be wiped from her face and invited us in, saying, "Well, please come in, I can most certainty shout my friends a cup of tea, ha-ha."

We followed her in, by the front door to the living room again, as she announced to Miss Vera, "Its official, thank you for your services. You and your husband may stay in one of the wings for free; and after today, I extend the same offer to the butler and mad also and are only to work five days a week, with a break."

Daniel and I took a seat opposite miss Vera and her husband, Aldrich as Esther ran through to the kitchen to inform her staff of the good news. Noting miss Vera appeared more snobby than prior as she starred in distain, as though it were our idea and asked, "So will you two be staying long?"

"I don't know," I answered, "are there any Germans to fight here?"

"You have a nerve mistier," she snuffed,

"Smith," I answered, misinterpreting her uncongenial attitude, "and yes I'm now more fearless than ever out there in the wilderness, despite the dangers. But here I cannot stand, though quite confident I am far from danger. Because I really was in no more danger out there then here, as the One who protects us, also protects Mis Limos. Any more questions?"

Esther re-entered just in time with a tray of teacups, as Vera spitefully stared at me, and Esther asked, "Would you like some tea?" While offering it to her, the elder women grinned, nodding, "Why thankyou darling, I shall."

Esther smiled and turned back to the kitchen, as Miss Vera continued, "You two won't be able to control her forever, she'll see things our way and then everything will be as I wanted it. You two are out of place in this world, in this high-end environment and you now make me even madder, as if it weren't bad enough, she is a fool with money, it seems her resigning is taken from the bible. But you rather rely on God then money, like fools. And now you wish to bring me down with your charitable views, but it will not happen; I'll be running things as I have planned and there's nothing you can do about it. Esther will either leave or stay, it's up to her, but her points of view will change in this upper world…"

As she heard her husband's footsteps and held her tong, as he entered by a doorway; beside the piano behind Vera and Esther reappeared from the far doorway to the kitchen and sat with a cup of tea, I asked her, "Are you sure these people can be trusted?"

"Oh, aren't Vere?" She clarified, "She's nice and uncle Aldry; my fathers' cozen loves all the changes I just made and trusts my judgment. So, what do you mean…?"

"Their scroungers for both money and power," Daniel huffed, "that's what he means. I heard it from the old bat's lips."

"Esther is this how your father raised you," Vera gasped, in her defence, "to be around such harsh people who stick with you, only for a piece of inheritance; I'm disappointed."

Aldrich then appeared to have tires form in his eyes, saying, "It's not true child, not a word. If I'm lying, have me beaten and thrown out. I've been nothing but loyal; putting my time into maintaining this house and did as was right in the family property. Please if I failed, show me my floors so I may soon correct them, help me to see things your way?"

"You already do," Esther replied, "now I think it's time for our guests to leave. Your tires are more than sincere enough,"

Daniel and I stood, whilst Esther pointed and showed us to the door, Virar gave us another sharp look with a grin, as we left to the atrium without a struggle, Esther asked, "What's wrong with you two? Can't you see their loyalty or is it that I'm rich now that really bothers you?"

"So, you don't believe us?" Daniel huffed, "Well just stick around, it will come to you. We'll return in a matter of days, perhaps to see you again,"

"Well Smith?" She asked,

"He couldn't have said it better," I nodded, "but I'll add this, many go after the security of wealth, just don't forget the days when you were on a remote island, living off not what you found, but were given; goodbye Lady Limos."

We then turned and walked out the door as Daniel exited to the jeep, Esther turned back to the living room, with tears in her eyes, as I saw Vireo come out from the lounge and close the door behind, on approach, as I assured, "She won't give in, you're finished,"

"She'll soon be too busy to worry about how I run things," she grinned, "even if she never gives in, she'll be married in time and pregnant with too much on her mind to worry about such things, and I'll see she marries a snob, as you say, ha, ha…"

"I said you're finished," I snapped, "there is no use making it shorter by antagonising me. Indeed, you cause me to justify it more, and stay away from Esther. Although she will find you out for what you are, a snake grown out of lust for power and wealth, I'll pray for you."

Then turned and left to the Morris, saying to Daniel, "I hope she'll be ok with those two,"

"She'll be fine, stop worrying," Daniel commented, "oh and by the way, do you have anywhere in particular you would like to go, this Morris is quite economical?"

"In fact, I do," I nodded, "when you went into the solicitors, I rang the French police; under Parelli and asked them what became of my car. An officer contacted on duty told me it was being shipped back to England, following the fairies non-extended rout and Parilli aboard on course for Bawdsey, on somehow hearing about my return to England."

"Well in that case," he nodded, "let us be off to the coast, I think the military have moved in tight, but we should get there in this."

Before turned around and out the drive, as he turned left and up the road, we After a few miles came out onto open road again, pulling up to get gas, Daniel filled while I made a further phone call and got the bill, before continuing with haste toward the west coastline, east of Colwyn Bay, as the sun begun to set, and we proceeded through the night. Stopping for food punter wagons and discussing military secrets on the way, we eventually arrived out the front of the now closed restraint, by the oceans' edge. Spotting few soldiers stood before the pier, while looking out to sea, Daniel parked the Morris eight outside the closed down small French restraint, as he and I stood from the car and ran over to the docks' entry. Approaching the four soldiers stood guard and noting the faint sound of a boat coming in.

One of the men guarding the pier, ordered, "Halt, who are you?"

Daniel showing him his badge, "Do you really want to know or is this badge enough for you?"

"Sorry sir," the private gasped, "it won't happen again, can't be to carful sir."

"No," Daniel assured, "I would have been angry if you hadn't stopped me, but I do enjoy mucking around with the lower ranks and always find it interesting to see how they react." Hinting toward proving the subject's identity.

Before walking passed as I followed him by the small group of soldiers, finding their officer otherwise focused and using a pair of binoculars to observe from where the ever loader sound had originated, gasping, "What is that?" On spotting a boat, racing in from the open waters piloted by Pirelli with my Rolls Royse secured upon its deck. He swiftly pulled into the right of us and slowed to a halt, two armed French soldiers of sorts, lowered a ramp over the side to the dock and threw Daniel and I a line. We secured the vessel, and the second lieutenant asked the French soldiers, "So, do you men speak English?"

The one on the left turned around to Pirelli; at the helm, as he approached to meet us, while the officer and soldiers stood their ground at the end of the dock and kept their eyes on Pirelli as he greeted, "Ha, Smith you like the change, I was in need of a larger boat for the smuggling of weapons to the resistance."

"Resistance in France?" I asked,

"Yes," he nodded, "I'm part of it, I came over to drop this fine automobile off and pickup shipment of weapons, to fill space in my warehouse." Then drew a badge and held it up, saying, "All a shore, let's go ashore!"

The soldiers soon lowered their MAS 38 machine guns and Pirelli stepped out onto the dock, pinning the badge to his shirt, whilst his men ran ahead upon the dock and followed the soldiers to assist with unloading the jeeps, he lit a cigar and smiled, "So Smith, I see you lost someone, I hope she is safe or otherwise died well for the cause."

"She's alive," I assured, "though only now sorting out her inherited estate; in fact, a large manor,"

"Wow," he smiled, "with her looks and now you say she's inherited a mansion. She has it all, I'd call that Ms right if it weren't for my wife Lysander, I was fortunate to had married before this war."

"So how are things," Daniel politely changed the subject, "in the resistance I mean?"

Pirelli holding a brave face, answered, "France will probably never be the same again. They have taken everything and as much as it angered me when it happened. I now thank Briton for sinking our naval fleet; the Germans would have certainly used our marine Bataille vessels. So, they saved us the job of blowing them up ourselves."

"So, you justify their actions?" Daniel gasped,

"Only a fraction of light, in your country's darkest hour," Pirelli replied,

"And I see you have been promoted?" I asked,

"Promoted, after you helped me overcome fears," he smiled, "by the way, what was your secret?"

"No secret," I assured, "I simply relied on God, I hope you will also seek him sometime,"

"That was before I became married, over three weeks back." He replied, "I found that it was you, a new you, who was brave enough to stand up to the Germans. Since then, I made my piece with God as I seen you had, and now, I am a lieutenant general in the resistance, as we're still sorting ranks."

"That's excellent!" I replied, "You have no idea how glad I am for you."

"Thank you and I would like to give you two, theses," reaching into his right pocket and handed Daniel and I a small medal of rank, saying, "I now give the rank of officers, whenever your about in France; show the resistance theses and they'll help you. Even follow you to the death."

"Thank you," I excepted.

Pirelli then turned to the two French naval men, as they brought crates of weaponry over, "Francize, Figaro start to unload the Rolls Royce, we found its owner."

They then started to release the ropes, securing the vehicle, whilst Daniel and I stepped forth to help free its chase and once all clear, quickly got in and drove off the boat by the gangplank to the dock, as we stopped beside Parole, "Well, I'll see you again," I commented, "be sure to dim all light on crossing and keep your heads down,"

"Right, you are Smith," he reapplied, before shacking my hand as I drove off the dock and up the road like a maniac, keen to go for a drive.

"Now we best head to my house in northern Norfolk," Daniel suggested, "if it's not too much to ask, I shall direct you." I then sped down the same narrow lanes and prayed to God for Parley's safety as well as Esther's and our own, and thanked God for yet another Christian brother.

Continuing through the night till thick fog set in and eventually pulling up to sleep before proceeding and eventually turning down an unsealed road as the sun had begun to rise and after thirty miles, came alongside a six-foot stone wall of a large property and neared its front drive entrance. "And here we are," Daniel nodded,

"A noble man?" I asked, entering by its twin open rort iron gates with bronze deer statues either side, he stayed silent and continued down the long drive passed a well-established garden, consisting of scarlet English rose and a small iron fence. Surrounded by large shade trees to mark the outer extremities, before a three story, rendered brick, Victorian era grand hall stretching near two hundred feet. Noting the drive appeared to curve around the garden till outside the large buildings' central entry door, with many slender windows in its front face, either side the door and small landings to rooms upon the second story above.

Spotting a large garage to the right of the hall, before the surrounding grounds and a far corridor of trees before forest surrounding the property more than two hundred yards off and an airfield set up behind the large building, with a small hangar housing a Hawker Hind biplane and Gloster SS 37 biplane. Gaining a better view as I drove closer and circled around the garden, Daniel announced, "Well, here's the house I am based at and you too Smith, this is where we'll set up to attend missions in secret. I hope you'll enjoy your stay?"

I pulled up outside the front entrance; Daniel drew a key from his pocket, "Here is your key,"

"Wait," I commented, "you are not attending?"

"I've been thinking about what you said before and what Livens Pirelli had said and with three months leave, that I believe is a sign. It's time for me to see my fiancee, Marry Lushly and prepare for a swift wedding. I suppose we'll no doubt celebrate at an appropriate time, I have already invited any who could attend after this war and now I invite you a true ally."

"That's a change, but was it truly in what Pirelli said?"

"No, not all." He smiled, "I've just seen a man pas up what seemed to me, two peoples very destiny. I realised that I to have a destiny and it would be best not to fight what is planned and have grown tired of running. So, I'll take my permitted leave and flight to her family's estate, where I shall openly except her hand, as her mine if she should have me in marriage, no doubt fulfilling a vital part of my destiny."

"But the war, have you already forgot?"

"The war will end, whether I'm married or not and now I except the fight is not merely in flesh and bone, but something more and by God's grace we'll be saved. After all we've been through Smith, have you reason to doubt?" Then stood from the vehicle and tossed me the key, "I hope you fulfill what God has planned for your life. But as for me it has been revealed, we'll continue this convocation when I return, and I believe when you get back,"

"No chance," I answered, "how would I know what's meant to be?"

"You, going ashore an island with me aboard a patrol boat, you overtook, and further on helped liberate islanders that were under attack. Oh, and found a rare, beautiful flower, that has been with you all this time? But make up your own mind Smith, though it's obvious to me."

He then closed the door and avoided the large empty house as he walked down to the left along its front, and followed a path toward the rear hanger, I pondered on what was said, till soon hearing the SS 37's Bristol Mercury VII engine start and prepare to tack off. Realising what he said, and the importance of what God was telling me, I restarted the engine and took off with hast, following the drive around the central garden and back up the straight.

Daniel taken off, spotted the Rolls and immediately performed a loop over the forest and banked hard into a barrel role, to celebrate as I pulled through the open gates and veered left as I speed down the winding country roads and lanes over weirs and narrow bridges. Finding my path cut off by men leading sheep, I slowed noting an opening to a large meadow and spotting there a far gate into the lain ahead of the mob. Instantly I pulled into the field and raced on, till re-entered the lain ahead of the sheep, and swiftly proceeded towards Chelmsford and the mansion, Esther had inherited.

TRUE INHERITANCE

I arrived at eastern Chelmsford and followed a series of lanes along the northern out skirts down towards the mansion as I pulled up outside the front gates and stepped from the vehicle, to run through the garden and approached the buildings front door. I then straightened my uniform shirt and knocked, hearing voices coming from around the left side of the building, I turned and ran around its corner. Finding Esther in a light blue silk frock sat upon a stone bench, with two well-dressed men in tailored made cotan suits, one on the left in yellow and other in white with a red carnation, both sat either side of her, while another stood before her dressed in dark burgundy silk. Noting the two men seated appeared to have been drinking and heavily placed their arms over her shoulders in a controversial manner.

I watched as the young man stood before here, boastfully pleaded, "Well listen and please here me out. My family have invested as yours has and you should as accustom merry me, to honour their wishes and further your wealth, if nothing else."

The one sat left of her then stood, as the man before her took his place beside her in similar fashion, the well-dressed man now stood, dictated, "And if not my cozen here? How about I dear lady, my parents invested just as wealthy?"

The more sober man in white, sat to her right quickly stood, as she attempted to stand in protest, pleading, "I really must go…"

The less sobor man sat to the left violently pulled her back as she sat and the one stood to the right, huffed, "No, my family is richer than theirs, but if we wed, I'll pay generously for you to have my children."

Esther belted the man attempting to secure her, up the side the face and pulled free as her dress partly tor and she stood, protesting, "I'm not marring any of you, I thought this was a traditional welcoming party!"

The one stood to her left grasped her arm, as she struck his face and the other two forced her back down to her seat, grasping her arms, "Help me hold her down!" the man on the left gasped.

The one who Esther had struck with her fist, huffed, "We've got her now, Vireo said we can do whatever nessusery to persuade her,"

"I thought you were gentlemen!" Esther gasped, as the man in maron stood before her reached toward her, only to be kicked between the legs and fell to the ground, attempting to grasp her foot.

The less intoxicated man sat to the right, let go with one arm and grasped her left leg from sticking the one fallen to his knees, as the other threatened, "You will marry one of us, even if by force, we won't stop; even if we have you beaten or blackmailed, disgraced or simply force to sing the certificate, now drink up…"

I stood from the garden and ran forth enraged, "Get away from her, you evil loveless vial filth of society!"

They released her in shock as she ran to me and embraced, "I'm sorry," she gasped,

"Don't apologise for those who relish evil," I assured, "go now, you must change your gown and leave me with them." Releasing my arm from around her, she nodded and gave the bewildered attackers a stern glace with a grin and passed around the corner to the front of the house. The man who was struck in face, rubbed his forehead and the one kicked below belt, dressed in maroon, threw his silver flask aside and stood, "Well just who are you?" he slurred.

"Stay away for your own safety," I cautioned, as they pointed toward, no doubt inherited, military badges of rank pinned upon their collars and the man huffed, "We're in the army, Charles a high rank officer. Once we've delt with you, pathetic fool, we'll finish our courting the lady."

"Think twice," I huffed,

"Ok boys," the deluded drunk, encouraged, "I'll show you how it's done,"

"Marriage is put in place by God," I commented, "The Bible tells us to love our wives as Christ loves the church, not in acts of indecency and adultery, but to live the way he instructed."

The more sobor dressed in white, huffed, "Let's kill him!"

The first in maroon ran toward me, swinging his right fist toward my face, as I blocked his arm with my left and hurled my right fist into his face, as he stumbled. I quickly grasped his right arm and pulled him forth as I swung another hard right into his face, before throwing him hard against the wall of the house, head and left shoulder first, he fell nonconscious. The other two ran forth, the left swung his right foot toward me and other, of a supposed high rank in yellow, attempted to throw a fist toward me, and grasp hold of my arm with his free hand.

I stepped to the right to dodge the one on the left's forward kick toward my upper body on quickly blocking the other's fist and struck his face, then grabbed the others foot as he turned only to attempt a further strike with his foot. Then place a hand over the head of the man in yellow I dazed and pulled him down as I kneed him up the side of the head and rendered him nonconscious. Then stepped forth as the other balancing on one foot, attempted to kick me in the face with the other leg and struck my right shoulder hard.

As I realised his foot and he stood to regain balance, in anger I quickly grasped both his feet and pulled them out from under him, as he fell, and his head struck the ground. I released to grasp him by the scruff of the neck, as he my wrists and franticly tried to kick at my legs. Quickly I pulled him forth and threw my left knee into his face, near knocking him out before grasping his left leg, to slightly pick him up and swung him clockwise into the wall of the house, as few nonconscious.

Catching my breath, I saw the man of a suppose higher rank, swear under his breath, on attempting to crawl toward the front of the house and stumble to his feet with a small knife clinched in his hand. He must have planned to use when he confronted me, as he turned in anger, with a sneer and gritting of bloody teeth.

"Ha…" I huffed, "Come-on, really?" In incredulity, he leaped forth and swing the knife at me, I court his arm and pushed him back with the soul of my boot to his left shoulder, near dislocating his arm, as he released the blade and fell against the brick wall unconscious.

I then quickly pursued Esther, thanking God I arrived in time, then entered the houses and found her crying in the foyer, "Smith, I'm sorry I doubted you,"

"I too can be wrong at times," I smiled, then heard Miss Vera's irrationally exasperated voice emitting from upstairs, as I turned to the left staircase, "Come on, let's see what's all the commotion." And ran up the steps to a walkway, leading left and right to a hall and turned left to the distinct voice finding it to originate from a summer room in the west wing at the end of the run. Passing the doors of vacant rooms to the left and right, before the last partway opened to the left. I carefully peered into the room, discovering Miss Vera speaking into a French stile, ceramic phone stationed upon a well-polished white marble table, before a side window overlooking the subdued men.

She continued to speak unaware, while arranging a vase of both white Dalmas and yellow English roses pulling one apart, "Yes Ross, I've called the police… He just beat on them, like an ill-bred ruffian; after your nephews were gentlemanly courting lady Limos. Brutally interrupted them and has taken the pour girl to ravage… Yes, I know it's a pity; I wanted one of the nephews to have her and so she might mother a child, once consecrated of course. Now could you send around any others, whilst the police do their jobs; to give comfort to the pour girl. She'll come into the house once the stranger has gone or he'll soon flea…"

Easter and I entered as she turned and dropped the phone in shock and stood speechless, I shook my head, "You have been found out for the embezzlement of estate funds once used to afford a ruthless assassination attempt on the Limos family. However, you didn't bet on an exemption clause written by Sir Samson, Esther's all too wise uncle; that the estate remained under guardianship with no access to funds. Apart from the final proof of Mis Limos undisputed death. Though I'm sure this suited a woman such as yourself a lifetime caretaker. You evil person, you betray the blood of your master and persist in the rejection of God. Do you not know that Christ died for all and so you might too live, yet you in your own greed bring in wolves to maul one of He's children?"

Esther approached her and threw the phone unit through the closed window, before snatching an open phone log from the table, huffing, "I think you'll find new accommodation, to your contempt. Because once the police take you away and even before that, I am signing over my money to charity and making this house a refuge for those struggling in wartime. Keeping only enough to see them healthy and you like those savages out there, will go down poor. For you, like them, have rejected what is good and eternal life for ill gains."

We then saw few police entering the grounds within morose Cowley passenger vehicles and step out to search the grounds, suddenly discovering the beaten men, calling for help and disconnected phone beneath the shattered window. Esther called to the officers, "Police, pleases take them away; they are the men who tried to attack me Mis Limos and arranged by Miss Vera up here beside me."

Vera maliciously went to grab Esther and slapped her face with her left hand on attempting the window, Esther forced her from the sill, calling, "Quickly up here…!" and pushed Vera to the floor, replying, "I forgive you, only because God forgave me. I hope you'll turn to Him."

As Vera wept at here prospects, and we quickly exited the room, as two officers entering and a constable asked on approach, "Are you ok?"

"Yes," Esther smiled, "those men out there are her accomplices, she was planning them to force me into a marriage. So, I might leave this mansion, of which I just inherited, she was the caretaker. Mr Smith here, came to my aid just in time, they had planned to force themselves upon me, that I might concede to a marriage."

The constable shook his head in anger for the attackers, Esther offered the diary, "Here, all evidence is right here,"

He glimpsed over the open page and latest entry, nodding, "You've done well, I'm pleased to see the evidence, are you sure you are all right?"

"Thanks to God on my side and Smith here," she nodded,

"I assure it's by His grace," I commented.

One of the officers securing Vera, reported to the constable, "We found her,"

"Are, the women spoke of," the constable clarified, "a miss Vera, I take it."

"And further she admits to arranging, a Mis Limos attackers outside," The officer affirmed.

"Excuse me," the constable pleaded, and passed to the room and other officers.

Esther took a breath, "mined if we leave?"

"Shale we," I nodded and continued to the stairs, before following them down, I prayed aloud, "Fathered, thank you for keeping her safe."

Another officer, this time an MPC constable, approached with a saluted, asking, whilst the officers escorted Vera down the steps, toward us, "So what just happened captain sir? Who do we arrest?"

Recognising him officer sergeant Conner Teller of the eight battalion, I saluted, "The supposed militants outside were attempting to force themselves onto Mis Esther Limos here, in so to take control of her family's fortune: recently inherited. That old bat, Miss Vera organised such an offence, in hope to regain this very mansion.

She was caretaker and didn't agree with Mis Esther the last of the Limos, being found a commoner, nor the handing over of the Estate, as I had expressed in my concerns for the matter. But don't charge them for any more than a violent attack, while disturbing the peace, and issue them each a Bible if they so choose and have the bill sent to me, by your superiors, that's an order."

"Right, now all that was said on the phone is made clear, even that eight thousand pounds that was stolen from the estate, was indeed clarified and evidence forwarded by a Mr C R Simpson, not two days ago. And as it turns out was indeed issued by nonother than your Mis Vera Sturt," he assuredly explained, before sighing, "Though I can try to sway the courts, the result I fear rather unlikely given the evidence put forward by Mr Wells there will be a thorough investigation and after all this isn't Falmouth. By the way, I have been passed that way, not much left of the old fort is there?"

I then offered him few bills, "This should cover it,"

"Thanks, old boy, but we tend to give the accused the good book for free," he assured, "and might I say that diversion of the segments radar HQ, rather quite strategic, as it turned out."

Miss Vera then being escorted down the stairs, was about to call a snide remark, only to be hushed by an officer, "Silent you, we don't want to hear it..."

"But how did you know he is a captain?" She asked,

Conner answered, "Because everyone in the area knows Captain Smith. He fought the corruption cases against former lieutenant Jason Tallery."

Esther silently asked, "Who was that man C R Simpson? Is he a judge?"

"NO," I answered, "my people, a lawyer group comprised of exe Scotland yard. I refused to use during the trial, but as a last resort, I needed a third person; your family's solicitors, Mr Wells, mightn't had listened to me, being one so freshly escaped the nose."

"Do, you still fear, are you not free?"

I walked on with Esther, nodded to her, "It's funny, all this time running and living in fear of the authorities, only to have their trust acquired all in God's timing; this wouldn't had been so, three months ago; indeed, I was already a suspect by axis and allies alike. Now let us not mention follies and regrets but live in the light. I'm so proud of you, it's quit a generous thing you have chosen to do with the estate,"

"You really think so?" she smiled,

"Of course, though there is always the treasure of saint Morake on Kuoiti island," and quickly walked out to the Rolls.

Esther eager to leave the grounds got in ahead of me, asking, "Then, Smith where are we going?"

"Well," I pondered, "I thought you'd like to see the family farm in Australia,"

"Is it wormer then Briton?" She asked,

"Ha, you could say that" I laughed,

"Smith," she asked, "I had thought about it and so much more during the hearing and the last two days; will you marry me?"

I smirked, then turned to her, accepting, "Only if you stay as you are, for God, and I'm the one who asks?"

"Well then?" She inquired, I saw the constable step from the front door and another police car pulled into the drive, then started the Rolls, before turning the vehicle around and took off out the drive answering, "I haven't even a ring."

"A ring," she sighed, "can't it be any gift?"

"How about this car for now?" I answered, in love for her,

"Only if you get a ring to replace it?" She smiled, I laughed and continued speeding from the village and toward Falmouth's dock, where I first set off. Soon pulling into its front entrance, noting ships docked either side the pier, set to sail and stepped from the car, as she followed. Then ran around before the stone railing overlooking the bay, in joy as she embraced and I her as we kissed for the first time, filling as though the moment should last forever, just as the sun had begun to set.

We followed the steps with its sandstone hand railing down to the dock and ran towards the small both ahead of us. I thanked God it all worked out and for Esther and life He has given me, as it was a new beginning.

The end, or not; for like a Book that never
ends, so I shall live through Christ.

Lightning Source UK Ltd.
Milton Keynes UK
UKHW041504170822
407409UK00017B/73/J